Pandemic

To order additional copies, please contact us.
BookSurge, LLC
www.booksurge.com
1-866-308-6235
orders@booksurge.com

Pandemic

Joan J. Johnson and William E. Rose

2005

Pandemic

To The Reader

This book is fiction. Any resemblance to persons or places mentioned within these pages is coincidental. While the likelihood of a pandemic called the avian flu is being reported on television and in the printed media, this book does not pretend to know where the first outbreak will occur or if it will ever occur.

Several people have been instrumental in the development of *Pandemic* and are owed our gratitude for the time and effort they willingly gave to it. Carol and Gerry Gariepy for connecting two strangers, one who had an idea and one who writes books and for their careful reading of the book's first draft; my sisters, Marjorie Brown and Norma Wagner, for their preliminary editing; Pat Consentino, for her critical comments and advice; Marilyn Haynes, Sarah Dyer, and Betty Burkett for their feedback; Ann Hannon, Irene Cronkright, Millie Cronkright, and Jim Doyle for their encouragement and efforts to help us find an agent; Kay Gleason for nagging me to get this published long after I had given up hope, and finally Louise Chrysostom, perhaps the most diligent copy editor I've ever encountered.

Part One

OUTBREAK

I

Bangkok, Monday, Mid-October

Trailing its ghostly fingers along the valleys and riverbeds leading into and out of Bangkok, an early morning fog pressed thick, wet hands upon the city. Just north of the post-war reconstruction, its sleek high-rises housing the international businesses, banks, and apartments of the wealthy, hordes of men and women on their way to work swarmed from the tenements in Kwang Tri. A suburb of Bangkok, Kwang Tri is ten minutes from the business district. Here the poorest live elbow to elbow, crowded into dark, airless rooms stacked carelessly and connected by rickety staircases. Windows look into other windows, all of them shut to minimize the ceaseless noise of mopeds and the stench of their noxious exhausts.

Lying on a mat near one side window, Phrati called softly to her teen-age daughter lying nearby on her own mat. "How do you feel, Dai?"

Dai groaned, coughed, and then mumbled, "The same."

Phrati threw back her blanket, feeling dizzy as she lifted her head and struggled to rise.

"Where are you going, Mother?" moaned her daughter.

"We have to eat," Phrati whispered as she rose and shuffled slowly to the window. Beneath her, vendors had laid out their wares. Their chatter was subdued, as if the fog had driven all of them into themselves. The street was teeming. People rushed this way and that, hurrying to jobs, to school, and to market, often doubled up on a moped or bike. The bright colors of their shirts washed gray in the clammy gloom. Phrati watched them through the myriad cross-hatching of wires strung haphazardly from building to pole to building like the scribblings of a child. She sighed.

"Stay in bed, Mother," Dai coaxed. "You're sick." But Phrati dressed, patted her hair in place, and left.

On the street, aging streamers sagged from poles and second story windows. Phrati saw the blue and white striped banner of Chang's, where she bought her rice and ginger. The crush of people caught her up and swept her along, bobbing and weaving like a bubble in a stream. She was dizzy. Her limbs ached, and it took everything she had to remain upright. She yearned to close her eyes, but she was buffeted by others and forced to side-step women gathered about the fruit and vegetable stands on the sidewalk. She coughed, a dry, hacking bark that angered the dragon in her throat. Those around her were in such a hurry, they didn't see the way she trembled and swayed or the blue-white pallor of her skin and the darkness beneath her eyes. They were busy; they were late.

If her daughter had been well enough, she might have watched her mother from the window as Phrati disappeared and reappeared again from beneath the tan and gray awnings lining the street. Dai would have seen her mother emerge below the blue and white banner carrying a small burlap bag of rice and then watch her cross the busy street to Mr. Chi's. But Dai was too weak to stand at the window and too feverish to care.

At Mr. Chi's, Phrati pointed to a chicken, a black one among the others bent old Mr. Chi displayed in a small wooden cage not sturdy enough to sit upon. Phrati haggled half-heartedly, and she was too sick to point out the bird's flaws. She could not know that illness, not age afflicted this bird; it was about to die anyhow. The price agreed upon, both knew that she was paying too much for the sorry bird. Phrati watched weakly as Mr. Chi deftly grabbed the chicken and twisted a string about its feet.

Home again, Phrati laid her bag of rice upon the table. In the other room, Dai's eyes were closed, but from her limp jaw, a trickle of drool descended in a silver thread to her mat. She touched Dai's forehead, which was hot and damp, and then her own, which was the same.

Carrying the chicken, Phrati moved slowly down the stairs again, every movement a torture. Behind her building lay a patch of dirt littered with garbage and trash and surrounded by a high fence. She stood dazedly in its midst, swaying solemnly in the dank October air, her eyes closed, while at the same time she stretched the neck of the chicken by rubbing it between her thumb and forefinger. The chicken remained still.

Taking the ax in her hand, Phrati laid the bird across the stump placed in the yard for exactly this purpose. Without hesitation, she brought the ax down hard, a clean and quick dismembering. The chicken's wings fluttered. The legs danced. Its blood spurted, a red fountain spraying the stump without artistry. Its head fell to the dirt where one eye looked up at her as if to question the meaning of life. Still, its severed body struggled in the woman's grasp, and feces squirted her hand. Disgusted, she let go. The bird danced frantically in the dirt while she wiped her hands on her apron. Dizzy again, she was anxious to pluck the feathers and clean the innards so that perhaps she might rest on her mat, if only for a few hours. She sneezed, her eyes tearing. She wiped her nose with the back of her hand

and then dabbed at her eyes, brushing the tears away and clearing her vision. She was terribly sick, this woman. Her fever was rising and her body ached. Still, she knew her duties. Soon her children would return from school full of life and energy; her husband and older sons would follow, famished and surly. All of them would want their dinner. It would be hours before she finished her chores and stored the dinner things.

But now she was ready for sleep. Her nap would be fitful. Her body had already hosted a marriage of sorts, the human virus she had caught from Dai, asleep inside, and the H5N1 virus she had just caught from her sick chicken. In the dark recesses of her bloodstream and tissues, these viruses had begun recombining and reproducing at quantum speed. By dinnertime their progeny would be neither one genetic strand nor the other. A new, dark child was being born, a roughly spherical child only 200nm in diameter. Minuscule rigid spikes would encircle its negatively stained virus particles, but its spiked halo indicated no messiah. This was a child no one wanted, but it would not care about that, its only purpose being to survive and reproduce, which it would no do unhindered. No angels heralded its momentous birth; no star shone across the desert for wise men to follow. In this busy Bangkok suburb, a destroyer of worlds was about to be born, the spawn of disease and death, and no one would know of its coming until it was too late.

2

Patterson, Massachusetts, Monday, Mid-October

Route 2A runs parallel to Route 2 across central Massachusetts, but it's a slower road, and in Patterson it is dotted by new and used car dealers, delis, a police and fire station, and several restaurants. As it moves away from Patterson, east or west, it runs into towns that grew larger when the railroad laid tracks through Massachusetts. Patterson should have grown as well, but the terrain just wouldn't cooperate—too much ledge, too steep hills. Years ago, railroad engineers decided to go through Almont instead of Patterson, and so the thriving machine companies that had provided jobs followed the rails, leaving the town without sufficient employment to attract newcomers or to keep its youth from moving on. For much the same reasons, Patterson farmers were enticed by the siren song of the fertile mid-west—"Plow all day and not hit one stone." They sold off or abandoned their rocky pastures and headed for easier soil. Patterson's town center, two miles south of 2A, is accessible by a two-lane, wandering and sparsely-developed road. The center boasts a Town Hall, a library open on Wednesdays and Saturdays, Patterson Elementary School, and a Congregational church. Some of its residents smile when a newcomer calls it "town". "Outpost" is more like it, they say.

The walls inside the church have not been painted in two hundred years. They are the original plaster and the pews are their original natural wood. People step up into a pew and close a small door behind them, just as their forebears did when the church was first established. The history of the church includes a battle over its ownership between the Methodists and the Congregationalists, a battle so spirited that it led to a showdown one Sunday back in the early 1800s. Methodists, wishing to establish their ownership of the building, secretly plotted to start their own service an hour before the Congregationalists arrived and then refused to leave when they did. Armed with sticks and bats, a fight broke out in the vestry that became Patterson's version of a holy war. That day is probably the most passionate Sunday Patterson churchgoers have ever experienced, and even today people still talk about it.

The talk this afternoon could become almost as spirited. The Ladies Benevolent Society had decided to meet in the vestry to discuss their plans for church improvements. High on the agenda was whether to spend their limited funds on carpeting or new appliances.

Laura Block had had just about enough discussion. She had things to do at home. Laura was writing a book on edible plants for a small western press devoted to survivalist literature. The advance wasn't great, but she had not been able to resist. A PhD. from Yale and several years of teaching and researching at the University of Massachusetts had made her eminently qualified to tell people what they could or should not eat from the plant world. She could still be teaching if she wanted to, but she'd taken leave when she became pregnant several years ago, and then, after the child miscarried and her marriage subsequently miscarried too, she found she could make a living writing for specialized presses. She was already well known for her epic dictionary of herbs and herbal medicine. And another big book was already being discussed with her editor from Henry Holt. Carpeting or new appliances were of little concern to her and she was edgy to get back to work. With just a little more to go, maybe five or six hours of concentrated writing and editing, she would be free, with no commitments to interfere with the arrival of Taylor Farr. Just the thought of two weeks with him made her dizzy with impatience.

Laura touched her neighbor's arm, both of them at the back of the group slowly filtering into the sanctuary. "I've got to leave early," she explained. "I've got a deadline."

Ethel Card wished that she too had a deadline. She hadn't worked a day in her life, at least by some people's standards. She'd raised three kids and all of them were grown and married. The two boys had families of their own out west, and her daughter lived in Paris with her newest husband. Ethel had once explained to Laura that her family was down to one yearly obligatory visit and three holiday cards per child. Ethel's husband Arnold worked for L. S. Garrett, the precision toolmaker in Almont that was a primary source of employment for several towns around, and he wouldn't be home for hours. She had no pressing obligations or appointments. If she made up a doctor or dentist appointment, she knew she'd get caught in her lie sooner or later. "Go," she said, resigned. "I'll tell them." She watched Laura shove her arms into her pea jacket and button up. Ethel had never been happier with a neighbor. Since Laura had moved next door, Ethel had once again become neighborly. Laura had transformed the property from a disgraceful junkyard of rusting pickups, tractors, old chain link fencing and debris to lovely gardens and a verdant lawn. Those awful Kents had finally gone, along with their ragged German shepherd and their nasty, brawling children. The street was once again peaceful, and

Laura was a fine neighbor. She watched as Laura slipped out the door.

The cold air made Laura's eyes water as she hurried toward her car. Once inside, she snapped on the radio, put the gearshift into first, and pulled away from the curb. She rolled her head back, still eyeing the road, and raised her shoulders as high as she could, holding them there and then letting them fall. A wave of relaxation washed down her neck and out to her arms. She was thinking of how to proceed, how to start the last chapter, when the anchor from WPVM began his newscast. She paid no attention as he reported that millions of chickens in at least six countries had either died of avian influenza or been destroyed in an effort to contain the outbreak. The sun was cheery and bright, not a cloud in the sky. Her book was almost done. Taylor was arriving in three days. Life was good.

3

Bangkok, Tuesday, Mid-October

Li Kan had barely begun to sense the gray dawning of another school day when she heard her father's urgent whispers. "Li Kan, go get Doctor Ghi now. Get up!"

Li Kan raised her head, yawning and stretching lazily. As she swallowed, she realized how parched her mouth must have been, for far in the back of her throat, a sliver of pain surprised her. She looked about the shadowy room at her still sleeping brothers and sisters and wondered why she had to be singled out to do an errand this early. And then she remembered her sister and mother, how last night while she ate dinner, her mother's eyelids closed even as Li Kan bragged about her teacher's compliment. Madame Wu was not one to praise students; more often, her eyebrows arched with disdain at their ignorance. But yesterday, Madame Wu had leaned over Li Kan's desk, her hand on her shoulder, and actually smiled. "You understand numbers," Madame Wu had acknowledged, nodding her head and then passing on down the row of bent heads and scratching pencils. Li Kan's heart had pounded with so much pride that she hugged herself to keep others from hearing it and thinking her vain. But she knew she would tell her mother in the evening, and her mother would clap her hands and say, "Yes! Yes! Little Kan. Yes! Yes!" She had waited quietly through all the preparations, had helped to serve, anticipating all the while the moment later on when she would sit beside her mother and share her wonderful news. But her mother had been breathing hard and coughing, coughing, all through dinner. Li Kan worried that she might fall asleep with the sticks in her hand. She had been vague, not quite there, when later Li Kan had pulled her sleeve and whispered, "Yia, today something wonderful happened."

"Ah, little Kan, I am so tired," her mother sighed. "Please can you tell me tomorrow?"

And her sister Dai, moved yesterday into her parents' room, had eaten nothing the entire evening. She had remained huddled on her mat, not even drinking the water her brother lifted her shoulders to sip. Worse, she ignored Li Kan's attempts to make her smile, something that never, ever happened, for she and her sister were best friends, inseparable. Li Kan closed her eyes again, thinking about Madame Wu.

Her father, already dressed for work, poured tea into a small cup and carried it into the next room, where her parents slept. He emerged again, seconds later, annoyed to see her still on the floor. "Get up," he hissed. "Your mother needs Dr. Ghi right now. Something is wrong."

Li Kan knew not to ask questions. Her father's temper was short, even in the best of times. But when he was angry or worried, all of them knew enough to move fast and keep quiet, and that is exactly what she did. Li Kan pushed herself up off her mat and rose, grabbing her school dress from the hook. She was gone in minutes.

Aroused by these rustlings, other children hurried about getting ready for school. The older boys, plaid shirts buttoned and shirt-tails hanging loose, peered into their parents' room to say good-bye to their mother, who lay wheezing next to their sleeping sister.

"Will she be all right?" Luang asked. He jingled his moped key, anxious to leave. At the auto factory, his supervisor was waiting for someone to commit the smallest infraction of rules, his delicate hands ready at the clipboard to record the name of anyone even a minute late. Luang was not about to be one of them. Chiang danced upon equally impatient feet, anxious to get a glimpse of the luscious legs of the seamstresses streaming into Thong's, the clothing factory for which he did maintenance. He already anticipated their giggles and the way they would modestly sashay past him and his buddies, their eyes lowered, their red mouths smiling. Both boys were relieved to hear their father whisper, "It's the flu," though they could see he, too, trembled. "Go to work. The doctor is coming."

By the time Li Kan returned, bringing with her the news that Doctor Ghi was on his way, only her father, mother, and sister remained in the gloomy rooms. Her father placed his finger to his lips, shushing her as soon as she entered the flat. He was clearly worried, for he barely spoke and his mouth was a tight crease in his face. "Go to school," he said. "I will wait for the doctor." He wished that he too could lie down, for his head was pounding.

"Are you all right, father?" Li Kan asked. He looked gray and weak, but she was not sure whether it was the darkness of their rooms that made him so ghostly or whether it was worry for Dai and her mother.

"I think I am getting sick too," he said. "This flu. It's a bad one."

"Should I stay to help?" she asked hopefully, not wanting to tell her father that her throat hurt and her chest seemed squeezed by invisible arms.

"No, no," he said. "You go."

Li Kan obeyed, pulling up her school socks and tying her good shoes as quickly as she could. She knew she was going to be late for morning exercises. That meant she would incur the wrath of Madame Wu. Yet she did not dare to ask her father for a note that might minimize her punishment. He was sitting on the floor beside her mother, unmoving, his head bent as if praying, his hands folded. From the doorway, he resembled the Buddhist statue she had seen in the public garden she visited with her class, the one that overlooked the small pool of goldfish.

Li Kan hurried out to the pavement, caught in the tide of hundreds moving east and west along the street. She tried to shake away the sickness she felt, but her shoulders and neck would not loosen. She ached everywhere, a dull, thudding ache that throbbed beneath the surface, one not yet intense enough to overcome her, but there, waiting as if gathering strength. She swallowed carefully, attempting to minimize the pain in her throat, and wondered how she would ever sit the long hours of hot, steamy classes and Madame Wu's afternoon detention. But swallowing carefully only made her choke. Despite her best efforts to cover her mouth, Li Kan coughed, sending a ragged pain down her throat and into her lungs. She paused momentarily on the street, repeatedly coughing as others brushed past her and hurried away. And then she turned right at the corner, her school in sight. This was not going to be a good day, she thought, and as if to punctuate that pronouncement, she coughed again, spraying a cloud of invisible droplets filled with her mother's new virus onto the hands and faces of those with the misfortune to be going the same way.

4

Patterson, Tuesday, Mid-October

Gold and red leaves skittered across the road amid spotty patches of snow from a too-early storm. Rob Grant thought, "Long winter." Rob knew winters in Patterson. He knew how ten miles to the east, south, and west, he could be driving through rain, but get close to home and suddenly rain froze to ice and then to snow, the roads often covered before he hit the hills that led to his farm. He'd been born there thirty-five years ago, spent his childhood roaming the forests northeast of the big Quabbin Reservoir with his dad, and shot his first deer minutes from where he was now. He left Patterson only for the years it took to get his degree in Horticulture at UMass, but by then he knew every back trail, tree stump, abandoned foundation, gravesite, and cave for five towns around. He had gotten used to calls from the local historical society or the police for information when no one else knew where some old stone culvert or silo foundation site remained buried by weeds or brush. Except for a few old-timers whose memories of families and their various accomplishments or disasters were first hand, Rob was among the most accepted authority on town lore.

Long winters were common in Patterson, relief coming only when the black flies appeared at the first burst of warmth in May, annoying everyone well into June. But it was not just the snow and cold that Rob sensed were about to make this winter a long one. The discussion he'd just left back at the Selectmen's meeting, the off-the-record one that had occurred after reporter Nose Bartlett was already halfway out of town, had bothered him, and left him with a general unease.

Nose Bartlett should have lingered, but once again he'd failed to measure up to his name. His real name was Lawrence, but the pronounced protuberance that dominated his face, the hooked nose that easily identified his family members, had somehow gone out of control in the gene pool that created him. In elementary school, he had been one of the outsiders found on every playground, always trying to appear "in" with the guys by sniffing around every conversation. Having what one might call a "nose for the news" got him his nickname, which then turned out to be his destiny. Once out of high school, Nose got his first job in the pressroom of the Almont Gazette. Later he had worked his way up to covering town meetings and football games and finally made a living doing what had always come quite naturally to him, nosing out news. But Nose had left early. He had missed the muffled conversation.

Rob refocused on the road, though mind-meanderings in this locale seldom endangered other cars or pedestrians. This was rural country, and on this road only chipmunks, squirrels, and a few errant dogs had anything to fear from inattentive drivers. Soon gravel crunched under his tires as he left asphalt and headed west. His farm nestled just a few miles beyond, well over two hundred acres of rolling hills, pastures, and forests, and all of it bordered by stonewalls and pine stands. His pride was the orchard he had nurtured for well over fifteen years now, one he'd planted on both sides of his drive so that in spring coming home was as fragrant as it was beautiful. He loved how white apple blossoms presaged the bounty to come, the way nature had of filling him with energy and hope. The orchards were work, of course, prone to diseases and easily victimized by insects that could devastate plans for a rich harvest. Through years of farm experience, his father's teaching, avid reading and meetings, a good aggie education, trial, error and analysis, however, he knew the warning signs, knew how to fight back. Because of that, not only the peach and apple orchards but all of his farming endeavors, the blueberries, raspberries, and tomatoes, the pumpkins, and the vegetable crops had served him well, providing for him and his family. Yet Rob knew also that nature was unpredictable and when it wanted to be, also uncontrollable, and he never let himself assume good fortune was his due.

He turned into his driveway and glanced up over the knoll, nearly a quarter-mile away, behind which his modest clapboard cape faced southeast, overlooking the array of valleys leading toward Mount Wachusett. Smoke rose from the chimney, and Rob thought that Terry must have left work unusually early to have already stoked the wood stove. It was only three o'clock.

When Terry saw the gray pickup come over the hill, she hurried to insert the last garlic slices into slits she'd cut in the pork roast. Turning to soap her hands, then rinsing and drying them, she watched as the truck slowed to a halt and Rob stepped down from the cab. She watched him, able by now to read the slightest tightness of lip or downturn of head, the quickness of his step, the rise or fall of his shoulders. She had loved him even as a child. When he'd begun spending recesses seeking her attention—pulling her braids or racing his buddies or hanging upside down off the top bar of the little kids' swing, showing off whenever she looked his way, she knew with a silent certainty that someday he'd be hers. Even when other girls giggled and flirted to catch his eye, she'd been unworried. She wondered how she could have known even then, in fourth grade, that someday that wiry, chestnut-haired, freckle-faced boy would grow into the man with whom she would make her life. How could she have been so right about such things at only nine years old? Smiling, she turned toward the back door just as Rob opened it.

"You're out early," he grinned, removing his coat and tossing it on one of the wall hooks. "Doc getting in one last round of golf?" Terry hugged him. She was nearly as tall as he, so that as a couple they had always looked the equals that they were. As respected and admired as Rob was in town, Terry's opinions and decisions held equal sway. They were, according to the knot of widows who served Sunday morning refreshments after church, a "fine couple". And among the rest of the parishioners, they were thought of as a unit, not two, but one, strong and permanent.

"Umm," he teased, "You smell like garlic bread."

"Pork roast," she said, pushing him away. "And roast potatoes." Terry checked the oven, and slid the roasting pan inside. "And yes. Doc says he can count on one hand how many more days he has before he'll be golfing in snow. How was the meeting?"

"Same stuff. Pete Howard's griping, as usual, about the oak tree. Says one of these windy nights it's going to flatten his house and kill all of them in their beds. His words, not mine."

"And Jack, of course, said it's the oldest tree in town and should be preserved."

"And it's on the common, not his property, Jack said." Rob smiled at the predictability of it all.

"That's it? The whole meeting?" She glanced at him, cocking her head.

"Whole meeting." Rob didn't like worrying himself about maybes that were probably impossibilities, and he certainly had no intention of communicating his anxiety to Terry, so he stepped into the living room, avoiding her gaze. "Fire feels good," he said, "freezing tonight."

"And we need more wood," Terry chimed from the kitchen. "Would you get some now, before you forget?"

Outside again, Rob positioned the kids' old red wagon next to the woodpile. Behind him he heard the familiar squeal of the school bus brakes and the faint muffled din of shouting children. He knew he would not be able to count to fifteen before the head of his oldest boy, Michael, appeared at the top of the knoll. As if on cue, there he was, running down the drive toward him. Despite the book bag that made him appear severely hunchbacked, Michael's speed and agility remained unhampered. An athlete, for sure, Rob knew and he bristled with pride. He also knew there was no telling how long it would take for Christopher to appear behind him. Christopher was easily distracted by colors or movements requiring closer inspection, details most people missed or plain ignored. Rob smiled at how much Christopher reminded him of his own little brother, the first Christopher. When Christopher did appear, book bag dragging from one arm and the other arm flailing the horizon, Rob was momentarily disappointed not to see his own brother's face grinning from beneath the Red Sox cap. "What've you got there, pal?" Rob called, for Christopher was waving an orange sheet, his bony arm barely steadying him in a run that was more a hurried stumble than anything else.

"A note from the principal," Michael answered for him, having pulled up panting beside the wagon.

"Ah. And it says?" Rob asked.

"Dad," Christopher exclaimed, now only feet away. "Look. The principal." And he pushed the sheet into Rob's hand.

"Are you in trouble?" Rob asked, feigning a serious tone. He could see that what he held was only a xeroxed notice.

"Everyone got one," Christopher responded. "I wasn't bad." Michael giggled and Christopher looked back confused.

But Rob had begun reading the letter from the principal. "Just flu shots," he said aloud when he finished. He looked up to see the storm door slowly closing, both boys already inside. Rob carefully folded the sheet into quarters, placed it in his jacket pocket, and then stacked the oak and beech logs until the wagon was full. He thought about the many more tasks needing completion before the snow blanketed his fields, and he was glad he'd have Charlie Grange to work with him. There had been years when he couldn't afford full-time help, years when the sun was already long gone, the kids already bedded down for the night before he could drag his dead tired body into their kitchen for the dinner Terry had set on the warmer.

"Winter," Rob said under his breath, taking the wagon's little handle in his big hand. "Flu shots." He walked the wagon to the storm door, dropped the handle, then headed toward the barn where he knew Charlie was already doing evening chores and tending his egg layers, chickens he kept to earn a little extra money.

5

Patterson, Tuesday, Mid-October

Principal Joshua Stone remained in his office until his stomach began growling. The yellow light from his desk lamp barely lit the farthest corners beyond his desk, so that the book shelves and file cabinets, shoddy old leather office chairs, and dusty trophies were more shadow than substance. His feet were cold, and beneath his desk he wiggled his toes to increase circulation. The Board had installed thermostats that automatically turned the heat down to fifty a good hour before the buses arrived, so that by this time of the day the concrete floors emanated a chill that crept through the soles of shoes, no matter how thick.

The computer screen in front of him began filling with yet another article he had found on www.google.com. He had been reading ever since the last school bus left for the day, and he intended to stay as long as it was necessary to begin to understand why for the first time ever the schools had been ordered to provide flu shots. Not that he didn't think it was a good idea. Many of the families he knew were hard put to provide decent health insurance for their kids. Too few made regular appearances for physicals because people could put off blood tests but not food in their stomachs. And perhaps this year, with the shots, the town wouldn't have to pay the outrageous substitute bills they'd had last year, when so many children were hacking and coughing in their steamy classrooms that teachers began dropping like flies. Some had been out more than a week, their upper respiratory systems hovering dangerously near pneumonia or bronchitis or whatever other serious illness might compound the effects of the virus. Even he had fallen, albeit only for two days, and the absentee lists had mushroomed so fast that the Board contemplated closing school for a few days to break the onslaught of infection. Fortunately, February vacation arrived just in time. Afterward, absences moderated, and by April things returned to normal.

This year the reports made it clear that the country was facing yet another nasty flu season. The particular strain the authorities predicted was to be an exceedingly virulent one, and the media stressed that all children and adults over 50 were strongly advised to get their shots. Last year, when the supplies of vaccine had run out well before Christmas, availability had been strictly limited to those most in need. This year the pharmaceutical companies were more prepared. And as if in response, this year the state had mandated free flu shots in all public, parochial, and private schools.

No one he knew thought much of this. And perhaps, Stone thought, neither should he. It was merely good public health policy and should have been instituted long ago. Though flu had never killed anyone in his family, at least the recent generations he knew about, it had taken its toll on Patterson the same as everywhere else. Last year, Sarah Shortliffe and Willie Good had both died in January because of complications stemming from the outbreak. True, Sarah was an asthmatic whose lungs and heart had long ago been compromised by attacks. And Willie was eighty-three, though in far better shape than some sixty-year-olds he knew. Many had been hospitalized and the nearest hospital in Almont, filled to capacity, had gotten pretty testy about admitting any but the life-threatening cases. There was reason, he tried to convince himself, for the bureaucrats to get involved, start passing laws and creating mandates. There was nothing more to it.

Perhaps because he'd been a science teacher, or perhaps because his brother was a doctor, Josh liked things to make sense; they had to add up. And mandatory flu shots didn't. Something else was at work here, he was sure. He didn't know what, and he didn't know if he could figure it out by himself, but he was going to damn well try, no matter how cold his feet got. Everyone knew that SARS had created quite a scare a few years ago, so much so that the World Health Organization and U.S. experts from the Center for Disease Control down in Atlanta had gotten actively involved the minute China admitted it had a problem. And he'd seen them contain it, though for a while things looked pretty dire. Lots of people had died, and videos of city streets crowded with people wearing surgical masks had sobered everyone. The offshoot, however, was that as soon as the WHO and China took the necessary steps to contain it, infections decreased and people forgot about SARS. The public was once again reassured that science and technology could or would solve any problem. Look at polio. Look at measles, mumps, and whooping cough.

So was there a problem that had led to this mandate? What did the politicians know that the rest of the public, including him, didn't? Stone pulled up an article from the Washington Post. Pictured on the right was a woman whose surgical mask covered all but her eyes. She was in coveralls, and she stood beside what could have been a towering stack of bagged turkeys ready for a pre-Thanksgiving shipment to Stop and Shop. But the bold print below the shot read

"Chickens to be Buried Alive." And the woman was no midwest farm wife; she was a health-worker from Vietnam.

Stone was no scientist, but he did know some things. He had spotted articles in the news and even in Time magazine that discussed scientists' fears of a potential pandemic. A lot of experts agreed that the world was ripe for one, not only because these things came in cycles, two to three to a century, but also because megacities were the perfect hothouses for the spread of infectious disease. Scientists said mushrooming populations were responsible for the destruction of previously untouched rainforests and jungles, where things lurked that no one could predict, diseases as yet unheard of. From consideration of these things, those who studied disease seemed to be trying to warn the world out of its complacency, and Josh thought that perhaps this new vaccination program was the government's response to their fears. But weren't flu shots developed a year ahead of the outbreak, their formula predicated on what was already known? And if so, wasn't he just being paranoid? He wished he could believe that as he logged off and shut down his computer. He wished he could, but feared that he couldn't.

6

Bangkok, Tuesday, Mid-October

Dr. Ghi's arthritic wrists could barely support him as he dropped to kneel between the two huddled women. Had he not known this family for forty years, he would not have even considered making a house call. He was just too old to be rushing about the city. Yet when he saw young Li Kan's face, a child he himself had delivered, he knew he could not refuse. He thought of her father Khun whom he had first treated as a young boy during the war. Khun had lost both his parents in the bombing. He had been brought to the hospital near death, one arm nearly ripped from his shoulder, his chest and legs badly burned. He had looked up at Dr. Ghi, and in his eyes Ghi had read the agony of that infernal time. Yet when Dr. Ghi spoke to him, encouraging him to hold on, to be strong, Khun seemed to muster some inner strength or resolve. He had seen it in others during that time, the pure will to live, to survive, that saved those who would be saved. And the boy had come to personify to him all that he admired in these people of his who could find the determination to bear wars and disasters, poverty and famine, and still go on. Khun had survived, though he would always wear the scars of his bad burns. And he had found a wife, Phrati, a woman Dr. Ghi had also delivered. Ghi followed their little family as it grew, administering to all of them from his storefront clinic, so that they had become to him the children that his barren wife had never borne. He cared deeply about them, and so when Li Kan ran up to him, pulling upon his sleeve just as he reached the clinic door, crying "Please, Dr. Ghi, my father begs please come now. My mother is ill. My sister too," he had stepped inside the clinic to tell his assistant that he would be delayed. He gathered up his bag and left immediately for their flat, his old legs wobbling as he made his way against the tide on the sidewalk.

"How long have they been like this?" he asked sternly over his shoulder. The women did not look right. Ghi immediately recognized the seriousness of their condition.

"My daughter has been sick for three days, but Phrati only one," Khun whispered, his head bowed in guilt.

Dr. Ghi felt the girl's faint pulse and leaned awkwardly in to listen to her breathing. Inches away he could feel the heat of her fever and knew without needing a thermometer that her fever was lethally high. She moaned and shifted to her back. "Doctor," she murmured, as if in greeting, and managed a half-hearted smile. He took the stethoscope from his woven bag and listened to her heart and lungs. From behind his stooped shoulders and white hair, Khun watched intently, leaning low, his hands on his knees.

"She's very ill," Ghi pronounced. "She must go to the hospital." Turning then to Phrati, he repeated the same examination, but she did not seem to recognize him or even to be aware of his touch. "Both must go," he said. "And Phrati became sick only yesterday?" Ghi worried that she was more desperately ill than her daughter.

"It's just the flu, isn't it?" Khun said. "I'm getting it too. We've been sick before." He tried to sound certain, a false bravado in his voice, but even he was unconvinced.

"Not like this," the doctor answered. "Your daughter

is barely conscious. Your wife is burning up. There are no choices here."

Dr. Ghi struggled to his feet and bent to retrieve his bag. "It is only a bad flu," he lied to Kuhn without looking him in the eyes, "but they need medical supervision. I will call an ambulance from the clinic. Get a bag ready for them."

"I have no money for hospitals," Khun pleaded, his face a sorrow. "Can't you just treat them here? Some medicine? I will watch them."

In his eyes, Dr. Ghi remembered the sad little boy who had lost his entire family. He put a kind hand on Khun's shoulder. "You're getting sick yourself. You said so. You must watch yourself or you'll be going to the hospital with them. Once they're gone, you lie down and rest, you understand? Send one of your children later for news."

With that, Dr. Ghi hurried away. He had patients waiting at the clinic, many of them sick with the same flu. Not quite the same, though, he thought as once again he returned to the street. These were the first he'd seen this season with such intense fevers and increased heart rates. And he did not like the sound of their lungs or that both were barely conscious when he arrived. They'd be all right once the hospital staff could oversee them, he reassured himself. But he knew intuitively that they were not all right. In the back of his mind, the knowledge of how dangerous influenza could be, how thousands died every year from the virus itself or from complications resulting from it, left him anxious. Both Phrati and her daughter were demonstrating pneumonia-like symptoms. Not good at all. Perhaps this hard-working family was in for more tragedy. And though he'd seen tragedy thousands of times in his long career, he was sorry to think that after all these years of tending to them, delivering the babies, inoculating them, prescribing antibiotics or whatever else they'd needed, his efforts might not see them through. He might just lose one. Or two, he added, shaking his head sadly as he opened the door to his clinic.

Seated hip to hip along the wall, mothers and children, punctuated by the occasional old man or woman, looked up as he entered. All nodded a greeting to Dr. Ghi, who hurried past the waiting patients without making eye contact. To do that would have been to chance speaking to one of them, and that would further delay the long list of patients his assistants had ready for him to see. He stepped inside his inner offices, called the hospital, and spoke to the emergency administrator, remembering the address from memory. "Yes," he said into the phone, "and have Dr. Wong call me as soon as he has seen them. I will be at the clinic."

With that he set down the phone, grabbed a file from the door of Room 1 and entered without speaking. Dr. Ghi was not known for his warmth or friendliness, but for decades he had been the only doctor treating patients in this poor suburb of Bangkok. He was well respected, and though certainly old enough to retire, Dr. Ghi remained the doctor of choice for all of the old families still in the district.

Many hours passed while Dr. Ghi saw patient after patient, peering into throats and ears, listening to breathing, taking temperatures, stitching wounds, examining slides, writing prescriptions. The day was a whirlwind of faces and symptoms, children crying at the sight of a needle, mothers wincing while holding their children still, old men coughing, hardy bones, frail bones, robust skin, papery skin, clear eyes, weepy eyes, pink nails, and yellow nails, the everyday parade of the sick. But when the call came in from the hospital, his assistant knew to put it through immediately, even though he was examining someone. His patient, an obese woman with onset diabetes, sat obediently on the edge of the table, her plump hands folded in her lap, her triple chins resting on her chest. "Excuse me," Dr. Ghi apologized. "This will only take a moment." She tried to look elsewhere, to pretend she was not listening, having learned politeness a lifetime ago. Intently she studied the chart of the upper respiratory system hanging on the wall just to her left. She could not, however, help but hear the short gasp Dr. Ghi emitted before saying "Both of them?" into the phone. Swiveling on his stool so that he turned his back to her, he seemed to shrivel into himself, huddling over the built-in office shelf as if by doing so, she might not hear him. "I will be right there," he said, his voice flat and grave. Dr. Ghi rose from his stool and replaced the receiver. His face was white, his eyes wide. He looked at the waiting woman, but she sensed he did not really see her. "You'll have to excuse me," he bowed. "I must go to the hospital."

7

Boston, Massachusetts, Tuesday, Mid-October

Jedidiah Stone had just finished dinner and was settling down with his most recent copy of the Journal of the American Medical Association when his brother called from Patterson. In his usual abrupt manner, Josh asked a question before even saying hello. Jed immediately knew his brother's voice. They lived hours apart, but they spoke frequently.

"What do you know about this avian flu?" Josh asked.

Jed leaned back in his armchair. Wasn't it just like Josh to think he knew about every disease that existed? As a kid, Josh always expected his older brother to know the answer to every question, and now, decades past childhood, he still did, despite all the evidence to the contrary. "Why?" Jed delayed.

"This mandatory flu shot program," Josh replied.

"That has nothing to do with the avian flu," Jed explained. "We're worried about this year's new virus strain, that's all."

"So the politicians up your way are just being good guys and protecting public health?" Josh's tone was cynical.

"Far as I know, Josh. We're bracing for a bad time of it at the hospital."

"This avian strain over in China and Vietnam, this has nothing to do with it?"

"Now, that's scary stuff." Jed nodded his head and rubbed

his chin at the same time. "You know what happened with SARS."

"But they contained it, didn't they?"

"They contained that epidemic. Viruses have a way of outsmarting containments."

"I know, I know. They mutate."

"They go dormant and wait as well." Jed was an Ob-Gyn, known in Boston as one of the best in the business. His knowledge of viruses was not cutting-edge and he knew it. But he knew how viruses worked. He knew that viruses existed in the hinterlands, beyond human concepts of life and death and that all a virus needed to come alive was a cell with the proper sticky surface for it to cling to. It could remain "dead," floating around in someone's blood or mucus indefinitely and then "BAM," it would latch on to some harmless cell and there'd be hell to pay. Someone had written that a virus is like a Trojan horse. The cell's natural inclination is to encircle it, pull it inside and thus conquer it. In fact, the virus is anything but conquered. Once inside, it begins replicating, using cellular material and systems until its numbers explode and pop the cell. The cell dies, of course, but worse, now thousands of new viruses float where only one had been.

"So these flu shots we're all getting are only for last year's flu strain. No protection from the Asian stuff." Josh sounded confused.

"The avian flu kills birds—chicken, ducks, sometimes other farmyard livestock, like pigs."

"People don't get it?" Josh already knew the answer. Yes, they could and occasionally did. "What's the big danger?"

"Recombination."

"What's that?" But Josh was already inferring a pretty good definition.

"Someone with a human virus picks up the avian virus. The two strains combine to create a totally new virus that can infect humans, one for which we have no natural defenses."

"Epidemic," Josh said flatly.

"Pandemic," Jed corrected. "World wide epidemic with enormous fatalities. Like the one in the early 1900s. The Spanish flu."

"Could that happen again, with all we know now about viruses?" Josh asked, knowing he was not going to like what he heard.

"Undoubtedly. We're due," his brother said solemnly. "We're overdue."

8

Bangkok, Tuesday, Mid-October

"We do not know," Dr. Wong explained to the agitated Dr. Ghi. "The ambulance brought them in not twenty minutes after your call. The admitting doctors immediately ordered ice baths for both and administered rimantadine and penicillin. The woman's heart rate was 150," he said, looking at the clipboard. "Her bronchial intake was near flat. She was bleeding from the nose and mouth, a thin, frothy stuff. Same with the daughter. She went into cardiac arrest, and all attempts to revive her were fruitless. Her lungs were like sponges. The woman's death followed the same pattern, not ten minutes later. Would you like to see the charts?"

Dr. Ghi sank in his chair, shaking his head. "I have heard of nothing this virulent. Do you know of anything?" Dr. Ghi made no claim to being anything but an old-fashioned doctor. He read what he could when he could, and he was a conscientious man. He dreaded telling Khun of their loss.

Dr. Wong pursed his lips, studying Dr. Ghi. "The husband said only a day for the woman?"

"Yes, only a day. But Dai was three or four."

"Yet the woman died within minutes of the daughter. Had she been ill, her system compromised?" Dr. Wong was hopeful of an explanation.

"Not as far as I know. The husband was getting sick as well. Just this morning."

Dr. Wong sat up. "Is he outside?"

"No, I told him to go to bed. He is unaware. I will go there now."

"Perhaps we should bring him in, just in case," Dr. Wong suggested. "Whatever killed them may be...you know... something we'd better watch. I've got the lab working on it, but if the woman's course was only twenty-four hours..." his voice trailed off. He gazed at the wall above Dr. Ghi's head for a second, and then looked back down at the old man's face. "Something tells me that I'd better call the health authorities. There is something about this that I do not like." Dr. Wong lifted the receiver, his fingers on the number pad.

Dr. Ghi swallowed, noticing as he did so the beginning of a sore throat. "A mutant. You are worried about a mutant strain," he said softly.

"Of course I am. Haven't we been warned for years now? And the avian strain is here, in this city. That I know for fact." Dr. Wong's memory had shifted into high gear, attempting to recall all that he had learned at the Geneva conference two years ago, the one organized by the World Health Organization. He remembered the keynote speaker, a Dr. Robert Schultz, famous worldwide for his work on emerging viruses. Schultz had warned that high density populations and modern-day travel were the perfect petri dish for contagion, making the spread of a virus impossible to quash once it entered the network of roads, rails, and airways connecting every person on the globe with every other person. Shultz had brought his point home when he said, "We are all, at most, a twenty-four hour plane flight from a hot virus." He remembered how still the audience had been at that moment, for all medical practitioners were at least vaguely aware of the horrors scientists like Frederick Murphy, at the American Center for Disease

Control, had pursued—the Marburg virus, and Karl Johnson, also at the CDC, who had discovered ebola. The thought of an ebola outbreak sent shudders through all of them that day, and later, when a few of the members of his delegation had met for dinner, Wong and the rest had whispered worriedly about the preponderance of disease that seemed of late to be coming primarily from Asia. These avian diseases that were jumping to human hosts were no laughing matter. What would it take, one of them had asked rhetorically, for some poultry virus for which we have literally no immunity to combine with a common, airborne human influenza spread by sneezing or coughing? And they had all agreed that it would only require the right circumstances—someone sick with flu who also became sick from a bird, or some other animal, a scenario so likely to happen sooner or later that the horror of the probability stunned them. He remembered the long moment at the table when all of them had sat back in their chairs, each staring off into a vision of such terror that no one wanted to speak.

"It is important to isolate the family. Get the father in, locate those children exposed, and quarantine them. Meanwhile, I will call the authorities. We'd best pass this on to them."

"I will notify the father. You can call me later…" Dr. Ghi had started to rise, but stopped when he saw Dr. Wong's expression.

"I will send a car for the father and the authorities will locate the other children. You had best stay here, Dr. Ghi," Dr. Wong said softly. "To be sure." He looked at the doctor with worried eyes.

Dr. Ghi stared back, the thin skin around his mouth creasing into a scowl. Half up, half down, he paused, thinking. "Ah," he said, sitting back down. "Ah."

9

Bangkok, Tuesday, Mid-October

General Chao bristled at being bothered just as he was sitting down to dinner. Before him lay a table glistening with antique Limoges china and polished silver. Massive fruit arrangements, flickering candlelight, ladies in their most glittering evening attire, and many of the men he was most anxious to impress chattering affably as his servants moved about, their trays laden. General Chao was upwardly mobile. He might only be Minister of Health right now, but the general had plans, imaginative plans, and he knew that dinners like this, appropriately timed, were essential to those plans. So when his secretary appeared at the dining room door, bowing humbly numerous times as he made his way to the head of the table, General Chao could barely contain his anger at being disturbed.

"What is it," he growled into the young man's ear, being careful to maintain a toothy smile.

"I'm sorry, General," his secretary apologized, groveling and bowing. "But I think you want to take this call. It's from your office."

The general considered a moment. To be called in the evening meant something of great importance, for he had trained his quavering staff well. None of them had the audacity to incur his wrath, and all of them knew that the general worked nine to five and no more. He could almost visualize one of his underlings trembling on the other end of the line, waiting to be duly chastised, or fired, as the case might warrant. But tonight, the image brought him no pleasure. If one of them had called, he had a problem. So he replaced the linen napkin on his plate, excused himself, exhorting everyone to begin without him, and rose to follow his secretary from the room.

"This had better be an emergency," he hissed, once out of earshot of the assembled guests. Only the housemaid heard him, and she was used to his abuse.

"I think it is, sir," his secretary replied, though clearly not assured. His secretary often felt himself caught, damned if he did, damned if he didn't. And every time, he worried that he might be looking for a job within hours. The general was neither a loyal nor an understanding man.

Inside his library, the general picked up the receiver and barked, "What!"

From the other end of the line, his Deputy Assistant began with profuse apologies. "I'm sorry, General. I know you have guests tonight. But I have just had a call from the Regional Office. We've got a situation in Kwang Tri that seems of the utmost seriousness. I think you'll want to make the decisions on this."

The general scowled. "Is this about chickens?" he sneered, having already dealt with the eradication of several poultry farms. "Destroy the goddamned chickens. What are you bothering me for?"

In the slight pause before his deputy answered, the general could almost hear him gulp. "No, sir. This is not chickens. We think perhaps chicken contact. We have two people dead in less than twenty-four hours, the rest of the family in critical condition and in isolation at the Kwang Tri hospital, and, we think, mass exposure at the public school, a clothier, and the auto factory. The officials at the hospital are worried."

General Chao's shoulders sank. Why now, he wondered. Why not yesterday, or tomorrow, or next week? Goddamn fortune I've spent for this dinner, and now I have to worry about the goddamned flu. General Chao had just about had it with all the whispering about avian flu and poultry workers getting sick from it. Just the other day, at the meeting of ministers, the room had erupted the minute the subject had been brought up. Colonel Iso, the agricultural deputy, that fat, officious chicken farmer, had roared when someone suggested that Thailand had a responsibility to report the seven outbreaks recorded in the provinces. "Are you mad?" he had roared. "You let this news out and we're going to be like China, bagging squawking chickens by the millions and burying them alive! This is our problem, and we can handle it quietly, with no one the wiser." And then the Prime Minister, leaning back in his soft leather chair, had begun worrying about revenues and trade problems. "Colonel Iso," he asked quietly, "What will happen if news does get out?"

Iso was good at assessing others' agendas. How else had he gotten this far, Chao thought. "Fiscal disaster! I tell you, sir, we'll have to destroy every chicken in the country. No one will want them anyhow. The WHO will be here within days, nosing around our farms, looking for health violations and pressuring us to do their bidding. The news will be all over the globe. And who is going to reimburse the farmers who lose everything? We will have to do it!"

General Chao was also good at assessing others' agendas. He saw how the Prime Minister's jaw worked, his muscles tightening and releasing. He caught the Prime Minister sizing up reactions among the ministers as they too thought about the dire consequences should the news get out. He knew the Prime Minister was also making a mental list of those he could depend upon and those of his advisors who might give him trouble.

Then the Prime Minister had looked directly at him. "What do you think, General Chao?" Chao had known that this was not the time to grandstand. Although he was a trained doctor, he had long ago become first a general. He hadn't risen to his elevated status by sticking his neck out. "I'm concerned, of course," Chao had squinted, nodding slowly. "But I'm willing to go along with Colonel Iso. If he says they can contain the outbreaks safely, then I say try that first."

A sigh of relief had passed from minister to minister. Iso's chest visibly inflated, his many chins rolling up smugly beneath his extended lower lip. All turned to the Prime Minister, who smiled benignly on Chao. "You are a good man, General Chao. We will deal with this ourselves." And later, as the men were leaving the meeting, the Prime Minister had spoken to him privately. "I am very impressed with your leadership," the Prime Minister said softly, patting Chao on the back. "I will remember this."

"I will remember this" still echoed in Chao's mind as he spoke to his deputy. "Tell the hospital to shut down admissions. Direct ambulance services to Bangkok Major. Don't give them any reasons. Just make it a temporary order. Tell the Kwang Tri administrator that he is to talk about this to no one, not even his staff. Proceed as usual. Meanwhile call Colonel Iso. Ask whether the chicken thing is under control. And tell him what you told me."

"Are you coming in?" his deputy asked weakly, afraid to say what he thought.

"I'm having dinner, you idiot," the general shouted, only barely aware that he had left his library door open. His secretary shook, looking down at his exquisitely polished shoes. "Two stupid deaths can wait until morning," he roared. Had his guests been listening, they would surely have wondered how such a generous man could sound so ferocious. But the ambassador had just told a wonderful joke, and everyone at the table laughed until tears came to their eyes.

Within the hour the phone rang in Dr. Wong's office. The underling on the other end was apologetic but uninformative. Dr. Wong leaned forward on his desk, using his thumb and forefinger to rub his eyebrows in delicate circles. His surgical mask, pushed down below his chin to his shirt collar, gave him a clerical look.

"You cannot mean it," Wong responded, stunned. "This is not something that we can sweep under the carpet, Deputy. This is not your ordinary flu. I have seen the victims and..."

"I am sorry, Dr. Wong," the deputy replied nervously. "I can do nothing without General Chao's permission. He has given you an order, and certainly I am in no position to remand it."

"I see," Dr. Wong sighed. And he did see. Wong knew how politics worked as well as anyone. Hadn't he also obtained his high position and held on to it by being politic? At certain times it was wise to be a team player, especially when money or power were concerned. If General Chao wanted to keep a lid on what was happening in Kwang Tri hospital, he wasn't going to be a problem. He would cooperate, of course, and know that by doing so, some day his cooperation would be rewarded. "Thank you, Deputy. I will do what I can. Will you ask the General to call me as soon as he arrives tomorrow?" With that, Dr. Wong gently hung up the phone.

10

Patterson, Wednesday, Mid-October

Michael and Christopher Grant stood just left of their driveway, waiting for the school bus. Michael picked up a few stones, tossing them lightly in his hand. "Bet I can hit Smiths' mailbox from here," Michael said, eyeing the rusting wreck the Smiths left when they moved.

"Bet you can't," Christopher dared, setting down his book bag and picking up some stones as well.

Michael threw and missed. He tried again and this time a small "thunk" resounded on the other side of the street. "Your turn, slugger," Michael challenged, looking down at his little brother.

Christopher wound his arm far too many times, as usual, and then let fly. The stone barely made it to the other side, landing three feet from the wooden pole to which the mailbox clung.

"Not bad, not bad. Try again," Michael encouraged, sending another stone hard against the box. But just then the roar of the school bus stopped Christopher mid-throw. Both boys dropped their remaining ammunition and grabbed their book bags. Though neither said it, both were loath to have anyone on the bus see them trying to do anything more than wait. To bring attention on themselves was to risk notice by Butch Jones.

Butch Jones was the meanest kid at Patterson Elementary. He had stayed back twice, once in first grade and again in second, so now he was nearly fourteen years old. His teachers finally threw in the towel on teaching Butch to read when in fifth grade he'd nearly suffocated a rather frail seven-year-old boy by sitting on his chest. Had Mrs. Lasky not seen them behind the wall, the little guy already turning blue while Butch patiently picked his nose, Butch would have succeeded. Butch had used the extra years of elementary school to grow huge, towering over his classmates and even those his own age. Having a father who used his fists frequently, Butch was an angry boy, and he turned his rage and size on anyone who had the misfortune to attract his attention. The brothers had narrowly escaped that fate several times, so Michael and Christopher both worked at the art of entering the bus with as little fanfare as possible.

This morning, however, Butch happened to be sitting in the last seat on their side of the road. The roar in the back of the bus coming from Butch and the sixth grade boys who curried his favor had momentarily quieted. They had reduced Martha Lang to quiet sniffles by calling her four eyes and turtle face and had yet to choose a new victim. In this brief hiatus, Butch happened to turn his moon face to the window just as the bus pulled to a stop. For some reason something about the quiet calm with which Michael shouldered his book bag made Butch grow angry. Little things could do that to Butch. So by the time the boys entered the bus, Butch had already planned an assault, despite his limited vocabulary and even more limited intelligence.

"Hey, Grant," Butch shouted over the roar of the engine. Young Christopher had taken a seat next to his second grade classmate. But Michael was making his way down the aisle, desperately hoping his best friend Jimmy had saved him a seat. He heard his name being called but he ignored it, relieved to see Jimmy slide over to make room for him.

"Grant, you hear me talking to you?" Butch challenged, his tone gruff. A few of the smaller children up front continued talking, unaware of what was going on far behind them. But the rest of the bus grew silent. Mole Travers, the driver, a surly twenty-year-old who as a kid had started many good fights himself, looked up into the rearview mirror, sensing Butch was at it again. But his attention wandered as it had consistently throughout his life. Mole, in fact, had missed most of what his teachers had to say and consequently failed to graduate. Driving the bus was about the best job Mole was going to get, and he didn't mind at all. He had his earphones on, totally against school policy, and was hip-hopping to his favorite beat. The road was clear ahead of him and the next pickup was two miles away. Mole loved the sense of power the bus gave him. He floored it, singing along, tapping on the steering wheel, and forgetting to check Butch in the rearview mirror.

"Grant, you going deaf or sumpin?" Butch's lower lip hung open, wet and pink. Butch's friends giggled, their eyes hungry for a good show, their faces relieved that it wasn't one of them Butch had chosen.

Michael kicked his book bag in front of the seat his friend had just vacated. He looked back at Butch. "I hear you," he said, sounding tired. He knew what was coming.

"Come back here, Grant," Butch ordered, relaxing back into his seat.

Michael knew he was in for it. "What for?" was all he said, looking now into the sorrowful eyes of Jimmy, who cringed against the window.

"Come back here and I'll tell you," Butch sneered. "Bring your lunch bag with you."

Now everyone knew Butch's plan. It had happened repeatedly, a peanut butter sandwich stomped flat and dirty under Butch's boot, an apple with a big bite out of it, a cookie swallowed whole with great burping, or worse, a ritual chewing and then a fake gag, followed by an ugly masticated wad spit at the closest target, usually the cookie's owner.

Michael had no intention of going back there, but he wasn't about to slide into his seat and hide like some pansy. He didn't want a fight, but he wasn't going to back down either. He knew he shouldn't say it even before the words left his mouth, and he knew that he was sealing his doom the minute he did, but he said it anyhow, "You're fat enough, Butch. You don't need my food."

Anyone who thinks fat people can't move fast has never seen the likes of Butch Jones. He was out of his seat and down the aisle, all fists and spit and red-faced before anyone else had a chance to register the insult. "You sonofabitch," he growled, throttling Michael's upper body and trying to get a good hold on him. Michael ducked, swinging back hard into Butch's stomach. Butch never even felt it. He wanted a hold and he got one immediately, first by squeezing Michael's face to his chest and then, by some turning and twisting, wrapping his arm around Michael's neck. Michael tried to bend out of the neck hold, but he might as well have been trying to lift the bus. Still he struggled, only slightly aware that the bus was now in an uproar. His ears pounded. Kids stood in their seats, shouting, "Get him, Mike!" and "Watch out!" and "Choke him, Butch!" and "Slug him!" Butch's friends had come forward, blocking other kids in their seats as the bus hurtled down the hill, veering nearly off the road to avoid a propane gas truck coming the other way. As children were thrown first to the right and then to the left, Mole saw the fracas in his rearview mirror but was too busy getting the bus under control to stop quickly.

Instead he kept his hands on the wheel and his eyes on the road, tapping the brakes to slow down.

Christopher had heard Butch's first call to Michael and frozen in his seat. On the second and third, he had dared to swing around and peek into the aisle. He saw Michael's body tense as he shoved his book bag out of the aisle and he knew that Michael was in for it. When Michael called Butch fat, Christopher's heart stopped, then began pounding erratically, the way it sometimes did for no reason at all. But this time there was reason. He saw Butch hurtling toward Michael and Michael's body disappearing into the hulk of Butch's dirty red windbreaker. Christopher was off his seat in an instant, running at full speed, arms flailing, then leaping onto Butch's back and grabbing him around the neck.

Butch roared as Christopher bit him hard on the shoulder, a mosquito with fangs. He momentarily released Michael to swing his arm back at whatever was causing him such acute pain. His wrist caught Christopher on the nose, sending him flying backward onto the girl in the nearby seat. But Christopher was up again in a flash, climbing the mountain of Butch's back as Butch tried to keep Michael from pummeling his flabby stomach. The crowd went wild at the sight of Butch looking like King Kong swatting at airplanes. While Christopher distracted Butch by yanking his hair, Michael swung up and caught him a good one on the chin. Butch howled, bringing his ham of a hand down hard on Michael's head.

And then the bus stopped. Mole was in the middle of things in a minute, jerking Christopher off Butch's back, grabbing Butch's meaty forearm, and roaring, "You f@@@ing kids cut it out!" When Butch tried to get in a last punch, Mole warned, "You're in so much trouble, Jones, I just dare you. You're gonna' be expelled for sure."

Butch cried out at the injustice, "That little sucker bit me!" and turned his shoulder toward Mole while rubbing the tender spot through his windbreaker.

Mole almost smiled, catching himself just in time. "He's in for it too, and so are you, Grant."

Michael rubbed his head where Butch had slammed him. Christopher wiped the blood from his nose. "Get up in front, the two of you," Mole directed the brothers. "And you stay in the back, Jones, until everyone is out of the bus, you hear me?'"

Butch grunted and turned, lumbering to the rear seat. Michael and Christopher preceded Mole to the front, where the driver made two girls move so that he could "keep an eye on them." Kids began talking again, buzzing about the fight. Mole put the bus in gear and pulled back onto the road. Over the roar of the bus, he shouted, "And don't anyone move. You're in big trouble when Stone hears about this."

From the back Butch continued to glare at the back of Michael's head. His friends pretended not to notice, but in secret sidelong glances, they all agreed that Butch had been bested by a couple of squirts. That news was going to spread like wildfire, and they were eyewitnesses.

When the bus halted in front of Carl Patterson Elementary School, Josh Stone stood on the sidewalk. Once he opened the door, Mole pointed his thumb backward, saying, "Trouble. Another fight."

"Who?" Stone asked.

"These two," Mole replied pointing, "and Butch."

Stone looked at Michael and Christopher and growled, "In my office. Now." The two boys hurried off the bus without looking at him. Then Stone released the rest of the kids, grabbing Butch by the arm as he stepped down. "Come with me," he ordered.

At Patterson Elementary, any violence among students, no matter who started it, required a suspension of at least three days. So when Rob arrived to pick his boys up from school, he knew there was no point in advocating for his kids. While it was a done deal, however, he did want to know the details. His boys had never been in trouble before, or at least not that kind of trouble. Occasionally they'd had to stay for some minor classroom misdemeanor or for failing to complete homework. Christopher was always forgetting to bring his homework to school, and Michael was no angel. But fighting? That was unheard of. So when he entered Josh's office, leaving the two miscreants outside, he wasn't challenging the punishment; he was just making sure he understood what had happened.

"Who threw the first punch?" he asked, after hearing the overall summary.

"Jones did," Josh said.

"But Michael insulted him," Rob added.

"More or less," Josh smiled.

"And Christopher bit him?" Rob was aghast, but also incredulous that Christopher would take on a sixth-grader.

"He was trying to help his brother," Josh explained. "From what he tells me, Butch had Michael in a headlock."

"But Michael started it, calling Butch fat," Rob continued.

"Look, I probably shouldn't say this, Rob, but that took more guts than I've seen from anyone in the school. Butch is notorious. We're just trying to keep a rein on him until he moves on to junior high. I have some female teachers who are actually afraid of him...and his father...remember, I never said this...his father is just as bad. You know him; the junk guy? He's mean as a junkyard dog too. Always looking for a fight. Always sure that someone's out to take advantage of him. So the teachers here...well, they've had all they can stand of him coming into school and accusing them of picking on his son, then slamming his son in the head as soon as they're outside. You understand?"

Rob nodded, then added, "That doesn't make it right. The boys are going to be punished." When Rob started to rise, Josh put up a hand and asked him to wait a minute. "Before you go, Rob...."

Rob sat back down.

"Have you been following this flu thing? Here, and the outbreaks in Asia?"

"Yeah. The chicken thing. The Department of Agriculture has contacted Jack Patterson about his chickens and Jack thinks something is up. He was talking to a few of us at the Selectmen's meeting yesterday. Everyone seemed worried." Then, as an afterthought, "Oh, and I got your letter."

Josh sat back in his chair. "Jack's got 50,000 chickens. What does Agriculture want?"

"They're going to send some monitors over to test them.... I don't know what they plan...but Jack thinks they're looking for something they don't want to talk about. Frankly, he's worried. He says that the bird flu was the talk at Regional."

"So am I," Josh added. "This required flu shot thing I sent home yesterday? Ordered, by the Department of Education. But something's not right about it either. Maybe it's nothing, but I've been on-line doing some reading, and I keep seeing the word pandemic."

"We've had them before."

"The last one was before we were born...the Hong Kong one," Josh interjected.

"Well, our parents lived through it. Any flu can be dangerous." Rob hadn't been worried about human flu, and he was surprised Josh was.

"This is different, Rob. It's more than that. I just know it." But Josh felt helpless to explain his anxiety. Rob was a farmer, after all. He dealt in specifics.

"Call Jed. He'll know," Rob encouraged.

"I did. He's checking." Josh rose from behind his desk, wishing he hadn't brought it up. "It's probably nothing," he said, holding out his hand to shake.

"Good seeing you, Josh. Sorry about..." Rob said, grasping Josh's hand.

"Don't go too hard on them," Josh smiled and followed Rob to the door.

In the outer office, Christopher and Michael huddled solemnly, studiously observing their shoes. Both quaked as the door behind them opened and they felt their father's presence.

"Come on, desperadoes. Let's go," Rob said in a deliberately quiet voice, a voice the boys knew meant big trouble.

Just then the hall door swung open with such force it crashed against the wall. A giant of a man with a long, black beard and ponytail, dirty coveralls, and muddy boots roared, "Where are you, Stone? And where's my boy?"

Michael's and Christopher's heads rolled back on their shoulders to look up at the man's red, pocked face. Rob put a hand on each of their heads and said, "Let's go. Now." But he had to shove them, so paralyzed were they by Butch's father.

"And where's the little snot-nose who bit him," Jones raved, not really asking a question.

At that, Rob had no trouble getting the boys moving.

Both bolted from the office as if fleeing a ticking bomb. Rob had to smile, but at the same time, he wondered as he headed toward the car how Josh was going to deal with Jones...or if he shouldn't turn around and stay to help, just in case. "He'll be all right," he said, but he knew that with Jones one could never be sure.

II

Bangkok, Wednesday, Mid-October

Throughout the evening Dr. Wong stayed at the hospital to supervise frightened doctors and nurses who knew that what they were facing was well beyond their expertise. He had personally questioned the family members, all of them now showing symptoms. Three were already burning with fever, and those who were fully aware of their circumstances were too sick and too grief-stricken to be of much help. Their mother and sister had died and their father, they had been told, was beyond help. It didn't take much for them to realize that the doctors had no idea what was happening to them or how to proceed to make them better. Through persistence and patience Wong had gotten some information, however, and what he had learned worried him even more. He knew that Dai, the daughter, had first come home sick with the flu several days ago. Her mother had moved her into the parents' room to better minister to her during the night, but no, they saw no bleeding from her nose or mouth. She was sick, but not that sick. In fact, she almost seemed to be getting better. Then yesterday morning their mother had awakened ill. They had all gone off to work and to school at her urging, but she had been too sick to make them breakfast or see to them before they left. Yes, she had gotten up to make them dinner though she was clearly very sick. That was how their mother was, they assured Dr. Wong. No one would have been able to keep her in bed. What had they had that night? Chicken, they all said. Their mother had gone to Mr. Li's in the morning and the chicken had been stewing when they arrived home. Yes, their mother usually purchased live chickens, they said. How else could she be sure of their freshness? Dr. Wong had gone from sister to sister, brother to brother, extracting every little tidbit of information, and the puzzle he was now beginning to assemble could possibly be nothing more than a localized incident. Food poisoning? Maybe. Some toxin might perhaps have caused this. Botulism. Salmonella. Any one of a number of staphs or streps. And in the women, with their already undermined immune systems, they might have spiraled downward into what he had observed this morning with the bleeding. It was not impossible. In medicine, nothing is impossible. He would think this through, set up some tests that might pinpoint the culprit. He felt a quickening, a tiny burst of hope. Perhaps this is all it is, he convinced himself. Perhaps I can save the rest.

Before going back to his office, Dr. Wong decided to visit Dr. Ghi. He prepared himself to be chastised by the chipper old man for keeping him from his duties. Wong would let him go home in the morning; he knew trying to keep the old fellow longer would be fruitless. If he had to, Ghi would leave in his undershorts.

Ghi was staying the night in staff quarters, at the end of the maternity wing, a few minutes' walk, and Wong hurried to apprise Ghi of developments and his new hunches. But when he opened the door, he was astonished to find Ghi stretched feebly on his bed, his mouth hanging open and his lips a pale blue.

"Dr. Ghi," Wong whispered, touching the old man gently. "Can you hear me?"

Dr. Ghi opened his eyes, taking a second to focus before

recognizing him. His eyes were rheumy and his face red-hot.

"I feel as if someone has beaten me with a stick," Ghi mumbled. And then he went into a paroxysm of coughing. Dr. Wong gently lifted Ghi from his pillow, helping him to sit up and catch his breath. With his arm around the old man's back, Dr. Wong lowered his ear so that Dr. Ghi could whisper to him. "My throat..." Dr. Ghi began, and then he coughed again.

If Dr. Wong had any hopes of a simple diagnosis, some toxin in the food, he despaired of it then. "You have become infected. This flu..." Wong began.

"This monster," Dr. Ghi corrected, despite his choking.

"It's airborne then," Wong realized.

Dr. Ghi visibly deflated, his breathing a liquid wheeze. Dr. Wong did too, for now he knew. The family members all sick from this thing could have been an anomaly, but Dr. Ghi's illness changed the equation. If he is sick, then it's more, Wong thought. Something highly infectious. Something deadly. Wong began, "The father is unconscious. The children are all showing the same symptoms, the same pattern as..."

"As me," Ghi said, straining to keep from coughing. As he did so, Wong noticed the thin, dried line of blood inside the opening of each nostril and the minuscule trail of red froth on the corner of his mouth.

"This is something new, something we have not seen before." Dr. Wong reached over to grab a wad of tissues. Tenderly he wiped Dr. Ghi's nose and mouth. But Dr. Ghi did not respond. His eyes had closed, his body gone limp. Dr. Wong put a kind hand on his forehead and whispered, "I will have them come get you, old friend."

In the hallway again, Dr. Wong leaned against the

wall. He allowed himself only a few seconds, refusing to let memories of Dr. Ghi surface, refusing to give into the mounting fear he felt. He hurried to the nurse's station, ordered all doors in the wing locked and the ward isolated. "Get some orderlies to remove Dr. Ghi to this area and seal off the staff quarters. I believe the room may be infectious now. No one is to leave this area under any circumstances," Wong added. The nurse's eyes shot wide open. It took her a moment to assess her circumstances and then she answered, "Yes, Doctor."

Next, back in his office, Wong called Bangkok Major, speaking softly to the chief administrator on duty there. Had they gotten much traffic from Kwang Tri, he asked.

"Yes, in fact we have," Dr. Osaki responded.

"What kind?" Wong asked carefully, trying to avoid suspicion but yet urgently needing to know.

"Two car accidents..." she said, reading from her computer. "One heart attack. You've got some influenza over there, I take it," she said innocently.

"What do you mean?"

"We've had a number with coughing and high fever. You're full over there too, aren't you? Isn't that the reason for the re-direct?"

Dr. Wong sank in his chair. "Dr. Wong?" he heard. "Are you still there?" He shook his head, biting his lower lip, and looked sadly at the wall where he had so proudly hung all of his medical degrees and certificates.

"Dr. Osaki," he said slowly. "Isolate them. Do it now. Take precautions."

A stunned silence followed as Dr. Osaki began putting two and two together. "Exactly what have you got there," she asked, having done the addition.

"Just do as I say," Dr. Wong responded. "I can't say

anymore." And then he hung up the phone, leaving Dr. Osaki listening to silence.

Dr. Wong headed back to the ward, where the head nurse beckoned him as soon as he came around the corner. "He is unconscious," she said, pointing to the room across from her station. Dr. Wong peered into Dr. Ghi's room. Wires, monitors, and IVs punctured his still body. His chest barely moved. Dr. Wong leaned against the doorframe, feeling tired. He had been at the hospital now for nearly thirty-six hours and his body knew it.

"Get some sleep," his second-in-command said to him. He had just emerged from the room across the hall. "We will manage for a while."

"Yes," Dr. Wong had said. "Perhaps I will."

His office sofa was anything but comfortable and far too short. He tried, but he could not drift off or even rest quietly. Dr. Wong swung his legs down and, placing his elbows on his knees, rubbed his eyes. He felt terrible. His throat was sore, and his neck and shoulders throbbed. He picked up the phone and called the isolation ward.

"What news?" he asked the head nurse.

"You'd better come back here," she said, her voice barely concealing her panic.

Li Kan died within minutes of her father, who the meager staff was frantically trying to save when her lungs gave out. The rest of her family succumbed nearly in order of birth, reversing the size of the family with such regularity that the exhausted doctors and nurses attending could barely believe what they were seeing. Dr. Wong stood by, letting the team do its work. He watched as one after another wheezed and coughed and gasped and bled unto their pillows despite the oxygen tubes and drips and monitors and medications administered to them. One by one, bodies left the ward, their faces covered, lying on stretchers bound for pathology. Never had Dr. Wong felt so inept. Calls to the lab, where the night staff technicians were preparing slides and samples, brought no definitive answers. Yes, Pfeiffer's bacilli were present in the blood stream. Yes, pneumocci also present. Neither was likely to be the actual cause of death. No, nothing other than a strange puffiness of the cells. It could be anything. They'd have to wait for autopsy reports from Dr. Min. An entire family decimated in less than three days. What the hell was going on?

And then Dr. Ghi's heart monitor went flat. The team had barely turned from the oldest son when the head nurse ran in, summoning them to come quickly. But there was nothing to be done. Blood ran from his mouth and nose, and his eyes and cheeks had sunk in so much that he looked like a cadaver despite the lingering warmth of his skin. Dr. Wong watched as Ghi was loaded onto the gurney, his face covered for his journey to the morgue.

At 1:00 a.m., Dr. Wong emerged from the elevator and turned right. He passed the labs where his busy technicians did not even look up, the morgue where he knew that the cold lockers were already filled with corpses, and opened the door into the autopsy lab where his oldest friend, gowned and masked, waved his gloved hand. "I'm glad you're here," Dr. Min said gravely. "Tell me what you think about this."

Dr. Wong replaced his mask and stepped close to the table on which Dr. Ghi's gaunt body lay. Wong was not surprised to see how arthritic and wizened the doctor had grown, but he winced to see the old patriarch split wide open, his chest exposed. Inside, Dr. Ghi's lungs were swollen and blue. "They were all filled with this same bloody froth, the whole family and now him," Dr. Min said, not looking up.

Dr. Wong knew what a healthy lung looked like. The membranes of the lungs are one-tenth of a millionth of a meter thick. As delicate as a soap bubble, the lungs contain 750 million tiny air sacks, the aveoli, where the body exchanges gaseous wastes for oxygen. The tissue must be light and elastic to be healthy. The combined area of the aveoli is twenty-five times that of a man's skin, their capillaries barely wider than the diameter of a single red blood cell. Dr. Wong knew that any grossness in the tissues or the presence of anything in them but air hindered the gaseous exchange necessary for life. Without that exchange, the patient suffocates.

"I'm going to cut away some of the tissue now," Dr. Min explained, using his scalpel to section off a piece about an inch square for them to examine. "See how this oozes fluid?"

"Blood."

"When it gets up near the large air passages leading to the throat, it mixes with the air, creating this froth."

"It happens in the last few hours before death," Wong said. "The same pattern, all eight times. The froth causes them to choke and cough in an effort to clear their passageways, and the coughing becomes incessant."

Dr. Min dropped the tissue section into a plastic flask filled with water. They both watched somberly as tissue that should be airy enough to float sank promptly to the bottom.

"It's not pneumonia," Min said, turning back to Dr. Ghi's cadaver. "Notice that there are no nodules. They haven't degenerated into that liver-like state we see so often in pneumonia cases." He sectioned off another piece and walked over to the microscope. "Let's see what we can find here," he said, slicing a thin sample and placing it on a slide.

"Any sign of Haemophilus influenzae?" Wong asked, looking over Min's shoulder.

"I can't see anything definitive here," Min answered. "But I'm going to contact Dr. Schultz in Geneva. See if he's seen or heard anything about this. And I'm going to make a set of slides and samples and send them off to him immediately."

"Send them to the WHO? You can't," Dr. Wong sighed. "We're to keep this inside."

Min's head jerked up and he searched Wong's eyes. Wong could see him assessing the situation, coming to grips with how the political agenda was going to play out. "We can't say anything," he said and blushed at the disgust he read on Min's face.

"Maybe you can't, my friend..." Min retorted, his jaw working. "But you wouldn't know that I did...and I didn't know that I couldn't, did I?" Min looked into Wong's eyes, not knowing what to expect, whether his plan would be countermanded, whether Wong would take steps to stop him. Instead, what he read there was shame and a clear sense of relief. He and Dr. Wong were going to be accomplices.

12

Geneva, Switzerland, Wednesday, Mid-October

Dr. Robert Schultz was surprised when his secretary slapped a pile of no less than 10 message slips on his desk. Edna had a way of speaking without moving her lips when she was angry, and she was doing that now. "Will you please call this man?" she said in a clipped monotone. "Otherwise I will get no work done today."

Schultz looked at the name. He knew of no Dr. Min or any Kwang Tri hospital. "Did he explain what he wants?" Schultz asked her.

She was already at the door; as she turned her eyes narrowed. "He was very cagey. He clearly did not trust me to convey any information."

Dr. Schultz smiled. Edna had been with him so long that anyone who knew anything about him or the WHO knew that speaking to Edna was almost as good as speaking to him. There were no secrets she didn't know. "Edna, I can tell that you like this man..." Schultz said, pretending to have missed her point, smiling broadly at her.

"Don't try to get a rise out of me, Robert," she said coolly. "You have a supervisors' meeting at 10:00 and lunch with President DeSans at 1:00. The rest of your day is clear."

"Get the man on the phone," Schultz said, tossing the messages to the end of his desk. "Then your day will be clear too."

She grimaced at him, for Edna never had a clear day. She

was the last line of defense between her boss and a thousand inane calls, people dying to waste his time and destroy his sanity. Often she worked well into the night beside him, especially during budget time or when his latest book was in its final stages. And even during the infrequent calmer times, Edna seldom stopped moving or typing or answering the phone. "Thank you," she said dryly, "I'll schedule a manicure." Before Dr. Schultz could snort, the door closed neatly behind her. "Good old girl," Schultz thought.

When she buzzed him, Dr. Schultz picked up the receiver. "Dr. Min," he declared. "How can I help you?"

"I have sent you some slides and lung and blood samples before my government has a chance to stop me." The man's voice was small and far away. He whispered and his voice was urgent.

"What government is that?" Schultz asked, a bit put off. Was this some quack targeting the WHO? He had seen it before. He'd also been through plenty of false alarms from paranoid scientists who thought they had just discovered a new filovirus. Especially after the ebola scare.

"The Thai government," Min replied. "We have a lethal influenza strain here, at least I think it's influenza. And I believe it's aerosol."

A bleak silence hung in the air. To an epidemiologist, an aerosol virus is a nightmarish enemy. It can travel the earth in less than six weeks, well before a vaccine can be discovered to fight it. While people can make themselves safe from viruses that require direct contact through blood or semen, even the killer ones like AIDS, airborne diseases are impossible, even when they emerge in rural areas. Almost no place on earth is truly isolated. Fortunately, most airborne strains have been dangerous only to the old and the very young, and most are only moderately dangerous. Most strains, he reminded himself. Not all.

"Where in Thailand are you?" Schultz was hoping that this Dr. Min was a country practitioner whose patients were rural farmers, isolated somewhere out there in the hills.

"Kwang Tri Hospital is in the industrial district of Bangkok."

"Figures," Dr. Schultz thought. "Are the samples collected from poultry workers, by any chance?" Schultz was now beginning the checklist of possibilities he carried in his quite capable mind. He was only too aware of the avian flu outbreaks in Vietnam and China. The chances were good that this strain might have predicated the call. Even when governments restricted the importation of birds from infected areas, the strain got through, probably because wild birds—ducks, geese, and the like, never went through customs. And Thailand was notorious for keeping its problems quiet.

"No, although one, maybe the first one, did handle a chicken purchased at market."

"In Bangkok."

"In Kwang Tri."

"And what has happened?"

"As far as I know now, she infected seven people, all of whom have died, including the doctor who first treated her."

Schultz's eyebrows knotted. He picked up his pen and began writing. "What relation to the index case?"

"Index case?"

"The woman. The first one with the chicken."

"She's the mother, then three daughters, a father, two sons, and, as I said, the doctor."

"Time period."

"A bit of confusion there. Apparently the daughter had

a virus and gave it to the mother. The daughter had been sick three or four days. But not that sick. Just an ordinary flu, from what I'm told. The mother only two days. Started with the same flu, but in her, something happened. We have some conflicting reports from the various family members. They were in the process of coming down with it themselves, and weren't all that helpful. But the gist of it is that the mother, even when she first had the flu, was still mobile. Made them all dinner. By the next morning, however, she was unconscious. The rest were prostrate in only a day."

"Just twenty-four hours?"

"Two days total. Onset aches, headache, sore throat, and coughing. Then a complete crash. Wheezing, great difficulty breathing. Lung tissue destruction and bleeding. They all drowned in their own fluids."

"What therapies did you try? Have you rimantadine out there?"

"Yes. We have all known flu medications. In fact, we tried several different courses, rimantadine and the others on family members, hoping that one of them would work so that we could use it on the others. Literally no effect. We also tried several antibiotics, thinking perhaps that pneumonia might be a consequence of their undermined immune systems. We checked for streptococci, pneumococci, and staph. But nothing."

"And your government knows about this?"

"Yes."

"And you have been ordered to remain silent?"

"The chief hospital administrator, Dr. Wong, has."

"Is the hospital under quarantine?"

"I suspect it will be. But before that order could come down, I shipped these specimens to you."

"Are you familiar with biohazard procedures, Dr. Min?"

"I am. Dr. Wong and I attended the conference in Geneva two years ago. You spoke there."

"I am going to alert my people and make some phone calls."

"Please do not use my name," Dr. Min requested. "Sooner or later they will find out. But for now, I'd prefer your being discreet."

Robert Schultz leaned back in his chair, looking out the window at the bright fall sunshine. Traffic was at a standstill in the street below, the sidewalks mobbed with shoppers and business people, the usual daily crush of bodies that only thinned after business hours. Dr. Schultz had never been an alarmist, and he wasn't really worried now. This Dr. Min probably went home from Geneva obsessed with emerging virus theory and spent the last two years approaching every mysterious illness as a potential discovery. Schultz knew that some doctors were like that. He'd seen enough of them, hungry to publish, to make a name for themselves, because with those two things came money, lots of it. Grants and speaking engagements and job offers too tempting to refuse. And even if the man's motivations were honorable, even if he really was fearful that he'd come across something new, the chances, my God, the chances were so slim that some third world doctor would be the one to recognize an emerging virus that it was absurd to worry. Surely the samples would be just another "same old, same old."

Schultz made the usual calls, alerting the incoming mail office of an overnight express shipment that should be handled with great care. "Send it to Level Four immediately," Schultz instructed the manager. Then he called Dr. Martin Linquist, the famed expert on Dengue fever they had recruited from the Microbiological Research Establishment at Porton Down in England.

"I could have a ninety-percenter coming in for you tomorrow, Martin," Schultz said jovially. He and his friend Linquist loved playing percentages. They had spent many evenings drinking Schultz's brandy while playing the percentages game. The bets had started when a reporter asked Karl Johnson at the Center for Disease Control in the US whether he worried that a rogue virus could wipe out the human race. Johnson had said that no, he wasn't worried, that more likely "it would be a virus that reduces us by some percentage. By thirty percent. By ninety percent." The stunned reporter had gasped, "Nine out of ten humans killed? And you're not bothered?" Johnson had replied, "A virus can be useful to a species by thinning it out."*

The comment had been picked up by Reuters. After that, every time something new came across the table—a new outbreak, plans for vaccines—he and Linquist graded its importance with percentages backed by an understood bet of $100, the winner being the closest without going over. Usually they passed each other a note or worked a percentage into some seemingly unrelated sentence, while others at the conference table remained oblivious. Both knew full well that their morbid humor would not go over well with some of their colleagues, or the public either, should the media ever get hold of it. The public might not want to think that the organization entrusted with the world's health was headed by doctors who placed bets on how many people might die from a particular outbreak and who took great delight in collecting when they won their bets.

One evening, when both had worked non-stop for nearly two days during the SARS scare, they had extended what was supposed to be a mere nightcap into a bout that left them both hung-over the next day. They had been postulating the what-ifs of SARS, the potential percentages, when Linquist had asked him if he knew anything about mythology, specifically Gaia.

"Mother Earth," Schultz had responded.

"You've seen all the pictures of earth taken from space," Linquist began. "How from that perspective the planet is one thing, a whole, beyond continents, beyond countries. A single organism, with its own biological systems that feed and water and remove waste and purge and correct and cleanse..."

"Of course," Schultz had said. "And life on earth is part of this being."

"So what are we in that larger system?" Linquist probed. "Are we part of the cellular structure? Or are we a parasite upon it?"

Schultz remembered how he had paused, wanting to answer that mankind is part of the structure but knowing that such an assumption would never hold up. Man hadn't been around that long. Man was not an essential ingredient in the life of the structure. In fact, Man had become detrimental to that structure, that being. Gaia. Man was quickly killing the planet, like cancer cells gone out of control. No, like a plague of locusts, a parasite eating up the forests, infecting the ground water, leaving behind in the rush to consume the planet huge dead areas of concrete and toxic waste. Man was worming his way inside as well, chewing tunnels through layers and layers of earth's epidermis in his constant hunger for oil, coal, gems, ore, leaving earth riddled and destabilized in his path. "A parasite," Schultz had conceded.

"How about a runaway infection?" Linquist proposed.

"Suppose these outbreaks we've studied, the Spanish flu that killed thirty, maybe fifty million worldwide, the Black Death, plagues that have wiped out large percentages of humans..."

"...With great regularity," Schultz interjected, "...two or three times a century..."

"...Yes, suppose these periodic waves of disease are really earth's way of defending itself against us..."

"...Like an immuno-response..."

"...We've seen the same thing when viruses attack a system. They get inside. They replicate. Multiply exponentially. There's a term, they call it 'extreme amplification'..."

"Yes, I know it. When the virus saturates the host."

"So maybe Johnson is right. Maybe what we do here is counter-productive to earth's future. Instead of saving Man, maybe instead we're ensuring his demise. Maybe the more people we save, the more percentages we lower with our science, the more likely it becomes that earth is going to have to fight back with another God-awful plague. Five billion people is too many, you know. The earth can't handle it. The host is endangered. It's got to kick in with its big boys, forces capable of flattening our so-called science and technology. Flattening us. Maybe we're going to come up against some new immuno-virus...

"...immuno-virus?"

"Yes, earth's immune response could be a virus that might exterminate Man once and for all."

They had both been sobered by these propositions. But as scientists, they also knew that in nature, life begets death begets life. They had watched these processes under a lifetime of microscopes and experienced them continually in the field. Perhaps, too, as they aged they could better accept the reality of Man's microscopic importance to the cosmos. So, in hearing he might be receiving a ninety-percenter, Linquist knew what Schultz was thinking—Not likely, but always possible, anywhere, any time because he knew it too, looking down from his office upon masses of people hurrying from concrete pavement to concrete building, the cars and taxis honking and exhaling their monoxide fumes upward in billowing clouds of poisonous gas.

Karl Johnson's comments are quoted from Richard Preston's The Hot Zone.

13

Bangkok, Wednesday, Mid-October

The quarantine order came down five hours after Dr. Wong called Assistant Deputy Ling. He knew the sample had gone out. He had watched the messenger that Dr. Min summoned load two cartons into the hospital van, cartons with the red-flower signifying biohazard printed on the box. For a time after the van had driven away, Dr. Wong stood leaning against the window of his office, thinking about how foolishly he had worried about protecting his position here at the hospital. For years, he had guarded it against any would-be up and comers with a ferocity that now seemed imbecilic. It was all coming to an end. A woman catches a virus, and now all was lost. What an irony. When he had first noticed the ache in his throat, he had dismissed it as tension, or sorrow about Ghi, or just lack of sleep. Then the razor-sharp pain began. At first, he refused to believe it. Not him. This couldn't happen to him. He was not Dr. Ghi, old and fragile. He was in the prime of his life. His immune system couldn't be better. And so he had paced, his heart pounding as he tried to find some reason that this was not the whatever-it-was virus that had already killed eight. But the pain spread into his lungs and soon he felt as if he could not get enough oxygen. Later, when there was no mistaking what was happening, he had locked his door and then called the Deputy Assistant to the Prime Minister, going right over General Chao's head. It would mean his job. Chao was known for truly abusive retaliations. But what did it matter now? He no longer cared whether he disobeyed an order or not, because any revenge Chao sought would come too late.

The coughing started soon after his call, not long after he had to lie down with an intensifying headache. When his phone rang, he answered it, gagging in his attempts to prevent the cough he couldn't stifle. His assistant guessed in a minute. Dr. Wong said that he was sorry, he was feeling under the weather, and asked his assistant to supervise the floor while he rested, but he knew he couldn't fool anyone. Even in his troubled state, he admired the steadiness of his underling's voice. "You must isolate yourself, Dr. Wong," the doctor had said in a hushed tone, and Wong guessed that his mouth was next to the receiver so that no one else could hear him. "I will manage the ward." Coughing racked his body again, but Dr. Wong managed to say, "I want to stay here, in my office. Just leave me here. It is better that the others don't know." Both put down their receivers, each wondering how much time he had left before the inevitable.

Both knew that only a minuscule change in the genetic code of a dangerous virus, which happens incessantly as viruses modify themselves, can endanger a species in direct proportion to the speed with which it can travel from one host to another. The spread of a virus that depends on direct contact of one victim with another can be halted because such contacts can be controlled or minimized. The AIDS virus should have been stopped before becoming epidemic, but it fooled everyone. Having begun when the virus jumped species from chimpanzee to man, it traveled down the Kinshasha highway in Africa through an untold number of sexual encounters occurring along the way because those infected didn't know it. AIDS does not become symptomatic for some time, and the virus itself is constantly mutating, changing the face it presents to the microscope with each new host, and often frequently within that new host. It traveled to the cities, and there it boarded boats and planes, freeloading a ride with its unsuspecting carriers to the far reaches of the globe, far, far from the steamy jungles where it first emerged. Not until a doctor in Los Angeles noticed that his gay patients were mystifyingly dying at an increasing rate did the medical world realize that something was amiss. By the time scientists got to work on it, it had already ensured its survival outside of the jungle and was happily mutating and infecting unsuspecting humans of every sort—homosexuals and heterosexuals, and no longer just through sexual contact but also through shared needle use in drug users and the blood they often sold to hospitals to support their habits. The population was rife with it almost before anyone knew what IT was. Thus, the AIDS virus compensated for its limited repertoire with its incredible stealth, cunning, and patience.

A virus that kills its host quickly, however, must find a better means to guarantee its survival. Otherwise, it dies with the host before it has a chance to propagate itself. Such a counterproductive aspect as speed of death is balanced by the ease of spread, and the easiest means of infecting other hosts is through the misty droplets produced by sneezing and coughing. As Dr. Wong lay dying on his sofa, his knees bent so that he could lie on his side, the virus that was destroying his lungs had already ensured its future. Three floors above him, the medical staff that had valiantly fought it were already incubating its progeny, already sensing the onset of head and muscle aches, the vague awareness of something in the throat, an as yet mild soreness that could so easily be excused as fatigue or stress.

Dr. Wong covered his mouth to quiet the coughing and immediately was aware of blood on his palm. Suddenly, all the things that he had believed so important, his name, his position, his career, his reputation, fell away in a wave of nausea and despair. All for nothing, Dr. Wong thought as he stared up at the ceiling. For nothing at all. The coughing crescendoed and he tried to sit up, but he was so feverish and weak that he fell back on his too-short sofa, still holding his stained handkerchief to his mouth. He dreamed fevered dreams. Strange purple faces gazed down at him from just below the ceiling. His late mother spoke sharply to him, calling him by his childhood name: "Come to me, my little Ohko." And when in his dreams he reached for her, she smiled a skeleton's smile and touched him with a curled, discolored nail. Computer voices discussed the traffic and the weather; someone denied that he was dying. Lots of people argued, all talking at once. But Dr. Wong was slipping away. He dropped deeper and deeper into the comfortable chill blackness where he knew enough to remain very still because that way he could feel almost nothing. When he finally achieved absolute stillness, Dr. Wong took his place as victim number nine.

The locked doors at Kwang Tri Hospital could not contain what had already traveled in delicate droplets of mist coughed up by the young people of Kwang Tri to Kwang Tri's upper school, the auto factory, and Chang's clothing factory. Already the virus was on the desks and papers, doorknobs and railings, clothing and hands, cheeks, lips, and eyes of anyone who came in contact with anyone already incubating the disease. Hundreds went home that night with sore throats and woke the next morning coughing exquisitely individual clouds of droplets that were then carried by family members to the lower schools, to restaurants, offices, mailrooms, cafeterias, government buildings, and eventually to Bangkok Major, where an unsuspecting Dr. Osaki admitted them because Kwang Tri was already overloaded. Such is the nature of a fast-moving flu.

Once Deputy Assistant Ling called the Prime Minister, who called a meeting of his ministers, the child conceived ignobly in the defecation of a chicken and the tears of a mother had already replicated billions of times. The ministers might muster their troops, the scientists their cell cultures, and the politicians their spin-doctors, but in Thailand it was all too little, too late. By the time the Prime Minister ordered the containment of the district, the Bangkok virus had been sneezed and coughed all over the city by workmen and servants, merchants and beggars. It had spread upward, knowing no class distinctions, to the wealthy who chatted in their salons and tea houses, drank and ate in their fine restaurants, or flew away for business or pleasure to the far reaches of the planet. By the time the Prime Minister and the King took their first definitive action, the Bangkok flu had already cycled countless times through the air filtration systems of airliners from at least 20 countries flying to Beijing, Frankfort, Paris, and London as well as to New York, Chicago, San Francisco and Washington D.C.

14

Patterson, Wednesday, Mid-October

After dinner, Rob and Terry settled down to watch NBC News. The boys were in the back bedroom doing their homework, barn chores had been completed, lunches for tomorrow had been stored in baggies in the refrigerator, and the kitchen was clean and dark. Terry blew gently across the top of her coffee cup and tentatively sipped to test its temperature. A few sips later she put the cup down and took up the sweater she was knitting for Christopher. Her needles click-clicked above the low drone of the TV. Rob settled back in his leather chair, his stockinged feet stretching and rolling to and fro on the ottoman. He opened his newspaper and began to read, only half listening to the TV in front of him. Peter Brokawn was discussing the primaries with an expert dragged in by the Washington bureau, the same old stuff Rob had been hearing for months as new candidates for both parties began declaring themselves and testing their policies on the public. Soon the news switched to a foreign correspondent in Thailand covering the avian flu outbreak with the World Health Organization. Rob immediately reached for the remote and turned the volume up. He guessed that these sick Thai chickens were somehow related to the state's agricultural department concern over chickens in the U. S., though he thought the connection a bit far-fetched. Still, Jack Patterson seemed to think there was more to the inspection of his farm than just the usual health code checks.

Terry raised her head, her needles still rhythmically lifting stitches, her fingers wrapping yarn and looping. She sensed the sudden tension in the room as Rob straightened and leaned forward. The reporter was quoting a member of the government who had spoken to him on the condition of anonymity. Apparently, the reporter confided to Brokawn, the situation in Thailand was not unique. Other Asian countries were experiencing similar outbreaks, and hundreds of thousands of chickens were slated for extermination because of it. In North Korea, for one, Thailand for another. Both kept their problems "under wraps," the journalist said. Censorship of reports from either country was a well-known fact, and it was hard to get information, because citizens in both countries feared angering the authorities. Still, rumors abounded of people getting sick from sick chickens. Rumor had it that a mysterious outbreak had erupted in Kwang Tri, a crowded suburb of Bangkok, the reporter said, but he had been unable to get further information. Avian flu, he finished, is highly contagious among all forms of fowl and easily spread from one geographic area to another via wild birds, primarily wild ducks and geese.

Terry looked at Rob. "Sounds bad," she said, wrinkling her brow. "You know, Doc heard something at that conference he attended last week, something about the CDC contacting several research campuses, you know, UCLA and Johns Hopkins and others. He said that some of the doctors were seriously worried about an outbreak... not just the maybe kind...the imminent kind...like people know something really big is about to happen." She quieted as Brokawn came back after the commercial. But all he said was, "We'll hear more from Thailand as soon as we get more information. This is a breaking story and a serious one. " Then he moved on to a story on an SEC investigation.

15

Patterson, Thursday, Mid-October

Laura Block slept late. She'd been up half the night writing the final chapter of Survive and Thrive, racing to the finish line as if possessed. She felt more than satisfied. The book was good and she knew it. She had covered all bases—survival through the four seasons in every section of the country and cultivation of edible bushes, trees, and flowers. She smiled as she stretched beneath the warm covers, thinking of some of the furry-faced survivalists she had met on her trip to Wyoming, their backwoods cabins and their anti-social mentality. She had been sent out to one such community last summer at the behest of Carl Brun, her editor, who assured her she wouldn't be shot as an intruder. Carl had a friend, an old college buddy who had left Wall Street years ago, sold his million-dollar house and his shiny Porsche, bought a Dodge Durango and headed west. He was a brilliant guy, but a bit of a nutcase when it came to the state of the nation, Carl warned. Out west he had become the leader of a group that bought thousands of acres about 30 miles west of Cody and there founded a survivalist outpost of about fifty people. Carl had already written him and set it up. She was to make flight arrangements and Carl would have him pick her up at the airport.

Three weeks later, she was met by a tall, craggy-faced fellow looking highly suspicious in his clean but worn jeans, cowboy hat and boots. The National Guardsmen waiting near the x-ray machines paid him no attention when he held up a sign, BLOCK, and she called over in her most professional voice, "Here I am. Thanks for meeting me."

The soldiers looked her way, checking out her legs. She hurried to the man with the sign, and he appraised her and then smiled broadly, showing the whitest, straightest teeth this side of Hollywood. That trip had been one of the most interesting research junkets Laura had ever taken. Two weeks in Northern Wyoming, much of the time spent on horseback or walking, always with Taylor Farr, her escort, had helped to resolve a lot of the confusion she felt after her divorce. Taylor was a handsome man, philosophically single, absolutely independent. But it hadn't been twenty-four hours before an electric tension began to grow between them, and Laura found it hard to hold his gaze lest she betray the desire she felt in his presence. She had thought she would never love another man after the disaster of her marriage to Tom. She had reconciled herself to a single existence and hardened her heart to any advances made by the men she knew or met in the course of her work. So sure was she that she had made herself safe from pain or heartbreak that Taylor had taken her unaware. A survivalist! She had laughed to herself. Of all the possible choices, a survivalist! What a romantic cliché. Used as she was to academic types, the cultured discussions about books and movies, politics and art, Taylor had seemed to come straight out of the kind of cowboy movie she had hated even as a teenager—Clint Eastwood westerns, Marlborough man demeanor. At first it was almost laughable as they rode from the Cody airport up into the rolling green Wyoming state forestland. He had a rifle, for God's sake, hanging from a rack behind their heads. A rifle! And she a gun law advocate who had marched for the Brady bill.

She got used to the rifle and the other gun he carried with them each time they rode out into the brown hills, just as she got used to his western twang and the slow certitude with which he responded to her questions. People really don't talk this way, she thought after the first "Yep." But indeed they did, all of them.

What was happening to her, Laura wondered after only a few days on the trail with him. No one could have planned it. No one would have believed it. As she rode her horse behind him, watching the trail ahead for plants she believed should be growing there, plants useful for both medicine and food, she found herself distractedly studying his back, the way his shirt, tucked so neatly into his jeans, moved back and forth with the slow clip-clop of his horse's hooves. She studied the straightness of his shoulders and their breadth, the easy way his arms had of hanging down at his sides. She noticed that his hair was sharply trimmed above his collar, that some fine gray hairs salted the black, that when he turned to speak his jaw was hard and strong, but his eyes were soft and kind.

And then began the looks. At first she disregarded the way he sometimes held her gaze, looking deeper than most men did. And she found herself smiling for no reason at all, and being ridiculously silly, like an idiot schoolgirl, for Pete's sake, and she'd silently chastise herself and pledge to recapture her original detachment. But it didn't work, because those looks would catch her off-guard and she'd try to deny they had meaning and berate herself for harboring feelings for this person she hardly knew.

Then came the touches, accidental at first. Touches that sent currents through her skin. Their hands touched as each reached for something, or in the midst of laughter, he'd reach out and touch her arm, or she'd find herself touching his. These soon became too frequent to be accidental. He'd put his hand on hers as she held the horse's reins. Or he'd brush something off her hair, a bug supposedly. Then one day he cupped her chin in his hand and looked at her for a long time, saying nothing. Laura couldn't bear the turmoil within her, and she'd broken away, pretending that she didn't realize his intentions.

Nothing she tried worked. She did know his intentions. How could she have helped it after the twilight evening when they camped along the trail, far from the community, alone, a radio playing softly beneath the stars? Their horses staked out behind them, they sat on a log near the fire, drinking coffee and talking, talking, talking. Laura could not remember how long it had been since she had talked so much about everything, including her life with Tom. That was a subject she never discussed, even with her closest friends, yet there she was, babbling on. For the first time since they'd met, Taylor seemed to open up too, and she learned about his life on Wall Street and the greed there that he had come to hate, the willingness of people to sell their souls for more and more money and their constant need to be richer or more powerful than others. How shallow it had all seemed to him—the one-upmanship that never ended because someone else always came along to top it.

Then terrorists bombed the World Trade Center the first time. That day Taylor had looked at his life from a whole new perspective and decided that if he had been killed in one of those buildings, he would never have lived at all. From the time he had been a youngster growing up in Greenwich, the Connecticut town that breeds CEOs and Presidents, the only thing he had really learned was how to be somebody else's idea of successful. He had nurtured his holdings and his bank account but never his spirit. He had played lacrosse well enough to be named captain, had joined the right high school organizations and belonged to the right country clubs, but he knew nothing about joy and appreciation for the earth and its creatures, let alone the air he breathed and the wonder of being alive. Within a week of the attack, Taylor Farr had quit, sold his stock, his apartment on Fifth Avenue, his Porsche, and taken all his Armani suits to the Salvation Army down on Third Avenue, refusing to take even a receipt to use for taxes. He no longer cared.

Laura sat listening, watching his eyes dance in the firelight, and she knew that she had fallen hopelessly in love. So when she had asked him why he never married and he had turned to look at her, studying her hair, her eyes, her mouth, before saying, "I hadn't found the right woman," she knew what was coming next, if not tonight, then tomorrow or the next day. Only it wasn't the next day. He reached his arm around her back and pulled her to him, took her chin in his hand and turned her face toward him, and when his lips touched hers, the moment was electric. There was no turning back. They made love on sleeping bags spread under the stars and stopped only long enough to step naked into the rushing stream and stand, exploring the wonder of each other in the milky light of a full moon before he took her hand and led her back to their prairie bed. Laura had never felt such passion or such beauty in her whole life, and if it never happened again, if this was just a transient thing for Taylor, well, then so be it, it was worth it, she'd do it again, because to have missed it would have been tragic.

Since then, everything had changed. Taylor could not call her from where he lived, but every week a thick, handwritten letter arrived, posted whenever someone in the community drove into the nearest town. And since then, Laura watched the calendar with growing anticipation, knowing that soon Taylor would arrive and they would be together again.

Finally, the day had dawned clear and dry, and it seemed nothing could undermine her optimism. Still in her bathrobe, she walked to the end of her driveway to pick up the Boston Globe. Returning she scanned the front page and immediately focused on the headline "Flu Now Reported In Eight Asian Countries". Laura stopped halfway back to the house, squinting in the glare of the morning sun. They had talked about epidemics out in Wyoming—Taylor and his friends—and Laura had silently scoffed at their fears that an emerging virus could possibly become a pandemic and destroy entire populations. Survivalists, she had learned, weren't just preparing themselves for nuclear war. They believed pestilence was an omnipresent danger. Humans have covered the entire globe in ever-increasing numbers, they said, and the consequence of the resulting population density is that germs are more easily transmitted, not only to individuals, but with travel and trade as it is today, to all continents as well. Worse, as the human population encroaches on wild animal territories and as poultry and meat farming becomes industrialized, the chances of an animal virus attacking humans increases exponentially. So here was this flu becoming rampant among poultry. All it might take is a chance mutation for a new plague that could spread as easily as wind-driven clouds spread rain.

Laura folded the paper under her arm and hurried to the house. Inside her sunny kitchen, Delilah purred and rubbed against her calves. Laura set the paper down and bent to rub the old cat between the ears. "Hungry, are you?" she murmured. Delilah purred loudly, her tail curling, her back arching under Laura's fingers. "Come on, girl. Let's see what we've got." She opened the refrigerator, taking the opened can of cat food in one hand, a quart of milk in the other, and setting both on the counter. The refrigerator door closed snugly behind her. Delilah meowed and continued to rub against Laura's legs. "Okay, okay," Laura replied, finally setting Delilah's dish on the floor. Delilah immediately began eating, her tail stiff and erect. Laura leaned against the counter. How she loved this old cat. Delilah was there when she first met Tom at the Faculty Tea and through all of their courtship. She was there when they married and he moved in, though she was not happy about this new intruder and always aloof when Tom had offered treats to buy acceptance. Delilah had been the first to share her joy when she came home from the doctor's office, brimming with the news that she was pregnant! Delilah had jumped up on the bed as Laura tossed off her cashmere sweater and silk shirt, circling as she always did before settling down on whatever of Laura's was available for a bed. "No, you don't," Laura had teased, gently pulling the clothes from beneath the annoyed cat. "Not on these." And Delilah had been there, too, three months later when Laura had miscarried. In the days afterward, Delilah waited anxiously not a foot from Laura's teary face as she grieved, curled on this very bed, these very pillows. Delilah had stared quizzically into her face, purring to comfort her yet keeping her distance, as if to give Laura her space. And finally, when Laura had reached out to her, Delilah had curled against Laura, her warm body and soft fur as reassuring as an old teddy bear. In the months afterward, Delilah had watched Tom with cool deliberation whenever he was about. Whether from Laura's lap as they read or corrected papers in the study or from her cat bed in the kitchen while they ate or from atop the quilt as the two read in bed, Delilah's critical gaze seemed never to leave him.

"What's wrong with that cat?" Tom had once asked.

Laura had looked up from her book expecting some sign of illness. "Wrong?" she'd replied, puzzled. "She looks fine."

"She keeps staring at me. Haven't you noticed? All the time, no matter what I'm doing."

Laura had chuckled. "Maybe you fascinate her."

"No, not like that. Like she distrusts me, like she's waiting for me to do something."

"Don't be silly," Laura had mocked. "You're a stranger, that's all. She's used to just me. You've changed her whole world." But Laura had looked up later, just before she closed her book for the night. Delilah wasn't purring, as she always did when she and Laura were alone. Her gaze was stony, cold and sphinx-like, as if she already knew what Laura didn't, that Tom would be gone for good in less than a year. He'd cleared his files from her computer by burning them on to a single CD, while Laura wished that he could so easily be erased from her heart. After Tom had packed his suits and shirts, books and papers into boxes, her marriage ended with both shaking hands like business associates. And when the door had closed behind him that final time, Delilah had been sitting in the hallway behind her, vindicated, looking up at Laura as if to say that she'd known all along that Tom was just a brief and annoying interruption in an otherwise perfect existence.

Animals play such a part in our lives, she thought as Delilah continued eating. Laura wondered just how many pets there were, not just in the U.S., but around the world. And then, how many domesticated animals as well. The cows and chickens, goats and sheep. That's what Taylor had explained to her that night as they all sat around the rough-hewn table in his cabin. Diseases such as smallpox and measles were mutations of old-world germs that had first infected domestic animals and birds before becoming recombinant and attacking humans. At first, humans had no resistance to them, and though mankind has evolved over the centuries, evolution itself is too slow a process to protect society from a new germ or virus that might occur at any moment anywhere, in any animal. Taylor said that increasing numbers of humans living side by side with increasing numbers of domestic birds and animals were like sparks and straw and that almost certainly a new pestilence was bound to emerge someday that could be worse than any that had come before.

"Why?" Laura had asked.

"Because of the density of human population," Taylor had answered. "Because of the way we live now. Planes, trains, trucks and cars, the whole population on the move. Before, vast continents had little or no dependence on other areas. People lived in rural pockets, protected by their isolation. But now everyone is rubbing elbows with everyone else. Everything you do is related to everything everyone else does. So a single virus, once it gets going, can wipe us out. All of us!"

"Come on," Laura had argued. "How many billion people are there? Once a virus is discovered, the scientists develop a vaccine. No disease is going to get to four or five billion people before we have a vaccine to protect them."

Taylor had leaned back in his chair then, shaking his head. But his friend Andrea had continued. "You know how long it takes for a vaccine to be developed?"

Laura had answered, "No, not really. A few months, I guess."

Andrea leaned forward. "Look, Laura. A few months to identify, a few months, actually three to four, to develop, then more months to produce...what's happening meanwhile? Suppose this is an especially virulent flu, one that runs its course in say twenty-four to forty-eight hours, one that's airborne, so that you cough and I breathe in the particles? How long do you think it would take before the cloud of particles become like dust in the sunshine.... you've seen them, haven't you, when the sun pours into a room? They're everywhere. Now transfer that to a city where eight million people are breathing and coughing and spitting and sneezing. And say a third of those people go home to their families in the suburbs. And another third drive or fly to other cities and suburbs on business or pleasure. You see what we're getting at?" Andrea's seriousness was evident in her eyes and the way her eyebrows knotted above them.

Taylor sighed. "Laura, what we foresee is apocalypse. Dead and dying everywhere. And the only way to survive is to isolate one's self, to be out in the middle of nowhere with literally no contact with the rest of the world until the thing runs its course. It's going to happen, sooner or later, and the only way to live through it is to be prepared...which is what we're doing out here. Becoming prepared."

And prepared they were. Hunters all, with supplies brimming in their cabins and in caves hidden by foliage... canned food, bottled water, batteries, solar energy panels and generators, guns, ammunition, blankets. They had accumulated enough for the entire community to ride out most any disaster, whatever it might be, man-made or otherwise.

Now Taylor was coming here to Patterson. No telling

what might come of this visit. Laura looked at her watch. She'd have to get a move on. It was seven o'clock and Taylor's red-eye flight was due to land in Manchester, New Hampshire at nine. She wondered as she hurried to her bedroom whether Taylor had seen the article, and had he known yesterday, whether he would have come at all. But, of course, that was silly. Taylor would come no matter what. They were in love.

16

Bangkok, Thursday, Mid-October

For all of its dingy exterior, crowded in among tenements and industrial buildings, Kwang Tri Hospital had been a model of cleanliness and order. Its new paint and the green vinyl chairs and sofas lining its lobby shone from twice weekly disinfectant sprayings. The rugs, vacuumed meticulously between midnight and five a.m., were free of lint or foot dirt, and the occasional tables, checked frequently day and night for litter, glistened from waxing. Beyond the lobby, brightly lit hallways led left and right into other hallways that led left and right, a maze so complex that every corner required signs with arrows. Yellow, red, and green lines incorporated into the floor tiles pointed the way to distant wings, splitting yellow left, green right, and red straight ahead through locked double doors. Taped on the doors was a hastily written sign: Absolutely No Admittance Beyond This Point.

The sign was unnecessary, however, for this part of the hospital was deserted. Security had locked the front doors, turning away visitors themselves until the military had secured all approaches. No one sat behind the information desk greeting visitors or finding patients' room numbers on any of the three computers set up for that purpose. A cold blue rectangle traced its repetitive path across each blackened monitor and from beneath the desk all three hard drives hummed softly. Abandoned notices, pens, pencils, and file folders lay scattered about.

The usually pristine lobby had not been cleaned; the staff had been told not to report. The offices where hospital business was usually conducted were locked, the desks unoccupied. On entering Kwang Tri from this side, one would surely think the hospital had been abandoned, for no nurses' rubber soles squeaked hurriedly along the floor, no doctors checked clipboards or flirted with staff, no patients gazed soulfully from wheelchairs as they were whisked into or out of Kwang Tri by white-coated orderlies. No one could enter Kwang Tri's lobby. Two armed soldiers stood guard.

The Emergency Room on the opposite side of the complex, however, was bedlam. Although all ambulances had been redirected to Bangkok Major, the streets running perpendicular to and the streets surrounding the Emergency Entrance throbbed with cars, trucks, mopeds, bicycles, and people on foot. The traffic could not move; it was blocked by two army tanks and a cadre of uniformed soldiers, their frightened eyes wide behind surgical masks, their rifles held tight in hands protected by rubber gloves.

The cars closest to this entrance had begun arriving two nights ago. Frightened drivers had been greeted by frantic nurses and doctors called back to duty by Dr. Wong's Assistant when he realized that the hospital could not possibly contain the hordes of sick and dying patients arriving in the early flood-tide of infection. Those with less than life-threatening injuries, the cuts and concussions, were at first turned away kindly. Then, as the evening wore on, the kindliness was replaced by bristling declarations that no, the hospital could not possibly handle them when desperately ill people were lining corridors and entryways. Military police came to control the ever-increasing numbers arriving at the hospital, close the business offices and lock the front doors. That way, the new Chief-of-Staff figured, they could monitor and control emergency arrivals and activate triage teams. The office staff still healthy and willing to volunteer had been set up at the Emergency Desk. They funneled newly admitted patients into the long hallway now lined two and three deep with patients waiting for vacated beds. Once one was in that queue, certainly only a few hours would likely elapse before being wheeled into an elevator and lifted to another crowded floor. There orderlies and volunteers stripped the bed sheets of the latest corpses while their still warm bodies were hoisted onto another gurney. As soon as one patient succumbed, the head nurse cleared the bed on her computer, which immediately alerted the Emergency desk of another free space. The similarity of this grim coming and going to the routine of a busy restaurant did not occur to those staffing the Emergency Desk; they could barely keep up with the flashes on their screens and the semi-conscious, slightly blue patients being wheeled inside by orderlies.

By evening of that day, the numbers arriving had increased exponentially. The streets and alleys leading to the front of the hospital had been closed, forcing traffic over to the Emergency Entrance, but the numbers of vacant cars left by the sick wherever they could pull over had so clotted the area that movement in or out was impossible. More frantic calls, this time from the lieutenant on duty to his commanding officer and from him to his supervisor and on up the line to General Fong, helped. Fong ordered reinforcements and then called General Chao to find out just what the hell was going on down there in Kwang Tri. When Chao fumbled and harrumphed and stuttered, Fong took matters in his own hands and called the Minister of Defense, who had his chauffeur drive him immediately to the Prime Minister's residence, who, when he heard the news, ordered an emergency meeting of all his ministers within the hour.

Kwang Tri was now outlined in bold red magic marker on maps of the city hanging in government offices in the capital. By mid-afternoon, the military was everywhere. Soldiers barricaded the thoroughfares leading into and out of Kwang Tri district, usually four or five of them with bayonets ready to turn back vehicles and pedestrians hoping to escape into Bangkok or out into the rural lands to the north. Within the district they prepared for martial law. Trucks roared past tenements, their bullhorns blaring instructions written by their commanding officer. Soldiers stopped cars and warned pedestrians of the coming curfew. Near the hospital, they began the work of untangling the traffic snarls created by the original soldiers sent to maintain order.

The ten blocks around the Emergency Room entrance were a chaotic parking lot. Cars had arrived with the sick only to be blocked by the soldiers, and when the drivers tried to turn their vehicles around, they had already been blocked by other vehicles. Some of the cars at the front had been pinned there for nearly twenty-four hours. A few were abandoned, and many had run out of gas while waiting with their engines running. Soldiers moved among the cars and trucks, their walkie-talkies crackling, telling panicked drivers to go home. No, the hospital could not admit them. No, they could not go to Bangkok Major because the roads were cordoned off. No, no doctors were available outside. The whole district was under quarantine. No, no one could leave the district. Go home, go home, they insisted. When they came upon cars whose drivers had died at the wheel, they passed wordlessly with only sidelong glances at the slumped figures. If a car was still running, they made no attempt to reach in and turn the engine off. They were afraid of the blood that dried on the chins and clothes of the corpses inside. And besides, they figured, sooner or later the vehicle would run out of gas. When someone leaned out to ask what he should do, that the family members within were desperately ill, the soldiers shrugged, despairing of an answer. "Carry them" was their best solution. When asked what to do with the dead inside their cars, the soldiers said, "Turn off your ignition and walk home. Leave them in the car."

The cars at the farthest edges of the jams leading toward the hospital were met with more soldiers waving rifles and shouting from bullhorns. The information was grim. There was no help for them at the hospital. They were ordered to make a U-turn in the street, return home, and stay there. Martial law had been imposed, and after noon any one seen in the streets would be arrested or shot. Radios blared from every car, as newscasters broadcasting from the seeming safety of Bangkok proper encouraged citizens to remain calm. The outbreak, and it was definitely an outbreak, was of unknown origin. No medicine was available, no known cure either. Kwang Tri was going to have to ride this thing out, and the safest way to do so was to stay inside, associate with no one, and wait. If anyone in the family became ill, that person should be isolated inside the house and those tending to him or her should take proper precautions. In the absence of surgical masks or rubber gloves, they should cover their faces with whatever they had available and wash their hands frequently, using anti-bacterial soap. Should anyone die, they were told they would have to wait until the army could come to remove the body. They should avoid touching the corpse or breathing the air nearby. Under no circumstances should the deceased be placed outside on the street, the announcers warned, or those responsible would face severe fines or imprisonment.

These announcements were followed by up-to-the-minute news from the Department of Health and from the Prime Minister. At mid-day a new deputy minister of Health had been appointed to replace General Chao, who had been arrested on leaving the Prime Minister's offices. The general had been charged with dereliction of duty and was widely believed to be responsible for the magnitude of the influenza outbreak in Kwang Tri. No further official details were available, newscasters said, but rumor had it that the general had been informed as early as seven p.m., two nights before, of the severity of this influenza strain and had done nothing but to order closing the hospital and isolating those showing flu symptoms. In fact, the fear was that in sending ambulances to Bangkok Major, the general might have increased the likelihood of the epidemic spreading to the city itself. Bangkok Major had fully isolated all patients that had arrived in the last 48 hours from the Kwang Tri district and was taking Level 4 precautions in their treatment to prevent further spread of the disease. No official statistics were available, the newscasters reported gravely, but the mortality rate of this strain of influenza had, so far, been astonishingly high, and because of this, listeners should stay tuned for word from the Prime Minister within the next few hours.

To citizens of Kwang Tri looking down on the streets from their windows, it did not take a newscaster to tell them they were in grave danger. People they knew, vendors they frequented, sat glassy-eyed along the sides of buildings, against telephone poles or fruit stands, while others lay gazing up at the sun from eyes that no longer saw light. From the clinic door, had any of the patients there been able to open it, one could see perhaps thirty bodies in various still-life poses along the street. Some of the sickened were barely alive, and occasionally one moaned or called weakly for help that was not going to come. Others trembled, pulling their shirts tight about them, coughing incessantly until their gasping for air crescendoed. Every so often, a foolish wife or daughter ventured along the pavement, holding a kerchief to her mouth as she searched for a missing father or husband. It was not yet noon. The army had yet to establish the curfew.

But no one in the clinic was moving. The three nurses who staffed it died tending patients, having thought their masks and gloves would protect them. Their patients were strewn about the outer office and the inner examining rooms like discarded wrappers, some curled into themselves, some stretched immodestly on the floor, some on their backs, mouths agape.

In apartments above the street people who as yet had no symptoms pressed faces to the glass of closed windows, trying to see up or down the street. They could hear trucks but could see no movement. Store doors were open to the street, fruit stands displayed wares, but no one tended them. Their owners had deserted them or lay dead beside them. Occasionally, a tenement door opened and some brave man or boy ran outside, his face covered, looked frantically about and disappeared into one of the stores. Minutes later he reappeared carrying bags of food no one had sold him. Those watching from above knew they should do the same and some followed suit, slipping out like cat burglars to a street where no one was healthy enough to arrest them. Others, fearful of disease, made mental inventory of their meager stores and prayed that this horrible nightmare would end before their supplies gave out.

17

Geneva, Thursday, Mid-October

Martin Linquist's subdued excitement as he entered the Level Four lab he had run for nearly six years typified his approach to these "scares" arriving periodically from across the globe. He made it a habit always to expect the worst, and that kept him careful and alert. He knew that accidents occurred when people working with bio-hazardous materials became complacent—either they underestimated the dangers of unknown specimens or they got careless while working with them. Mistakes happened all too easily, and a good friend of Linquist's had died ten years ago because of the second mistake. He had become some so engrossed in an autopsy that he failed to keep his gloves washed in Envirochem. The cadaver's blood hid a tiny tear he didn't realize he'd made in his gloves, allowing the virus entry into the plastic bubble of his Chemturion suit. By the time his friend had finally dipped his hands in the disinfectant, it was already too late.

His particular worry, however, was the first kind of mistake. Linquist had of late grown bored with the specimens he received. They had been just humdrum, Level One annoyances masquerading as Level Four terrors. He had spent the better part of two years in South and Central America chasing the sources of Dengue Fever, consulted with the CDC on the Marburg virus, and later followed up on some of the research done around Lake Victoria on AIDS. Linquist also was familiar with Karl Johnson's documentation of ebola, and while in Africa, had himself done some follow-up experimental research in Kitum Cave on Mt. Elgon, believed by many to be the elusive source of the ebola virus.

He thrived on danger. It made him wake up excited each morning and helped him to sleep at night, something his colleagues seldom understood. Ex-wives, either. They were all afraid of his being liquefied by some God-awful virus in some Godforsaken outpost. Even he found such madness difficult to comprehend. He was a contradiction to himself. Others thought him fearless, believing he loved danger. They could not know that each time he came up against the power of a deadly virus, his heart pounded, his gut ached with fear, and his stomach turned to an acidic mush.

Yet Linquist would not have it any other way. He knew that safety could be nothing more than a ho-hum existence for him. Linquist bored too easily. And with him, boredom led to snappishness and depression. Left without some new mystery to solve or some potential life-threatening virus to seek, Linquist worried that he might follow in his father's footsteps. His father, a lean, towering, muscle-machine of a man, had climbed Everest, rafted the entire length of the Congo, sailed round the world by himself in a twenty-six foot sloop, only to die in their cellar. Martin was just five when his father sustained a crippling back injury in a car accident on the way to, of all places, the grocery store. As a consequence, his adventures had been permanently sidelined by the resulting paralysis of his legs. While physically his prognosis for a long life was excellent, his father had spiraled down into a deep and brooding depression from which neither his mother nor his grandparents had been able to dislodge him. He never read his father's suicide note. He already knew what it said, and his father's view on how life should be lived had shaped him throughout high school and college football as an indomitable forward, as a Rhodes Scholar, and throughout his life as a virus chaser who'd rather be somewhere in a jungle than anywhere in an office.

So, whether Linquist would ever admit it or not, he hoped this new specimen would be worthy of his Level Four precautions and yet feared unwrapping it. He wanted, yet dreaded, something ferocious. He hoped to find some new configuration that would get his adrenaline gushing once again. He'd tested a hundred false alarms and had been disappointed after each one. And he was aching to get back into the field, to feel that rush upon getting off the plane in some far-away country, breathing in the foreign air, taking in the foreign landscape and hearing the foreign tongue, knowing that lurking somewhere nearby was a killer that just might have his name on it. It was insanity, this ambivalence, he admitted to himself. Or self-destructiveness. But it was what made his life worthwhile.

In his space suit, Linquist moved slowly about the lab, clearing an area where he intended to prepare the slides for the electron microscope. The two biohazard cartons were already in the lab's air lock. He carried the boxes to the worktable and then carefully cut through the packaging tape using a knife with an enlarged safety handle specially designed for working with triple-layered gloves. Nothing is more dangerous in a biohazard lab than steel blades, shards of broken glass from a dropped flask, splinters or other sharp edges that might catch the suit, creating a tear that could allow a dangerous virus inside. Glass, for example, had long ago been replaced by far safer plastic vials and flasks. But no matter how many precautions scientists took to protect themselves, accidents happened. They didn't happen frequently, but in a Level Four lab, the smallest one could be fatal.

Linquist removed all the specimens and vials from the cartons, noticing how carefully each had been labeled with the patients' names and times of death. A complete surgical report included organ preparation mode and other particulars. The serum samples were properly contained in plastic tubes packed with dry ice. Paraffin blocks contained lung, kidney, and spleen tissues, some lymph nodes, heart, pancreas, pituitary, brain, and liver samples.

This Dr. Min was pretty good, Linquist thought. Let's see what he's got for us. First Linquist wanted to observe the lung tissue under the electron microscope. He took his diamond knife and fitted it into the cutting machine and then watched through the attached microscope as the machine moved the sample back and forth across the diamond blade, slicing specimens too thin for the human eye to see. These fell onto a single droplet of water, where they floated, suspended. Linquist separated out the damaged or partial slices, then picked up his tweezers. After choosing a microscopically small copper grid, he inserted it into the water, slowly moved it directly under one of the slices, and lifted. This he carried to the adjacent windowless room, where the hulk of the electron microscope dominated the floor.

He turned on the overhead light and the machine hummed into action, casting a green glow over the dials, digital readouts and screen. After placing the specimen on the sample holder and locking it into place inside the machine, he turned off the overhead light and seated himself at the console. Linquist had a ritual he observed at these moments, and this time was no different. Instead of immediately leaning over the screen, adjusting the knob so that the complicated world of the specimen could be moved about at will, Linquist sat back in his chair and breathed deeply. It was as if he were taking the time to utter a small prayer. In fact, for Linquist this pre-viewing moment was ceremonial. Though he prayed to no God, he asked for guidance with what he was about to do. He had spent his life observing life under a microscope. The worlds he found there were, to him, worlds of exquisite precision and beauty, worlds well beyond what most men could ever conceive. Yet no matter how wondrous, Linquist always felt he was on the edge of the Nameless, the Horror, the Absolute Equation of Life=Death. No matter how far down he went into the sub-structure of living entities, his electron microscope probing what before had been beyond Man's capacity to know, always there was a deeper world to be discovered, Truth lurking just beyond his reach. In the sub-atomic particles that are the stuff of life, Linquist fully believed that Truth would be there for the knowing, if only he had the technology and the courage to see.

A moment passed, silent but for the quiet hum of the microscope. Then Linquist leaned forward, peering through the window of his helmet at a microscopic world he had never seen before. The sample looked like a midnight sky emblazoned with jostling halos. From each of these, needle-like spikes thrust rays of light. A battlefield of invisible armed angels. What was this he was seeing? Where were the tissue cells? Linquist moved the specimen, scanning the dark infinity for the familiar, the should-be. But what should have been no longer existed. The specimen was wrought through with a multitude of spiked halos, each packed thick with negatively stained virus particles, as if they had been devoured by darkness.

He sat back to readjust his vision. He stared into the green gloom, assessing what he had seen. Lung tissue no longer existed, or if it did, not in this specimen. Whatever this entity was, it had replaced the lung, either by digestion or destruction, rendering it incapable of functioning. The victims had suffocated, their lungs no longer capable of replacing gaseous wastes with oxygen. Before they died, they lived through hours of unspeakable distress, blood filling the aveoli, the sensation of drowning, the constant coughing to dispel the fluids gathering in the billions of sacs as microscopic capillaries gushed blood. Like drowning. Linquist had always feared drowning. He experienced recurrent nightmares of sinking into the cold ocean, feeling the numbing cold, the increasing pressure on his eardrums, and finally the accompanying roar of silence. Always Linquist saw his own hair floating upward, his arms waving like sea grass, his eyes wide and frightened, bulging really, but perhaps still able to see the impassive eyes of fish honing in for a nibble. And sinking, sinking into the bottomless gloom. To die by drowning was among the worst things he could imagine, and he wondered how these eight victims had endured their own slow descent.

Linquist snapped back into action, a shiver running across his shoulders and down his spine. He needed another sample. Perhaps this was an anomaly, a dead patch. What he wanted to see was some of the normal tissue. What was the process that led to what he now had in front of him? How had it happened?

He turned off the microscope and returned to the table. Hours passed. Linquist moved between the table and the dark room, each time returning to the sample table with greater excitement and yes, he'd admit it, fear. He could not believe what he was seeing and yet what he was seeing was something he had anticipated his whole life. This entity looked much like a medieval mace without the attached chain. The protruding rays he had observed jostling in the midnight sky of the first specimen were actually a kind of spiked armor that encircled and protected a nursery of incubating progeny, broods of future entities being readied for expulsion in an explosion of new life. The entity sacrificed itself so that its species could grow and multiply. A single spiked nursery, as far as Linquist could guess, was probably producing broodlings numbering in the millions before the entity ruptured, whereupon the foundlings came of age as new nurseries. The new nurseries repeated the same process, so that the number of nurseries within the lung cell quickly filled it, devouring or becoming the cell itself. He imagined how the wall of a cell packed with nurseries resembled the vinyl liner of a swimming pool. As the years passed, the once smooth bottom of the liner began to "grow" shoots reaching up into the water. These were roots and seeds that had worked their way up through the dirt and stone dust, tenaciously seeking light despite the weight of thousands of gallons of water and the resistance of a guaranteed vinyl liner. Nothing could be done about them, for to dive under and snip them off meant cutting the liner. And even if the liner could be quickly patched, the persistence of the plant prevailed. The liner stretched to accommodate the shoot as long as it could, but eventually the inevitable occurred. The shoot grew through the vinyl, born into water and sparkling light, destroying the liner. Similarly, the cell was helpless against the spikes. Once their numbers grew large enough to fill the cell, their crowded spikes protruded from and then popped the cell wall. Immediately the foundlings sprayed the surrounding area, billions of new viruses, all ready to attach themselves to unsuspecting healthy cells. Unlike a pool liner, however, this process took minutes, not years. If this Dr. Min was correct and death occurred from twenty-four to thirty-six hours after infection, the rapidity of cell destruction was mind-boggling. And so, thought Linquist, was the potential for pandemic. If this entity was truly airborne, as Dr. Min believed, and already eight had died because of it, how many people were already now infected, coughing as they died upon others who would also die.

Linquist stood for a minute, stretching his back, then hurried to the wall phone. Before he even reported back to Schultz, he wanted to speak to this Dr. Min, to warn him that he too must be in danger, having handled these specimens. While he waited for an answer, he paced back and forth in his space suit, an astronaut attached by a phone wire to what he sensed was a new world order.

The woman who answered spoke no English. The phone was passed about, and in the background, Linquist heard chaotic sounds. Sirens, he thought, and people shouting, as if there were an emergency to which all the staff had been summoned. And a radio blasting, unless it was a loudspeaker. And the fumbling sound of the receiver passing through many hands, being dropped on a counter once, and finally another female voice, one that spoke English:

"I am sorry, can we help you?"

"This is Dr. Martin Linquist of the World Health Organization."

He heard her muffled gasp. "Yes? Can we help you?"

"I must talk to Dr. Min, your pathologist. Can you connect me?"

She covered the mouthpiece, but he could hear her speaking with someone, a brief argument, both voices raised but unintelligible.

"I am sorry, but Dr. Min is unavailable at this time," she said. Her voice was stiff, as if repeating what she had been told to say.

"This is a matter of the greatest importance," Linquist pleaded. "I must speak with him now. This is an emergency."

Again she covered the receiver. Linquist did not know Thai, but, as the argument intensified, he feared that she might hang up. Then, suddenly, the receiver must have been grabbed from the woman's hands. A male voice barked, "What? Who is this?"

What kind of a hospital was this, Linquist wondered. What was going on? But he repeated what he had said to the woman, adding this time that Dr. Min had FedExed him some samples, asking for his opinion, and that he must speak with him immediately.

The man sighed. He paused. Linquist could tell he was deciding something. Then he said, quite simply, "Dr. Min is dead this morning."

18

Patterson, Thursday, Mid-October

"Well, it looks like I've got myself two new farmhands," Rob said, looking down at the blue flannel Spiderman pajamas Christopher had worn thin at the knees. Dawn was just breaking, and between the slats of their venetian blinds, gray light leaked silently into the still room. Nothing. No one moved.

"Well, it looks like we'd better get a move on," Rob said, this time louder. One leg moved, exposing a small white foot beneath the edge of the blanket. All movement ceased again. Rob smiled, knowing that normally, the boys would have at least another hour to sleep their boyish dreams.

"Well, somebody better get moving, or I'm going to have to get the ice bucket," Rob threatened, this time loud enough for Terry, sleeping in the next room, to hear clearly. Michael's head lifted off the pillow, his eyes adjusting to the incoming light. He squinted. His face crinkled. He looked quizzically at his father.

"Dad?" he asked. "What's...." he looked at his alarm clock's glowing readout. "It's not time to get up," he moaned, turning over and trying to deny his father's presence by pulling a pillow over his head.

"For farmhands it is," Rob insisted. "School boys sleep till 7:00. Farmhands get up now," and with that Rob grabbed first Michael's, then Christopher's blankets, flipping both backward off the sleepy boys.

"Dad!" Christopher howled. "Why'd you do that?" He tried to retrieve his blanket, but Rob held fast.

"Move! Both of you! Now!" Rob ordered, but a smile curled the corners of his mouth.

Still protesting, both boys dutifully rolled out of their beds, Christopher collapsing to the floor as if having a stroke. His eyes remained closed and he could easily have gone back to sleep, even in his contorted position. Michael stumbled to the bathroom and began peeing without even closing the door. Rob picked Christopher up by the waist, flipping him and then hanging him upside down. "This will get your blood moving," he barked. Christopher protested, writhing and twisting, but giggling as he looked for something to grab and right himself. His father began to shake him, as if he were trying to get hardened salt out of a shaker. "Dad!" he protested, but now he was laughing heartily and sufficiently awake. Rob put him down gently.

"Both of you. Five minutes. In the kitchen." Turning, he passed Terry in the hall.

"What are you...' she smiled, confused.

"Tough boys are tough enough for farm work," Rob whispered, grabbing Terry's wrist and squeezing. "I'll put the coffee on."

Farm chores are farm chores. Their repetitive nature— milking the cows, gathering eggs, mucking out the barn, feeding, cleaning, and the outside work of preparing the fields for winter might appear routine, but for the farmer, every moment was an opportunity for observations that added up to life or death conclusions. Some were simple conclusions, such as the obvious health the dairy cows, the robustness of egg production, the adequacy of stored supplies such as hay. Other observations required a skilled eye—catching the existence of a minor limp, a teary eye, or a strange smell. Rob had these farmer skills. The boys, however, were slave labor, unwilling farmhands uninterested in such opportunities to observe. Thanks to Butch Jones, their father was going to make them pay dearly for getting in trouble and missing school. He might smile, but behind that smile was determination that they should not enjoy their three-day reprieve. They were going to work, and work they did.

Charlie Grange arrived at eight to find them shoveling out the hen room, their boots covered with dung and their jackets growing shoots of straw and under-feathers.

"My, oh my," Charlie hooted, his wide grin exposing his crooked front teeth. "Ain't this a happy surprise?" He stamped his foot and slapped his left knee at the same time. "You boys looking to steal my job?"

Christopher shot him an embarrassed smile. Michael answered, "We got in trouble."

"Enough to miss school?" Charlie asked, surprised.

"At school. We got suspended."

Charlie leaned against the doorframe, puzzled. "You boys did something bad enough to get suspended? What? What happened?"

"A fight," answered Christopher, dumping another shovel full of hay and dung into the wagon.

"On the bus," added Michael, stabbing a forkful of hay with his pitchfork.

"Must a' been some good reason," Charlie mused aloud. "You boys don't seem the fightin' type." Charlie had known the boys for several years now, ever since Rob had stepped up when no one else would hire him. Charlie had been down and out, a drunk living on the street, sleeping in barns and empty summer camps up at Blue Lake for years after he lost his own little farm and his wife left him. After nearly freezing to death one night, he'd finally tried to turn his life around, but no one wanted to give him a hand up. "You're too unreliable," they'd all said, these men he'd known his whole life, men who knew his history. "I need someone who's going to show up. I can't take the chance."

He'd managed to get a few odd jobs, mostly from widows who needed a bit of heavy work done they couldn't do themselves, from people who needed a worker for a week or a month for harvesting some crop. But nothing permanent, not a living. Until Rob. Rob had been different. He'd hired him on a temporary basis, but after they'd worked together for a time, he had seen Rob appraising him, not saying anything, but watching. And Charlie knew Rob was pleased with what he saw when Rob began asking him what he thought about the looks of the celery sprouts in the greenhouse and whether he knew of a better way to tie the tomato plants. Rob made Charlie feel good about himself, that he was worthy of being trusted, that he still had some shred of value the alcohol hadn't destroyed. He owed his sobriety to Rob too, for surely he would have backslid into his old Jack Daniels ways had Rob not hired him and more importantly, believed in him. So now Charlie had a new family of sorts, and these boys were dear to him.

"We aren't fighters," Michael answered, and Charlie could see the set of his jaw and the tension in his shoulders.

"So what happened?"

"Butch Jones," Michael answered, stabbing another forkful of hay.

"That Pitbull's boy?" Charlie asked. Charlie surely knew Pitbull. He'd grown up with him, for Pitbull had been in every class with Charlie until fifth grade, when Bull had stayed back a second time. Charlie and his friends had been glad to leave him there, and later, see him quit school altogether after eight grade. No one had wanted Pitbull coming up to the high school. No one wanted anything to do with Pitbull. Because Pitbull had already eaten up and spit out just about anyone who'd crossed him, including his cousin, Officer Lorry, who once had tried to arrest him as a public nuisance and ended up with a black eye.

The Joneses didn't go to jail. The clan reacted like water buffalo; they made a circle around the culprit, lowered their horns, stamped their feet, and dared anyone to try to permeate their defenses. No one ever had, as far as Charlie could recall. The police stayed clear of the Joneses, and if they had to go up into the hills where the lot of them owned farms, they went with the state police assisting if they went at all. If this Butch was Pitbull's boy, his boys were in for it.

"Who won?" Charlie asked.

"No one. The driver broke us up," Michael said over his shoulder. Christopher's eyes shone, however, above a wide smile. "I bit him," he said. "Twice." He stood looking up at Charlie, waiting for a reaction.

"A real Mike Tyson, you are," Charlie said, shaking his head. "Did he feel it?"

"His father was mad. Came into the office looking for the kid who bit his kid," Michael told Charlie.

"Uh oh," Charlie responded. "If we're talking about Pitbull Jones, that won't be the end of it."

Christopher's smile vanished. "What do you mean?" he asked, and Charlie heard the tremor in his voice.

"He means you're going to be punished...which is exactly what is happening right now," Rob declared, coming up from behind Charlie at the door. "Are you guys finished yet? Because I want you to take that wagonload out to the rhubarb patch and spread that manure over the crown of each plant. One shovelful per."

Charlie stood straight again. "Well, guess I'll get to the greenhouse." And both men disappeared, talking as they went.

"What'd he mean?" Christopher turned to Michael.

"He's just talking," Michael lied, for he knew that Charlie didn't waste time just talking. Charlie knew everyone, just like his dad did. And he didn't like the name Pitbull. People don't get names like that without a reason. "Come on," he said. "Let's get everything done fast and maybe Dad will let us go up to the hut. I want to see if anyone's been there."

It was nearly lunchtime before Rob ran out of tasks for the boys and relented. They had worked hard without complaining for over four hours, the sun was bright, the air crisp, and the land all gold and orange. Rob knew the boys needed respite and were he still a boy, he'd have wanted to go with them. Rob's cultivated land stretched over 150 acres; the rest remained forest. Beyond that, Harvard Forest lay deep and green, the ground covered with pine needles and cones, the air smelling of pinesap and adventure. Rob himself had explored literally every inch of forest in Patterson and the adjoining wild lands in Almont, Baxter, Hammond, Ogle, and Eaton. He knew how a boy could easily fantasize a world undivided by railroad tracks, roads, and power lines, how, once beyond the visual markers representing the known, a boy could believe himself an explorer in a new land. He remembered all too well the excitement he used to feel, how his senses sharpened, how his eyes focused for sudden movement or hidden clues, how his ears sought sounds as if at any moment a bear or fisher cat might spring from the undergrowth. The life of a boy growing up in Central Massachusetts could be almost as rich today as it was during his grandfather's time, before the Quabbin Reservoir, when his ancestors had farmed land now under forty feet of water.

The boys climbed the trail toward their secret hut, passing into and out of the dappled light of a forest that would soon shed its leaves. Every footstep was an announcement of their arrival, crackling the newly fallen maple and birch leaves, most of them still red and yellow, orange and purple.

"Wait, Michael," Christopher said, panting behind his brother. "I want to take off my sweatshirt." The sun had grown hot and the climb, especially while he was trying to keep up with his older brother, was taking its toll on him. His heart pounded and his face dripped with sweat.

Michael paused, looking up through the trees to a cloudless blue sky. High above, a hawk made slow circles on invisible waves of air. To Christopher, watching Michael while he struggled with the arms and the too-small neck of his sweatshirt, Michael looked princely, like the heroes in his King Arthur book. He was growing taller by the day, and his athleticism was obvious in the small bulges of his upper arms and the cords of his neck. His blond hair riffled in the breeze; his neck arched back as he followed the bird's progress.

Christopher's whole life had so far been an effort to measure up to the easy strengths of his brother. Always, watching him run when Christopher could barely walk, watching him climb when Christopher lacked the agility and strength to pull himself up, Christopher had wanted to be his brother. But recently he had begun to realize that he couldn't be his brother. He didn't know why, but he was not as fast or as strong as Michael; he didn't have Michael's endurance either. Christopher was old enough now to remember what Michael was like when he was Christopher's age, what Michael could do then that Christopher still couldn't do. The comparison made him uneasy and not a little jealous. In the world of boys, Christopher sensed Michael was everything anyone would want to be. Hadn't he been the only kid Christopher ever knew who had the guts to stand up to Butch Jones? Hadn't he refused to wimp out like everyone else when Butch decided to make a fool of him? Butch was nearly twice his weight and several inches taller, yet his brother had stood up to him. Hadn't he always gone first when they were scared, like in the darkness last Halloween when they were sure that someone was hiding up ahead? Christopher could barely swallow the rusty taste of pure terror that night. Only two nights before, he had disobeyed his parents warning about watching Halloween II, and now the knife-clad fingers of Edward Scissorhands were surely waiting up ahead to eviscerate him like all those other victims. He had hung back, whining like a baby, "No Michael, I'm afraid." And Michael had scoffed at him and vaulted forward toward the rustlings they had heard, startling a very unhappy flock of wild turkeys out of the branches they had made their beds for the night. "See?" Michael had said. "Just birds. Come on, Chris, or we'll never get any candy."

Christopher hung his sweatshirt on the scruffy undergrowth beside the trail, planning to pick it up on his return. He pulled his jersey out of his jeans and pushed up his sleeves. "Okay," he said, looking at Michael. But Michael held his finger to his lips and pointed. Christopher immediately went limp with worry, and then froze, moving only his eyes in the direction of Michael's finger. Something was moving about thirty feet away, something dark and low. The bushes rustled and leaves and dried twigs snapped. Whatever it was was coming on a diagonal toward them. Coming fast. His heart stopped.

And then it broke through the underbrush, its tail

wagging. A dog. Thank God a dog, thought Chris. Michael remained still, unsure whether to run or hold his ground. The dog ran toward him, his back end wiggling in glee, and leapt upward, both paws on Michael's shoulders. Michael stumbled backward, kept his balance and immediately began laughing. The dog was licking his face as if he were a surprise ice cream cone, slobbering all over him, relentless in its joy to have found someone. Michael wrapped his arms around him and then went down, the dog as tall as he and probably ten pounds heavier. Christopher watched as the dog overpowered his brother, circling, swirling, rolling, licking, nudging, checking every inch of his brother from his tussled hair to his dirty sneakers, sniffing and nosing his jeans and shirt as if looking for treats. And then an instant later, the dog was running toward him.

Christopher squatted, burying his face in his arms to protect himself, but to no avail. The dog's cold nose pushed through every opening, lifting his resisting arms to find his face, and when Christopher rolled to the ground, the dog sought him out beneath his tee-shirt, behind his neck and above his jeans. The dog was wild with joy, prancing and circling.

"Where'd he come from?" Michael laughed, helping Christopher up. And then the dog was on him again, insistent in its friendliness.

"Bet he's a stray," Christopher ventured, patting his wriggling behind. "Look at all the burrs." Both boys ran their hands over the dog's fur.

"He's skinny," Michael said. "Feel his ribs." Christopher felt along the dog's side. Beneath the thick fur he could feel the animal's skeleton.

"Wonder how long he's been out here," Michael mused.

Christopher lifted the dog's ear. "Look," he said. "He's missing a piece." The dog lowered his head, patient while the boy examined his wound.

"Be careful," Michael warned. "He could bite."

But Christopher knew this was no biting dog. If dogs could purr, he knew this dog would purr like a kitten. The dog had a way of leaning into the slightest touch, as if it craved human contact. Though his fur was a ragged mess, loaded with briars, burrs and tangled leaves, his eyes were clear and happy. Friendly, Chris thought. This is no bad dog.

"Who do you suppose owns him?" Christopher asked. And then his eyes went soft. "Do you suppose..."

"Don't even think about it," Michael prompted. The two boys had been asking for a dog ever since Holly, their old yellow lab, had died. And each time, their father had gone rigid for a moment before he flatly answered no. Holly had been Rob's dog for fourteen years, going everywhere with him. Whether accompanying Rob to a Selectmen's meeting, hunting in the fall, or riding shotgun on the tractor, she walked or sat beside him as if joined invisibly to him. He never had to tell her to heel or come, because she was always heeling and never two feet away from his leg. When she had to be put down, the cancer beyond control, Rob's melancholy had been palpable, as if her loss had made empty spaces on the rug where she slept at Rob's feet or in the kitchen, where Terry had tactfully removed her bowls, or beside Rob in the pickup, where her nose had always tested the breezes through the open window. Holly was like Rob's oldest child, Terry explained to the boys... not as important as they were, of course, but his first baby, even if she was a dog. So when she died, Rob grieved for her just as he'd grieve for any of them. Terry had promised that eventually their father's sorrow would pass, and after a time most of it had. But at the mention of another dog, Holly's loss seemed to come back strong as ever. No, he always said. No more dogs. And that was that.

So here they were in Harvard Forest with what was probably a stray dog that their father would never let them keep. If they brought him home, their dad would probably call Animal Control, and the dog would be off to the pound. They couldn't leave him here. How would they ever get him to stay put when they turned back? The dog nudged Michael's leg, as if to say, "I'm yours." Michael looked at Christopher.

"Please, Michael? Please, let's try?"

As if understanding the importance of the moment, the dog sat on its haunches looking longingly up at Michael. Its brown eyes were so intelligent, Michael thought to himself. It wiggled on its backside, whimpering its own canine please. Christopher put a hand on its neck, feeling its thick ruff.

"Maybe he's just lost, you know," Michael said. "Maybe we'll take him down with us and find out he belongs to somebody."

"He's got no collar," Christopher stated as if that answered Michael's concern. Christopher knew that people who no longer wanted their pets often "dropped them off" out in farm country, fooling themselves that someone would take them in. Most often, the cat or dog starved to death or was eaten by coyotes.

"He could have lost his collar."

Christopher thought a minute. "All right. Then we'll save him."

The possibilities made Michael smile. They'd take him home and Dad would agree that they should put an ad in the paper and then while they waited for someone to come claim him, which Michael hoped wouldn't happen, Dad would get to like him too much to call Animal Control, and then he'd be theirs. "Let's go," he said out loud, and the two boys and an ecstatic dog headed back down the trail.

"No way," Rob predictably stated when the boys arrived, their new friend leaping about them as they ran toward Rob. Upon seeing Rob, the dog trotted toward him, but now some clear sense of strategy must have determined his behavior. Instead of leaping up to his chest, the dog stopped one foot short of Rob and sat, looking up quietly at him as if Rob had always been his master. When Rob ignored that, the dog whimpered. When Rob ignored that, the dog woofed softly. Still ignored, the dog's backside wriggled and he danced on his front paws, still sitting. When Rob made the mistake of letting his arms unfold from over his chest, the resolute stance meant to end all argument, he dropped his hands to his side. The dog was instantly on the left one, licking it and tossing it up so that Rob's hand slid over its head in a pet. Rob couldn't help but smile, though he knew manipulation when he saw it.

"See Dad? See how friendly?"

"See how well behaved he is?" Michael added.

Still stern and uncompromising, Rob said, "Let's go in the barn. See how he is around cows and pigs." Somehow Rob knew this would be a losing strategy. He knew a good farm dog when he saw one, and he'd be pretty surprised if the dog did anything more than sniff the livestock. Together the four walked into the darkness of the barn. An errant chicken, loose from the chicken room, suddenly strutted in front of them, exasperated. Rob watched the dog, who at first looked as if he might give chase. His body snapped to attention, his ears up, his eyes alert. As the chicken hustled past him, he trotted after it, sniffing. The chicken, frightened now by a stranger, flapped its wings and ran clucking, but the dog just looked after it with an expression of disdain that made Rob chuckle. "What a stupid critter, he's thinking," Rob snorted. The boys laughed and called the dog to them. "Good boy, good boy," they both congratulated. The dog danced about, elated by the praise.

"Can we keep him, Dad? Can we please keep him?" Christopher pleaded.

"We'd have to put an ad in the paper," Rob answered. "This dog belongs to someone. Chances are they'll claim him and you're going to be left feeling bad. It's better to call Control now so you don't get attached." His words dropped into the gloom about them like stones. The boys were silent.

"You mean so *you* don't get attached," Michael corrected. His words were slow and accusing.

Rob looked down at his older son. Their eyes locked. Had there been light in the barn, he'd have seen himself reflected not only in his son's face, in the high forehead, straight nose, square chin, and slightly clownish ears, but also mirrored in the light brown eyes that hinted tears.

"Please, Dad," Christopher touched his hand.

"Your mother isn't going to want to put up with some stray dog," he said, knowing he was going to lose this one.

"Let's wait. Let's ask her. If she says yes..." Michael also knew they had won. His mother was easy. She had missed Holly too, but she had even said that the best thing for Rob was to get another dog. She'd offered to go on-line and see what labs were available nearby only a few weeks after Holly's death. She loved dogs.

"I'm telling you, it's not a good idea," Rob insisted. "We

don't know whether this dog's had his shots. He could be sick or something."

"Please let's just wait for Mom," Christopher was excited now. He knew his father well enough to sense victory in the offing.

"Just till Mom gets home," Michael pleaded.

Rob knew the battle was over. And he wasn't that sad about it either. He looked down at the dog his kids had found and for a moment almost thought the dog was smiling up at him. He could tell this was no pedigreed animal, and yet the combinations that had created him worked wonderfully. Had to be part shepherd, part golden, he thought. Soft fur, good-sized head. Nice size too, big but not too big. A bath and a good brushing, and the dog was going to be something fine to look at.

The dog, sensing acceptance, began to dance about him, his long bushy tail wagging. Then Christopher cried, "Yippee! Yippee!" and ran around the dog and his father, skipping and jumping. But the final decision was made a second later when Michael slid his hand into his father's and though somewhat embarrassed by this childish action, said, "Thanks, Dad."

"Grizzly, we'll name him," Chris laughed. "Because we thought he was a bear."

"Come on, Griz," Michael called, slapping his legs. The dog, without a second's hesitation, raced to him, jumping up and once again knocking him down. Another face washing. Another wrestle.

As Rob watched, he remembered old Holly in the days before the boys had been born. How she loved nothing better than to wrestle with Rob, how impossible it was to defend himself against her insistent dog kisses, and how much he had loved that old girl, who'd never once failed to stand beside him through all the early hard times on the farm.

"Chores," Rob announced. "Go get yourselves a sandwich. Then you're going to have to brush that mutt and give him a bath before your mother gets home and throws a fit." The boys struggled to their feet, Grizzly running ahead of them. Then they walked out of the gloom of the barn into the bright October sunlight, a family with a dog.

19

Patterson, Thursday, Mid-October

Doc Strong was in a foul mood by the time Terry arrived at the clinic. He stomped out to her desk, growling orders for files, messages, and coffee before she could remove her jacket and put on her nurse's cap. Terry wanted to cock her head and ask about golf scores, but something told her to be quiet. When Doc chewed an unlit cigar, it was a sure sign of trouble. She bustled about, got the coffee perking, retrieved phone messages, and gathered the files he'd requested, ever aware of the storm cloud that Doc created on the other side of the open doorway.

"Look at this fax," Doc grumbled, shoving a creamy sheet at her when she brought him his mug.

Terry picked up the paper and read. The official impact of the U.S. seal, even if only on a fax, alarmed her, but the contents seemed innocuous enough. The Office of Health and Human Services mandated that all doctors read and implement the contents of an official government packet due to arrive by mail within the next two days. Direct reporting of all suspected influenza cases was to be accomplished on a daily basis through area public health departments that would now report directly to the CDC. To facilitate communication, all doctors would now be required to establish an e-mail address and register this address with the CDC Communications Center. The e-mail address followed.

Terry looked confused. "Is this for prevention? All the worry about this year's flu?"

"Hell, no," Doc said. "Damn government. Who do they think they're fooling? Bureaucrats. Didn't you hear the news last night?" Doc was slamming drawers, looking for something that wasn't there.

"Yes, about that avian outbreak in Thailand?"

"Bird outbreak nothing!" Doc harrumphed "That's just the tip, Terry. We've got pandemic. The government is trying to keep it quiet, but we've got it. It's in Thailand now. But how long do you think it will take to reach here? That thing is going explode all over Asia like nuclear fallout!"

"But it's a bird flu," Terry replied without confidence. She had worked with Doc for nearly ten years and she had seen him save lives and solve so many medical mysteries that no other doctor would ever be good enough for her family. Anyone who thought a country doctor a bumpkin had never met Doc, who read voraciously and was more in touch with research than most researchers.

"Not anymore it isn't." Doc grumbled. "What do you think they're doing up there in Kwang Tri, cordoning off the entire district. People are dying up there and those tractors you saw? They're for burying them."

Terry's voice trembled. "The bird flu...."

Doc interrupted. It's A(H5N1). At least it was. It's a sub-type of Type A. "

"Why do you say it *was* H5N1?"

"Because H5N1 only infected humans who came in contact with the birds who had it...their excretions, nasal secretions, saliva, feces. You had to be near the birds to get it."

"And that has all changed." Terry nodded.

"That's right. Kwang Tri's got a recombinant version. The thing can be communicated by humans to humans, but because the genetic source is birds, people have no resistance."

"What about drugs? We've got some right out in the cabinet.... Amantadine and Rimantadine...And I know there's more."

"They don't work. And the others, the Oseltamavir and Zanamavir might have worked before the mutation, but no more. We're in for it, Terry, and the goddamn government's worrying about e-mail addresses instead of shutting down all commerce and travel to Asia. Damn politicians," and Doc stood up, vigorously chewing his cigar.

"How do you know this, Doc? None of what you're saying was on the news." This wasn't an accusation, nor was Terry's voice challenging. She knew when she asked that Doc was right and had information he wasn't supposed to have.

"Doesn't matter where I got it," he growled again, "it's the truth. Mark my words, this is going to be something the likes of which none of us could ever imagine."

And then the phone rang. Doc picked up the receiver and waved her away. Terry wanted to grab her jacket, pick up the kids at school, and race home. Her heart was pounding and a sudden sense of dread locked her stomach muscles till they ached. But she knew she had to be rational. It's over there, she thought to herself. Nothing has happened here. We'll be safe. The government will protect us. We'll have scientists working day and night on a vaccine. We'll be okay. Still, no matter how hard she tried to reassure herself, her sense of dread increased. Just then Mrs. Lee, their secretary, arrived, huffing and puffing from door to desk, dropping her hefty body noisily into her well-worn swivel chair. "I'm here, darlins'," she called to the inner office.

Doc put his hand over the phone. "Don't say anything. She'll get hysterical."

Terry looked from him to the back of Mrs. Lee's head, bit her lip, and nodded.

"Close the door behind you," Doc whispered above his hand. And she did so just as Mrs. Lee turned to greet her.

"Well my oh my, don't you look worried today," Mrs. Lee crooned. "What's the matter, dearie?" Mrs. Lee's eyes were a bright blue above the rosiest cheeks this side of Denmark. She was seventy years young but had long ago lost the battle with dieting. Her chins folded neatly against her neck as she gazed up at Terry.

Terry forced a smile. "Sophia," she said. "Is that a new dress?"

Mrs. Lee looked down at herself as if surprised at what she was wearing. "Oh!" she exclaimed after a moment. "Yes, it is."

And then the first patient arrived, Mrs. Grogan, hobbling on crutches, mouth turned down and cold gray eyes darting about the office.

"Good morning, Patricia," Terry smiled.

"Umm. Yes," Mrs. Grogan managed before picking up the nearest magazine. "I suppose he's going to make me wait, as usual."

And so the day began.

20

Geneva, Thursday, Mid-October

The systems designed to protect the world from plague went into action within hours of Martin Linquist's call to Schultz. His faith in Linquist's conclusions sent him running toward the elevator at the CDC, telling Edna on his way out the door to hold all calls indefinitely and to cancel all afternoon meetings. Within minutes he was standing by the glass observation wall in Linquist's lab. Linquist held up a photograph of the spiked nurseries nurturing themselves on a human cell while he spoke on the wall phone. Schultz was confused by what he saw, and as he squinted, Linquist spoke into his phone.

"The damn thing sacrifices itself to reproduce more of its kind," Linquist explained, his eyes wide with excitement. Schultz tried to offer other possible conclusions, but Linquist destroyed all of them with the evidence he had. Both scientists recognized that this was a first, a virus for which humans had no immunity, a virus programmed to reproduce in such quantum numbers that the sacrifice of one insured survival of thousands of others that would make the same sacrifice hours, perhaps even minutes later.

"You may have been right," Linquist frowned now, shaking his head.

"Right?" Schultz asked, surprised. What he had just seen was totally foreign and unimaginable to him.

"About a ninety percenter..." Linquist reminded him. He looked out at Schultz, the creases around his mouth deep and serious. "Min's dead. The hospital is in chaos." Schultz was stunned. "He handled it only hours ago," he muttered, his shoulders sagging. Both recognized the staggering implications—everyone at Kwang Tri who had any contact with the victims had already incubated the virus. If they had gone home to their families, they had brought the virus home with them. If this morning, everyone infected had gotten up and gone about their usual routines, everyone they came in contact with today was likely to contract it. If any of them traveled anywhere outside Kwang Tri the virus was already on its way around the world. By now it could be anywhere—Europe, the U.S., South America, Africa, Asia, the mid-East. No place on earth could be ruled out.

Their conversation lasted only a few minutes longer. Then Schultz was back in his office where Edna was removing from the fax machine a facsimile of the photograph Schultz had just seen, sent up by Linquist before he left the lab and began disinfecting himself. Other pages followed, all further proof that what they had in Level Four was something none of them had ever seen before. Schultz was not a man given to trembling, but today something in him had begun to quaver as he hurried to initiate The Plan. Edna could see it the minute he flung open the office door, sending it flying backward hard until it slammed the adjoining wall. But Schultz was oblivious; he was already out of her office and into his own, barking over his shoulder that she'd better have no plans for dinner, that this might be an all-nighter.

Edna gathered up the faxes and followed him into his office where Schultz was flipping open the notebook that she knew contained The Plan, the system the WHO and other organizations working with it had devised three years ago after a very close call with ebola. The Plan was a step-by-step procedure meant to be implemented whenever a Level Four danger was discovered in the field. It listed the people and organizations to contact and in what order, the defense systems to be initiated to limit the spread of the disease, and the mechanisms to wipe out the disease at its source if its source could be determined. All of these had taken months to finalize, but in its final form, The Plan was something that Schultz and his colleagues had hoped would be the best defense possible.

When Schultz had returned from their final meeting that day three years ago, what had surprised her was that he seemed mildly depressed instead of elated to have reached an accord. When she had asked what was troubling him, Schultz had waited a long time before answering. He was sitting at his desk and he had swung his leather armchair in such a way that the lowering sun cast deep shadows across his craggy face. One side of his face was bathed in a rosy glow while the other was in darkness. Edna watched him, sipping her tea. When he answered, the sun streaming in across the three o'clock sky blinded her. She placed her hand over her eyes to better see him, but as he spoke, he seemed less her long-time boss and friend and more a dark visage with pronouncements she did not want to hear.

"The day is going to come," he said solemnly, "and I hope it's not on my watch. But it's going to come soon, I think, when this system or any system we can devise, is going to fail. It's just too complex, this world of ours. We've been lucky so far. The worst diseases, you know, AIDS, ebola, Marburg, the lot of them, have lacked one single capacity—their spread has been controlled because they're not airborne. One minute change in the RNA of any of them, and they could be slate wipers, because we can't stop airborne viruses. There are just too many people."

Edna had watched him as he placed his cup on the desk and picked up the notebook. "See this, Edna?" he had said. "It's going to work on the things we know about so far...It's a good plan. But everyone there, all of us who wrote this thing, we all know that when the time comes, when some new adaptation emerges out of the jungle or the cities, something deadly and aerosol, this book," and he dropped it disgustedly on his blotter, "this Plan won't be worth the paper it's written on."

Edna remembered that moment as she laid the faxes on his desk. Without looking up, he said, "Okay. Those are going out to everyone on page three. Now. You do that; I'll make the calls. As soon as you're done, come back here."

Edna heard him ask for the head of the American CDC as she set down the faxes and turned to page three in her own notebook. Then she began the fax. She knew that at the other end of her own phone line, someone was retrieving each sheet she sent. She looked at the photographs in her hand as she waited for the machine to complete its cycle. They looked like photos of a Wyoming sky, she thought, remembering a childhood camping trip to the U.S. with her parents, how stretched out on her sleeping mat an infinity of stars had danced above them. How the American West had seemed to her a great frontier just barely discovered, as if Lewis and Clark might appear at any moment to share a hot chocolate by their campfire.

"Edna," Schultz called. "Call Linquist. Tell him the CDC had already gotten wind of something. They've got their team in the air. Tell him to get his staff moving, FAST!"

21

Bangkok, Friday, Mid-October

Granted permission by the Prime Minister, who promised them complete cooperation, Dr. Ralph Sloan and the nine members of his team landed at Bangkok International Airport soon after sunrise. That the CDC had pre-empted the WHO was of special delight to Sloan. For the entire length of his career he had nursed a burr in his side over a slight by the former director of the WHO. Jenkins had cost him some embarrassment and the loss of considerable credit for the work done on LaCrosse encephalitis in the midwest. Others had made off with the publicity Sloan knew had been due him, and the rage he felt at being bested had surely prompted the ulcer he now nursed. He had spent the last decade making sure the same thing didn't happen again, and while the WHO had since retired the man responsible for his digestive irritation, Sloan had never really trusted anyone even remotely connected to the WHO. Of course, he would make it look like he was going through the proper channels. His staff back in Atlanta were at this very moment probably drafting a letter to Schultz in Geneva, detailing the reasons for his hasty departure for Thailand. But the letter would not arrive by FedEx until tomorrow, and by then, Sloan hoped he'd already have a handle on things here.

He brought with him the usual handful of people the CDC sent, one of them a respiratory pathogens expert named Doug Gorham. Gorham had a tendency to get on Sloan's nerves. He was a little too righteous, Sloan thought, and that often made him uncomfortable. Good people always did. They were just too simplistic. They somehow knew they had a handle on what was right and were always ready to tell everybody what they should be doing, and even worse, what they should be feeling. Sloan didn't come naturally to such moral diligence. His father said that he had been born with a "killer instinct" to win and had encouraged little Ralphie to use it whenever he could. His father had been a billionaire before he was forty, a Wall Street entrepreneur and later a real estate mogul of no little fame in and around Chicago. So Ralph Jr. grew up knowing the importance of one-upmanship and getting there first, and today he had done it again.

Gorham was at his side as they disembarked at Gate 5, hurrying on his short legs to keep up with the long, easy strides Sloan took. Sloan noticed Gorham's tousled hair and his wrinkled shirt. Sloppy, Sloan thought to himself, really just a slug. If Gorham hadn't been so good at what he did, such a goddamned bookworm when it came to research, Sloan would rather have had McMahon accompany him. McMahon knew how to look professional. This guy was an embarrassment.

He increased his stride, noting how Gorham fell slowly behind. He was struggling with a heavy equipment bag they hadn't trusted to the baggage guys, shifting it from arm to arm and using his paunch to keep it chest height. Good, Sloan thought to himself, and walked even faster. The others followed like baby ducks, gabbing among themselves but keeping up, so when Sloan turned back mid-stride, he saw that they too had passed Gorham. The nerd looked as if he were with some other group.

Two reporters were waiting, one the woman who had

tipped Sloan off with a late evening call just after the closing of Kwang Tri Hospital. Karen Klein was a correspondent for the Washington Eagle Times; they had met at a cocktail party a few years ago. Their affair had been brief and disappointing, but it ended well, with both happy to move on and neither looking back. And while Sloan was surprised that she'd chosen him to call with this tip, he'd been glad that she was one of the few women he hadn't alienated. Karen had a source, an American friend who was engaged to a nurse who told him that while she was on duty at Kwang Tri Hospital nine people had died within hours of each other. The source told Karen that an entire family and the doctor who treated them had been quietly sent to the morgue. The nurse had reported for work the next day only to call later, hysterical that she was no longer able to leave the premises and sure that her life was in danger. No one was doing anything about it, she had wailed, and could he somehow get her out. Her fiancé had tried to get into the hospital but had been barred by security, and the only thing he could think of to do was inform the media. He had called Karen. She did some checking and in no time at all concluded something was deeply amiss in Kwang Tri.

"Karen," Sloan crooned. "So glad to see you."

"They've cordoned off Kwang Tri," she said matter-of-factly.

"I've spoken to the Prime Minister. They had to." Sloan had not been instrumental in this decision. It had already been made by the new Minister of Health, the Prime Minister, and Thailand's king before Sloan called. When his request to speak to the Minister of Health was immediately granted, Sloan knew something was up. He had worked with enough politicians to know that emerging viruses and public health issues put the fear of God in all of them—for monetary, not medical reasons. He had yet to be sent to any country that welcomed the presence of the CDC or the WHO, because outbreaks that became public crippled tourism and trade, and if a country didn't depend on one of them, it depended on the other. So to have the new Minister seem so anxious to cooperate, so grateful for his offer to bring the CDC's vast expertise to bear on "the issue," meant it was already wobbling out of control.

"So what are you going to do now?" Klein readied her notebook, turning as she did so to walk along with him toward the front exit. "What's protocol?"

Sloan loved these questions. He had been through the whole spiel so many times over the years that the words flowed without his expending any intellectual energy. "First we have to find out what we've got here. We've got to locate the infecting agent. Identify the causative pathogen. We're going to canvass the area where the first family lived. Track down everyone who had contact with them. "

"Are you going to request a quarantine?"

"The area is already cordoned off. That's enough until we have substantial evidence that there is need of quarantine. That requires samples from the sick and the dead. We'll send them back to Atlanta. The guys there have the facilities for culture and molecular biological analysis." Sloan was not really talking to her, just reciting the usual litany. Instead, he looked straight ahead to where he saw his name on a placard held aloft by a young Asian man in uniform.

"Do you think it's a filovirus?" the reporter asked.

"You mean like ebola?' Sloan had a way of wrinkling his eyebrows and sneering that could make the most confident people shrink. He turned to her with a disdainful smile, for she clearly had no idea what a filovirus was. "This isn't some jungle in Africa, my dear," Sloan added. He loathed people who pretended to be knowledgeable and loved putting them down.

Karen was offended. "Look, I may not know much about emerging viruses, Dr. Sloan, but I had the good sense to call you, didn't I? Otherwise, you'd still be in Atlanta sipping your mint juleps."

Sloan heard the edge in her voice and knew there was no point in making her an enemy. Reporters can be useful in so many ways, and truly, she was responsible for his getting the jump on the rest of them.

"Now, now, Karen. No need for sniping. Your diligence may well save some lives. And when I've got something, you'll be the first to know." He feared she'd hear the patronizing tone, but apparently she missed it. Sloan noticed when her frown faded to a smile that the skin around her lips was absorbing her red lipstick, so that tiny lines blurred what should be defined. She had a full mouth, but under the fluorescent lights it looked oily and slick. Above it, her greedy eyes appraised him. He wondered how he'd ever let himself get involved.

"That's more like it, Doc. One hand washes the other."

"A very good suggestion, in view of this situation," Sloan replied, thinking himself quite witty for a man up all night.

Four hours later, his team was set up and ready to go. They had unpacked all their equipment on the main road leading into Kwang Tri. Between Bangkok and Kwang Tri there were no visible demarcation lines. Bangkok proper petered out into industrial and manufacturing buildings, then support companies like paper goods providers and plumbing contractors, then tenements, then hovels built along the road in thick clusters that grew denser as one got closer to Kwang Tri, where the skyline rose from one and two story stores and buildings to the occasional four and five story government-grant buildings. From what he had been told by a colleague, the entire area teemed with people living six and seven to a room and, to no one's surprise, with backyard goats, pigs, chickens, dogs and, outnumbering all of them, rats. It was dirty, it smelled of garbage and sewage, and the air was bleak with noxious smoke from chimneys, street vendors, and vehicles.

Sloan shook his head in disbelief. "This roadblock is what you call 'cordoned off'?" For of course there was no way to cordon off Kwang Tri. Soldiers could bar the roads and monitor the streets surrounding the infected area, but anyone who wanted to escape could use the millions of windows, doors, cellar ways, and alleys inside to escape to the outside if they had a moment's opportunity—the distraction of a soldier, a shadowy area where the spotlights the government had installed could not reach, or even if one knew or could pay off a guard. Sloan knew all too well how these things worked. What was worse, the soldiers themselves were spread too thin.

"How many people are inside?" Sloan asked the captain supervising the soldiers who were helping Sloan's team set up.

"Perhaps two hundred thousand," he said without emotion. Sloan noticed that the officer looked down or to the side when answering, and wondered why he seemed so incapable of directness. Was he embarrassed? Ashamed? Fearful?

Before them, perhaps thirty of the captain's men bustled about the tents they had already erected. The captain turned away, barking orders Sloan could not understand. The team was nearly ready.

Four jeeps driven by military men in gas masks and protective clothing and carrying AK-47s carried the nine-man team into Kwang Tri proper. As Sloan looked about through the protective plastic of his helmet, he was struck by the complete lack of human activity. No one was on the streets. He could see faces in the windows, ghostly pale ovals pressed to the glass. They seemed impassive, almost disinterested, Sloan thought. Why weren't they coming down to the street in droves, begging for help and medical supplies, begging to be let out of Kwang Tri? Sloan remembered the dusty village in Kenya, the reaching hands of the entire tribe, the pleading calls, the horror on the villagers' faces, all of them turned out to greet the plane in the outbreak he had snuffed back in '96. He had felt like a conquering hero that time, coming to save the people. This place, though, was like nothing he'd ever seen. Empty. Desolate. Sloan turned to the captain. "What's keeping them inside?" he shouted from inside his protective helmet.

The captain raised his rifle in answer, then looked away again.

"For how long?" Sloan shouted again.

"Two days."

"Any revolts?"

"Several."

"You use force?" Sloan watched the captain and now knew why the captain could not look him in the eye.

"Yes."

"How many killed?" Sloan wondered what it must have been like, quelling a panicked district and forcing everyone into their homes. He knew how panic got started, and he knew the human tendency to flee an overpowering force. To have a district of two hundred thousand laid down like this, thousands cowering in their homes, they must have used brutal force against their own people. That was why this captain couldn't look him in the eye. He was wrestling with his own moral dilemmas. Sloan wondered whether the captain and his men might even have family in here. How would that affect their ability to follow orders? How many people had slipped through the line thanks to relatives working for the military? He tried to put the situation in perspective. He did not even know how widespread this thing, whatever it was, had become. Maybe he was conjuring up scenarios that had never happened. He'd take control. He'd figure out what the problem was. He'd....

And then the jeep turned right on to what was probably one of the main streets in Kwang Tri. Ahead of them, a truck had stopped at the sidewalk, its exhaust puffing clouds of monoxide into the street. Sloan squinted. The flat bed of the truck was piled high with what he first thought were bundles of clothing. The bundles, however, were corpses in varying positions, stacked four or five high behind the cab of the truck. On the flatbed, two soldiers in gas masks and protective gloves were dragging the rearmost corpses forward, making room for new arrivals. The driver honked and the door to the next building opened. Sloan watched two young girls and an old man carry a corpse out to the street, where it was received without ceremony by the stackers who took it by the feet and under the arms and hefted it onto the rearmost pile.

Sloan's vehicle swung around the truck. Ahead, another truck on the other side of the street was working its way toward them. Sloan noticed that doors to some stores and businesses were locked and barred, but others besides them stood open, as if someone might at any moment emerge from within. The bins where vendors displayed their wares had been picked clean and Sloan guessed that the stores that had been left unlocked were empty as well. He looked up again and noticed that the numbers of faces looking down at him were far fewer, and often they did not linger to watch. He glimpsed a curtain moving here, a blind closing there, but the sense of an audience was missing. He imagined the smells here must be unbearable.

As the jeep convoy moved along the street, other trucks passed, each carrying more bodies. Sloan asked where they were going, and the captain merely pointed behind them, where for the first time, Sloan noticed billowing black smoke in the western sky. He guessed the dump had become a crematorium. For the first time, Sloan shuddered. The enormity of this was beyond anything he had imagined.

"How many so far?" he asked. The captain merely shrugged his shoulders and looked ahead.

"How far is the hospital?" Sloan asked, hoping to get a response this time. The Captain did not have to answer, however, for at that moment the jeep rounded another corner and he saw in front of them a street being cleared by a band of soldiers with flatbed trucks. A path to the hospital had just been opened enough so that it was now possible to get close to the hospital. The jeeps halted and the captain motioned for Sloan to get down. The soldiers began unloading the equipment he wanted carried in. The others in his team walked forward in their field suits, looking like an alien invasion from some orange planet. None of them spoke; Sloan knew they, too, were stunned by what they had seen and were fighting to stay calm.

"We'll use the hospital facilities," Sloan turned to the team, resting a hand upon the roof of a parked car. Before he could give further instructions, he looked down and jerked his hand away. Inside the car, a middle-aged man, blood caked on his chin and shirt, looked up at the sky through the passenger window. Gaseous decay had bloated his face and torso; his clothes bulged to contain him. Sloan's team members turned to follow his gaze and stared. "Jesus," one said.

The captain blew a whistle and soldiers came trotting. "Get this man out of here," he shouted through his mask. "You were supposed to have this area cleared." He trembled with anger. "Move!" he shouted, stepping back while soldiers flung the door open to remove the staring corpse.

Perhaps for the first time in his life, Ralph Sloan felt his legs trembling beneath him. The realization of what was happening here and what it likely meant for the world was not lost on him. He was only too aware that humans are subject to the rules of evolution the same as every other species. While it might be possible to assuage the fears of the general population with the promises of science, Sloan knew full well that humans do not occupy center stage of life on this planet any more than Earth occupies center stage in the universe. Humans are as prone to species disaster as dinosaurs and perhaps, having been producing out of control for millions of years, are due for disaster at any moment. Somehow, as Sloan looked from the body now being carted away to what he guessed was an empty hospital, he sensed that they had just arrived at a cataclysmic moment in time. And as he and others like him had predicted, it was occurring not in the jungle but in the megacity, the perfect petri dish for a virus to infect an infinite number of hosts, the critical opportunity a virus needed to insinuate itself quickly and flourish.

Sloan felt Gorham nudging him and turned. "We'd better go take a look," Gorham said pointing to the hospital's emergency doors. Sloan looked into Gorham's eyes and saw there the same realizations he was experiencing mixed with unspeakable sorrow. Almost imperceptibly, Gorham shook his head. This time, Sloan didn't find Gorham annoying. Gorham was experiencing his own future, Sloan knew. His very own apocalypse.

Sloan nodded and together the two led their team inside.

"They've cleared the area," Sloan said aloud, although it was obvious to everybody. A momentary sense of relief washed over the lot of them. Each had expected to see bodies everywhere—behind the admitting desk, in the small, curtained alcoves, and as they walked into the adjacent hall, stretched out on the cots lining the walls. The cots remained, as did the bloodied sheets. But the real evidence of the ravaged hospital, the hundreds of children, men, and women who had died here in the last thirty-six hours now burned in the fire billowing black smoke into a perfect blue sky.

"The morgue should be downstairs," Gorham said, pointing to the hastily-drawn hospital layout the captain had furnished. "The first ones are there."

"You know what to do," Sloan said. "Take Rodman, Gress, and Scoll with you. Get the samples we need and let's get out of here." The three men nodded their understanding and followed Gorham to look for the elevator. Sloan sent the remaining four to investigate the hospital lab. "See what you can find there." As they followed the first group, Sloan headed down the hall toward the administrative offices. There he hoped to find records, even hastily scribbled notes that might shed some light on things.

Though it appeared that all the doors along the hallway had been left open, he grabbed the large brass ring heavy with keys that lay on the Assistant's desk, just in case.

He slowly made his way down the hospital wing, peering into rooms as if at any moment someone might jump out at him. Though Sloan had seen plenty of deaths in his career, he felt a tight ache in his stomach. He did not want to find a forgotten body, stiffened into some obscenely crooked position where it had fallen; he did not want to stifle the gag that nearly always left him fighting not to vomit. He tried to control his discomfort, to look upon this scientifically, but his insides would not cooperate. He tried to tell himself that the empty hospital offices were merely abandoned, not the scene of hysteria and panic, but he kept imagining the chaos that must have occurred, the rushing, the shouting, the fearful exchanges between doctors and nurses, the groans, the wails. These voices were relentless, no matter how hard he tried to concentrate. He berated himself. Hadn't he relished jumping on the plane and beating everyone to the scene? Hadn't he yearned for something big to come along that would allow him to once again razzle-dazzle the world? Wasn't this exactly what he wished for?

Sloan thumbed through the papers in one office, hoping to find something useful but, realizing they were invoices, he tossed them down. He worked his way along the hallway, entering each office, looking around, sifting through papers left scattered on the desks, and then moving to the next office.

At the far end of the administrative wing, one door remained closed. He twisted the brass knob, but the door was locked. Sloan tried three or four keys in the lock before the handle turned. He opened the door slowly, not knowing what might lie behind it. At first, the sun streaming in through the venetian blinds blinded him. The room was awash in light, and the desk that sat in front of the window seemed a huge black hulk. This had to be the Chief-of-Staff's office. As his eyes adjusted, he stepped inside and walked directly to the desk.

Sloan flipped through the sheets on the desktop, realizing as he did so that this might be the information he was looking for. Completed surgical, autopsy, and lab forms, a stack of them in a single folder, had been left open on the desk. He picked up the entire folder and walked to the window, turning the venetian wand so that the light would be diverted, the papers easier to see. There he stood for several minutes, flipping through the sheets.

When he turned back, he realized with a sudden sinking feeling that he was not alone. Had he not known better, he would have thought that a man was sleeping soundly on the sofa. Sloan jumped as he did the double take, an involuntary gasp seizing him. The man was curled in the fetal position, his feet hanging over the arm, his hands tucked up under the side of his face. He was absolutely still, but for a moment, perhaps as Sloan quavered, he seemed to breathe. Sloan froze, waiting for something to happen. But nothing did. The man was clearly dead.

Though he did not want to, Sloan forced himself to walk over to the body. This had to be the Chief of Staff, Sloan thought to himself. The man was wearing a shirt and tie, and as Sloan looked back at the desk, he saw a suit jacket hung over the back of the office chair. How had he missed that? He was missing a lot of things, he thought, nervously working his jaw. What else had he missed?

Sloan looked closely into the staring eyes of the man. They stared back at nothing. The blood that had poured from his nose and mouth caked the skin around his nostrils and the lines around his mouth. Where it had dribbled, it left a brown stain on the suede sofa. He had been dead at least 24 hours, Sloan guessed, wondering why the doctor had chosen to lock himself in his office rather than have his staff tend to him. Had he felt guilt for letting this thing spin out of control? Sloan wondered. Or had it all happened so fast that he was merely another lost victim caught up in the wave? Whatever it was, Sloan decided to leave him where he lay. If they ever got control of this killing thing, if Kwang Tri ever got back to normal, the Thais could come and remove the doctor themselves. If they didn't, what would it matter if the lonely soul rested here, where he had chosen to die? Sloan stood up straight and slipped the folder under his arm. At the desk, he gathered all of the remaining papers, just in case they might be informative, picked up the brass ring, and slipped silently, almost considerately, out of the office, locking the door behind him.

It was nearly 6:30 p.m. by the time the last biohazard carton was loaded on the jeep. The team stood watching the soldiers, too exhausted and tense to do much more than point to objects and indicate placement. Those who had done the autopsies and samples were spattered with dried blood that they would wash off in the disinfectant shower set up beyond the barricades. Sloan noticed how the soldiers shrank from them, fearful of the blood. In their orange field gear and their bubble helmets, the team must have looked like alien enemies. If they had any sense at all, the soldiers must be wondering why they hadn't been provided with equally protective gear. Perhaps they did not dare dispute orders. If this outbreak was what Sloan thought it might be, they had reason to be frightened. Most were wearing only surgical masks. Those wearing gas masks were no better protected, for gas masks are designed for chemical bombs like mustard gas. The masks could protect them from chemical vapors, but despite the two charcoal chambers and layers of fabric designed to inhibit inspiration, the openings in the filters were like doorways to a virus. Countries where outbreaks often got their start were frequently the least prepared to deal with them. They had no budgets to adequately clothe and protect their workers, which was half the problem. Same with the hospitals and clinics, which Sloan knew often had been instrumental in the spread of disease rather than its cure. Look what happened with the nun who spread Marburg to countless patients at the little hospital in Africa.

Sloan made a mental list of what had to be done first. One of the things he would insist upon was a true isolation ward at the hospital in Bangkok and the proper precautions for the staff there. The other was that no more soldiers work inside the perimeter without adequate protection, even if they had to beg or borrow field suits from other countries. It was ridiculous that the men on the trucks were physically handling corpses when no one knew for sure how this disease was being communicated, whether the virus died with the host or hung around to latch itself on to the first sorry fellow foolish enough to come close.

Night had fallen by the time they had all been through the disinfectant showers and gathered in the low brick building the government had evacuated just outside the barricades. The team buzzed with theories, anxious to begin serious analysis of the problem. But before they sat down at the card tables set up for them by soldiers, the roar of a new series of jeeps arriving and the bustle of people, doors slamming, and orders being barked by officers drew Sloan's attention to the window.

In the bright spotlights, he immediately recognized Martin Linquist, not only because his picture had been featured in magazines and books in every language, but also because Sloan had been in the front row at a number of conferences where Linquist had spoken. "Damn," he thought, realizing that now everything was going to change, that instead of being the general in this battle, he was going to have to work with someone equally powerful, if not more so.

Seconds later they heard the ruckus in the hallway, just before Linquist ducked his head to enter the room. Behind him stood several of the WHO's team. Sloan couldn't help but equate the two groups with a pair of lacrosse teams about to do battle; he smiled.

"Martin Linquist! Come in. We are just about to discuss the situation here." Sloan pointed to a few extra folding chairs leaning against the wall. "Grab a seat."

"You have no idea what is going on here," Linquist growled.

"We've been inside. We've got the samples." Sloan's voice was even, despite the anger pumping his blood faster.

"Have you analyzed them?" Linquist knew the answer, of course, because only an electron microscope could see the virus, and there was none here. Even Linquist's cell cultures, already prepared and growing back in Geneva, would take days to be fully readable.

"We're sending them back to Atlanta shortly," Sloan smiled his fake smile. "We'll take some to Bangkok Hospital as well."

"If you'd bothered to inform us you were coming, we could have saved you some time." Linquist's stare was cold and accusing.

Sloan was aware that everyone was staring at him. Gorham's eyes were shocked. "You didn't inform the WHO?" Gorham gasped, then realized his mistake.

Sloan had been in tricky situations before. "There wasn't

time," he stated, as if this made everything perfectly clear. "The government had an emergency. I was contacted, and I came," he lied.

He could sense Gorham's sorrowful gaze and once more he knew why Gorham annoyed him so much. The way those hangdog eyes sought an answer in his, it was as if Gorham somehow pitied him.

"No cell phones? No secretaries?" Linquist's sneer made Sloan's blood boil. The tension in the room sizzled. No one moved. Sloan stood at the head of the assembled card tables, Linquist at the foot, and between them lay an ethical gulf so great that they might have been ten million miles apart.

Sloan tried another tack. "What do you know?" He thought that Linquist would have to give in. He had the samples, after all. His team had already been in there. They knew what was going on. Linquist was just a Johnnie-come-lately. Linquist would have to put aside his anger at being bested if he was going to get any information from him. Sloan was holding all the aces.

Linquist stared at Sloan in disbelief. He had never met Sloan personally, but he'd heard a few things over the years. Some scientists spent their time trying to make a name for themselves, and after a while other scientists tended to avoid them. You couldn't discuss a scientific problem with one of them—they were too likely to make off with your ideas and claim them as their own. And you could never be truly at ease with them either, because it'd be stupid to put yourself in a position of possibly disclosing something about your work that might be a clue. That's all some of them needed. And Sloan's was a name he'd heard when he got together with some of the Americans down at Fort Detrick, the military research facility in Virginia, and even the Director at the CDC in Atlanta, with whom Linquist had shared many a fine brandy. A pregnant silence often followed the mention of Sloan's name. These men were not ones to gossip or attack a colleague, but in their silences, Linquist had long ago garnered an impression of Sloan that at this moment seemed pretty accurate. Sloan was here to make a name for himself. The hell with the health of the world.

"I know it's a new virus. One we've never seen before." Linquist wondered as he spoke whether Sloan would soon be figuring out how to steal credit for this discovery. "I think it's a recombination, and it has some of the attributes of the avian influenza. I think the thing has jumped species, and I think it's aerosol."

Sloan's eyes narrowed, but he tossed his head. "Is this guesswork," and he emphasized guesswork, "based on anything observable?" He was sure Linquist had to be talking off the top of his head, maybe basing his theory on reports coming out through soldiers' gossip.

Linquist shook his head and sucked in his lower lip. The way he stared at Sloan made Sloan uncomfortable. Then he set his briefcase down on the card table and opened it, taking his time to shuffle through the papers there. From the briefcase he removed a file of pictures, and choosing one carefully, he handed it to Gorham, who sat at his right. Sloan was livid. How dare he pass the picture to an underling, Sloan raged. Everyone at the table was now leaning toward Gorham, who gaped at the photo, trying to make sense of what he saw.

"You're the respiratory pathogens expert, aren't you?" Linquist asked, ignoring the fuming Sloan. "Gorham? You wrote that article last month in Scientific American?"

Gorham looked up, surprised. "I am."

"What do you gather from that?" Linquist asked.

Gorham studied the photo. "Where are the tissue cells? I can't figure out what's what in here."

"The tissue cells have been destroyed," Linquist said, now removing more photos from the file and passing them left and right up the table, effectively making Sloan the last person to get a look.

"Where did you get this stuff," Sloan sneered. "We've got the samples."

The room was abuzz as Sloan's team passed the photos and discussed among themselves what they were seeing. No one was paying any attention to him.

"Quiet!" he ordered, and suddenly the room was silent. Everyone looked at him. "I asked you, where did you get this stuff?"

Everyone turned the other way to look at Linquist. "If you'd bothered to call the WHO before you left, we'd have told you, Dr. Sloan. In fact, we called the CDC to inform Atlanta just after your plane took off. The pathologist at Kwang Tri sent these to us. He died soon after."

A collective sigh from Sloan's team made it clear to everyone what they thought. They realized Sloan, who hadn't followed protocol before he left, had duped them. Gorham looked up at Linquist, shook his head and looked back at Sloan.

Perhaps for the first time in his life, Sloan could think of nothing to say.

Linquist looked at the stunned group while his team, still gathered about the doorway and leaning against the walls, watched. Seconds before anyone spoke, the hush of scattered sighs, the rustle of data sheets and photos being passed about, the occasional murmur as one person pointed out something to another disguised the seething rage of the man still standing empty handed at the end of the table. If was as if by refusing to look at the evidence Linquist had disseminated, Sloan thought he could erase the now obviously huge blunder he had made. He kept his arms folded over his chest, knowing even as he did so that he was a caricature of a spoiled child and that everyone in the room saw it. But he could not help himself. He felt his ulcer awakening, like a dragon long asleep in its dark, humid cave, the familiar ache that preceded pain that preceded agony, and hoped that in his hurry he had packed his medicine. No one looked at him, which made it worse. It was as if they all were too ashamed of what he had done to acknowledge him.

Lester Savant, an aging CDC scientist and the only African-American on the team, was the first person to speak for the group. "If this is what I think it might be, Dr. Linquist, we've got to alert the Minister of Health. They've got the military in there picking up bodies off the street with gas masks and rubber gloves their only protection. I don't think they've sequestered their troops. For all we know, they're going back to barracks and infecting others."

Linquist was grateful that at least one member of Sloan's team could see beyond his nose. "We know. Unfortunately, what you don't know is that this morning, over half of the men who worked in there yesterday reported to the infirmary. They've got it. And all day there's been a steady stream of more. Worse, Bangkok Major began taking in secondary cases the night before these samples..." and he swept his hand around the table to indicate the photos spread there..."were sent, but they didn't know what they had until the early hours of the following morning. By the time they began isolating, their doctors and nurses were already exposed. I don't know what the Kwang Tri hospital looks like, but Bangkok Major is shut tight. We know a few people in there are still alive, but the disease has spread throughout the wards, staff, and crews."

"Kwang Tri is a ghost town," one of the women on Sloan's team said. "The hospital had been emptied by the time we got there, but the borough itself..."

"...They've got martial law there. The people are confined to their homes..." added another.

"They're burning corpses a few miles out of the city. They have no idea how many," Savant added, having listened to Sloan and the captain on the way in.

Linquist seemed to know all of this. "That section of the city houses approximately..."

"Two hundred thousand..." Sloan had finally found his voice. Everyone turned in his direction and then looked back at Linquist, relieved. The standoff was over.

"They estimate they've picked up approximately five thousand dead. They've come from literally every building on every street, which means the dead are a good indicator of what is to come. The people in their apartments there can only survive if no one in their immediate family unit has been exposed."

"But what about the rest of the city?" the first woman asked. "If it's there, then isn't the whole city..."

"...The Prime Minister is being consulted as we speak. The Minister of Health is going to recommend closing all roads into and out of Bangkok, the airport as well."

"The whole city?" Gorham's mouth hung open.

"Of course the whole city," Sloan jeered. "They've got to. That means that they've got to go public..."

"This is what worries the Minister. The Prime Minister is not going to be happy about the world knowing what's going on here. The Minister thinks this may be a hard sell." Linquist spoke directly to Sloan. Between the two of them, on every continent they had seen politicians obstruct policies designed to save lives. In their shared gaze, both communicated the message that this was something that went beyond borders and individual agendas, that they had to work together or they were all going to lose.

"The world has got to know. By now, pockets of infection could be springing up anywhere planes went yesterday and the days before. If the doctors don't know what they're seeing..." a younger man, new to this kind of detail, showed clear signs of panic. He whined like a child.

"If they close the borders, we're not going anywhere," Sloan said matter-of-factly. "We didn't bring all of our equipment. We're going to need a planeload of lab equipment if we're going to be stuck here." The woman and the young man looked up at him, horrified as they began to realize their situation. If they were stuck in a dying country, the chances were good that they would be among the victims unless they could find a cure quickly, a vaccine, something. Even the experienced team members swallowed hard. Trying not to write scenarios that might never occur, they used their long experience in the field, some of them with Level Four pathogens just as deadly as this one seemed to be, to control their fear. Still, they were afraid because this monstrous hatchery of a virus had arisen on a grander scale than anything they had ever seen. This was history book stuff, another Spanish flu, another Black Plague, corpses stacked high in trucks. This was going to be a devastation. And they were sitting in its center.

The discussion went on far into the night. They made plans of what must be done, the systems that had to be set up to control the spread of the disease, the supplies that the

UN was going to have to provide immediately, how they were going to arrange, what they were going to arrange, who was going to arrange, all on a scale that the already weary scientists could barely grasp. Finally, before dawn the group decided that they could no longer be productive without sleep. One final agenda item had to be decided, one that none of them really wanted to tackle, but timing required they decide who was going to stay and who would go back to Atlanta and Geneva, because the science, the potential cure for this thing was not going to be discovered amidst the hysteria of waves of dying people. It was going to come out of a quiet, sterile, technologically cutting-edge laboratory, and they could never assemble that here. Not in time.

Once again, the room was deadly quiet. Some dropped their gaze to the papers before them, pretending to study what had already been studied. "We've got to face facts," Linquist said. "We need a group here to carry out the tests that those working outside require. We need people who know what they're doing, experts. Not just Thai doctors and nurses. They can't be expected to accomplish what needs to be accomplished. But the thing is, and I know I don't have to say it, but the thing is, whoever stays..."

"I'm staying," Sloan said, but this time, instead of looking about for approbation, he looked directly at Linquist. "And you should go back tonight, before they close the borders." The room was silent again.

"I'm not going back either. I want to see this one through." The words came out of his mouth almost without his willing them. Something in the way Sloan volunteered himself, knowing as he did that he was probably not going to come out alive, had surprised Linquist, taken him off guard. The man had guts, Linquist realized. He might have been a grandstander, but this time his courage and honor prevailed. And seeing that, Linquist wanted nothing more than to stay himself, because between the two of them, maybe they could stop this thing. And if they couldn't, well, what was there to lose?

"I'll stay," Gorham raised his hand as if still a student.

"Me too," another said.

"If you're staying, Gorham, then you, Lester, have to go back to lead the team in Atlanta."

Lester Savant had been on the verge of volunteering to remain with the others, but he knew that if Sloan and Gorham stayed, his leadership would be needed back in Atlanta. Reluctantly, he nodded his head.

Before the meeting closed, they had decided that six should go back with the additional samples to Atlanta and Geneva. The rest would ride it out in Bangkok. The groups broke up amid tearful hugs and a lot of harrumphing, and before first light, the plane taking them to Luxembourg, where they'd split for Geneva and Atlanta, lifted its wings above the doomed city.

22

Patterson, Friday, Mid-October

Taylor Farr stretched his long, angular limbs, and turned on his side. The late afternoon sun lent a pale, dusky tone to Laura's bedroom. She lay sleeping on her back, her blonde hair a chaos on the satin pillow. Farr used his forefinger to order some of the strands, delighting as he did so in the feel of it under his rough skin. Laura's eyelids fluttered and then opened, needing a moment to adjust to the light and the fact that a man was with her in her bed. Then without looking at him, she smiled.

"What's so funny?" Farr asked, cupping his hand on the side of her face to turn her head toward him.

Laura continued to smile, gazing up at him, her eyes crinkling at the corners.

"Yes?" he said. "Does that beautiful face have a voice?"

"You've been here..." she looked at her watch. "...thirty hours and we've been in bed...." and she calculated again..."twenty of them. Do you suppose we ought to do something other than make love and sleep?" Now Laura was grinning widely, and Farr knew it wouldn't take much to convince her to make it thirty-one and twenty-six. But he was hungry, and he had to go to the bathroom, and he was aware that with night falling soon, they'd be back for more of the same before midnight.

"How about a steak," he said, twirling her hair. "Do you feed lovers or just wear them down to exhaustion?"

Laura laughed. "I keep them fattened up. You really want steak?"

"I need meat," he said, swinging his legs over to the side and sitting on the edge of the bed. "Red meat." And then he stood, stretching his arms upward almost to the ceiling. Laura appraised his back, how the muscles in it rippled as he stretched, how perfectly Apollonian his butt and thighs were. So different from her ex-husband's white body and almost girlish build.

"Steak it is," she said, making a mental list of the items she had in her refrigerator and what it meant in terms of menu. "But shower first," she added, jumping out of the bed and running for the bathroom. "Me first!" She laughed as she reached the door one step ahead of Farr, who caught her arm before she could slip inside. He hugged her to him, turning as he did so that he was closest to the door.

"You know how much I love you?" he asked, but he was teasing, she knew. His hand was reaching backward for the door handle and he had a gleam in his eye.

"How much," she responded, waiting for the punch line.

"This much," and he let her go and slipped inside first. "But you can come in too." At which he stepped back, turned on the shower, and lifted the toilet lid to pee.

"Whew!" she said. "Thanks for the sentiment. I don't know if I can handle such flowery language."

"Can you handle a shower with a strange naked man?" he asked, his eyes gleaming with lust. "I can show you lots of sentiment in there."

"I'll bet you can," she replied, stepping into the enclosure. "But prove it anyway." Laura did not think she had ever been so happy. Something about Taylor Farr made her smile just to look at him. When she let herself believe that this was all really happening, that this wonderful man wanted her, that he had come East only yesterday and they had been making love ever since, she felt she might burst with joy. So different from anything she had ever known. So perfect. He was everything that her ex wasn't—so real, forthright, down to earth, and yet brighter in so many ways than her academic snob of an ex-husband could ever be. She felt she could truly be herself with this man, no pretending to be girly when she had strong opinions and beliefs, no pretending to be witty when she wanted to just be frank. Time flew when she was around him and she wanted it to stop. Laura wouldn't have minded if time never passed at all.

Later, Taylor was piling charcoal into the Weber grill and Laura was washing lettuce in the sink while the television blared the six o'clock news. Laura had not been paying any attention, for she hardly ever turned the set on, and when she did so, it was usually far later at night for a PBS special. Taylor, however, was getting a kick out of watching TV again, having forfeited it along with everything else when he started the community out in Wyoming. Taylor had spent much of the time, as a matter of fact, glorying in hot tap water, phones, electricity, mail delivered to the door, and a host of other modern conveniences that his community managed to do without, so that Laura had teased him that this trip might just corrupt him completely. "You're not going to be able to go back, Taylor," she'd warned, laughing. "You just might have to stay and live among the infidels."

"If I stayed, it wouldn't be for this stuff," he had leered, narrowing his eyes impishly beneath one raised eyebrow. "Not the conveniences." He smiled, thinking about how soon it would be time to go to bed.

So Laura just barely heard Peter Brokawn as he explained that NBC had just obtained breaking news from Thailand:

"In a story you heard Sunday night," Brokawn began, "NBC reported that a section of Bangkok called Kwang Tri had been cordoned off, though the government at that time refused to comment on the nature of the problem. Our reporter in Bangkok has now obtained evidence that the Thai government has been hiding an outbreak of a mysterious illness that is spreading out of control in the district. In Thailand, here is our correspondent, Karen Klein:"

A tall woman with long red hair and very bright lipstick fiddled with her earphone for a long moment before realizing that she was on. Immediately she straightened her shoulders and looked at the camera. "Yes, Peter, this seems to be a very serious situation. The CDC arrived yesterday morning. I managed to speak with the CDC team chief, Ralph Sloan, when he arrived at the airport and he told me that Kwang Tri had been cordoned off but not quarantined. That's because they weren't really sure what they were looking at." Karen took a breath. "But before the day was over, Peter, not only had the Kwang Tri district been quarantined...but I know for a fact that people are actually confined to their residences. And what is more interesting is that the primary hospital here, in the city center, Bangkok Major it's called, is now closed."

Brokawn interrupted.... "Karen, are you telling us that the illness has spread to the main city?" A slight pause ensued while Klein pressed her earphone to her ear, looking down as she listened to Brokawn in the twenty-second delay.

"Yes, Peter, that is true. And apparently, the fatalities occurring from infection with this thing are huge. Rumor has it that the virus or pathogen or whatever it is, is airborne, so that even the slightest contact with someone coughing or sneezing can result in infection. I have not been able to verify all the reports I've been hearing, but that smoke you see billowing in the sky behind me?..." and Karen turned, holding her microphone close to her lips while she extended her arm to the ominous black sky, "may well be the government incinerating the bodies of the dead." The camera paused on the shot, the hold obviously planned prior to the broadcast. Brokawn's voice over the shot asked how many were thought to have died. Klein turned a sorrowful face to the camera as she waited the delay. "Yes, Peter, I could confirm no figures but the estimate is over a thousand," she said. She stared at the camera, which then cut left and zoomed in on the rising clouds of smoke.

"Thank you, Karen," Brokawn said. He looked at the camera and said, "Now for a station break," but before the camera switched, Brokawn seemed to be shaking his head at someone off camera. Then the NBC logo appeared on the screen and the station broke for commercials.

Behind her, Laura heard Taylor say, "Shit." Surprised, she turned from the TV to see him leaning against the doorframe. "So it's finally happened," he added, almost under his breath. Laura realized that what seemed so removed and unreal on the television was absolutely real to him. This is what Taylor had told her was going to happen someday, but "someday" felt so far away when she was falling in love back in Wyoming amid the vast mountains, the bright blue skies, the down-home folks who couldn't do enough to help her with her project. "Someday" was not in her lifetime, just some place in time generations from now in a world so different from hers that imagining it seemed like writing science fiction. Could this be it? Could the impossible really have happened?

Part Two

CRISIS

23

PanAsia Flight 4551: Bangkok/Singapore/ Tokyo/Honolulu, Sunday, Mid-October

On the first leg of its journey from Bangkok to Honolulu the 747 jumbo jet experienced only mild wind turbulence and one drunken businessman. The second leg, however, had been unusually difficult for Liliana Chi. A head stewardess with over 10,000 hours of flying time, Liliana was in charge of all cabin operations, and because of the events on this flight, she was frazzled. Problems began just after the second take-off in Singapore, although as she later thought about it, she should have noticed that the man in 12B looked sick well before they landed there.

She should have, but she didn't. His wife and the three children traveling with them had been scattered about the plane, typical standby seating assignments, so he was sitting with strangers. When they had boarded in Thailand, Liliana had noticed how grateful they were for seats; they dragged their bags along the aisle, bowing humbly to whoever made eye contact with them to apologize for delaying the seated passengers waiting for take-off. They had been very lucky. The flight was filled to capacity, an anomaly for a Wednesday with no holidays near. And from what Liliana gathered, the standby line was thirty deep. They got on only because five ticket holders had failed to report, and they were first in line.

Liliana and Chen, the Assistant Head, hurriedly helped them store their bags in the overhead compartments. But then the family had created some confusion getting seated, for everyone on the plane had already buckled up. This was nothing new to Liliana; she was used to last minute arrivals and standbys; this was part of her job. She helped them find their rows. Several passengers had to move into the aisle to let them in. Then one of the children, the youngest, began weeping because she could not sit with her mother, since none of the standby seats were together. The old man on the aisle struggled to stand to let her pass, grunting with the effort, and she had looked up at him and begun to wail inconsolably, tears streaming down her face. With great shushing and urging, her mother had tried to convince her that she would be all right, but the child was unconvinced.

Then the father, who had already belted up, once again had to climb over the people in his row and hurry back to the commotion in the rear. It looked like it was going to be a standoff, with child adamant, father angry, mother humiliated, until the old man, embarrassed that the child seemed so afraid of him, offered to take the mother's seat so that she could take his. That solved the problem, but added at least twenty more bows and thank yous before Liliana could hustle the old man to his new place, forcing yet another passenger to unbuckle and stand to let him pass.

Still, the whole process had taken only five minutes or so, and soon Liliana was on the intercom, telling the captain that they were finally ready. The plane began rolling almost immediately. As Liliana moved about the cabin, checking the overheads, insuring that everyone was belted, smiling as she worked her way down the aisle to the flip-downs the stewards used on take-off and landing, she mistakenly thought that this would be just another boring day.

Liliana did not love her job, although she knew very

well that she had been lucky to get it with only a lower school education. In the back of her mind, she guessed that her prominent family had pulled some strings for her, despite the fact that they had thrown up their hands and nearly renounced her. Liliana's father was a world-famous violinist and her mother played the cello. They had trained her since childhood, providing her with the best teachers, supporting her every step of the way. Yet she had failed to become the concert pianist everyone expected her to be.

Well, she hadn't failed. She'd chosen. She'd been flying now for over twelve years, and though she had loved the original excitement of seeing new cities and getting away from her whining children and slothful husband, the experience had worn thin. Restaurant food, countless boring nights in hotels while on layover, ignorant passengers with their demands, and arrogant flight captains ogling her had become so routine that Liliana had learned to live life outside herself. She was good at what she did, of course. Regular, responsible. She had risen to Head Flight Attendant within only a few years. Not that it mattered to her husband, whose livelihood she provided. And not that it mattered to her parents, who to this day remained cold and aloof, their disappointment in her palpable.

What Liliana appreciated about flying was that she could live inside her head. She could smile and serve passengers their coffee and tea; she could provide them with pillows and blankets and keep the overheads latched. Yet with a constant parade of strangers coming and going, Liliana didn't have to relate to anyone, and that allowed her to follow her career, the one she should have pursued, in her mind. If a passenger could have tuned in his earphones to Liliana's head, he would have heard Chopin, complex chords that spoke of sorrow and disappointment, poor choices and failure, played so beautifully that he would sink back in his seat and be carried off in reverie. That is what Liliana did once silver wings lifted her above the earth. She gave concert after concert.

So perhaps it was the music that prevented Liliana from noticing. Later, as she thought back, she remembered that it was when she and Chen and the other attendants began the long task of serving passengers juice, coffee, and small packages of biscuits that she should have noticed something might be wrong. The father, seated at the window, seemed shaky and hesitant when she asked him what he would like. His eyes had been closed when she reached his row, but when he opened them, he appeared disoriented and feverish. No, he didn't want anything, he said, but before she could complete serving the others in his row, he changed his mind. Please, could he have some water, he asked, and she noticed how his hand quivered when he grasped the cup. Still, she'd seen people get airsick enough times to know that such symptoms were common, and she moved on to the next row, forgetting about him the second she did so.

And then later, she remembered, when she was passing his row she became aware of his coughing. He had a handkerchief over his mouth to muffle the sound, but she saw him leaning forward, his shoulders shaking as he hacked into the white linen. Still, people got sick all the time. Many came on planes with runny noses, teary eyes, and barking coughs. People paid good money for plane tickets and weren't about to forfeit them because of a common cold or flu unless they were really too sick to get out of bed. Liliana knew that anyone sick on a plane coughed or sneezed his or her germs up through the ventilation system, sending them through the ducts, and back over other passengers like invisible mists settling on everyone's hair, shoulders, hands, and laps. She knew, for example, that the woman in the very last row of the plane would probably be breathing in this sick guy's germs within a minute or two. She herself had never been sick until she started this job, but in the time she'd been flying she'd contracted bronchitis almost every year and pneumonia twice. So when she saw him coughing, she felt mild annoyance and thought, "Oh, no, here we go again." But again, she forgot the man almost immediately as she moved on with the usual chores.

He became seriously ill soon after she began serving dinner with Chen. Chen had been on the other side of the cart, working the three rows behind him, when the woman on the aisle seat tugged his jacket to get his attention. Liliana had seen him turn, annoyed at what he thought was just another pushy passenger, and then she had seen his face instantly concerned at something in the row. He looked back at her with an expression that said it all: "Uh, oh, we've got trouble."

By the time they pushed the cart out of the way, setting the brakes so that it could not move, the commotion had alerted other passengers to a problem. A woman had struggled to her feet to stand in the aisle, her husband climbing out behind her, and both were gaping at the sick man. Other passengers were leaning into the aisle to see what was going on, and a small boy stood facing backward on his seat, looking quizzically at the sick man behind him. By the time Liliana reached the row, the familiar rustlings of worried whispers had spread throughout business class.

"Sir," she had said, stepping into the row to keep her voice down. "Sir, are you all right?"

The man stirred, opening his eyes, then began coughing almost uncontrollably. The fit lasted several seconds.

Then he fell back against the seat, murmured something, and seemed to go back to sleep. Liliana touched his arm, shaking it softly. "Sir, are you all right?" As she spoke, she noticed the bloody handkerchief he held limply in his hand. Despite her gentle urging, the man did not respond. He merely murmured again, something she could not understand, and from his nose a small trickle of thin, bloody froth worked its way over the hairs on his upper lip toward his mouth. Liliana used the back of her hand to feel the man's forehead. It was damp with sweat; he was burning up.

Still, she remained calm. This was textbook stuff, she told herself, despite the growing alarm she felt. Chen had already seated the displaced couple in two Attendant seats, apologizing profusely for the inconvenience and promising that PanAsia would make this up to them. As he returned, Liliana told him to go get the man's wife while she tried to make him more comfortable. As she stretched to reach inside the first storage bin where they kept piles of light airline blankets and doll-sized puffy pillows, she heard the wife's "What? Sick you say?" even at the front of business class. The woman rose, panic-stricken, and ran forward with Chen, then dropped to the seat beside her husband. "Sabi, Sabi," she called, shaking his inert body. Before Liliana could return to comfort her, the woman began to sob. "Sabi, Sabi," she cried, her arms around the man now, her face against his chest. "What is wrong, Sabi? Speak to me," she wailed, frightening the other passengers, who sat straight in their seats trying to get a glimpse of what was going on.

The sounds of their mother's cries now alerted all three children to the problem. The small girl ran up the aisle, crying "Mama, Mama," and the other two scrambled over other passengers in their hurry to get to their parents. So much wailing! Liliana could not believe her ears as the family called to their unconscious father between weeps and wails, moans, and lamentations. The entire cabin seemed on the verge of panic; Liliana heard the worried clamor as she hustled the children back to their seats and asked strangers to contain them, while Chen asked over the loudspeaker if a doctor was present.

Two men stood up in first class, one of them pausing to remove a medical bag from the overhead before following his friend backward. They urged the woman away from her husband so they could look at the patient. Liliana gently pushed her forward to the food area, where she gave the trembling woman a drink of water. Out of the corner of her eye, she could see the doctors moving the man to lay him down, so that now his feet stuck out into the aisle. She noticed how one of his socks drooped loosely at his bony white ankle. For a minute or so, the plane became eerily silent, as if everyone was listening for a heartbeat. She heard, "He's dead." The doctor had not meant to publicize the fact, but like so many travelers, he spoke over the roar of the engines and his voice carried everywhere.

After that it was pandemonium. Liliana and Chen tried to restrain the wife, who on hearing those words scrambled back to her husband's seat and threw herself on him. The children, hearing their mother's cries, began wailing anew. Liliana was surprised at the compassionate way several passengers came to their aid, holding them, soothing them, and effectively keeping them out of the way. Their mother, however, would not let go of her husband, and the two doctors and Chen had to literally drag her away from him.

All this had happened so quickly that Liliana had not yet told the captain. Since the cockpit door could not be opened, she lifted the intercom phone, trying to speak softly so that passengers could not hear her. "We've got a man dead here, sir," she said.

"What?" the captain could not hear her.

"We've got a man dead here, sir," she repeated, this time louder, shielding her mouth and the receiver with her other hand.

"What the hell happened?" the captain asked. She could almost see the expression on his face because she knew his reputation from other attendants. He was rigid as steel and did not like to hear about problems from his crew. Inevitably, it was going to be her fault. Liliana took a deep breath.

"Sick," she said, "coughing, then bleeding from the nose, then dead." She waited a long several seconds while this registered. They'd heard, of course, what had been going on in Bangkok. When they landed to pick up passengers, the Captain had switched on the radio, listening sleepily. He hadn't debarked, but that was not uncommon. The clean-up crew swept through the cabin while the Captain napped in his seat and the co-pilot spoke with air traffic control. She, Chen, and the other attendants walked to the service lounge, washed up, and met in the cafeteria for a cup of coffee. They'd heard it from other attendants sitting near them, the way people do in crowded places. It was weary talk, without excitement. When they returned to the plane, they told the captain, but he already knew from the radio. None of them had really considered the implications. So what if people were getting the flu in Bangkok? People were getting the flu at every stop they made. They thought the entire hubbub was just another media story, nothing to be seriously concerned about.

Until a man died on their plane, that is. She could hear

it in the captain's voice. "Got any doctors on board?" the captain asked.

She gave him the details. She could hear him conferring with the co-pilot, then he said, "We've got four hours until Tokyo. Do what you can to cover him up. Keep things calm." Then the line clicked.

Liliana signaled Chen and the other section attendants to gather in the front kitchen. Everyone was nervous, and Liliana tried her best to convey a cool demeanor. If the team showed fear, the entire cabin could become hysterical, and if that happened, she'd be the one who paid. She instructed Chen and Laso to cover the man, and, looking back where he lay, added, "See if you can get his feet out of the aisle." She ordered the rest to carry on as usual. "Keep the family quiet. Do whatever you can." By now the family was huddled together, children and mother sobbing, and Liliana expertly ushered them to the remaining attendants' flip-downs, where all four continued to sob loudly.

By the time the plane reached Tokyo, an ambulance was waiting to take the body, along with Japanese officials to record what had transpired during the flight. No one was allowed to debark while pilots, officials, the two doctors, EMTs and the government doctor conferred. Liliana watched them arguing, but at last the EMTs entered with a stretcher and removed the body while everyone in the cabin craned their necks to see a covered corpse deplaned. Liliana escorted the crying family off the plane behind the stretcher that carried their father and introduced the mother to the PanAsia official waiting to help them make arrangements.

The order then came over the speaker that all passengers could now debark. Those whose destinations were Tokyo or connecting flights could go immediately. For those continuing on, however, the captain said they were making a lengthier stop here while the plane was inspected. He assured them the delay would last no more than a few hours and apologized for the delay, adding that those planning additional connecting flights once they arrived in Hawaii would have to wait until they got there to exchange their tickets for later flights.

Though she didn't remain on board to watch what happened after the plane had been evacuated, Liliana knew one of two things would occur. Either they'd change planes, which would mean flying a new one in from Singapore, or they'd disinfect their plane, let the gases do their work, air the thing out, and put the continuing passengers back on. Either way, Liliana knew she had time for a brief rest, and she took advantage of it. She was tired and the whole experience had been depressing. She'd never had a guy die on her watch; she'd aided passengers with heart attacks and fainting spells, and probably a hundred airsick ones who'd sheepishly handed her their still warm, vile-smelling vomit bags, but never a death until today.

By the time the order came to re-board Flight 4511, Liliana had grown impatient with the delay. She'd napped, she'd eaten, she'd once again washed up and combed her hair. She'd read, she'd paced, she'd watched countless other planes arrive and depart. Chen dozed quietly beside her in the lounge chair while the younger attendants shopped the boutiques and magazine stores. Liliana did not go with them. Instead, she sat thinking about her life. Her parents had so desperately wanted her to become a concert pianist. Her teacher had too. Even the government had offered her scholarships if she would go to the conservatory to study. A genius, her parents had raved. No question, her teacher had seconded. But she had fallen in love. She could think of nothing better to do than to be with Saoto, the boy who lived a few blocks away. Her parents' admonitions meant nothing. The teacher's disappointment when she stopped practicing meant nothing. The retraction of the scholarship meant nothing. She wanted Saoto, he wanted her, and the two of them spent all of their time finding ways to be alone where they could kiss and hug, rub and fondle each other. No amount of chastisement had worked on her. Finally her parents had given up in disgust, telling her to do as she pleased. She had.

By eighteen she was married and pregnant, and now at thirty-three she had two teenagers at home, a husband who worked only sometimes, and a life that had gone sour. She watched her foot bounce her black leather pump up and down. She adjusted her jacket. She touched her hair, feeling for loose strands. She looked at Chen, an ugly young man whose face had been scarred by acne. She saw the young attendants returning with their packages, laughing, joyful despite the delay. And in her mind she played Chopin, imagined herself tapping out the silvery threads on ivory piano keys, and felt the tugging complexities of notes and chords. Barely, as if out of the phantom prelude itself, she heard the order to board.

Liliana greeted the passengers as they boarded, recognizing only a small minority from the last leg. New standbys took the places vacated by the dead man and his family, so that once again the plane was full. Liliana smiled widely, a habit she had learned in the early days of flying, but she did not feel like smiling. She knew she had every reason to be tired, for the last leg to Tokyo had been a nightmare. But beyond that, she felt shaky. She looked at Chen, standing beside her in front of the captain's door, and noticed that he, too, looked tired. His facial muscles sagged, and his eyes looked feverish. "Are you okay?" Liliana nudged him. He looked at her as if surprised to find her there, then shook his head no. "Sore throat is all," he whispered as the lines of people filed onto the plane.

By the time the plane set down in Honolulu, Liliana's breathing had changed. She found it hard to get enough oxygen, so that instead of unconscious intakes of breath, she had to consciously breathe deeply to feel she'd gotten enough air. And she was exhausted. Thank God that this was her destination. She would go straight home, take a shower, and go directly to bed. Liliana wasn't one to give in easily to feeling sick, but in the back of her mind, a niggling worry beset her. She wondered whether the dead man had trouble breathing. She wondered whether he had had a sore throat, which she now felt growing more intense. She wondered whether, in the beginning, he had just felt very tired, and she tried to remember her first impressions of him, before he got sick. When he had hurried to the rear of the plane to quiet his daughter, had he looked tired? She struggled to remember his face, his eyes. Certainly, he had seemed so when she offered him refreshments. He was sleeping, she remembered. And he seemed disoriented.

Chen, Laso, and she took the taxi together, leaving the other attendants on their own. Chen lay back against the seat, his eyes closed. Laso looked at him and then at Liliana. "He feels lousy," Laso said confidentially.

"I do too," Liliana said, and coughed as if to emphasize the fact.

"A good night's rest," Laso advised, smiling, then turned away to look out the window. The traffic was heavy, requiring the driver to stop frequently. Thank God he had air conditioning, Liliana thought, feeling the sweat beneath her hair and on her forehead. She looked at the back of the driver's head, noticing how his thinning hair thickened closer to his neck. And then she began coughing again, before she could get her hand to her mouth. Embarrassed, she said, "Pardon," but no one seemed to notice.

Finally home, Liliana entered through the back door. The house was silent; everyone was sleeping. Liliana took a fast shower and put her pajamas on, tiptoeing quietly to the bed where her husband snored peacefully. Twice she had to choke down a coughing fit, which aroused him only slightly. Downstairs again, she made tea and toasted a muffin, although by then she felt too sick to eat. She did sip the tea, however, and put her cup on the end table. She propped the pillows on the couch so that she could sit up and pulled the afghan over herself. Sitting up seemed to help the coughing. At least downstairs she could watch television. She picked up the remote and flipped it on. Its flickering images flashed in the darkened room like blue neon lights. Liliana muted the sound and soon was only mildly aware of a montage of nonsensical images. She laid her head back against the pillows and closed her eyes. Her breathing became increasingly wheezy and difficult. But Liliana barely noticed. She was playing Chopin's Prelude in C Minor. The blue spotlights flickered across the stage while she, at the piano, spread her fingers across the ivory keys in a complexity of chords. The grand piano's lid rose in front of her, its rich, deep mahogany lustrous. Cool and elegant in her white gown, Liliana felt the audience's pleasure as they too were swept up in the exquisite beauty of the music. Out there in the darkness, she knew familiar faces watched her. Finally, she had pleased her teacher. Finally, her parents were proud. Liliana never felt the light trickle of bloody spittle that traced a path down the left side of her chin. Her mouth hung open in the wonder of finally doing things right.

24

Bangkok, Sunday, Mid-October

Karen Klein finished her interview with Brokawn, supervised the capture of useful shoots that they could feed to the techs in New York, and then checked her cell phone for messages. As she sat atop the hotel roof overlooking the city, she held her cell phone, tapping in the message retrieval code. Although she didn't entirely trust Sloan to honor his promise to call, she hoped that he had, for she guessed she was sitting on top of the story of a lifetime, one that would seal her status as a top journalist. The first message was from the guy who tipped her off in the first place. He wanted to know if she'd made any progress getting his girl out of Kwang Tri Hospital. He also wanted her to know that the army had imposed strict quarantine measures on Kwang Tri and that he was trapped in his apartment, unable to do anything himself. He alluded to some violence he witnessed on the streets when the army first came in, intimating that he had more stories for her, if and when she came through for him. Karen had trouble understanding much of what he said, for reception was poor, the connection fuzzy, and he coughed a great deal. Apologizing for his cold, he begged Karen to do more for his fiancée.

Karen dutifully wrote down his phone number and moved on to the next call. It must have come in moments after her broadcast, while she and Chet, her cameraman, were finishing up. It was from the office of the Minister

of Health. An underling for the Minister requested that
she come immediately to his office for an interview. Days
before Karen had had a most unsatisfying interview with
the former Minister, an arrogant, militaristic ex-general.
She had walked away frustrated with his brusque answers
and superior attitude. But that was Chao, not the new guy.
Maybe this one would be more forthcoming. She wrote
down the number and, just in case, pressed the star to
save it. Then she moved on to the last message. Her heart
jumped when she heard Sloan's voice:

"Karen, this is Ralph. If you can get down to our
headquarters here, I have some information for you. They
might not let you come in on your own, so I'm going to
speak to Captain Chang, the officer in charge here. He's
surly, but I think I can convince him to chauffeur you in."
She heard muffled voices and then someone calling Sloan.
He put his hand over the mouthpiece and answered, then
came back on the line. "Call me. Unless I'm asleep, you
can get me at this number." Sloan dictated the number and
Karen, holding the notepaper down against a rising breeze,
copied it carefully.

An hour later she climbed out of Chang's jeep, leaving
her cameraman to unload his equipment. The captain
had not been happy to help her through the various
checkpoints now in place throughout Bangkok. He barely
spoke to her, and when he did, his dislike couldn't have
been more obvious. His heavy-lidded stare reminded her
of a snake's. Karen had exchanged knowing glances with
Chet, her camera guy, every time he looked away, and Chet,
always the comedian, had crossed, rolled, squeezed, and
bulged his eyes back at her. Neither was really offended.
An investigative story always included reluctant contacts,
people unwilling to give even a crumb to the media for fear

that doing so would come back to bite them, that somehow the reporter would make them look bad or would discover something about them that they had managed to hide. She had often been forced to be rudely aggressive to get the answers she needed, and her skin had thickened with each rebuff. Surely, this Captain Chang wouldn't have given her a ride if she were dying on the street. He had been strong-armed into bringing them to Sloan, she was sure of it, and Karen smiled to herself that if anyone was capable of strong-arming, it was Ralph. He was uncompromising as hell, and she'd seen him win a confrontation many times because of it.

Inside the building, the team had set up their computers, several bunkrooms and office/conference areas. As she passed them, looking for Sloan, she saw several people concentrating on computer screens. Beyond them, Karen saw familiar red-flower warning signs on a door to the right. A soldier stood at the entrance to the makeshift lab, and stepped in front of her when she tried to enter. He spoke no English and seemed to have no idea what she was talking about when she asked where Ralph Sloan might be. He continued to shake his head and refused to stand aside. Then she saw Ralph striding hurriedly toward her. He took her arm and guided her into a small room nearby.

"My cameraman..." she said, momentarily resisting him.

"He'll find us. Let's get started. I don't have much time."

Karen studied Sloan's face and decided that he looked considerably older than at the airport. She wondered how she had missed his papery skin when she saw him there, and whether he wasn't actually a lot older than she thought. She hadn't noticed his age when they'd had their little fling back in the States. "Tsk, tsk," she thought, "love is blind."

"You look tired," she said, unusually tactful.

"I'm exhausted," Sloan agreed, closing his eyes momentarily as he leaned back in the desk chair. "but it's important that you get this story and get it out now. We're afraid that the Prime Minister is going to shut down communications altogether, and people have got to know..."

"I've seen the smoke..."

"That's not the half of it," Sloan said. "We want you to have the facts, because this isn't the only place that's going to try to hide what's happening. People have got to know..." he repeated, and Karen for the first time saw that beyond the tired, aging appearance, something about Sloan seemed incredibly sad and hopeless. She watched him run his hand over his face, rubbing his forehead as if to stimulate the flow of blood. Karen took out her notebook and pen and sat forward, leaning on the table. "For starters..." she said and waited.

"For starters, at last count over five thousand have died." Sloan watched to see her reaction, expecting what it would be. She gasped, her eyes wide with disbelief.

"Five thousand?" she said, wondering if she had misheard him. During the broadcast, she had thrown out the thousands figure because it made her story bigger and because she had actually heard that figure in the rumors. But she hadn't really believed it, not thousands of people. Certainly never five thousand people.

"That was yesterday. There are two hundred thousand quarantined in their apartments waiting for someone in the room to show signs of infection. They know the illness is rampant. They know their chances of having been infected are great. Someone starts coughing and everyone in the room knows it's just a matter of time. They're dying with deadly regularity. We can't save them, only isolate them and hope that this thing burns itself out. We can't help them because we haven't got the facilities or the people. We have to keep them in there because that's the only way we have to contain the outbreak. If they step out on the street, they will be shot. Several hundred have already been killed by soldiers."

Karen suddenly remembered her source's call about the quarantine and the violence. And then a chill ran down her spine as she remembered him coughing "Once the coughing starts, how long?"

"From what we've gathered, less than twelve hours."

She did a mental calculation and realized with a quiver that by now her source could be dead. "What is this thing?" she asked, aghast.

It took Sloan a few minutes to explain what they knew and what they didn't know. He showed her the pictures Linquist had brought and promised to let her have a copy. He explained how the virus worked, taking his time to describe how it destroyed lung tissue, effectively smothering or drowning the victim. He told her they weren't yet sure if it was aerosol, that the cultures would take some time to grow and analyze, but that in his and Martin Linquist's opinion, it had to be. How else to explain the sudden spread throughout the district? He explained how viruses work and, without patronizing her, he talked about the different kinds of viruses, reminding her of her question at the airport. "You asked me about filoviruses," he said, "but this isn't a filovirus and it doesn't require direct contact with blood. At least not at the present time," he added.

"At the present time? Can they switch?"

"They adapt and mutate constantly. Change is the

absolute given in the world of RNA viruses. We've been lucky that those filovirsuses you mentioned haven't taken that path. Yet. But this one is different, we think. It's a different type, first of all. And we think it's a combination of the avian virus that decimates the fowl population and a human influenza. It's jumped species by "marrying," and he used the two fingers of each hand to indicate quotation marks, "a human virus that's spread by coughing and sneezing. The thing is, people might have some immunity to the human side of this thing, but they have literally no immunity to the avian side."

"Aren't the influenza viruses we get each year...aren't they always a bit different from the year before?"

"Yes. Look, Karen, new viruses usually retain the properties of their parents. Think of a family line over a hundred generations. You know how the individuals may look somewhat different—a slightly longer nose or greater height or...well, you know. But they all carry certain genes that are like themes in their family line. In the same way, viruses have themes that repeat themselves over the generations. For example, arena viruses spread among rodents. Whatever the mechanism is, it guarantees that the next generation will spread between rodents as well. Not birds. Not coyotes."

"So how can the avian virus be attacking humans?" Karen wanted to argue the impossibility of such a phenomenon, because it was just too scary.

"The thing we've seen in emerging viruses, and influenza viruses particularly, is something we call antigenicity. Influenza viruses, as you said, change from year to year because the human immune system is damn good at recognizing and fighting an enemy from within. Once the immune system learns to recognize the virus, it tracks it down and destroys it with a vengeance. Unfortunately, viruses are good at what they do too, so as soon as the human population catches on to them, a virus has to adapt if it is to survive. It changes its antigenicity so that it is unrecognizable. If a virus can't do that, it's a goner. The ones that survive are really good at changing, and the *really* good survivors are the ones that obtain for their structure an entirely new gene that the human population hasn't experienced before..."

"Voilá...avian flu..." Karen rolled her eyes and sighed.

"The smallest change in the genetic makeup of an influenza virus can have drastic effects. Its whole character changes."

"But we've got flu shots..."

"No good..."

"But you'll figure this thing out, just like regular flu..."

"Maybe, if we're lucky."

"And if we're not?" Karen had trouble believing Sloan now. She thought he was just hedging his bets, making the situation seem dire so that when tomorrow or the next day he and Linquist announced they had a vaccine, he'd be a big hero.

"Let me tell you what we're up against, Karen, and then you can get that cynical look off your face. My guess is that by tonight, twenty-five thousand people will begin coughing. And if you think it's just Kwang Tri..."

"...I don't. I know it's gotten out."

"If you think it's just Bangkok, you're wrong. For forty-eight hours planes have been leaving this city going all over the world. The only reason you haven't heard anything yet is that their passengers only started dying yesterday or the day before. And the doctors and nurses where they're dying..."

"...Have caught it?"

"...Have caught it and have begun infecting others. Not to speak of their families, friends, and co-workers."

"What you're saying is that by tomorrow it's not going to be twenty-five thousand..."

"That was just a figure."

"...But twenty-five *million*..." Karen purposely exaggerated. Such numbers had no reality to her. She expected Sloan to give her an exasperated look, as if she hadn't a brain in her head. Then he'd correct her with a reasonable increase. Instead he looked at her despairingly.

"...Not for a few more days..." he said, hunching his shoulders as if to ward off a blow.

Karen sputtered to a halt. "*Twenty-five million?*" Her eyes were wide, her jaw dropped. "Twenty-five million *in a few days* you say?"

Sloan rubbed his forehead again. "In a few days," he repeated.

"But then..." and Karen finally got it; this wasn't just a big story she was covering. "Ralph, what are you telling me? Are you forecasting the end of the world?"

"Maybe," Sloan said. He paused for a second, running his fingers back and forth along the edge of the table, and then stood abruptly. "There's your story, Karen. I wish it were something else." He reached out to shake her hand and Karen felt the good-bye in it. "I have to go now. Run with it, my advice. You haven't got much time."

Sloan opened the door. In the hallway Chet was sitting on the floor, his camera at the ready. Always the journalist, Karen wanted Sloan on camera.

"Wait Ralph," she said, reaching for Sloan's sleeve. "I want some footage of you. Let me get you explaining..."

But Sloan pulled away. "No time," he said over his shoulder as he hurried down the hall.

"That's a first," Karen said, thinking of the many times Sloan had done everything he could to get before a camera. Then she looked at Chet. "Let's go. We'll get the captain to drive us to the Minister's office. I want to hear what he has to say."

While the captain seemed reluctant to do anything more than drop them off at their hotel, Karen's insistence won out. He told his driver to take them to the government building where the Minister of Health had offices, and once there, they were whisked directly up to the fifth floor by a receptionist who for some reason treated them like visiting dignitaries.

"Madame Klein," the Minister said, rising and holding out his hand as his secretary them into his office. He was crisply dressed in a shirt without wrinkles and a perfectly cut black pin-stripe suit. His hair gleamed, and the nails on his small hands had been manicured. He came quickly around the desk, and while his demeanor was calm and utterly polite, Karen sensed something else. She was used to the personae people developed in their jobs and daily lives, the way they pretended to be someone they wanted people like her to believe they were. Personae were instrumental in accomplishing one's goals, Karen knew, and the most successful people, in her experience, were the people who used them skillfully—people who could smile graciously while plotting murder, people who could lie to their own priests. If she had learned anything over the years, it was to listen to the words behind the words and see the person behind the face he presented. She was good at this. So she crossed her legs comfortably as she sat down, then reached inside her purse for the steno notebook she always carried.

"Now, Minister Leu, what can you tell me about this

mystery illness?" She had her pen at the ready, waiting for a quote.

The Minister looked at her quizzically. "Did you come here thinking it was for a story, Ms. Klein?"

Karen was now the one confused. "Is there some other reason I would come?" she asked.

"I believe you came because I requested that you come. I did not have an interview in mind," he said, leaning backward and folding his small, white hands on the edge of his desk. Then he smiled, but Karen knew a fake smile when she saw it. His lips drew tight over his large white teeth, but his eyes were ebony.

"I summoned you here because I am aware that it was your call to the American CDC that...let us say... publicized our little problem here. You have caused us... no end of embarrassment, Ms. Klein, and your meddling has interfered with our efforts to deal with the problem. We..."

"How?"

"How? How, Ms. Klein, is not your concern. However, I will tell you this. The Prime Minister has ordered a temporary but complete shutdown of all communications. We want all foreign journalists out of the country today. We will be putting you and your colleagues on a plane at four this afternoon. You have been ordered to report to the airport immediately. Our people will escort you there directly. You may stop at your hotel to pick up your belongings. Other than that, you will be on your way home this evening."

"You can't just..."

"Oh, but we can, Ms. Klein. Especially after your most... "and his fingers spread wide on both hands " inappropriate report this morning. You are here on permission of the Thai government, and that permission is now revoked."

Karen could not believe her ears. Never, in any country she had visited had anyone ordered her out. "Who can I see to..."

"There is no one who will countermand this order," he said quietly, looking directly at her. He did not seem to need to breathe, so still was his body.

"The Prime Minister..." Karen began, but he interrupted.

"The Prime Minister has accompanied the King on an unofficial visit to Beijing." He picked up his pen as if to begin signing some papers, looking away from her as if she were no longer there.

Karen stayed her fury and sat back in her chair. It took little mental effort to put two and two together. The King and the Prime Minister had fled Thailand. She bet their entire families were gone too. And this pompous guy in front of her was probably waiting until nightfall to escape as well. She wondered how many others had already slipped away, rats running for their lives, while people like Sloan, who was down there in the trenches, stayed to face things head on. Damn, she thought to herself. Damn, damn, damn.

"What if I refuse to leave?" she asked. But she already knew the answer. If she refused to leave, they just might make her stay here to die. She might take some calculated risks and make some imprudent enemies, but she had no intention of being a martyr. She had an important story the world had to know. And if she couldn't get her story out of here, at least she could get it out once she returned stateside. She had to make the best decision she could. And she heard Sloan's voice, "Run with it, my advice," in her ear.

"Thank you, Minister Leu," she said coldly, with no

thanks intended. "Will you be leaving today as well?" Her sarcasm was thick and it hit the mark.

His eyebrows shot up as he watched her stand, her head held high.

"You will thank me," he said quietly, putting his pen down.

"I doubt it," she snapped, turning on her heel and heading for the door.

"We shall see," he said wisely, a dark-eyed prophet in a Versace suit.

By three o'clock Chet and Karen stood with the other reporters who had been rounded up during the day. Those who hadn't been picked up by the military had gotten calls from their networks about the order to leave. None were happy, and they all knew the reason for their ouster. "What the hell were you thinking?" one asked Karen. "You know you can't just circumvent the censors that way." Another disagreed. "She's got a breaking story, Al," the correspondent for the BBC said. "She had to get it out." "She televised rumors," a Los Angeles Times guy accused. "She knows better." Karen argued passionately for herself while the guards supervising the group stood silently watching. Whether they understood what was being said or not, they showed no emotion and when the order to board the plane came, they merely shouldered their guns and herded the angry journalists aboard.

The reporters were not long gone when another exodus began. Karen had called it when she asked the new Minister how long he was staying, but he was only on the third or fourth level in a society that was slicing itself off at the head. The King and the Prime Minister, of course, had been the first to find reason to get out. They took with them their entire families, beloved uncles, aunts, and cousins, aging parents, and complete staffs. The staffs resented being taken from their families for an indefinite holiday, but those who dared to speak up were summarily fired. That was the least of their problems, but at the time they didn't know it. The rest quickly made their arrangements and reported to the bus assigned to transport them. Dragging worn canvas duffels and shopping bags, the maids and secretaries, butlers and chauffeurs bumbled their way up the steps, obediently finding their seats and then looking expectantly out of the windows. Not privy to the information the King or the Prime Minister had, they could not understand why they were leaving so abruptly with the problem in Kwang Tri as it was. But what would they know anyhow? They shrugged and looked ahead.

The Ministers, several army generals, and the close advisors to the Prime Minister followed quickly on his heels. Each found reason to leave the country quickly. Their wives, aware of the growing danger, found it expedient to cancel dinner invitations they had already accepted, apologizing profusely for their husbands' short-sightedness and promising to make amends soon. They also removed their children from school, assuring the mistresses that they would supervise their children's studies and return them current with the curriculum. Ah, teachers said, grateful for their polite consideration. Of course, they said. But in the rooms where teachers congregate, and in the living rooms where hostesses entertained, looks were exchanged. "What is going on?" the servants asked each other. "What is going on?" the hostesses asked each other and their husbands, when they returned from work. And their husbands, back at the office, asked, "What is going on?" when they could gather in small groups around a computer or water cooler or in the men's room. Like a trail of smoke lifting and twisting from an ashtray, a cloudy awareness began to settle and swirl, lift and float about the city that had already cut off one of its limbs in Kwang Tri and another at Bangkok Hospital. Before flights were canceled, the people who could not leave already knew that they had been deserted. The wealthy, never ones to be caught unprepared, decided a vacation was in order. They booked flights and left in such growing numbers that soon no seats going anywhere were available. That did not stop them, however. Within a matter of perhaps thirty-six hours, those in the know and those who watched those in the know had planted themselves elsewhere—in Cairo, in Hong Kong, in Beijing, in India, Turkey, Italy, Germany, France, Spain, Russia, Brazil. And even after the no-more-flights order came down, small Cessnas and helicopters lifted off the tarmac against a midnight sky, transporting all manner of escapees—drug lords, crime bosses, politicians, CEOs, CFOs, real estate moguls, all fleeing the shadowy enemy, most of them fearful that they were too late.

On the planes, they looked at each other for symptoms. Old men, their nails yellow, puffed themselves up to look healthy. Those feeling feverish carefully wiped their foreheads when no one was looking. If someone coughed, heads everywhere lifted and turned. "No, no," the cougher might explain, "I had a cold even last week." Some told the truth. Others lied. All felt the same urge to get out and get away. Within a few days one might take a paint brush dripping with blood and spatter in on a world map, just one quick flick of the brush, and the bloody spots would drip from every major city on every continent. The human will to survive knows no ethics. If they were bringing the disease with them, well, they had to seek better medical attention, they had to go where they could get help, they had to make their families safe, they had to do whatever they could to survive.

On her flight to Luxembourg, Karen Klein could only guess what was going on behind her. But she knew that the Bangkok virus, like her, had lifted in the wind, its seeds of destruction blown to all corners of the planet. She guessed correctly that those seeds not only followed her, but that many seeds had preceded her, so that when she landed, she would be landing on an earth already incubating new seeds that she could not escape. As she leaned forward, looking out the small window into the darkness, she knew that the land she could not see below had become a deadly incubator for a disease her old friend would not be able to cure. She had no proof, but she was as sure of that as she was sure that she would never see Ralph Sloan again.

25

Patterson, Monday, Mid-October

Terry Grant felt foolish, but her instincts told her that Doc Strong might be right. Office hours didn't begin on Monday until 1:00 and she was using the morning to head to BJ's in Leominster to stockpile groceries.

She had been worried since Doc Strong's outburst on Thursday, and it was only when she came home that Rob had been able to calm her. When she told him the details of their discussion, Rob had seemed only mildly concerned. "They've got it under control," he said, stroking her arm. She'd wanted to smack him. Rob might know farming, but she was a nurse, and she remembered only too well what she'd learned in training about viruses and bacteria and how dangerous both could be.

"But you don't know that," she said. "Viruses are emerging every day now. It has to do with a lot of things — our taking over jungles, for one. And crowding for another. Look what's happened with antibiotics, Rob. They're not working anymore against some strains of bacteria. We can't stay ahead of the mutations." Terry recognized the high whine in her voice and purposely dropped an octave. "I know you're worried too; I saw you when you were watching the news."

Rob scratched his head and stretched. "We don't live in the jungle or the city," he said to reassure her. "We're out here in the country breathing good air."

"You talk like we're isolated," Terry argued. "We're not.

Everyday the kids go to school and sit in classrooms with other kids and play on the playgrounds with even more kids. Every day I go to Doc Strong's office and interact with sick people of all sorts. We eat food shipped in from God knows where that we stand in line to buy at supermarkets and go to movies in Grayson where people who work in Worcester also go..."

She would have gone on, but Rob said, "You've made your point, Terry. I know what you're saying. But the thing is in Asia. Thailand. That's a world away."

"Only hours by plane, Rob," Terry interjected. "Doc Strong says we should be canceling all flights in and out."

"We can't do that, Terry. We can't just close our borders. There're other things that get flown in and out that we need. And ships. We're a country dependent on trade. What happens when we prohibit shipping? You'll have no strawberries for breakfast, that's for sure."

"Don't belittle me," Terry warned. She knew she was right, but she wanted to believe Rob. Sometimes he could be so bullheaded though, she thought. She wasn't going to depend on him now to keep her family safe. She might not be able to do anything about the outbreak if it came to the U.S., but she sure as tooting could stockpile supplies.

That night, Terry had begun surreptitiously taking stock. While Rob helped the boys with schoolwork, she ventured down into the cellar, ostensibly "to clean out the freezer." If Rob made the connection, he didn't show it. He was happy to do figures with Chris, keeping the newspaper on his left to read while Chris worked problems.

Terry lifted the lid to the freezer, holding it up while she surveyed the contents. They'd bought this freezer years ago, just before they butchered their first pig. Now, as she looked down into the bright light below, she saw that it was about half full. She began sorting the packages, looking at their dates. Some of the stuff was over a year old. She'd have to get rid of those, she decided, but at least that would make more room. What if they lost electricity, she wondered, stopping short. Then she laughed at herself. Come on, we're not talking doomsday here, she whispered aloud. She pulled a tall plastic pail close to the freezer and dropped four or five packages into it, then re-organized the meats, frozen pastas, vegetables, and breads so she could see what she needed.

Finished there, she went to the pantry, her pride and joy. Rob had built it for her when he expanded the garage, and there she kept rows upon rows of cans, preserves she'd put up, and paper goods.

"What are you doing?" Rob asked, having suddenly appeared at the door. Now he seemed suspicious.

Terry was quick. "I'm on a roll," she lied. "It feels good." She'd looked at him and smiled, and if Rob doubted her, again he didn't show it.

"The boys are waiting for a kiss," he said, turning to leave.

"Tell them I'll be right up," Terry said. And to avoid giving her plan away, she snapped off the light and followed.

Sunday Terry had gone on-line to see what she needed. Survivalist information was plentiful, and as Terry made lists, she thought that she was glad they lived on a farm. At least they could use the land. And they had tools. Rob could hunt. What would city people do if services stopped? Terry had seen what happened on a small scale at Home Depot and Stop and Shop when a hurricane or blizzard was forecast. People ravaged the shelves, buying ten times more than they could ever eat or need during the course of the storm. One woman had actually knocked her off balance trying to grab the last two twelve volt batteries remaining at Aubuchon's; the only reason Terry managed to get them was that she had slapped the woman's arm away. Later, she had everyone at the office laughing about her "cat fight" and calling her Tiger. But funny or not, people got weird even before they panicked, when something was just "in the air". She wasn't going to fight crowds, Terry swore silently. Her family would be prepared whether Rob helped her or not.

So when she finished filling her cart, she pushed it up near the bank of cash registers and asked the closest cashier if she'd mind her leaving it there while she got the rest of the items on her list. After filling the second cart, Terry got in line, retrieved the first cart, and waited patiently. She thought she recognized the woman in front of her, though the man was a stranger. Terry was not good at names, but faces stuck and she was sure this woman lived in Patterson. She'd seen her somewhere, maybe at one of the functions in town. And then she remembered. She lived out by Ethel Card. Ethel had told her about her new neighbor and introduced them one sunny afternoon when she had seen them walking along the road. She thought Ethel had said the woman was divorced. Was this a new man or the old one? He was wearing a cowboy hat, for pete's sake, and boots. Definitely a poseur, she smiled to herself.

And then the woman turned around. She recognized Terry immediately but seemed embarrassed. "I know you," she said, and Terry saw her struggling for a name.

"Terry Grant," she helped, "and I know you too. You're Ethel's new neighbor."

"Laura Block. Not so new anymore," Laura smiled. "Nearly four years now." Laura saw Terry glance at Taylor. "Oh, and this is my friend Taylor Farr." The man offered Terry his hand. "Handsome," she thought.

"He's visiting from Wyoming," Laura added, almost as explanation for the western clothes.

For the first time, Terry noticed their carts. Two of them, piled high with canned goods and batteries and staples like flour and pasta. "Looks like you're stocking up too," Terry said. And the minute she said it, she regretted it. No one knew what she was doing, and she wanted to keep it that way. If Rob quaked at their bills at the end of the month, well, she planned to point out that they'd have to buy all this sooner or later anyway.

The thing was, Laura blushed. Terry thought it strange, so she went into a lengthy explanation about being a pack rat, stockpiling things she wouldn't use in five years let alone one. Taylor, however, merely leaned against the counter and smiled. Then the cashier began totaling their order. It wasn't until their order was packed and paid for that Laura turned once again to say goodbye.

"Stop in sometime," she said. "I'd love some company." Then she realized Taylor was standing right there, obvious company.

"I will," promised Terry, now piling her packages on the counter. "I will."

On their way to the car, Laura began laughing. Taylor watched as she tilted her head to the sun, her long hair falling behind her. "What's so funny this time?" he asked, smiling broadly.

"What must she think?" Laura asked. "Patterson's a small town, you know. And she's got to wonder what I'm doing stockpiling groceries with a cowboy. It'll be all over town before nightfall." But Laura didn't seem to mind. "Look at this stuff, Taylor. You've got me buying more than I could eat in three years. And all these batteries. And this emergency kit!" She laughed roundly again.

Taylor was laughing too, because he couldn't resist the way Laura could just open up and hoot when she thought something funny. An old couple on their way into BJ's smiled as they passed, as if they were in on the joke, but Taylor knew that Laura's laugh did that to people. It helped them find humor in things, just as it had for him when she first came to Wyoming. Taylor couldn't remember when he'd last had a good laugh, but there she was, and suddenly he was laughing all the time. Giddy, almost.

"I'm going to have to transfer funds to my checking to pay for all this," she chided. "I'm not used to buying on this scale." She looked at her bill. "Taylor, six hundred dollars this cost me! Six hundred!"

"Money well spent," he said. "And we'll get more this afternoon. If nothing happens, you won't go shopping until next November." He put his arm over her shoulders, hugging her to him. "And if something does happen, you'll be safe out there in your little house in the woods."

In Laura's car, Taylor's long legs bent awkwardly against the dashboard. "Why ever did you buy a car like this," he said, rubbing one pained knee.

"I'm not buying a pickup!" Laura said, knowing exactly where he was going. "This car is just right for me."

"It's a girly car," Taylor teased. "Suburban wives and yuppies."

"It's a safe car," Laura said. "Side impact bags."

"It's a girly car," Taylor repeated. "Did Tom talk you into it?" Now his grin spread ear to ear.

"No he didn't," she said emphatically. "I picked this out." She put on her signal as they approached the next turn.

"It's a girly car," was Taylor's final statement before she pulled to a stop.

Laura stuck out her tongue, "Neah, neah, neah," she said

as if she were four years old. Taylor reached across the seat and pulled her to him. "You just wait," he leered before he kissed her. "You won't be neah, neahing me later."

On her way home, Terry planned how she would hide some of the things she'd purchased—the obvious survival ones like batteries and the emergency kit. Rob never went near her sewing room and she could devote half the closet to storage. The food in the freezer he'd never see; she did all the cooking. The pantry stuff, however, was problematic. Her pantry would explode once she stored the cases of soups, canned veggies, dog food, beans, and the rest. And if things looked worse on the news tonight, she decided, she'd go back to BJ's tomorrow, and Stop and Shop too, until she felt confident that the entire family could ride out an outbreak. As she came over the hill toward her exit, she slowed, looking at the orange and gold beauty of the valley stretched out before her. With barely a car on the highway, the sun at 11 o'clock, the sky a vast, clear blue, Terry's anxieties diminished. She probably was just being foolish. No one else seemed worried except Doc. Maybe he was just an old man, the way some old men get. No one else was racing to the supermarket to stockpile groceries. Then she remembered Laura.

26

Atlanta, Georgia, Monday, Mid-October

The emergency meeting called by the director of the CDC, George Parker, had given those notified only two hours to cancel their appointments, finish up their experiments, and do whatever else they had to do before heading upstairs to the conference area. By the time Parker arrived, carrying with him sheaves of photographs and papers, nearly twenty high level personnel were sitting around the long table. The room was crowded and humming with anticipation. Most of them had only heard rumors. A few had spoken with the three who had returned to Atlanta days before. They had been strangely silent and non-committal about what had happened in Bangkok. No amount of probing seemed to work on them, but in the world of health scares and plagues, they had become used to people sealing their lips when something really big was afoot. They knew that sooner or later they'd find out, because that's how things happened in Atlanta. Initial silence, hush-hush stuff. Then a few days later either a general meeting or a public announcement. So today, everyone was anxious to hear the news. What were they facing?

Parker, a short, stocky man whose Caribbean-blue eyes were icy clear, ordered the papers he had brought with him into three piles. He concentrated on sorting, fully aware that the room was quieting as if a slow wave was washing over those assembled there. He waited for absolute silence.

Parker didn't ask for silence, and he made it a habit never to begin speaking until he had it. Only a fool continued talking when he arrived.

Finally he looked up, sweeping his eyes slowly over the assembled men and women watching him. "Folks," he said, "we've got a problem."

No one said anything. He lifted the first pile and handed it to the woman on his left, who took one of the stapled sets and passed the pile on. She immediately began reading the data contained there, and as each person passed the slowly diminishing pile on, he or she did the same. Parker waited while people read, watching as some finished and looked up. The room was deathly silent except for the rustle of pages. When the last person finished, Parker looked long at the assembled group. "It's not that we haven't expected this for some time," he said gravely, "and it's not that we haven't prepared for it either. Now it's here. I've called you together to let you know the situation. We're going to do some re-assigning today. All of you will set aside your own projects and go to work on this."

"What *is* this," one of the men asked. "I've never seen anything like it." The others concurred, and a general hubbub arose as scientists pointed out the anomalies they saw, flipping the data sheets and photographs back and forth.

"When you're all quiet," Parker said, his voice low. The chatter stopped instantly. "Lester here was on Sloan's team. He's going to give you an overview." Parker laid a thick hand on the shoulder of the man to his right, and Lester took up some of his own papers and prepared to speak. His report took less than 10 minutes, during which time he described the characteristics of the virus, the fact that the cell cultures they set up immediately on their return showed conclusively that not only did the virus destroy cells from the inside, literally becoming the cells, it did its job in twenty-four to thirty-six hours. Lester told the group that the WHO had come up with the same results with their samples, ruling out the likelihood of error. Finally, and he said this reluctantly, they were one hundred percent sure the thing was aerosol. The room was quiet.

"What's the recovery rate?" a hawk-nosed scientist asked timidly.

"We don't know. We think it's fatal," Lester said carefully, "one hundred percent of the time." He looked at their blank faces. Something made him say, "At least we think so." But that changed nothing. Everyone at the table recognized that whatever Lester thought was probably accurate. He had been with the CDC for decades, he was a revered member of the society of scientists, and he had mentored most of them when they first came to Atlanta. Lester didn't over-dramatize anything. In fact, he had a tendency to understate, and his calm exterior never wavered, even under dangerous conditions out in the field.

"And it's airborne," the woman reiterated, hoping she had misheard him.

"Yes," Lester said. "We've got more tests to run before we can take that public. But all the signs are there. Yes."

A few members of the group wanted to know exactly what tests had been run and some of the methods Lester and his group had used. Some of them were Level One and Two people, not yet qualified to work in the Level Four lab, and Lester could read the fear on their faces as they questioned him. Lester answered their questions, watching as some of his colleagues took notes on the back of the packets they had been given.

When Lester finished his part of the meeting, Parker

thanked him, and picking up the third pile in front of him and passing it to his right, he began to tell them what he had done just prior to the meeting. "I informed the Secretary of Health and Human Services yesterday afternoon," he began, "but I wanted you to know that for two days we have been flooded with calls from doctors. We've got reports coming in from San Francisco, Honolulu, Seattle, Chicago, Dallas, Houston, Miami, New York, Philadelphia, Kansas City, and Phoenix. There are suburban and rural outbreaks as well. State boards of health are deluged with calls from country doctors who haven't a clue what they're looking at, and they're calling us asking for answers. "

The room remained silent, while Parker flipped through some memos. "Okay," he said. "Lepkowski met with the President last night. I spoke with him this morning. Before lunchtime, all air traffic will be suspended."

"Out of the country?" the woman asked.

"In and out and everywhere in between," Parker scowled, not appreciating the interruption. He let the realization settle while he waited. "The President will call a news conference at noon. I suggest you listen. Meanwhile, Lester has drawn up a plan that he thinks will facilitate our efforts. We've got no time, folks. This thing is rampant and it kills everyone in its path. I don't have to tell you that unless we can create a vaccine quickly, we won't have anyone to vaccinate."

"It's 11:45 now," someone pointed out.

Parker picked up the remote that sat beneath the TV on the wall. He flipped it on but pressed the mute button so the meeting could continue until the President appeared. "Keep your eye on that," he said to the woman on his left. "Let me know when you see something." And then Parker and Lester began explaining the plan Lester had devised, writing on the chalkboard the names of the scientists present and the groups dedicated to particular tasks each would be in.

Fifteen minutes later, as if on cue, everyone looked up to see the Presidential Seal on the screen. Parker picked up the remote and aimed it at the TV, restoring the sound. People had been moving about the room, gathering in groups once they were assigned, but now, standing or sitting, everyone's attention was on the screen where President Riordan would appear momentarily. When he did, it was clear that the man was shaken. His eyes seemed smaller and his head sat rigid on his shoulders. He looked directly into the camera:

"My fellow Americans," he began, and the paper in his hand shook visibly. "My fellow Americans," he began again after clearing his throat. "What I have to tell you tonight is something no President ever dreamed could happen in this fair country of ours. A terrible blight is upon us, an illness brought here from foreign shores. It has decimated Thailand, where we believe it began, and has moved to China, Saudi Arabia, Africa and India, and to countries in Europe and South America, as well as to the United States. The best estimates we have today are that more than 200,000 have died, with many more infected. This is a virus that attacks everyone, not just the very young or very old, but everyone who comes in contact with it. The coughing and sneezing of its victims convey it, and its incubation period is abnormally short—twenty-four to thirty-six hours. We have utilized all the known pharmaceuticals to stave off the infection, but so far to no avail. As yet, we know of no one who has survived the infection.

"I have spoken today to the leaders of all countries experiencing outbreaks, and they all assure me they are doing everything they can to halt the further spread of this virus. Thailand has closed its borders. No one can go in or out. Other countries have closed their borders as well, canceling all flights, halting railroad cars at their borders, and stepping up their border patrols. Not even cars or foot traffic will be allowed to cross into their countries until this contagion has been identified and a vaccine developed.

"My discussion with these world leaders has convinced me of the efficacy of doing the same. I have instructed U.S. Border Patrols, Customs, and Immigration to close our borders as of twelve noon today," he paused, looking at his watch, "...about five minutes ago. I have also instructed the FAA to cancel all flights, not only flights into or out of our country, but also within our borders because it is believed that the planes themselves have played a major role in transporting the virus from Asia to our shores. To aid these agencies in their awesome task, I have called upon the military, the Coast Guard, and the National Guard to cooperate fully with local authorities at all ports of entry and border highways.

"It is of paramount importance that you, the American public, understand the importance of individual cooperation with local authorities. During past national disasters, Americans have always united in a strong front against the enemy. This time, the enemy is not easy to see. It is not a country or an army or a band of terrorists. This time, the enemy we face is invisible. We cannot fight it with superior arms or a robust army. This time, we have to rely on our scientists, the world's scientists, to find a way to protect our citizens from infection. But that, my fellow Americans, will not happen tomorrow or the next day. Identifying and analyzing a virus takes time. It takes even longer to develop a vaccine and then to produce it so that every man, woman, and child can receive the serum.

"Until that time, it is my responsibility as President to do what is necessary to protect our people. Closing our borders is going to have a drastic effect on our lives. From foodstuffs imported from Mexico and Central and South America to oil from the mid-East, Americans are going to feel the loss of products on which they have come to depend. As in the wars of the past century, we will have to learn to ration and to do without until the danger passes. Meanwhile, I have instructed my cabinet," and the President indicated the men standing behind his podium, "to implement emergency plans to insure America's safety and food supply. In the days to come, you will be hearing about these measures.

"My fellow Americans, this enemy can only defeat us if we falter in our resolve to protect ourselves and our children from it. We are a resourceful people. We have time and again demonstrated our indomitable spirit, a spirit that has in less than three centuries made us the greatest, strongest nation on earth. I ask you now to join with me in a united front to stop this pandemic in its path. God bless us all."

The President did not take questions. He turned from the podium and, surrounded by his Cabinet and Secret Service agents, immediately walked from the room. A general uproar erupted as newsmen raced to get their stories to their news agencies, while on the TV, NBC had Jennings Prescott ready to interview several experts.

Parker pressed the remote and turned to his staff. "Well, there it is. It won't be the last official announcement is my guess," he said. "Let's go, people." He looked solemnly at them all. "Let's stop this thing." Then, like the President, Parker turned and strode out of the conference room, leaving those remaining clamoring for answers from Lester, arguing among themselves, and studying papers and photographs. Slowly, groups left the conference area heading for labs, computers, and other meeting places. Within the hour the room was empty. Jennings Prescott had long since returned the broadcast to its regular programming, a soap opera. Coincidentally, on the screen a man lay dying in his hospital bed, tubes and monitors connected to his body like tree roots. A woman seated beside his bed held his motionless hand, sobbing. "Don't leave me, Robert." But no sound came from the conference room TV. No one had thought to turn it off.

27

Patterson, Monday, Mid-October

Laura Block stood in the doorway staring at the gray TV screen. Taylor sat on the sofa, leaning forward, his elbows on his knees. He had just pressed the remote, cutting Jennings Prescott off in mid-sentence.

"You were right," Laura said, stunned. She stared at the empty screen as if an answer might appear there.

Taylor sat back on the sofa. He thought it ironic that he was here in Massachusetts when the catastrophe he had envisioned and prepared for so long ago occurred. Back in Wyoming, he had a totally-equipped cabin and barn, rifles, traps, a generator, gas, batteries, a hand-pumped well, and enough canned food to last him a year. He had prepared himself to ride out just about anything other than a direct nuclear attack. He had friends equally prepared, a support structure that included several carpenters, an electrician, two nurses, and several ranchers and farmers. They were ready. They had been for years. And now where was he when disaster struck? In Massachusetts, for God's sake. He knew nothing about the land here. He couldn't buy a gun here. He couldn't even get to a store on his own.

"Taylor?" Laura asked. "Taylor?"

"Sorry," he said, turning to her. "I was just thinking."

"About how to get home?" Laura asked, knowing that he must be angry that he was here with no way to get back to Wyoming. "You could take my car," she offered.

Taylor looked up at her thoughtfully. "It would take

us three, maybe four days." It never occurred to Taylor to leave Laura in Massachusetts. "Anyway, we've made some preparations. Today, we'll make more."

"What do we do?" Laura asked, suppressing the joy she felt at Taylor's use of "we".

"We prepare ourselves to ride this out in isolation. If we can get what we need for the long haul..."

"How long?"

"Figure six, eight months." Laura's eyes went wide. He continued, "If we can do that without picking up the virus in some store. Then after we stock up, we avoid everyone. We don't answer the door, we don't speak to anyone except over the phone or through e-mail. We don't go anywhere where people are. Essentially, we stay here, in this house. If we go out in the car, we can't stop to talk to anyone. We can learn the woods around here...I can hunt...I can teach you...but if we see anyone in the woods, we have to go the other way. We cannot get within ten feet of anyone until this thing passes or until they have a cure. Are you up for that?"

"At least I know what we can eat out there, that's one thing..." Laura was suddenly thankful that she knew every edible plant for miles around. No longer was her vast knowledge of plants an effete luxury. She was going to be useful.

"And we'll need fuel for the winter, Laura. You've got a woodstove. Call right now and order twenty cords. You want delivery tomorrow. Go. Do that right now."

"You think we'll lose electricity?" Laura was aghast. This was a world she could hardly imagine.

"We're not going to take a chance. Get the wood. I'll start a list of things we didn't get yesterday." Taylor rose but stopped short when he looked at Laura's crumpled face.

"Are you getting teary on me, girl?" he asked, opening his arms. She stood her ground.

"Taylor, what would I have done if you weren't...And here you are, stuck with me on the wrong side of the country..." Laura's eyes rained tears.

"We're going to be all right," Taylor murmured, hugging her and patting her back. "And I'm not stuck with you. You're the one I want to be with. Now stop crying and make that call. I need you to be strong."

Laura pushed away from him, wiping her face with her hands. Then she nodded her head, turned, and walked to the phone. Taylor sat back down on the sofa. For a minute he stared at the blank TV. Then he picked up some notepaper and a pencil from among Laura's clutter and began to write.

28

Washington, D.C., Tuesday, Mid-October

In the parking garage below the Washington Eagle Times offices, Karen Klein hurried from her car, her trench coat still wrinkled from the packing job she had done in Thailand. Since she had returned, she had been on the run, interviewing scientists at Fort Detrick, the Army's famed emerging viruses study center, at the CDC in Atlanta, Cabinet members and politicians in Washington, and even an impromptu few minutes with Vice President Springer as he walked from a hearing on Capitol Hill. She had talked with hospital officials from San Francisco to Portland, Maine, and if that wasn't frightening enough, she had managed to obtain data and statistics being compiled by the Department of Health and Human Services, information not for public perusal. Karen had sources, and one of them was a long-time friend of hers whom she had promised would remain anonymous.

Karen had reason to hurry. Reporters everywhere were on the story as soon as her exiled group of correspondents returned to the U.S. Even before they returned, actually, because they were on their cell phones as soon as they could, sending the story ahead of them to all the major media. While it certainly wasn't her nature to help fellow reporters or to sacrifice an edge she had on a story, Karen had given them her scoop because this time things were different. This time Karen knew that the story had to get out fast. She knew her editor would chastise her for losing her scoop, and he had. The facts about what was going on in Thailand had hit the front page of just about every major paper in the U.S., and Ed Karl had been giving her the cold shoulder ever since. Karen, however, had the interview with Sloan, and that gave her story a veracity the others couldn't have. What did it matter, she continued to repeat to herself. If this lethal virus Sloan had described was going to destroy the world as she knew it, would it matter in the long run who broke the story? Who was going to care?

But then a strange thing happened. She supposed she could have predicted it, but she had hoped things would be different. When the news about Thailand had broken, instead of creating a profound sense of danger, life had gone on as usual. Yes, people had talked about it over cups of coffee in cafeterias across the country, at dinner parties and coffee klatches, but the distance—Thailand, Asia, the other side of the world—had rendered the news merely interesting, mildly disconcerting, only slightly worrisome. Penetrating the complacency of modern-day Americans who had lived so comfortably and safely for so many decades had proved to be beyond even the power of a highly contagious lethal virus. So, Karen had taken a very deep breath and begun the onerous task of trying to save the world from its apathy.

She had been in the White House yesterday when the President made his speech to the nation. She had covered DC long enough to know that Riordan would take half-measures in order to protect his corporation buddies, and corporations required open borders and unrestricted transportation systems. Not that she actually believed the President would purposely risk public health, but he was too easily influenced by people who would, power people for whom money was everything. The same ones who owned the newspaper monoliths that could decide what the American public was going to know or never know. Closing the borders and shutting down the airports was a half-measure. From what Karen had learned, he should have told people to stay in their homes, postponed all public events, cancelled public schools, and warned people to stay away from people not in their families. But he didn't do that. He held off. Because of it, everyone would pay a very steep price.

Karen's briefcase was heavy with data. She carried her laptop in a black nylon bag over her shoulder. Leaning forward as she walked, she was already writing in her head the story that she would give to her editor before deadline at 5:00. She had only to make a few more phone calls, and she would be ready.

By the time she reached her desk on the ninth floor, she already had a pile of messages stuck on the spindle by various people on the night shift. On her chair was a hand-written note from Ed to see him as soon as she arrived. She tossed off her trench coat, set the laptop and briefcase on her desk, picked up the note and walked directly to his door, lifting the note to the glass to remind him that he had summoned her. He saw her immediately and waved her inside.

"Close the door," he said. Ed Karl was never one to precede business with pleasantries.

Karen closed the door behind her and sat down in one of the black suede chairs positioned in front of his desk. She didn't say anything. She waited.

"Upstairs wants us to back off on your story." As he said this, he watched her over his spectacles, gauging her reaction.

"You've got to be kidding," Karen snorted. "Back off?

What do they mean by that?" Karen leaned forward, her long red hair flaming in the morning sunshine.

"They've gotten calls from the brass..."

"The brass?"

"Washington is worried that too much information might cause a public panic."

"The public ought to be panicking. The alternative is dying!" Karen was outraged that someone might try to censor her. Yet, in the back of her mind she knew that outright panic could be as disastrous as the virus itself. She'd been covering a concert years ago, a novice reporter, when the crowds outside the theater tried to rush the doors, crushing eleven young kids to death. She knew that when the public moved as one, whether frightened or angry, it became a being of its own, one to be feared and avoided at all costs. People could go crazy when they lost themselves in a group, do things they'd never do as individuals. She realized that the so-called "brass" might have a point.

"I've got some discretion, here, Karen, but I've been warned. No one's trying to undermine the First Amendment, but we've got to be careful. Already I'm getting reports of Doomsday groups gathering in San Francisco and New Mexico. The end of the world, they're saying. Judgment is upon us."

"They may be right," Karen said.

"And there's been a rush on the grocery stores, pharmacies, and hardware outlets. You can't buy a battery anywhere. Churches are calling prayer meetings as if "The Old Rugged Cross" is going to save them."

Karen sat back in her chair and looked directly at her editor. He seemed so cool, so detached. Not a wrinkle in his shirt. Not a hair out of place. "That might be the only thing that can," she said, holding his gaze. "Do you have any idea of the magnitude of this?" she asked gravely. "Do you have a clue about how bad things are?"

"Tell me. Give me what you know."

"Try this for starters. They've tracked the disease out of Thailand on 151 flights. On those flights, an average of 125 passengers were exposed to the virus. Of those nearly nineteen thousand," she paused for emphasis, "nineteen thousand passengers, officials believe that two thirds then traveled on connecting flights to every major city in the world. Again, on planes averaging about 125 passengers. That's over a hundred and twenty-five thousand more exposed. Those people then went home to their families, jobs, schools, you name it."

"But not everyone gets sick."

"True, not everyone. I could bore you with stats, but every sneeze, every cough from an infected person creates a cloud of millions of these little bastards that lifts, pauses, and then descends on everything and everyone within ten feet. Railings, door handles, tables, all the things people touch. And they can live there indefinitely as long as they have moisture. People don't even have to breathe them in by being in close proximity to an infected person. All they have to do is hold on to the same railing going down to the subway or push open the same door. Then they touch their lips or their eyes. Maybe they have a cut. HHS believes that of those exposed to the virus, most will incubate the disease for twenty-four to thirty-six hours before becoming symptomatic, and then another twelve to twenty-four coughing their way to and from work. They don't start coughing blood or become prostrate until near the end, and by then who knows how many people have breathed their infectious clouds, how many objects they've sprayed. I've talked to representative hospitals from all regions of the country. In the last twenty-four hours, their emergency rooms have spilled over into the streets; they can't isolate because the numbers getting sick are too great, their own staffs are down as well, and some of them think it's a matter of a few days before they're going to have to shut down."

"Shut down?" He almost scoffed.

"Yes, shut down. And here's something else you might want to know. The President has ordered the Nuclear Power Regulating Agency to implement a standby plan for shutdown if their employee absentee rate reaches forty percent. They're going to flip the switch and initiate cool down because there might not be anyone there to monitor or maintain the reactors."

"That's just an emergency plan. The reactors shut down all by themselves when something goes wrong. They've always had that."

"That's different. Emergency shutdowns may be automatic, but the reactors have to be monitored. People have to do that. The absentee rate at Millbrook and at Three Mile has risen 10 percent in the last two days."

"It's flu season."

"Last year, same dates, a two percent rise." Karen had no reason to feel smug about the thoroughness of her research. This wasn't an Easter egg hunt she was on; the facts felt like stones in her chest.

Karl tapped his pencil on the blotter. "What else?" he asked grimly.

"How about the mortality stats?" Karen asked, folding her long hands in her lap.

"Two hundred thousand."

"Half a million, and climbing."

"Where?"

"Everywhere."

"How many here?"

"Twenty thousand as of yesterday. Best guess estimate is that by tonight, you can quintuple that." Karen bit her lower lip, tasting the perfumed oil of her lipstick. "Each day thereafter, quintuple the last."

Ed was at a loss for questions. "What does HHS think?"

"That it's a slate wiper."

"A what?"

"A slate wiper. Wipes the slate clean. Everyone is likely to get it. Everyone who gets it dies."

It took Ed a minute to digest what she had said. He shook his head. He looked out the window. He flicked his thumb and forefinger at least twenty times. Karen was one of his best researchers. What she wanted printed had always been fully verified. And she was not hysterical, like some of his people. She was cool and analytical. If what she said was true, and it indubitably was, the paper had an obligation to get that information out. He had an obligation, despite the consequences. "Go with your story," he leaned forward to say. "To hell with the brass."

"I thought you'd say that," Karen answered as she stood.

By the time the Eagle Times headlined her story on Wednesday morning, Karen was on her way to New York. Not able to fly out of Dulles, she had taken Amtrak, for she had heard on the evening news that the interstates near every city along the way had exceedingly heavy traffic. The train had nearly emptied before it reached New York City, but as it hurtled past stations and over thruways leading into the city, Karen saw long lines of traffic jamming the highways. Grand Central Station was a nightmare of people hurrying to get out of the city, most wearing surgical masks.

Its cavernous lobby resembled a science-fiction movie she had once seen. People moved with an urgency she could literally feel. As they approached her, their eyes scanning the walls for their appointed tracks, she found herself jumping aside to avoid collisions. Panic trembled just below the surface. Karen realized she could be in the midst of a riot were these fleeing people denied access to the tracks where they mistakenly believed escape was possible. Their jaws were set; the hardness in their eyes glinted. Every bodily movement was tense and bent forward toward the trains they thought might save them. The masks had their own effect, as if now with their identities hidden, these people were no longer mothers and fathers, husbands and wives, grandparents and children, but beings bent on one thing: their survival. She remembered something Sloan had said—that the virus had one goal, and for just a second the crowds became a horde of masked viruses pouring toward her, without compassion or ethics. Not so different, this higher species. People buffeted her left and right, for she was going against those surging out of the city. She jumped frequently to avoid suitcases rolling on their little black wheels behind fleeing refugees

Finally outside, Karen hailed a taxi just pulling up to the curb. She waited as yet another family unloaded itself from the back seat, then quickly jumped in.

"Something going on here?" Karen asked innocently.

The cabbie, an Hispanic man, looked at her in his rearview mirror as if he couldn't believe her ignorance. "Is scared," he said, his accent thick, his heavy eyebrows knitted. "Fraid of flu."

"Where are they going?"

"Families," he said. "Outside city." He said more, but Karen could not understand him. He had begun talking faster. She heard "many die" and "no doctors" and "stays inside."

"But you're working," she said. "Aren't you afraid?"

"Oh, yes," he said, his eyebrows shooting up, his eyes wide. "Oh, yes, very. But need work. Seven family." His hands were broad and hairy on the steering wheel. She noticed the frayed cuffs.

As they paused in traffic, he grew silent, listening to his dispatcher. They watched the cars inching forward in the other direction, the drivers staring straight ahead, their hands clutching steering wheels, their families silent, often packed two layers deep in the back. Karen watched a small boy watching her, his face pressed to the glass, his eyes following her progress forward. She smiled and waved. He merely stared.

Along the way, cars were double-parked everywhere. Families milled about as they loaded suitcases, duffels, and black plastic garbage bags full of necessities into their cars. Those who thought they could ride out the flu with relatives in the suburbs were abandoning the city. Karen thought about the germs they might carry, how surely many of those living elbow to elbow in the city were now about to pollinate more distant areas with the virus. And once outside, how long could they stay away? Most people lived week to week on their incomes. She tried to remember an old statistic that had surprised her when she first heard it... that most people's savings reserve was less than a month's salary? Was that it? If that were true, they'd be creeping back into the city, just like the cabbie, needing work to eat. Yet there they stood, loading their trunks with belongings, their cars with loved ones, running from something they could not see and only barely understood.

Karen leaned against the leather seat of the cab and

looked at the back of the driver's head. The two of them encapsulated in this yellow bubble traveled the frightened streets as if they could somehow be immune to the danger. She thought about Sloan in Thailand. Was he still alive? She wondered. Could he have survived this long? And here she was, a messenger from hell, herself likely to contract the virus at any time, more intent on a story than on protecting herself. She should go home to her family. She could be safe, at least safer. She might even be able to survive this outbreak if they isolated themselves, her parents and her younger sister. What was driving her to follow the monster that she too could not see, that she too could not even imagine?

"U N," the driver announced, slipping the cab into a vacant spot on 44th Street. He looked at her in the rearview. "Forty dollars," he said, his eyes challenging.

Karen looked up sharply. "Your meter says $20." She stared back at him, eyes to eyes, her fingers grasping the bills in her wallet.

"Forty dollars today. Look at the streets. You want a taxi, forty dollars."

For the first time Karen realized how few taxis were on the streets. She opened her door, slipping a twenty and a five from her wallet. Then, with one foot on the pavement, ready to spring from the cab if he floored it, she said, "Twenty-five. Look at the streets. You want a cop, go find one." And out she jumped. She heard the driver yell something at her in Spanish, a curse she was sure, but she was already running across the pavement to the glass doors of the United Nations building.

Five minutes later Karen slipped into a press seat at the rear of the crowded auditorium where Dr. Robert Schultz was addressing emissaries and ambassadors, scientists and doctors. She knew that Schultz, as Director General of the World Health Organization, would have the latest information available through the WHO's rapid response component, the Emerging Viral and Bacterial Diseases Surveillance and Control unit and that here she would get the latest international information she needed for her follow-up story. Karen had been delayed by the traffic, and Schultz was now in the midst of his report detailing the steps the WHO had taken in Thailand and the course of the global outbreak. She flipped on her tape recorder and set it on her knee, then began hand notes on her steno pad.

The report was grim. Schultz knew he was speaking to a mixed audience, scientists and doctors mixed in with lay people, mostly ambassadors, who hadn't a clue how a virus or even a cell worked. He explained how a cell is a stand-alone entity able to eat, grow, and reproduce. In the human body, cells are continually replicating, he said, keeping bodily organs and tissues supplied with fresh, healthy, new cells to replace old, dying cells. A virus, on the other hand, is a minuscule particle about one-millionth of an inch long that inhabits the netherworld between life and death. A virus lacks the machinery to carry out the chemical reactions for life; it contains enzymes that can decode its genetic instructions only if and when it finds a living cell to inhabit. So it waits.

While a virus cannot function outside a host cell, Schultz went on, it can lie around waiting for a potential host to come along, sometimes for long periods of time. Coughed or sneezed, spit or bled out of a living host, the virus then waits patiently for a new victim to breathe in, ingest, or touch it with injured skin. Because this new Bangkok virus kills its victim in record time, it could have died out for lack of victims had it emerged in a rural village where isolation is a way of life. Once it killed all the residents, it would disappear. Unfortunately, the first known case of the virus occurred on the outskirts of Bangkok, population a quarter million and, like a flame in a hay barn, it spread with astonishing speed throughout the district, then to the city proper, then, disseminated by travelers like sparks in the wind, spread to other cities and towns in a global bonfire. The only way to extinguish the coming conflagration, Schultz concluded, would be to eliminate the possibility of its spreading to new victims. In the world we live in today, with populations so dense and people so dependent for their survival on goods transported from other places, doing that is nearly impossible. The virus couldn't have a better reservoir of victims.

Schultz went on to explain the process the WHO, the CDC, and other associated organizations were taking to develop a vaccine, and then he began taking questions from the audience.

"Dr. Schultz," a tall, graying man asked, "it is the WHO's single most important task to stay on top of these emerging viruses and take the steps necessary to contain them at their source. It seems to me that what we have here is a serious breakdown of your system. Have you determined who is to blame and have you taken the steps necessary to correct the problem?"

Schultz paused for a moment, staring at the questioner as if he were an imbecile. "The emergency response unit, headed by Dr. Martin Linquist, was sent from headquarters in Geneva to Bangkok within twenty-four hours of the receipt of the samples sent us of the first known cases of the virus. Within twenty-four hours of that, the Collaborating Centre on Viral Haemorrhagic Fevers at the

Centers for Disease Control and Prevention in Atlanta, which I might add also sent a team headed up by Dr. Ralph Sloan, confirmed what Dr. Linquist's preliminary studies had postulated, that this was, in fact, a new aerosol virus that likely occurred as a recombination of the avian flu afflicting poultry in that country and a more common form of human influenza. By the time the two teams arrived, the epidemic had already spread beyond the borders of Bangkok, primarily through air and rail travel, and insinuated itself on literally every continent on the globe. We couldn't have responded faster, but even if we could have, it was impossible to be fast enough."

"But why did it take so long to discover a problem existed?" another man shouted, standing and raising his hand as he did so.

"As you know, sir," Schultz said coldly, staring through the footlights on the stage, "the WHO does not have the power to send its intermediaries to a country without the permission of that country's government. It is my understanding that the samples sent to us were sneaked out of Thailand against government orders by a coroner concerned about what he was seeing. It was not until we had preliminary proof that intercession was absolutely essential and contacted the Prime Minister through his new Minister of Health that we received that permission. By that time, the Thai government realized that the disease was out of control and they were on the verge of contacting us. Unfortunately, by then, many days had passed. The WHO cannot be held responsible for the delays of the Thai government, sir. I suggest you address your question to the Prime Minister, if you can reach him. I believe he is on holiday in China." The audience gasped. Schultz turned from the man. "Any other questions?"

Another man stood. His bald head glistened in the light. "Dr. Schultz, what do we know about the lytic cycle of this virus?"

Schultz took a deep breath. "We know that the time this virus takes to attach itself to and enter the host cell, release its genetic instructions, recruit the host cell's enzymes to reproduce itself, and multiply enough to burst the cell is less than an hour."

"And from infection to death, how many hours?"

Again Schultz took a deep breath. "Less than forty-eight."

A woman stood, raising her hand as she did so. "Dr. Schultz, do you have statistics on the spread of this virus? What is the prognosis?"

Schultz's chin jutted forward, his lips in a straight, grim line. "The disease has traveled everywhere. The numbers of outbreaks are now so great that we no longer have the ability to track its course. Our affiliated agencies and organizations are overwhelmed. Reporting agencies can no longer keep current. Hospitals, which have traditionally been a primary source of data, are closing their doors, unable to care for the ill, their staffs afraid to deal with the disease or too sick themselves to help others. So we no longer have accurate numbers. The prognosis, as you can imagine, is dire. We believe that before the virus runs its course, unless a vaccine is created to stop it, millions..," he paused, looking at the audience, and the next thing he said was nearly a whisper, "...perhaps billions will die." He looked down at his notes.

The buzz from the audience rose. People looked at each other, shaking their heads in disbelief. From the back, Karen watched as people began talking over each other, their eyes wide. The woman two rows in front of her cried, dabbing her eyes with a tissue. Others were doing the same, though many tried to hide the fact by whisking tears away with their fingers. Above the clamor, a man in a white lab coat stood. "What course does the WHO suggest our countries take, Dr. Schultz?" he shouted.

Schultz waited for the audience to quiet. "Some will have...a chance to survive if three things happen. First and foremost, our scientists must develop a vaccine. That, I'm afraid will take time. Months probably. Two, when the vaccine is created, we will need the workers to produce serum and transport it to distribution centers where those who are still alive can be vaccinated. That will depend on the spread of the infection, whether we'll have the workforce to do it. Three, every country must quarantine its citizens in their homes until the virus dies out or subsides. This last requirement is perhaps the most important one and the hardest. The only way to avoid getting sick is to isolate oneself from others. Eventually, those already carrying the disease will die and the virus will exterminate itself. The virus's survival depends on contact with humans. No other species. It is specific to humans. Eliminate human contact, and it will die. But isolation of this sort in our world...well, you understand how difficult...."

The room broke into chaotic questions and yelling. "What will happen to human services if everyone is isolated?" a black man three rows in front of Karen shouted. "What will happen to water? Electricity? People need heat. And where will food come from if...." The room was bedlam. No one could listen to anyone else, for the roar of frightened, angry people would have overridden even a bullhorn. Almost immediately, people rose, hurrying to the exits.

Dr. Schultz remained at the podium watching people

fill the exits, but soon a crowd of delegates surrounded him. Karen could barely see the silver-gray top of his head above the throng. She wanted to speak to him, but she knew trying now would be fruitless. She wanted to ask if he had heard anything about Ralph Sloan. Perhaps he could tell her if Sloan was still alive. She decided to wait for the crowd to disperse. Setting her notebook and purse on the now empty seat beside her, she opened her laptop and waited for it to boot. She thought about the last few days, how much like an out-of-body experience this had all been, as if she, the reporter, were somehow removed from the world she was watching as it collapsed around her. And in her head, a familiar poet she had loved in high school dictated his lines into the headline she typed: "This is the way the world ends, this is the way the world ends, this is the way the world ends, Not with a bang but a whimper."

29

Patterson, Tuesday, Mid-October

Josh Stone watched the school bus pulling up to the front door, its air brakes squealing as it slowed. Stone had gone out long before the first bus was due, his wool jacket buttoned tight against the cold as he paced the sidewalk, wishing he knew what to do. Stone was certain that school should be cancelled indefinitely. He knew that it was only a matter of time before somebody's son or daughter brought the virus to Patterson. Parents in Patterson worked in Leominster, Fitchburg, and Worcester. Some even commuted farther east, to Boston. And Springfield, to the west. All it would take was one parent to bring the virus home, and the next day, the school's hot air system would pump that virus into every classroom. Stone was accustomed to runny noses, sneezing and coughing. Elementary schools are rife with germs that never cease spreading from one child to the next in hundreds of cycles during the course of a school year. He had been watching the kids unloading every day since last week, when his brother had given him the real story about what was likely to happen. His brother and he had talked a long time about what the virus could do, how easily it spread. Ever since, he'd wanted to inspect every child as he stepped down, hold each one by the chin and look for runny eyes or noses, ask if anyone had a sore throat or a cough. Send the kid home immediately if he suspected anything. But he couldn't do that. He couldn't just single kids out that way. Working parents depended on the schools to care for their kids. There were laws, and parents knew them too.

Laws, Stone thought. Protections of individual freedom might this time turn out to be the weapons that destroy us. Stone had watched avidly as Meet the Press reporters argued over the issue of quarantine. The Director General of the World Health Organization's warning had been in every Sunday paper, and now the litigious and the contentious from every activist group and every major newspaper had a new issue to intellectualize and debate. Meet the Press thrived on that. Stone hated the way the five journalists argued, often shouting over each other to make their points. None of them listened; they only expounded. Yet he had watched the show hoping that from their predictably oppositional stances he might be able to form his own opinion. He hadn't. Because the whole situation was impossible. By comparison, wars are easy, he thought. In World War II his parents had lived through rationing and blackouts and drafts because they had something to fight, a visible enemy, and a simple strategy—fight back. But you couldn't fight this thing, this virus, with sacrifices and parades and men with guns. At least the lay public couldn't. Maybe the scientists in their sterile labs might be able to feel they were doing something productive, but how could a people that prided itself on action suddenly retreat to their homes and wait out the disaster? Shut their blinds to the death around them? Wrap their own family members in plastic sheets and cart them outside to rot in their backyards? Remain passive while their food supplies diminished? He had come to school this morning as confused as yesterday. Now, stepping to the edge of the curb, he waited as the bus driver pulled up.

The door sprang open, and Josh looked up at the

weaseled smile of Mole Travers. "No problems today, boss," Mole reported, pulling the emergency brake up hard.

The youngest students, who sat in the front seats, swarmed down the steps and onto the pavement. Stone tried to catch a glimpse of each one, but they were like a cloud of blackflies, buzzing about him, then zooming away toward the school doors. He felt a growing sense of panic, as if at any moment he was going to miss the one child who could bring disaster to his school. He had to stop himself from ordering them all back onto the bus so that he could observe them one by one. But they were gone, clamoring into the school, shouting, running, pushing, rushing and dragging their heavy book bags along the polished floor. Inside, their teachers were already trying to quiet them, standing cross-armed at their classroom doors, chastising them for running, for shouting, for bumping and pushing. Stone's day was beginning, as it had for decades, first as a child himself, then as a teacher, and now as principal of Patterson Elementary. But for perhaps the first time in his life, Stone felt dread.

Michael Grant appeared at the top of the bus steps, and Stone remembered Michael's father from years ago when they were both boys. Michael was a ringer for his father, no question. Even the calm decisiveness of his movements was identical to his father's. Michael looked up to see him watching and smiled a broad, happy grin. "Morning, Michael," Stone said.

"Good morning, Mr. Stone," Michael said, stepping down from the bus. "My dad said to tell you he's going to miss his new farmhands." Michael smiled but looked down, embarrassed by the trouble he'd been in.

"Made you work, did he?" Stone smiled back, placing a hand on Michael's shoulder.

"Yes, sir. Every day."

"Do you good," Stone nodded, glad that he had parents like Rob to make his job easier. Michael moved on, and Stone's momentary distraction ended when he heard the boisterous laughter of Butch Jones above him. Butch filled the doorway, his hands grasping the frame, blocking others from exiting. Inside, his friends were pushing and shoving against him, trying to get out. Butch was immovable, and he used his rear-end to shove back. "That's enough, Jones," Stone ordered.

Butch looked down at him, considering Stone just long enough to let Stone know that when he let go of the doorframe, he did so in his own time. His smile was mocking beneath hard little pig eyes. Then, without even acknowledging Stone, he jumped to the bottom step, then off, shoving others in front of him aside. Stone was about to grab his shoulder, but Butch was out of reach in an instant, rocketing toward the school. Stone looked up to see Mole watching him with his snide smile.

"He's a hummer," Mole said, enjoying Stone's loss of authority.

Stone sensed the insult, but didn't rise to the bait. "Notice anyone with a cold today, Mole?" Stone asked, hoping against hope that Mole might have had the sense to notice.

Mole rubbed his face. "Maybe. Someone was coughing back there," he said. "Might have been that little Rainier kid. The one with the asthma?"

"Let's hope it's asthma," Stone replied, turning toward the school and making a mental note to check on little Robert. Behind him, he heard the bus doors close. A few children lingered along the sidewalk, and Stone gently herded them toward the entrance, asking a group of little girls about their class art show, two older boys about the weekend football game. Then, looking outside one last time, his hand on the glass door, Stone headed for the office.

Inside, a group of office staff and teachers gathered in a hushed and intense discussion behind the office counter. As soon as Mary Rogers, his secretary, saw him approaching, she said something and everyone turned, some looking guilty and upset.

"Okay, what's up?" Stone asked, already knowing. He prided himself on the staff he had assembled here over the years, a dedicated crew who worked hard for kids and who took their jobs seriously. One thing he had encouraged was openness. Stone was never afraid of debate, and he and his staff had done a lot of it over the years. Sometimes he had to convince a group that what he wanted accomplished was the best course, and sometimes a group or individual convinced him that he was wrong. That give and take was essential to education, Stone knew. Otherwise, the faculty became brain-dead. Brain-dead teachers seldom taught kids much about real life. If they couldn't think for themselves, how could they ever teach kids to do it?

Jeff Brown's red face exploded in anger. "I don't think any of us should be here," he said. "We should stay home, like that guy Schultz said."

"Yes," Mary Rogers agreed. "The President should order it."

"The President can't order people to stay in their homes," Milt Franks sneered. "This is a free country. Nobody is going to force me to go anywhere!" He folded his arms over his chest and pouted. Franks believed himself a champion of the Bill of Rights and never hesitated to use the Bill to win a political argument.

"The President would be undermining our basic rights," his wife Liz Franks agreed. "You let the President start telling us what to do and out goes the Constitution!"

"And the Bill of Rights!" Milt predictably added.

"Bullshit," said Jeff. His face grew redder. Jeff and Milt had often engaged in disputes about everything from tardiness policy to the war in Iraq. He was one of the few who would argue with Milt, because Milt could be nasty and pompous once he got going on a topic, and many on the faculty had walked away from arguments with him humiliated or frustrated by his condescending attitude. Brown, however, was well versed in debate and logic and definitely smart. Some of the faculty thought he egged Milt on just to sharpen his skills. "Don't use Dicto Simpliciter on me," he huffed. "Just because individual freedom is a good thing, you can't use it as an excuse to infect and kill your neighbors. They say this virus *depends* on human contact. Eliminate that and the virus dies."

"You let the President begin stepping on the Bill of Rights," Milt spit, pointing his finger at Jeff, "and it's all over. Democracy as we know it is a thing of the past."

"Aren't you jumping to conclusions, Milt?" asked Mary, always a tactful mediator. "Just because in a state of emergency the President temporarily has to override your ability to congregate with others doesn't mean that democracy is destroyed. When it's safe, the quarantine will be lifted and everything will go back to normal."

"For those who survive," Irene Lamb added grimly.

"How can you be sure?" Sally Maier said. She pushed her glasses up the bridge of her nose. They were always sliding down, and the habit had become unconscious to her. "The next thing, they'll be telling us what to wear and what we can read."

"Why are you arguing individual freedom when this flu may just make the argument moot?" Sarah Lewis declared. "You guys waste your time debating issues while the real issue gets ignored. Jeff is right. We are putting our lives on the line coming to work here. We should stay at home."

Then Jeff spoke again. "I don't care what any of you think. They should close the schools and quarantine people in their homes. People are dying by the thousands, and here we are in little Patterson pretending that it can't touch us because we're rural. I saw people on the news wearing surgical masks. Seen anyone here doing that? And look at us, for God's sake, stuck in classrooms with sneezing, coughing, spitting, nose-picking kids, any one of whom could be already infected. I'd take sick days if I could, but I can't risk that with my back needing surgery. So here I am, a sitting duck!" He grabbed his folders off the counter, sputtering, then turned and stormed off to his classroom, leaving the group suddenly silent.

Stone watched him go, then said, "He's right, you know. We're all in danger here. I want you to spread the word. I'll put it on the Faculty Memo today. I want to know if you see anyone exhibiting the symptoms—sore throat, coughing, sneezing, fever, exhaustion, anything...okay?" he asked, looking from one to the other. They all looked back at him, surprised that he agreed with Jeff.

The bell rang and the group broke up. Stone lingered at the counter, looking down the hallway and thinking that they were all crazy to be here. Teachers had no choice but to be on the front line, because the idea of closing the schools indefinitely was so preposterous, so consequential, that the President would probably wait until the very last ding-dong of doom before he ordered it. Not until he was ready to order quarantine. And when would that be and would it be in time?

At her desk, Mary Rogers picked up the ringing phone. "It's for you, Josh," she said, holding the receiver out to Stone. She silently mouthed the word "Superintendent."

"I'll take it inside," Stone answered, tapping the counter a few times before heading into his office.

He closed the door behind him and lifted the receiver as he walked around the desk toward his chair. "Stone here," he said in his usual curt tone.

"Josh, it's Brad," the superintendent announced, his voice worried and hushed. "Tell me," he said confidentially, "you have anyone sick down there?"

"It's too early for attendance, Brad," Josh said, thinking it just like this guy not to know the late bell had only rung a minute ago. Teachers wouldn't take attendance for at least ten minutes. Josh stood over his desk, fingering the spirals of the phone line.

"We've got trouble," Brad continued after a short pause. He took a deep breath. "At the high school. One of the Almont kids reported to the nurse a while ago. Said he was getting a cold. Couldn't stop coughing, he said. The nurse used a tongue depressor to look at his throat, and while she was peering in, he coughed on her. She's sure it's blood, Josh. Said it went in her eyes and that she breathed some in. She's hysterical."

"I don't blame her," Stone said, groaning. He knew Thelma Gleason well. She'd been born in Patterson and they'd gone to school together, though she was a grade behind him. She had kids in Patterson, her daughter Haley only in second grade.

"That's not the worst of it," Brad went on. "The kid has two sisters, both home sick today. So's the father."

"Both high school girls?" Josh asked.

"One is a sixth grader over at Almont Elementary.

The other is in middle school." Brad sighed. "Jesus, Josh, Thelma's sure this is it. The Bangkok thing. And we've got a family sick with kids in three different schools. The boy says his sisters started getting sick yesterday. That means a huge school population exposed. And the father works at Garrett's. Assembly line."

"Where's the mother?"

"She works for Verizon. All over the state, engineering work for cell towers."

"Is she sick too? Where is she now?"

"She called them last night from Pittsfield. The Four Winds Motel out there. She was sick. They can't reach her this morning. No answer on her cell."

"So she's the spreader."

"Probably."

Josh dropped heavily into his chair. "Why the hell are we holding school, Brad? We're asking for it."

"I can't cancel school, Josh. You know that. Even during snowstorms, I have to wait for the highway department to tell me yes or no. I called Leslie White to see if she'd order an emergency meeting of the school board. They'll decide."

"What did she say?" Josh wished just about anyone other than Leslie White was board chairman. She couldn't do something decisive if her life depended on it.

"She's called the others. They're meeting tomorrow night to..."

"Not now? Not tonight?" Josh wanted to slam his hand down on the desk.

"She can't get a quorum tonight. We've got to hold on to things until then." Brad didn't sound convinced, though.

"Listen here, Brad," Josh tried to control his anger, "Listen here. I've got teachers ready to walk out, they're so scared. And I don't blame them. They've got families. They don't want to die. When they hear about Thelma Gleason, they're going to start calling in sick. I might have to call school for lack of staff."

"You've got to hold on to it," Brad pleaded. "Just through tomorrow night. I'll come down there if you think it will help."

"Yeah, you come down here, Brad. Teach some of the classes where kids are coughing and sneezing. See how it feels to be standing in front of a class where germs are flying around you as you speak. Yeah, come on down. I'm sure that's going to help." Josh's sarcasm was so bitter that even he was surprised. He almost never lost control, but today, he just didn't care what Brad or Leslie White or Milt Franks or anyone else thought. Weeks ago, damn it, weeks ago he had worried about this very thing...suspecting an impending danger. Guessing what it might be. And here he was sitting in his office while all around him his staff, their families, his family, his own kids, all of them were being set up for disaster. He had guessed it and done nothing. He was furious. "I can't promise you anything, Brad. We'll see how things go."

A long silence ensued as both men tried to calm themselves before they said anything more. Josh watched the big black hands of his school clock tick ticking away the seconds. Then Brad sighed a tremulous sigh. "Who'd ever have thought..." Brad said, drifting off without finishing his sentence.

"Yeah, who would have?" Josh murmured, hanging up.

30

Patterson, Wednesday, Mid-October

"They're not going to school. I don't care what you say, they're not going," Terry slammed her closet door shut. "I've talked it over with Doc and he agrees."

Rob looked at Terry in wonder. She had come home from work hours ago in a panic. "Where are the boys?" she had yelled to Rob as she got out of the car. "Aren't they home yet?" Rob had watched her grabbing things out of the back seat, her jerky, angry movements, seen her slam the door with a vengeance. Poor Griz had run over to greet her and she had ignored him, storming toward Rob. He leaned on the shovel, almost amused at her intensity. As she neared, he made the mistake of smiling, a smile that vanished quickly when he saw her red eyes and puffy lids. She had been crying hard from the look of her.

"It's here, in Patterson," she wailed as she got close, her face twisted with despair. Rob let the shovel handle drop as he opened his arms to her. "Good God, Rob, what's to become of us?" she sobbed. "It's in the schools. Thelma Gleason was rushed to the hospital, and the boy is unconscious. The state police found his mother dead in a motel, and the whole family is down with it."

Rob could barely make sense of the story. A mother dead in a motel, a boy in high school, Thelma Gleason rushed to hospital. "Come inside," he said, rubbing her back and smoothing her hair. He looked at his watch. "The boys will be home in twenty minutes. They shouldn't see you like this." Using his arm to guide her, Rob urged Terry inside, sat her down in the kitchen and put the teapot on to boil.

"Now tell me again. What happened?" he said, setting a teabag in her mug and placing it in front of her. "We'll have some tea and calm down."

Terry's sobs had already subsided, but she now had the hiccups from so much emotion. "Wait," she said, "let me take a breath." She held her breath, and Rob could see her counting to ten, a trick she had taught him and the boys, one that never failed to work. Then she slowly let out her breath and swallowed. She wiped her face with the napkin Rob had placed by her cup and waited to be sure the spasms were gone.

"Doc got the call around ten from the hospital. Thank God he persuaded Dr. Long to set up isolation just in case. At least they were prepared when the EMTs brought Thelma and the boy in."

"Who is the boy?" Rob asked, his eyebrows knotted.

"An Almont boy. I'd never heard of him. McArthur or McCarthy I think. He came to school sick and by 8:30 or so had to go to the nurse. He infected Thelma, at least we think he did."

"So that's not a definite."

"He coughed blood in her face! It went in her eyes and she breathed it!" Terry was annoyed with Rob's calm. She could not understand how he could be so placid. "Just listen, Rob. Stop minimizing things!" Terry's eyes blazed, and Rob decided to keep quiet and ask no questions. He could put things together later. The teapot began to whistle, and he stood, reached for it and poured her a cup. As she went on, telling him about the boy's family and the chances that the kids had passed the virus on to classmates, he grew more concerned. He thought back to the last Selectmen's meeting and Patterson's chickens; he thought about his discussion with Josh Stone when he picked up the kids at school. He remembered how complacent he had been, thinking not here, not in Patterson. He had dismissed every clue. Terry was right about his minimizing the importance of the news from Asia, about emerging viruses, about everything. Even now, he was trying to find a way to minimize this Almont family and Thelma Gleason. He was pretending his family was safe when clearly they couldn't be...not if it was in the schools. And suddenly he thought of Michael and Chris in their hot crowded classrooms.

"Nothing at Patterson...." he said aloud. "Terry, nothing at Patterson, right?"

Just then they heard voices at the back door and Michael and Chris tumbled in, throwing their coats on hooks, dropping their book bags, laughing, and calling "Dad? Mom?" as they burst into the kitchen. Griz ran beside them, jumping so he could look them in the eyes, his tail wagging. Chris threw his arms around the dog's neck and wrestled him to the floor while Griz got in as many licks as he could, sniffing behind Chris's collar, washing his face with a long red tongue. "Yuck!" Chris cried, "Dog breath!" and then laughed and crawled under the table, hiding from the affectionate dog.

Later, as Rob and Terry watched the news, Rob became convinced that the whole world was going crazy. Michael Lane and Kristen Call, doing a special news follow-up, detailed the madness. They covered the supermarkets in New York City, their shelves emptied by people hoarding in preparation for a rumored quarantine. They showed the miles of cars packed in traffic jams along the thruways out of New York, Boston, Chicago, and San Francisco, and interviewed several families on their way to relatives' homes. They covered Home Depots across the nation, where people were fighting over the last tools and goods such as plastic, tape, plywood, hoes and shovels. No lumber store they could find, Call announced, had a generator to sell. Vegetable seeds had been wiped out at every Walmart, Home Depot, and Agway within 200 miles.

After the next commercial, NBC affiliates covered some of the events occurring nationwide to deal with the problem. A huge Mormon audience held vigil Sunday night out in Salt Lake City, the grounds of the Tabernacle thick with crowds waving candles from side to side in the darkness as if trying to catch God's attention. In San Francisco, Reverend Willy Grant held an all afternoon prayer gathering, thousands upon thousands singing hymns and swaying together in prayer. The camera panned the faces of men, women, and children, their faces streaming with tears as they looked up at the empty blue sky. Kansas City police had only just managed to quell a riot started by some anti-abortionists who claimed the outbreak was God's punishment for Roe vs. Wade. They tried to storm the Mayor's office and police finally used tear gas to disperse them. Another riot broke out at a grocery store in Naples, Florida as residents there flocked to stockpile groceries. The store had not opened because half the morning staff had called in sick, including the store manager, and the three who did show up were afraid of the looming crowds outside. When opening time came and went, the crowd began to shout and someone finally grabbed a metal signpost to smash through the doors. Once inside they began looting, using the store's carts to gather anything they could get. The store had been picked clean before the police even arrived.

Michael Lane, at his desk in New York City, faced the camera, his expression grave, and assured listeners that what they had just seen was only a sample of the news items coming across the AP lines, even as they spoke. "Stay tuned," Lane said. "And we'll take a look at what is being done to maintain public services."

After the station break, they began anew with the utilities. Northeast Electric had so many linemen absent in the last two days that they were unable to maintain the lines effectively. Wherever a tree branch had fallen on a line or a transformer had blown or any of a hundred other daily problems had occurred, Northeast had not had the technicians to go to the sites to fix them. One harried official explained, "We are thirty-six hours behind schedule." Thousands were without power, and more outages were expected as new problems arose. He asked the public to be patient.

Call interviewed the New York City fire chief, who explained that they too were having serious problems fully staffing firehouses. "We've got guys calling in too sick to show up," the chief said. And when Call asked if the fire department was capable of dealing with a major fire somewhere in the city, the best the chief could answer was "Depends on where it is".

Michael Lane then spoke with Arthur Jablonski, Police Chief for the City of New York. "We've got our people out there. The streets are safe," he said, but his attitude was half-hearted. He was desperately trying to appear in control, but the grim lines around his mouth and the circles under his eyes told the real story.

"We understand that you have had to curtail normal police activities, undercover and other details, to put your men out on the street to maintain a police presence," Lane said. "What about the terrorists? Can we continue to believe that the NYPD is keeping us safe from an attack?"

Jablonski looked down. "Well," he said slowly, as if choosing words carefully, "right now we're under a terrorist attack, aren't we?" The camera switched to Kristen's face. She looked totally confused. "You mean this is a biological attack?"

"Well," the chief said, "we're looking into that. Right now there's no way to know."

The network went to station break, but Rob and Terry were so stunned they continued to stare at the screen without speaking. Michael, standing in the doorway, said, "Dad, why is all this happening? Are the terrorists making everyone sick?"

Rob turned around in his chair. "You done with your homework? Let me see your math."

But Michael was immovable. "Dad, what's happening? Is this like 9-11?"

"Come sit with us," Terry said, realizing how frightened her son had become. She patted the seat next to her, and repeated, "Come on."

Michael settled himself down. Terry put her arm around him. "I don't think this is terrorism," she said. "Doc says that the virus got started in Thailand from chickens. Every country has it; it's not just us." She tousled his hair. "But you've a right to be scared, honey. Everyone is. We're just going to have to be careful."

"Careful how?" asked Michael.

"We're going to have to make a plan," she said. "Find a way to stay away from crowds of people, because that's how you catch it."

Suddenly Griz's cold nose was moving Terry's elbow aside, pushing his head under her hand. Michael patted the dog's long furry back. "Does that mean that we can't go to school?"

"No school?" Chris asked, just entering the room. "How come?"

"Of course you're going to school," Rob said. "That's the law." He looked over at Terry, saw her eyes flash in the semi-light of the television. Chris climbed onto his lap, curling up comfortably, his head just below Rob's chin. Then the lights flickered and went out. The family sat for a minute in the darkness, no one saying anything. Minutes later, the screen came to life again, the reading lamp flicked on, and in the kitchen, the dishwasher continued its cycle. Terry sighed with relief, but the relief fled quickly. That's how it's going to be, she thought. We're going to be sitting watching TV or reading or cooking and, out of nowhere the power is going to go off. Only when it does, it's not going to come back on. She looked at Rob and knew he was thinking the same thing. He gave her a long look and in his eyes, she saw her own fear.

Once the kids were in bed, Rob and Terry began discussing plans.

"Continue keeping things normal," Rob insisted. "We've only got one case out here."

"Six!" Terry corrected. "The family, that's five, and Thelma."

"One instance, I mean," Rob tried not to change his tone, though he hated it when Terry corrected him. "We can't get panicky. Tomorrow I'll go buy extra supplies—grain and stuff. And you go for groceries."

Terry knew she mustn't withhold information from Rob any longer. "I already have. I went to BJ's three times and to Stop and Shop as well."

"You what?" Rob shrugged, wondering how this could have happened without his noticing.

"Check my sewing room. And the cellar," Terry admitted.

"You just..." Rob was flabbergasted. "Like what? What did you buy?"

"I hope enough to maintain us for a few months," she said, "if we're careful."

Rob was already heading for the back room where Terry sewed. He opened the door and stood staring. "Jesus!" he said under his breath. She had stacked the room with staples, mostly dried foods. Bags of wheat flour. Sugar. Boxes of noodles.

"The canned stuff is downstairs. And some bins of potatoes, beets, that kind of thing."

Rob's astonishment showed in his eyes. "This must have cost thousands..." he trailed off, scanning the room again. "Where did you get..."

"My vacation account," Terry smiled. "Guess we're not going to Disney World this year."

Rob shook his head in wonder.

"There's nothing wasted, Rob. If nothing happens, if this is all just panic, well, I won't have to go shopping for a very long time. Except for meat. I didn't buy meat or frozen food. Just stuff that will last if the electricity..." Now Terry trailed off, for both of them quickly remembered the sinking feeling they'd had upstairs in the momentary power outage.

Rob put his arm around her shoulder. "You are something else," he said, his pride in her plain to see. Terry felt good. She knew he'd have scoffed at her a few days ago, but tonight, with all that was happening near the cities, she knew she had been right. She bet that by tomorrow night, things would be the same at the Victory and Stop and Shop and even BJ's. She had beaten the crowd; she had made her family safe.

"And the kids are not going to school tomorrow," she said emphatically.

"Now, wait a minute," Rob straightened. "We're not taking the kids out of school. They've already missed school."

"We have to," Terry insisted.

"No, we don't have to," Rob maintained, over and over again, and it wasn't until bedtime, when Terry slammed her closet door and flat-out stated that she didn't care what he thought, the kids weren't going in tomorrow, that he finally acquiesced. Doc had agreed that she should stay home for a few days while they saw what was going to happen next. Life was too precious to risk it for a few reading and math lessons. Rob decided he would be the first man at Agway tomorrow, loading his truck with enough grain for their animals to last them until spring. Five, six months maybe. He'd have to make more than one trip, but Charlie could help him.

"If we keep the kids home," Rob began...

"Not if," Terry interrupted.

"I mean, while the kids stay home, what else will we be doing? They say human contact is the source, so what are you thinking? We don't get near anyone? We don't go to meetings? It's just us? No one else?"

Terry had settled back on to the pillows. She pulled the blanket up to her shoulders. "Even tomorrow, when you go down to Agway, you've got to be careful. Don't get near enough to anyone who might then cough. Wash your hands the minute you get back. Don't touch your mouth or eyes until you do. Stuff like that..."

"What about Charlie?" Charlie lived in the center of Almont, in a rented room up over Mary Louise's house. If he were going to be in town every night, what good would it do to isolate themselves, Rob wondered.

Terry thought for a moment. "We've got to convince

him to come live in the garage loft. I can fix it up tomorrow. It's nice out there, and we have a kerosene heater. He's got to decide, Rob, one way or the other. Otherwise, we might as well let the kids go to school and keep on pretending we're safe."

Rob slipped under the covers, reaching for Terry and pulling her close. "I'm glad I married a nurse," he said, kissing her about her forehead and gently rubbing her back. "Even if we can't go to Disneyland."

Terry nestled against Rob's chest, and for a few minutes it was tempting to believe that nothing had changed, that life would go on as it always had for them, that no enemy was waiting for the sun to rise.

31

Patterson, Wednesday, Mid-October

Ethel Card held her husband's hand in what he thought was fast becoming a death grip. After dinner, they had decided to watch the Lane/Call special, and Ethel had snuggled close to Arnold on Laura Block's sofa. Everyone in the room stared silently at the images on the TV screen, occasionally looking at each other with increasingly horrified expressions. When the station broke for commercials, Arnold had to pull his hand away, holding it up so that they could all see the nail imprints on his palm. "Ethel's going to kill me before the bug does," he said mockingly, a smile crossing his face. The second of lighthearted teasing died quickly when he looked at Taylor. Laura rose to get the coffee that had been perking in the kitchen. Taylor leaned forward on his chair.

"You've got some guns, don't you?" Taylor asked, scowling.

"He's got an armory downstairs," Ethel said, pushing Arnold's hand out of her face. "If our house ever catches fire, it's going to blow sky high." She looked at Arnold crossly. "I've been trying to convince him to get rid of them for years."

Arnold folded his arms over his ample belly. "Not so foolish now, am I, Taylor?" He knew exactly why Taylor had asked the question, and realized his wife didn't.

"I'd say you're smarter than most," Taylor replied, nodding his head. "What've you got down there?"

Arnold sat back against the sofa, putting his hands behind his head and spreading his elbows wide. With one elbow, he tapped Ethel on the back of the head. "Hear that, girlie?" he said smugly. Ethel moved out of his reach, warning him to watch himself. "I've got several shotguns, most of them automatics. A Remington, a Benelli, two Winchesters. Oh, an old Weatherby, and that gun I bought last spring from Ed Sommes up by Otter River, a black powder .45."

Ethel sighed in disgust. "How many guns can a man shoot at one time, Taylor?" she asked rhetorically.

"My uncle left me his Colt .38, and I have three Smith and Wessons, one's a 38, the other two are 44s. That's it for handguns. They don't interest me much." Arnold was in his element, enjoying the increasingly pleased look on Taylor's face.

"Any 30-06s?" Taylor asked, his face hopeful.

"Yup. I bought a WWI Springfield years ago. Then a WWII Garand M1 at the gun show down in Hartford. And there's my dad's Enfield 308."

"No Remington?" Taylor asked, disappointed. His bottom lip pushed up over his teeth.

"Nah. That your choice?" Arnold deflated a bit, realizing he didn't have the one gun Taylor most wanted.

"Yep. A fine gun," Taylor replied. "Ammunition?"

"Not for everything. Well, some for everything, but plenty for the hunting rifles."

"You didn't mention the hand grenades," Ethel added, her voice stern. "There's a box of them down there from the service."

"Nam," Arnold added sheepishly. "I kept a few souvenirs." Arnold looked a bit guilty, but only a little. He was already assessing the need he might have to lob a hand grenade or two. He remembered a time when he had thrown a pile of them to keep the VCs off his injured buddy until the medics could reach them.

"Think we could go tomorrow and buy that Remington and a shitload of ammunition for it?" Taylor asked, looking at Arnold knowingly. Taylor had no gun permit for Massachusetts. He could use his Wyoming permit, but by the time the gun dealer shipped the gun to a Wyoming dealer and it was shipped back to Taylor, he knew it would be too late. He wanted the rifle now, and plenty of ammunition. Arnold could get it on the spot, and while both men knew they were "adjusting" the law, Taylor guessed that it wasn't going to matter in the long run.

"You've got to have a Remington?" Arnold asked.

"The best hunting rifle money can buy. I'll pay for it. We get through this, you can keep it."

"That's an offer I can't refuse," Arnold said smiling. "I've got plenty of weeks coming to me at Garrett's. What say I take some time off, girlie?" he turned to Ethel.

Ethel had been listening intently to what was not being said. Now she understood. The men were foreseeing a long-term problem, one that might require them to hunt for food. "I've been telling you to take some vacation for months now. It's about time," she said, moving back closer to Arnold.

Arnold moved his arm off the back of the sofa and sat forward. He paused, clearly wanting to say something but reluctant to do so. He worked his mouth, looking down at the carpet. Then he looked up at Taylor. "They think one of the guys is sick with it," Arnold said, "over in Building C." Arnold couldn't say the name. "It" was all he could muster. "It" had been worrying him ever since he came home from work, ever since Larry Weeks had called him over when the shift ended, the sun cold as they stood in the parking lot. He hadn't said anything to Ethel, because he knew what her reaction would be. He hadn't even thought about what he might do to protect himself. As if "It" were one of those forces of nature, like lightening or tornados, that people had to learn to live with because they had no alternative.

Taylor sat up fast. 'You have any exposure?"

"It's at Garrett's?" Ethel exclaimed. "Why didn't you tell me? It's at Garrett's?" Ethel voice rose two octaves. "Arnold, doggone you, Arnold, why didn't you tell me?"

"That's why," Arnold said, pointing at her. "She gets hysterical over things."

Ethel stood up. "You're not going back there, Arnold Card, until this thing is over. You hear me? You take your ten weeks now. That's it. No discussion." Her hands on her hips, she stamped the floor as if ready to charge.

Laura heard Ethel's raised voice and now stood in the doorway. "What's going on?" she asked.

"Just Ethel being Ethel," Arnold explained. He waved a hand at her as if that could make the angry woman disappear, then looked at the muted television. He was clearly embarrassed.

"You won't believe what this man just told us," Ethel began, but Taylor interrupted.

"I asked if you were exposed." His expression was stern.

"Naw. Don't know the guy. He works way over in C. He just got sick yesterday." Arnold was annoyed at Taylor's intensity. He heard the man's anger. He also heard and sensed his fear.

"Look," Taylor explained. "Laura and I were planning to isolate ourselves the minute this thing got out here. Once we do, we're not going to have any contact with anyone who might be a carrier. If it's at Garrett's, you could be one." Everyone in the room looked at Arnold. He squirmed noticeably. He could almost feel everyone draw back.

"Naw, couldn't be. The buildings are different. It's too soon."

"Well it's *too late* now," Laura said, trying to smooth things over. "Arnold isn't sick, but even if he was, we'd already be exposed. The question is, where do we go from here?"

Taylor knew Laura was right, though he had to fight to control his anger. How could a man "not mention" that he worked with someone who had the virus? How could anyone be so ignorant? But then he also realized that Arnold, like most people, hadn't even begun to make a plan. He was one of those people who let things happen to them, the kind he and his friends discussed back at the community in Wyoming. Never pro-active, but a good guy, nonetheless. And it would be Arnold who could solve the one problem Taylor hadn't been able to solve: guns and ammunition, because he knew they were going to need both. He guessed that Arnold had just realized the same thing. If the virus was going to run its course, if the scientists down at the CDC didn't come up with a vaccine, the dying was going to go on for months. Who knew how many? They'd need meat, and thank heavens Laura lived out in Central Massachusetts where there was still enough forest to support wild turkeys and deer, beavers and pheasant, raccoons and rabbit. Thank God she hadn't come from Boston or New York, where the survivors could be eating each other once the electricity went off and the freezers died.

"Tomorrow we get the gun and ammunition. Laura and I have stockpiled food. Ethel, you and Laura can go tomorrow and see what's still left so you can add to our provisions. Arnold, this is how it's got to be. Once we get what we need, we've got to cut ourselves off. Right now, we can do that by just staying here. No more Garrett's. No more meetings. No more Ladies Benevolent, Ethel, not even church. Once things get bad, when people from the cities come looking for food, when the people here who didn't have the sense to prepare themselves start raiding, we can close off this road easy enough. We'll lay some trees down across it. And we have guns."

"What?" cried Ethel. "You think we're in danger from people we know?" Ethel trembled with fear. "You can't mean it, Taylor," she said. "Our people are good."

Arnold put his arm around her shoulders. Her eyes filled with tears.

"People will do what they have to, Ethel," Taylor explained. "Once the food is gone, they'll come looking."

"We have to protect ourselves," Arnold said. "The alternative is..."

"We have to share," Ethel protested. "We have to help those who can't help..."

"They're carriers," Taylor interrupted. "That's the point. And if they're not carriers, we still can't let them steal our provisions. In no time, we'll be just like them, wanderers looking for food. You've got to decide, Ethel, whether you want to survive this..."

"I do," she interjected quickly, but then thought about what that meant. "I guess I do."

"Of course you do," Laura added. "We all do, and we will. We'll have staples. The guys can hunt, I can teach everyone what's growing out there that we can eat, and we can work together to survive. But we have to make a pact. That's what Taylor is saying. We have to decide that we can't let anyone in. They could be carriers, and even if they're not, we wouldn't have enough food. And we have to protect our stuff, at all costs. Because Taylor says the day is going to come when somebody is going to try to take it..."

Ethel moaned at the thought.

"...And we have to be ready, Ethel."

"We will be ready," Arnold said, hugging her closer. "Right, girlie?"

They spent the rest of the evening planning, making lists and looking at the storeroom where Taylor and Laura had arranged the provisions they'd purchased at BJ's. Five times they had driven there, Laura explained, loading her station wagon every time. "Some of the clerks got suspicious when we showed up three times in one day," Laura laughed. "The office checked my bank account to see if I really had the funds to cover all that food. It was weird, the way they treated us."

"How much did all this cost?" Arnold marveled.

"This and the stuff in the cellar and out in the garage?" Taylor smiled, knowing that the amount would stun them.

"Don't ask," Laura said, play-punching Taylor's arm. "It'll scare you. Suffice it to say, I'm broke."

"We'll get more tomorrow," Ethel said. "We'll go first thing, and we'll take the pickup. Arnold, how much do we have in the checking account?"

"Taylor and I will hit Buck Rub's, get him his rifle and me some more ammunition." There was something infectious about all this planning. They all felt it, a kind of excitement, despite the horror of what it meant. They intended to survive at all costs. The world might be a far different place when this was all over, but the four of them were going to stick together, and together they would make it through.

32

Grayson, Massachusetts, Thursday, Mid-October

Officer Bobbie Nye tried to ignore his phone that had begun ringing incessantly somewhere around 4:00 a.m. At first he thought it might be something wrong with one of his kids. His son lived up in Keene, New Hampshire with his family, and his daughter in Winchester, a hairdresser at the Shear Bliss Salon. His heart had raced as he turned on the light, searching dazedly for the phone hidden by the Newsweek he had been reading before bed. The magazine slipped to the floor and took his box of cough drops with it.

When he had picked up the receiver and recognized the familiar phone number on his caller ID, he'd put the receiver back down, turned off the light, and covered his head with his pillow. Down there, underneath the fresh smell of detergent and Clorox, he tried to make himself believe that he had a right to his day off. O'Reilly, down at the station, had no compunction about calling men in on their days off if somebody was sick and they needed coverage. And truly, Bobbie didn't mind the overtime. But yesterday he had been feeling poorly. He had fallen asleep in the middle of *Cops*, and if Clara hadn't wakened him, he'd still be in there on his recliner, snoring away. Then he'd had trouble getting back to sleep because, somewhere between dinner and Clara waking him, he'd developed a minor sore throat and a ticklish cough that had kept him sitting upright for a while, propped against the pillows and reading a magazine until his eyes had begun crossing and his lids closing down. As he thought about it, down there under the pillow, he wasn't feeling so good even now. So ignoring the phone seemed like a good idea until, after two hours of recurring sixteen-ring summonses, rings he'd counted while waiting for them to stop, Clara had said, "For God's sake, Bobbie, answer it. Tell them you're sick and can't come in."

He'd said "Ah, shit," and picked it up.

He pressed the answer button, putting the receiver to his ear, and dramatically croaked "Hello," hoping that O'Reilly would hear sickness in his voice and let him be. Instead, O'Reilly cursed and said, "Bobbie, where the hell've you been. I been calling for hours. Didn't you hear the goddamned phone?'

Bobbie's face flushed. "We had the ringer turned off," he lied. "Got some crank calls kept waking us up." Bobbie looked over at his wife, who shook her head in disgust, then flipped her flabby body over so that all he could see was the bare spot on her scalp where her hair swirled flat.

"You gotta' come in," O'Reilly pleaded. "We've got three men down sick, and the captain is worried about riots." O'Reilly was breathless, his age and extra fifty pounds getting the best of him. Bobbie could hear him panting.

"Riots!" Bobbie scoffed. "On a Thursday morning? You gotta' be kidding me." His eyelids were closing even as he spoke. He was already dreaming about how nice that pillow was going to feel over his head. Clara began snoring.

"You been listening to the news, you idiot?" O'Reilly said angrily. "Get the hell in here. We need you now. There's a line a half-mile long at Stop and Shop. The parking lot is jammed. Same at Victory and EZ Mart. Guys there are afraid to open their doors. You heard what happened down in Florida. We got it here."

"Man, I'm not feeling so good," Bobbie complained. "Got a sore throat and a...."

"Nye, if you're breathing, you get in here. We need police presence and we're short-handed. I'm not asking, I'm telling ya'." Bobbie heard the urgency in O'Reilly's voice, and something in him responded. He'd always wanted to be a cop, just like his dad and his older brothers. He'd always felt heroic, powerful, once the uniform was buttoned and his holster hugged his hip. Even directing traffic, Bobbie loved the power: making cars stop, letting them go, holding up his hand, hurrying people along. Just as hearing the National Anthem brought tears to his eyes, Bobbie sometimes got teary just thinking about himself as an officer of the law, an instrument of order and justice. So he swallowed hard. He'd had sore throats and coughs before, but O'Reilly had never ordered him in. This must be something important. He threw the blanket aside and swung his feet to the floor. "Yeah, yeah. Okay. I'm coming," he said. He heard his wife turning over behind him, but wouldn't look over his shoulder. "Half an hour," he said, pressing the off button while O'Reilly was still talking.

"What strength of character," she murmured, pulling the sheet up to her chin, her eyes still closed. "I think I'm getting your cold."

"Yeah, well, stay in bed," Bobbie said, pushing his feet into his trousers, and then standing to pull them up. He coughed, holding his hand over his mouth, then bent down to pick up his box of cough drops, stuffing two in his mouth and the box in his pants pocket. "Wish *I* could," he said, heading for the bathroom.

By the time Bobbie arrived at the station, O'Reilly was

frantic. "Four down," he yelled at Bobbie the minute he swung the glass doors open. "Take the cruiser to Stop and Shop. You're on your own. I'll send someone as soon as I can." In the yellow light of the station house, O'Reilly was looking a little sick himself. His clothes were rumpled, his face pallid. Under the fluorescents his thinning hair looked greasy. Before he could say anything else, the phone rang and Daniels, at the desk, called him. O'Reilly gave Bobbie one last desperate look of appreciation and turned, striding down the hallway to where Daniels held out the phone.

Bobbie grabbed the keys to the cruiser and headed out the side door to the parking lot. In the gray morning light the lot had a ghostly look that Bobbie found somehow comforting. Cruisers were parked neatly in their appointed spaces. The MacDonald's people just beyond the station were getting ready to open up, their lights dim in the morning fog. He heard sounds of morning traffic just beginning, the swishing sound of early birds' tires on the street. Far away the familiar squeal of the garbage truck stopping, the clang of emptied cans thrown back roughly onto the street. If he didn't feel so lousy, he thought, this would be a lovely morning.

Minutes later Bobbie rounded the rotary and sped off to the right. When he crested the hill, he had to blink in the dim morning gray before he could believe what he saw below him. The mall parking lot throbbed with cars and people. Even before he got close, he could see the ruckus near the door as people crowded the entrances, pushing against each other or ramming them with their steel carts. Two men were exchanging punches during the tug-of-war they were having over what must have been the last available cart, and cars were stopped three deep in the lot's traffic lanes, blocking other cars in their parking spaces. Cars idled two deep along the street as well. "Uh oh," Bobbie thought as he turned on the siren and flashing lights, pulled out of traffic and sped through the intersection.

He could not drive into the parking lot. Abandoned cars effectively blocked all entrances and exits. Bobbie called the station to alert them that things were out of control, asking for backup now and suggesting O'Reilly call the State Police. Parking his vehicle, he grabbed his nightstick and climbed out of the car, leaving the siren wailing. A few people looked his way, but his presence seemed to make no difference to any of them.

Bobbie hitched up his pants, patted his revolver, and trotted to the trunk, where they kept a bullhorn. Then he headed into the lot, trying to get to the crowd at the door as fast as he could. He had to shove people aside as he worked his way forward, and some of them thought nothing of shoving back, as if they didn't realize he was a cop.

"Move it," Bobbie spat, trying to contain the urge to cough. He raised his bullhorn and shouted, "Make way, make way, move out of the way!". The crowd did not part easily. People in front of him knew he was coming but didn't want to relinquish their spots. Bobbie saw the panic in their eyes as they turned, looked at him and turned back. He pushed, trying to stay calm although he knew he could do very little if the crowd got out of control. What was he to do? Shoot mothers and fathers trying to buy groceries?

As Bobbie neared the glass doors, he could see the frightened clerks inside standing far back from the glass. One was on her cell phone, and Bobbie figured she was begging for help. Their eyes met for a second, and Bobbie could see her relief that the police had finally arrived. "Little does she know," he thought, forcing body between the crowd and one of the doors. As he looked out over the crowd in front of him, he barely noticed that even more people were pouring in from the street, their cars abandoned haphazardly along the main road.

"This is the police!" Bobbie called into the bullhorn, not that the crowd didn't already know it. "I order you to disperse now. Go back to your cars. Move away from this door. That's an order!" He put his hand on his gun, his fingers teasing the snap on his holster. It was then that Bobbie realized he'd made a mistake. He'd pushed his way in and now he had no way out. He should have started dispersing way back, where the crowd was forming, not here at the front of the crunch.

Suddenly a man in front of him lurched forward, pushed from behind by unseen hands. He tried to stop himself by putting both hands on Bobbie's chest, pushing Bobbie backward against the door. "Get back, get back!" Bobbie shouted as the man tried to right himself, but again he was shoved, this time harder, so that Bobbie had to gasp to catch his breath. He began coughing in spasms, unable to speak. The woman to his right said, "Jesus, cover your mouth," and tried to wipe her face where his spittle had landed. She'd have backed away, but pressed from behind, she couldn't. He dropped the bullhorn and with both hands pushed the man away, swearing and spitting curses at the guy. The crowd surged into the small void he had created, pressing him still harder. He could barely move his right arm and from somewhere in the back he heard a kind of chant growing louder. "Let us in, let us in," the voices urged.

Bobbie forced his arm downward, the compression growing more intense. The people around him cried out, realizing they too were in danger from the constricting crowd pushing toward them. "Help," one elderly lady managed to gasp before she fainted, still standing, her head lolling to one side, her face blue-gray. Another woman tried to turn to confront the people behind her, but she couldn't budge. "Stop it!" she cried out. "Stop it, move back!" Her voice was a mere whimper beneath the growl of the crowd.

Bobbie's hand finally inched down to his holster. He snapped the cover and edged his pistol out, but he couldn't get his arm back up. His finger was on the trigger, but no matter how he squirmed, he couldn't move his arm. Finally, in desperation, Bobbie pulled the trigger, shooting downward in the hope that the crowd would respond to gunshots. A woman just to his right screamed as the bullet hit her foot. For an instant the crowd paused, giving Bobbie a chance to move his arm. He raised the gun above his head and sent two shots skyward.

But it was too late. The crowd surged forward, crushing Bobbie into the glass. He could smell mothballs on somebody's sweater, the stale smell of beer on someone else's breath. He felt bones pressing into his arms, and someone was standing on his left foot. The man in front of him had black hairs growing from his ears. He had passed out, his chest pressed to Bobbie's by the force of the mob behind him. Bobbie tried to take a breath, but he couldn't. There was no room for his chest to expand. He could feel the glass flexing behind him and knew it was only a matter of seconds before it would shatter.

As the glass burst behind him, Bobbie felt a momentary, heavenly release. Falling backward onto the blue tiles of the supermarket floor, Bobby gasped for air and looked to see others falling forward, many of them unconscious, onto the floor around him. Bobbie thought about his wife, sleeping soundly in their sweet smelling sheets and the soft, gray light of the morning, how peaceful it had been, just as hundreds of legs and feet overtook him, stepping on him in their race to the shelves.

33

Patterson, Thursday, Mid-October

Josh Stone raced down the hallway of Patterson Elementary, the school nurse close at his heels. They'd been summoned by a frightened student who burst into the office crying, "Come! Help! Mr. Franks' room!" and then turned on his heel and disappeared. Marie Lasky already had her bag in hand as Josh burst from his office. Josh was a weekend runner, a former sprinter in college, and his legs were long and muscular. Short, plump Marie was no match for him. Still, she did her best to keep up, her bag flailing her right thigh with every step. By the Marie turned into Milt Franks' room, Josh was already kneeling over the small boy who lay on the floor, his hand on the boy's head. An anguished Milt stood beside him. "He just collapsed," he explained to Marie. "I called him to the board to do a problem, he stood, swayed, and fell."

Marie knelt beside Josh, her fingers feeling the boy's neck for a pulse. "His heart's erratic," she said, "but he's breathing." Just then the boy moaned, trying to turn to his side. He was a bony child, all elbows and knees, and his hands were half-hidden by a hand-me-down shirt too large for him. "Not feeling so well, honey?" she crooned to the boy. His eyelids fluttered. "That's okay, we're going to get you some help." The boy's mouth hung slightly open. "Look," Marie said quietly to Josh, pointing to the trace of blood along the edge of his lip.

Josh had his cell phone in hand, dialing 911. He looked

in the direction of her pointed finger and quietly groaned. "Patterson Elementary," he said. "This is Principal Stone. I've got a Robert Koontz, aged 9 or 10. Fainted in the classroom. Nurse said his heart is erratic; the boy is breathing but unconscious."

Marie watched Josh out of the corner of her eye, one hand soothing the child's forehead, the other holding his thin wrist, monitoring his pulse.

"What do you mean delay?" Josh hissed. "We've got a sick child here."

Marie looked at Josh, her eyes wide with fear. "Tell them we think we've got a case," Marie said, omitting the words she could not say aloud.

Above her, Milt jumped back, his eyes wide. "I'll get the kids out of here," he said, turning. Children had gathered in a huddle to watch with horrified interest from the back of the room. "Let's go, let's go," Milt ordered, flapping his arms as if to herd geese. Reluctantly, the children began moving toward the door, murmuring "What's wrong, Mr. Franks?" and "Is he going to be all right?" in a worry of whispers.

Josh spoke softly to Marie, his hand over the mouthpiece, "All the ambulances are out. They're being deluged."

Marie wondered what she was supposed to do now. Get a stretcher from the office? Put the child on one of their cots? Leave him on the floor and cover him? A chill overtook her as she realized she was touching someone who had the dreaded virus. She was surprised at her calm. She should be running away as fast as she could, but as she looked at the helpless child on the floor, she knew she wouldn't desert him any more than she would her own babies. "He's burning up," she said. "Ask them..."

"Listen here," Josh spat into the phone. "This is a public

school. We've got a boy down with the virus who needs help and we have 300 other kids who need protection. We should take precedence!" Marie watched her boss's face grow red with anger. Josh stood, walking away from them toward the teacher's desk. "Who is this, anyway?" he growled. "Well, let me tell you something, Dan Coe, I'm going to let the parents of every kid in this school know who delayed getting this infected boy out. I don't care who else is ahead of us in line, you get the EMTs here, now! You understand?" Josh turned, looking down at the still kneeling Marie, his eyes flashing while he listened. And then Marie was shocked to hear his low snarl, "Fuck you!" He snapped off the phone and shoved it in his pocket. In one fluid movement he strode back to the boy, bent, lifted him in his arms and headed for the door. "I'm taking him. Let Mary know. Call his parents. I'll be back as soon as I can."

Five minutes later Josh pulled into the emergency driveway at the back of Almont Hospital. Three ambulances idled at the entrance, their crews nowhere to be seen. Josh parked the car beside the third ambulance, ran around to the passenger's side, and lifted the limp child out. A minute later he was inside, shocked to find the emergency room throbbing with coughing people seated on lobby chairs and on the floor along the wall. A few stood, looking as if they wouldn't be standing much longer. One seemed asleep; his mouth hung open and a thin line of spittle ran down his chin. Another sagged, her knees bent slightly, as if at any moment she'd begin sliding down the wall. Several others stared, emotionless and bleary-eyed as he passed. Josh recognized two, both from Patterson. He was almost certain the woman with the long blonde hair had two kids at Patterson.

Josh could hear hurrying footsteps and voices in the hallway beyond him, but the front desk was abandoned. Just then two EMTs burst through the steel doors, rolling an empty stretcher ahead of them toward the exit. Josh stepped in front of them. "Where's the admitting nurse?" he asked. "I've got a sick boy here." He held the child forward in his arms, half-expecting them to sweep him onto the stretcher and race back.

The men looked at Josh as if he were an alien. The taller of the two, an Hispanic with a short black moustache, spoke as he swerved around him. "Take a look," he said, his hand sweeping the room, "they're all sick." The two men rushed through the exit doors and disappeared outside. A second later, Josh heard the wail of their siren, a sound not unlike the desperate cry of a calf brought down by wolves.

He pushed his way through the heavy steel doors, being careful to protect Robert's lolling head from banging against them. A nurse heading his way spoke sharply, "You can't come in here..." but Josh paid no attention. He was looking for a doctor and a place to lay Robert down, and even though she stepped in front of him, he kept moving, knocking her aside. "Stop!" she cried. "You can't come in here." But to no avail. Josh kept going, turning right into the first brightly lit room he saw.

A surprised doctor and nurse looked up from the man they were examining. The man coughed and Josh knew immediately what the nurse quickly wiped away from his lips. He watched her gloved hand toss the bloodied cloth aside and looked up to their masked faces. "I need help!" Josh spoke calmly, even though his heart was racing. "This is one of my students. Collapsed in a classroom." He saw the moment's hesitation as both nurse and doctor made the decision; then the doctor nodded and said, "Lay him on the table there. We've got no more beds."

Josh gently laid the unconscious Robert down. His little body couldn't have weighed more than sixty pounds, and as Josh pulled his arms out from under him, he grieved to see how frail the child was.

"Step aside," the doctor ordered, insinuating himself between the boy and Josh. Josh was only too glad to do so. Now that Robert was safely at the hospital, a wave of sadness swept over him, and he had to fight to keep the tears back. He walked to the doorway, pulling out his cell phone to call Mary. "Did you reach the Koontzes?" he asked as soon as she answered. Both parents were on their way, she told him. "How's Robert?"

"Not so good, I'm afraid," Josh said, looking at the doctor's broad back and little Robert's legs splayed on the table. "Mary, this is what I think we have to do. I've been exposed, so I can't come back there. Marie has too, so she should go home or come here. You have to ask Milt about what happened before, whether he touched the boy, if any of the kids did. You know what I mean. Anyone with possible contact, send them home. Tell Donna she's now acting principal."

"You can't stay here," the doctor said over his shoulder. "Not unless you're already sick." He never turned around, but his tone was stern. The nurse, though, did turn, looking at him with huge, sad eyes.

"Tell Marie..." but Josh had no idea what to tell Marie. What advice did he have to give? He had no idea where he was going to go. What could he tell her? "Tell Marie they say she can't come here unless she gets sick. I don't know where I'm going, but as soon as I do, I'll call you."

Mary's voice was soft on the phone. Josh knew she was near tears. "They've got to close the school, Josh. They should have before. Now you're..." and her voice trailed off as she fought for control.

"I'm okay, Mary," Josh insisted, though he didn't really believe it. He had been too close to the boy. In the car he had breathed the same air. He had touched him. His hands tingled as if germs were already attacking him. He had an overwhelming urge to run for the bathroom, to scour his skin, rip off his clothes. He would not let himself think of his wife, his kids. That was more than he could handle, the possible loss of his family, leaving them to fend for themselves.

As he leaned against the doorframe, the steel doors burst open and a young couple, seeing him there, raced forward.

"Where's Robert, Mr. Stone?" Mrs. Koontz cried. "Where is he?" Her husband had already looked inside the room, recognized his son's thin legs, his dirty Nikes. He pushed past Josh, a suppressed "Eawwww" issuing from his throat. The woman let go of Josh's jacket, following her husband into the room, and Josh, taking one last look, strode toward the steel doors just as the EMTs burst through with yet another patient.

Outside in the parking lot, Josh leaned against his car and sobbed. He had no idea what to do, what might prevent the virus from getting him. The sense of helplessness was overpowering. None of this should have happened, he thought. I should be home with my family, safe from this thing. Now look what I've done. Now I'm one of the sick ones. He opened his car door and slipped into the driver's seat, pushed the key into the ignition, and turned it. The car hummed to a start, idling smoothly. He ran his hand along the leather of the passenger seat, thinking about his wife's warm thigh resting there. He smelled the leather, the new car smell that he loved. He looked at the gray November sky, the clouds hanging low on the horizon. Then he put the car in reverse and backed up.

Retracing his course along 2A toward Patterson, Josh noticed that Joe's Deli was closed. He slowed, trying to read the badly-lettered white sign, the word "Temporarily" misspelled "Temperarily". A mile later he reached the Patterson Inn, the corner where normally he'd take a right toward Patterson Elementary. Suddenly he realized he could stay in one of the motel rooms along the back. Sam, the manager, would wonder why he was renting a room, but he'd just ignore the quizzical look and pay for three or four days with his credit card. Sam would probably think he and his wife had had one heck of an argument and would forever after wonder about his marriage. The thought prickled. Then Josh stopped himself. Forever? What a laugh, he thought bitterly. What forever? He glided into the parking lot and pulled up short before the peeling office door.

Sam was at lunch, the girl at the counter said while picking something out of her lipstick. A surly girl, Josh guessed. He took the keys she handed him and drove to the parking space outside #12. Opening the door, he cringed at the smoke-dank smell of the darkened room. Cigarettes, he gagged. How he hated that smell. Before closing the door behind him, he glimpsed two double beds. Josh felt the wall for the light switch and looked about the room. Like most motels, it was impersonal but clean. It seemed somehow appropriate to his situation. No bag, no clothes, no reading material, no anything. He was an escapee, a man on the run. Too bad he had to bring his body along. Then he threw open the draperies and stared into the gray day. His was the only car in the lot except for a battered old Chevy with a red heart painted on its hood. The girl's, he bet. He saw a black pickup pulling in, its blinker flashing, and across the road, the assemblage of DeMarco Brothers' trucks and backhoes. No one moved about the lot.

The sky looked ominous, as if a snowstorm might be coming. Josh searched his memory. He hadn't paid close attention when Channel 5 did the weather. His wife had been babbling on about getting stuff ready for the Senior Lunch, some presentation she was to give, his kids were still upstairs dressing, and he heard the familiar patter of their hurrying feet. Josh remembered the coffee perking and English muffins toasting, and he could see his wife's perfectly oval face in the warm yellow light of the recessed overheads. He could see her black hair hanging loose and straight, how the lustrous black strands glistened, even inside the house. He fought back a sob. He hadn't paid attention to the weather. Stupid. He hadn't paid attention. Because he thought it was just another day, back then. He should have known, but he didn't, and now he couldn't be sure if it was going to snow or not.

Josh was never a man to engage in self-pity, but he had to fight hard to ignore the ache he felt constricting his heart. His chest was so tight he found it hard to breathe. He sat on the floral coverlet, his fingers running across the quilted squares, still staring into the empty lot and at the shining hood and grillwork of his car. Ten, maybe twenty steps, and he could be outside, into the car, and on his way home. He could smell the familiarity of his house, the warm, clean air. He could see Lila turning as he opened the door, her smile wide, her soft, brown eyes welcoming. He shook his head as if to shake away the images and thought about what he was going to say to her. Then he pulled his cell phone from his pocket and dialed.

When Lila answered, she knew immediately that something was wrong. The flatness of Josh's voice made him sound lifeless. "What's wrong, sweetie?" she asked.

Josh told her all that had happened. Lila listened without

interruption, her occasional "uh-huh"s and "oh"s and "oh, baby"s soft and sorrowful. Her hand was weak as she held the receiver, and she had to pull out a kitchen chair and sit down because her legs began to tremble.

"I want you to pack me a suitcase, enough for four, maybe five days here. Grab that *Hornet's Nest* I'm reading and that pile of books I've set aside in my office. A pad and some pens, so I can write. And pack me some snacks. I'll order my food in, but just stuff in case I'm hungry. Pajamas. My razor. And my pillow, Lila. Put that in so I can dream I'm home, okay?"

"Come home," Lila tried to insist. But she knew as well as Josh that he couldn't. Not yet, not until enough time passed to be sure. Josh was right, as he always was. He was putting her and the kids first, but right now Lila wished there were no kids to consider. Then she could make him come home, and she could nurse him if it was necessary. And she could die beside him if that was God's will, because she couldn't imagine life without him.

"I'm in #12. I want you to deposit the stuff outside the door. I'll be waiting. *Don't come in, Lila.* Just leave the stuff. As soon as you're gone, I'll go out for it."

"The bus is going to be here in a few minutes," Lila said. "As soon as I pack your stuff, I'll call, so you'll know I'm coming. Okay?"

"Promise me you won't try to come in," Josh insisted, knowing that everything in Lila would tempt her otherwise.

Lila imagined the motel, imagined Josh standing in the window, imagined how warm and secure his arms would make her feel. "I promise," she said. But as she set down the receiver, she wondered if some promises were impossible to keep.

When Becky and Raymond emerged from the school bus, Lila already had Josh's suitcase in the car. They burst into the kitchen just as she finished filling a grocery bag with food. "What are you doing, Ma?" Becky asked, picking at the elastics of her braces. "Ouch!" she said absentmindedly.

"Where are the cookies?" Raymond asked, holding the empty jar toward her. "This was full this morning, Ma. You binging on tollhouses?" Raymond smiled, teasing.

"I'm taking them to your father," Lila answered, preparing herself for the inevitable explanation. She looked at Becky and saw Josh's forehead and eyes. She looked at Raymond, who was suddenly very quiet, and saw Josh's hair and the set of his jaw.

"Why?" Raymond asked, sensing something important. His father was down at the elementary school, so why would he need food? He'd be home in another hour. Becky looked at Raymond, then at her mother. She watched her mother fight back tears, the way her mother had of swallowing to gain control, of grimacing to keep her face from crumpling. She had seen that look already more than she ever wanted to...when Grandpa died. Then Grandma.

"Dad's been exposed," Lila said softly. "A boy at school." She took a deep breath and looked at them. "He's going to be fine. But he doesn't want to take any chances. So he's going to stay over at the Inn." Lila hoped her false bravado rang true. She straightened, grimacing.

"How long?" Becky wailed. "Why not come home?" She was suddenly fearful. He father had never not come home. Not once. Who was going to help her with her French? Who was going to tease her about new boyfriends?

"You heard her," Raymond reprimanded. "Just to be safe. Right, Ma?" But Raymond knew instinctively that things just weren't that simple. The word was all over the middle school, and a lot of kids had said their parents were thinking of keeping them home tomorrow. And he'd heard the school committee was holding an emergency meeting tonight because there were a lot of absences. A lot of empty seats in his classes. Even gym seemed empty. They'd had to double up some classes for lack of teachers. And because they couldn't get enough substitutes, his principal, Mrs. Mallory, had monitored a temporary study hall in the auditorium most of the day, her sour disposition wrecking the fun they thought they were going to have with some unsuspecting substitute. You didn't tangle with Mallory. She'd eat you alive.

"I'm going over right now," his mother said, picking up the bags.

"Let me take one," Raymond said, grabbing for the fullest.

Lila tried to protest, but Raymond wasn't going to let go. She could see Josh's tenacity in Raymond's face, the strength she loved so much in her husband in her eighth grade boy. She let go of the bag. "We're coming," he said. And that was that.

Lila made her call to Josh, then, and a few minutes later the three of them pulled into the Inn. The Honda slowed as they searched the numbers on the doors, then stopped before #12. Lila could see Josh standing in the window. He looked the same as he always did. Neat. Clean. Handsome beyond words. She jumped out of the car, everything in her urging her to make him open the door and let her inside. But she had the kids, and they too were jumping out of the car. Becky cried, "Dad!" when she saw Josh, and started to run toward the door. But Raymond grabbed her arm. "You can't," he said, looking sorrowfully at his father. "You promised."

Lila opened the trunk. "Raymond, Becky, help me unload this stuff." She tried desperately not to look at her husband. She knew that if she gave in, all of them could be lost. Not just her, but Raymond and Becky too. Out of the corner of her eye, she could see Josh leaning into the window, both hands against the glass. His face was a torment. Becky had run to the window, her hands on the glass. He was mouthing something to her. "Daddy," she cried. "Daddy, I'm so sorry."

"Help me," Lila ordered. Raymond was beside her, lifting the suitcase out and then walking to set it down at the door. She carried one bag. He came back for the last one. She returned to the car and closed the trunk. Then it was time to say goodbye.

Raymond stood beside his sister, fighting back tears. Josh, on the other side of the glass, was mouthing, "It's okay. Everything is going to be okay."

Lila said, "Come on, guys. Get into the car. You'll see your Dad in a few days. You can talk to him on the phone as much as you want. Come on. Get in the car."

Becky's sobs had subsided to sniffling. Raymond's face was white, but dry. Lila urged them backward and into the car. Then she returned to the glass, where Josh stood quietly.

"I love you," he said, his eyes brimming.

"I love you too," Lila said, reaching her hand up to touch his through the glass. What else was there to say? Lila knew that this might be the last time she saw her husband. How could she let him know her sorrow? How much he meant to her? How empty life would be without him? How much praying she was going to do from this minute forward that he wouldn't catch the virus. Or that he would somehow survive if he did? People seldom have words for such times, and even if they do, they rarely can say them.

Josh watched Lila turn and walk back to the car. He could see Raymond's dim figure in the front passenger seat, and after the car backed up and turned, he watched both of his children waving to him as the car pulled slowly away. For a long time he stood at the window, reliving the sight of his family, wishing he could see them again, hoping that maybe they'd forgotten something. But when the car didn't return, he walked to the door, opened it, and lifted the suitcase inside. Then he went back and picked up the bags. With his left foot, he kicked the door closed behind him. He was exhausted and emotionally spent. All he wanted to do now was take a shower, change his clothes, and close his eyes. He'd order dinner later. A steak, maybe. And blue cheese dressing on his salad. Baked potato. Sour cream. And he'd read. And watch TV. The night would pass, somehow. He'd make it pleasant. And tomorrow? Well, he'd see about tomorrow when it came. Until then, he'd just relax. Get a good night's sleep. His body ached, and his throat felt sore. A good night's sleep would be a blessing.

34

Boston, Friday, Mid-October

Governor Derrick Taggert had not had a chance to comb his hair, wash his face, or even straighten his tie from the time he arrived at the State House this morning until this stolen moment when he stood before the mirror in the bathroom adjacent to his office. He looked carefully at his face, running his hand along his cheeks and chin, feeling the stubble growing there, then opened the cabinet door and removed his Schick. A quick shave would make him feel a whole lot better, he hoped, and look better too, for he was going before the cameras in less than half an hour.

Taggert did not often request network time. Once, when an ice storm had coated the state, weighing down and then breaking power lines, turning secondary roads into skating rinks for cars, he had called a state of emergency on the six o'clock news. His speech had been brief, and then he had rushed off for a photo op down at the DPW, where bucket loaders filled sander after sander with road mix. They'd had a few traffic deaths by then, idiots who thought that their SUVs were immune to ice. And a few die-hards who had to get to work, despite the roads being impassable. Taggert had assumed a careful, worried demeanor for that speech so that no one could accuse him of minimizing the gravity of the situation and so that the newly created widows would always remember their fifteen minutes of fame. But that was then.

This time, he didn't have to fake anything. In fact, he

had never been so worried in his whole life. The updates being passed to him by his people, the calls coming in from all over the state, and the desperation of the entire Boston health department were sobering enough. He already had several key people sick, friends who had supported him throughout his career, and yesterday his wife's family lost two cousins and an aunt. The worst of it was that funeral parlors would no longer pick up bodies or process them because the undertakers, the ones still healthy, were afraid to touch the corpses. That job was being shifted to Civil Defense and the National Guard, because everyone agreed that decaying bodies had to be disposed of immediately, though no one was sure how long the virus remained infectious on a corpse. Unfortunately, the director of Civil Defense and Unit 576 of the National Guard wanted assurances that their people would get Biohazard field suits that the state did not have, at least not in the quantity needed. The program set to begin at midnight was tentative at best.

Taggert had spoken with the President around 3:00 p.m., indicating that he planned to call a State of Emergency for Massachusetts and asking how the President planned to provide aid. Riordan was sympathetic. He was always sympathetic. Riordan was a likeable guy. But he didn't have anything worthwhile to offer because already the nation's emergency systems were stretched to the limit. "Look, Derrick," Riordan had explained, "the kinds of things you need, field suits, oxygen helmets, protective supplies, just don't exist in the numbers required to protect the forces going out to collect bodies or interacting with the public. We can send you some, but it will be a fraction of what you're asking for. And yes, we can truck foodstuffs up there, but we can't feed the people of your state and all the others calling me for anything but the short haul. A few days maybe. That's if we can find people to transport it. I'm on the verge of calling a national state of emergency myself, and when that happens, you guys up there in New England are going to be on your own."

"But Massachusetts is being hit especially hard," Taggert had argued. "We're the ones with an international airport *and* a seaport. What's Nebraska got but cornfields?" In this respect, Taggert was justified. The states along the Atlantic, the Pacific, and the Gulf were experiencing the worst outbreaks and consequent disruptions of everyday services, while interior states with primarily rural populations continued to function somewhat normally. California was the worst nightmare, Taggert knew, having spoken to California's governor just after lunch. California's situation would make Taggert want to throw up his hands, he had told Governor Lefkowics, who advised that he'd better think of something fast, because he was only a few days behind California in level of emergency. Taggert had gotten off the phone more depressed than ever and sat for some time staring out the window at nothing.

"Close the schools, shut down all non-essential government offices, request that the private sector do the same," was Tim Palermo's advice, and Tim was his main man, the best counsel he'd ever had. Tim might not have Derrick's prestigious Harvard education, but he was five times smarter and twenty times wiser, Derrick knew. When Tim spoke, Derrick listened and most of the time, he took the advice and thanked his good fortune that he would never have to run against Tim in an election. Tim had been begging him to take this action for days, and now Derrick knew that his failure to act faster might have exacerbated things.

Then his friend Jack Forziadi, over at the Department of Ed, had called at nine to say that the schools were rife with infection, kids dying, for pete's sake, in the nurse's offices and teachers threatening to strike unless the governor called off school. Derrick had to act, and he had to act today, Forziadi said, or he was quitting at 5:00. Forziadi meant what he said. The man hadn't wanted the job in the first place, back when Taggert won the election. But Taggert had begged and insisted that it was Forziadi's civic duty to help Massachusetts raise its standards, crack the damn unions, and fix the broken busing policies. If Forziadi had any ethical integrity, Taggert had wheedled, he had to come work for the state and make things better for all children. Taggert had saved the trump card, "better for all children," until last because he knew that the one thing that made Forziadi tick was improving the lives of children. Forziadi had grown up in Roxbury and knew the streets and the traps laid there to waylay lives. He had risen above poverty and apathy to become valedictorian at Yale and a Rhodes Scholar, but he had the passions and dreams of Martin Luther King, his childhood idol. Taggert's trump card had worked. Forziadi had signed on, albeit reluctantly, and the state's schools had reaped the benefits. Until now. Now Forziadi was threatening to quit, and between Forziadi and Palermo, Taggert saw no other course of action.

Over the buzz of his razor, he heard Monica tapping lightly on the door, calling him. "The make-up guy is here," she said. One? Taggert wondered. Last time, they had sent three. "Be right out," he called back, unplugged the Schick and replaced it in the cabinet. He looked at himself in the mirror, feeling only slightly better but considerably more professional.

A minute later, Taggert sat back in his chair, a towel

wrapped around his collar and beneath that, a barber's apron protecting his shirt and pants. Standing directly behind him, the make-up guy patted his face with foundation cream and began rubbing it in. Derrick was so pre-occupied with the notes his assistant had just typed for him that he paid no attention to the fingers gently working his cheeks unless the man's arm or hand blocked his vision. Then he watched the pale, almost blue-white skin, the hint of wrist veins, and the deep lines of the man's palms. "Where is the paragraph on quarantine?" Taggert asked Monica, who was re-reading her notes beside him.

"Down here," she said, leaning over to point to a paragraph at the bottom of the page. "You wanted to fix the wording, but never got around to it." She offered him her pen. Taggert crossed his legs and wrote a sentence above the printed line. It was in the silence that ensued that Taggert noticed the breathing of the man above him. A minor wheeze, he thought, straightening. But the man was fat. Taggert could feel his belly pushing against the back of his chair. Fat people often wheezed. They got out of breath easier than most, he knew, and this guy probably had to hurry down the long hallway to his office if he wanted to keep up with Monica. He read the improved paragraph. "Okay, this does it. The suggestion that we might have to quarantine, but that as yet the situation does not warrant it. Closing the schools and all non-essential services." He looked at Monica and said, "Let the feds deal with the mail." Then he turned back to his papers. "Working on temporary program to process the victims who succumb by instituting a 933 dial-up. With cooperation of the National Guard. Good. Inform them that our police and fire departments have been adversely affected. Higher than usual absentee rates. Consequent delays in response time. Yahdah, yahdah, yahdah."

As he scanned the last page, his pen running along the margin, he almost missed it. The first one was so minor, so quiet, he was only dimly aware of the man behind him who was running a comb through his hair with one hand while he reached for the hair spray with the other. It was a kind of "ach," almost whispered. The second was louder, two syllables: "Ah ach". Derrick lifted his head from his reading and looked straight ahead. On the third, the man used his comb hand to cover his mouth. The third was polysyllabic: "Ah ach ach ach. Eh ach ach." And it was loud, because the man could not stop coughing. Taggert jumped up from his chair.

"God damn it, you're coughing all over me," he snarled. Monica looked up, shocked.

The make-up man's eyes widened. Being admonished by the Governor might mean his job. The state troopers outside might burst in any minute. It was just a cough. "I'm sorry, sir," he whined. "I couldn't help it. I just..."

"Get the hell out of here," Taggert shouted, backing away and wiping his suit with his hands as if some invisible substance had spilled there. Monica stood, taking the man's arm and leading him forward, toward the door, her face frightened. "Please, come with me," she urged, and the make-up man scrambled to throw his sprays and vials quickly into his satchel before he was yanked away.

"I'm really, really sorry," he implored while Monica tugged at his shirt. The man's face contorted. He looked like he might cry. "I didn't mean to..." but then, Taggert could see he was seizing up, convulsing, and suddenly the fellow let loose with a barking, gurgling, fluid cough that seemed to last forever. He bent forward, gasping for air and, too late, covered his mouth. Monica jumped back, letting go of him as if he sizzled.

"Get out," Derrick screamed, and at the door he could see Joe, the security guard, appear, his hand on his holster. He looked at Derrick and then Monica. "Get out, get out, get out," Derrick shouted, but Monica couldn't move. She wasn't going to touch him either. The man shook his head, embarrassed, humiliated, frightened. "I'm sorry," he said one last time as he shuffled away, his wide back filling the door as he left. Joe nodded at the doorway. "Everything okay?"

"Shit," Taggert hissed, hurrying to the bathroom to wash his hands. Monica just stood there, not knowing what to do. "You're on in five minutes," she said. "Shall I tell them to cancel?

"No, no," Taggert called over his shoulder, scrubbing his hands under the hot tap water. "I'll be right there." He stood, looking in the mirror at his made-up face and wishing he could wash it right then and there. Instead, he resolved not to touch his face or hair or clothes until the broadcast was over, and then he'd fling himself into the shower and stand under the pulsing jets for the next twenty minutes. Now he had a job to do. He had to make the speech. He had to let the people of Massachusetts know what he was doing. He had to get those kids out of school and keep them at home. He had to convince people they should avoid public places. He had to shutdown non-essential government services until further notice. He had to do what he could to curtail the spread of the disease. And he would. He would. But the first thing he was going to do after the broadcast was dump his clothes in a plastic bag and take a shower. Then he could start off fresh.

35

Patterson, Monday, Late October

"Good God, Rob, what were you thinking," Terry wailed, holding out the Almont Daily News and shaking it so that the single pages began slipping loose. Terry's face was red with anger and frustration, and she was out of breath from running to the barn.

"What'd I do?" Rob asked, setting his shovel aside.

"What did you do?" Terry mocked, "What did you do? You just told the towns of Almont, Patterson, and Ogle that we stockpiled enough food to last us until June, that's what you did!" Terry shook the paper in her hand, then threw it down and crumpled to the floor in tears. "Rob, how could you be so naive?"

Rob suddenly realized the consequences of yesterday's encounter. He had let Nose Bartlett in yesterday when the reporter had stopped by. Nose had driven out to get his opinion on closing the schools and the town's plan for the flu emergency, and the two of them had sat talking on the very hay bales Terry now leaned against. How stupid! What an idiot! He hadn't been thinking. He hadn't been careful. But he hadn't expected Nose to come by, to come sidling into the barn where he was stacking dried goods. He'd nailed up shelves along the wall of an unused horse stall, using some old lumber from up in the loft, and then he'd organized alphabetically the boxes Terry had bought. He and Charlie had been admiring the results of their effort when Nose appeared outside, calling "Hello? Anyone here? Rob?"

Rob had responded, "Over here" before thinking and then he and Charlie couldn't have run outside looking guilty when they realized who it was, or yelled, "Stay where you are; we're coming." Nose would have been even more suspicious. So they waited for Nose to walk in and Nose had surveyed the stores of dried foods, whistled through his buckteeth and said, "Looks like you guys are prepared for the worst." There wasn't much Rob could do then but smile sheepishly, pull the light string, and hustle Nose back outside. But Nose had seemed reluctant to budge. Even in the half-light of the stall, Nose was taking inventory.

"Damn," Rob said. "Nose Bartlett." But all the damns in the world weren't going to change the fact that now everyone knew they had food. It probably wasn't going to make a difference right away. People could still get some supplies. Some of the trucking lines were still functioning and some factories were still producing, mostly the ones in the mid-west, where things weren't quite so bad. But sooner or later, and Rob's guess was sooner, people would have to go out looking for food, and once they picked their neighbors clean, they would remember. Rob wished he'd built the shelves in the cellar, a place he could protect far better than the barn.

"Yes, Nose Bartlett, Rob. Why did you let him know?" Terry had stopped crying now, though her eyes were red and her eyelids still puffy. She wiped her face with her hand and straightened up, pushing back against the hay bales.

"It just happened, Terry," Rob explained. "He caught us red-handed. I had just finished the shelves." Rob sat down on the bale next to Terry, putting his hand on her hair and petting her the way he petted Griz, soft and gentle. Griz, who had been sleeping in the corner, lifted his head and woofed, his long, furry tail sweeping up floor dust. Then he rose and walked over, smelling Terry's hair and licking Rob's hand at the same time. Rob bent down to pick up the paper, searched around for the page with the article, and sat up to read.

"Where are the boys?" Terry asked. She put her arm around Griz's neck and hugged the dog. "You good boy," she intoned, patting him. Griz dove in for a quick lick of her face. "Yuck," she cried. "Dog kisses!" And hugged him some more.

"Says Patterson and Almont town leaders have failed to prepare for this kind of emergency," Rob said disgustedly. "Yeah, what were we supposed to do? Like we're not dependent on everyone else. You'd think it was still 1760, for pete's sake." Rob shook his head and continued reading.

"He's getting a story," Terry said. "Got to have someone to blame. Why not the Selectmen?" Terry thought how much she disliked Nose Bartlett. She remembered that back when she was a teenager, Nose had decided she was the woman for him. He had stalked her, appearing everywhere she went. She'd go to the basketball game with her girlfriends and Nose would be waiting outside for her. She'd sit with her friends in the bleachers, and Shirley or Carol would soon be poking her, whispering, "Look behind you." And he'd be there, his knees practically in her back if he could get close enough. He'd try to pretend he was watching the game, but she knew that the minute she looked away, Nose's nose would be pointed at her. Nose Bartlett. Worse than dog kisses. Sometimes at night, back when she was growing up, she'd look out the window into the darkness and know that he was down there watching. She'd caught the glint of his glasses once. The living room lights were on downstairs while her parents watched TV, and just that little bit of light thrown onto the lawn had caused a reflection as Nose peered up into her window. She'd opened her window, stuck her head out, and shouted, "Get out of here, Nose, before I call my dad," and heard the bushes rustle as he skulked away. But he'd be back, she knew, when she wasn't watching, because he was a creep and creeps don't give up that easily.

Later, when she and Rob decided to go steady, she'd hoped Nose would sniff out some other poor girl, though she didn't truly wish him on anyone. She started wearing Rob's senior ring on a chain around her neck, and every time Nose passed her in the hall and every time she sensed him watching her in class, she'd purposely fondle the ring, sometimes pressing it to her lips as if she didn't know anyone was watching. And eventually Nose had given up. It took several months, but finally the word around school was that Nose was nosing after Sarah Lewellen, and Sarah had threatened to deck him if he didn't leave her alone. Terry, Shirley, and Carol had laughed when they heard that. Deck Nose. Punch him in the Nose. The Nose knows. Enough of the jokes, but they didn't stop for a long time, because all three girls had been so relieved to be let alone. Though they never said so, all three instinctively distrusted the kid. There was something that was "not right" about him, but back then none of them had the experience or the education to know how right they were. Now, here he was again, disrupting Terry's life, nosing around her barn and publishing information that she had tried so hard to keep secret. And Rob had let him! She couldn't get over the irony that he had gotten back into her life through Rob.

"Where are the boys?" Terry repeated.

"Down with Charlie, checking the fencing," Rob answered absent-mindedly. He was still reading the paper, this time the headline story. "You see Almont Memorial is closed?" he asked. "Have you spoken to Doc today?"

"He says it had to. They have no more beds and can't do anything anyway. Doc says Dr. Howard died yesterday. And Elsa Greet, that nurse you had when you broke your leg? Her too." Terry moved up onto the hay bale with Rob, trying to read the paper at the same time.

"He want you to come in?" Rob said, still reading.

"He told me to stay home and take care of my family," Terry said, slipping her arm inside Rob's. "I'm sorry for before."

"I was stupid," Rob apologized. "That guy..."

"I know," said Terry. "That's how he is."

Terry stood, slapping loose hay off the back of her legs. "Think I'll go make an apple pie," she said, thinking aloud.

As Terry went up the path to the house, she was surprised to see two cars in their driveway. Shirley Young stood by one, the driver's door open. Carol Green was walking back from the front door. "Oh there you are," Shirley waved, and Carol turned to look.

Terry waved back as she walked toward them.

"We thought you weren't home," Carol said as she drew closer, "but your car is here." All three looked at Terry's Jeep as if it had suddenly appeared.

"Yup," Terry smiled. "We were down in the barn. Come on in," she said, beginning to unbutton her jacket. The women followed her to the side door and then inside the warm kitchen, where all three shed their coats and hung them along the line of hooks on the wall.

While Terry filled the teapot and set it on the stove, Shirley reached inside Terry's cabinet for cups. Carol slipped three napkins out of the napkin holder and folded them, one at each place at the kitchen table. The two guests were as at home in Terry's kitchen as in their own; the three had been best friends for years. Shirley's farm was next door, and Carol three farms down, in the opposite direction. Carol was the oldest. She had five teenagers, one ready to graduate in June. Shirley and Terry grew up together, but Shirley had married just out of high school and her girls were older than Michael and Chris, her boys younger. Ellen was a senior too.

Once the tea was poured, Shirley wasted no time getting to the point. "I see Nose is at it again." That meant both of them had already read the article. "Is he ever going to leave you alone?" Shirley asked, putting her hand on Terry's.

"He's just doing his thing," Terry said, her tone flat. She wasn't going to let on how upset she'd been and hoped that by now her eyes were back to normal.

"But now people know..." Carol said, stopping short. "Listen, Ralph and I have done the same thing. So has Shirley. We've both been preparing for this, just like you."

"I didn't tell you..." Terry began, feeling guilty because she hadn't told her best friends. In her race to gather supplies without being noticed, she'd been afraid to tell anyone.

"I didn't either..." Shirley said, holding her hand up to stay Terry's apology. "I knew from the news, you know? But back then, people didn't seem to think it could happen here. Everyone just went on like they were immune."

"Then we bumped into each other at BJ's," Carol laughed. "Shirley had groceries piled into two carts, and she was dragging one and pushing the other, so I knew..."

"...Because Carol had one, and each of her kids did too. It looked like a parade heading to the register..."

"...I used my real estate tax account..."

"...She spent three thousand dollars..." Shirley howled, "Three thousand, Terry!"

"I've got five kids," Carol explained, as if they didn't

know. "And they eat everything in sight. And Ralph does too."

"So Carol tried to look like she buys groceries like that all the time…" Shirley went on, slapping her leg. "She's looking, you know, this way and that, and asking me how my kids are, and saying we ought to go see that movie with Brad Pitt together, and all the while the register is going ka-ching, ka-ching, ka-ching."

"…And I'm dying, because Shirley's watching all this stuff being put into cartons while I'm talking…"

"The same thing happened to me," Terry squealed. "You know that writer up by Ethel Card, that herbologist? Well she was there once when I went…" and then the coincidence struck her, "…and I bet she was doing the same thing, now that I think of it. She was with this cowboy guy…"

"…A cowboy?" Shirley's eyes grew bright. "Boots and hat?" Shirley had only been divorced a year, but already she was looking hard for a father for her kids.

"Boots and hat!" Terry laughed. "They had loads of stuff too. And they were looking at my carts with a kind of knowing attitude, as if we were all in on some secret."

"Well, we are," Carol said. "And now we have to decide what to do. Because Ralph says we've got to make our alliances and promise to stay clear of town and other people, you know, because…"

"…Because it's all around us," Shirley said quietly. For the first time, she looked scared. "I've told my kids they have to stay at the house, at least for now."

"Ralph says that if we make an alliance, we all have to promise total isolation…no meetings, no going shopping, no nothing…"

"We're ready," Terry said. "We had Charlie Grange move his stuff into the barn, and he's staying with us. And I would have pulled my kids out of school even if the Governor hadn't done his thing last night..."

"Me too," Shirley said.

"I pulled mine out two days ago," Carol said "as soon as that Almont boy..."

"He died," Shirley said. "His whole family too."

"Did you hear about Josh Stone?" Carol asked, her hand on her heart.

"Josh Stone? What?" Terry sat up straight, leaning forward. "Josh? At Patterson?"

"Yesterday," Shirley said.

"One of the kids at Patterson. Right in class. Josh took him to the hospital in his own car. No one at school knows where he is. He couldn't come back because..." Carol purposely let her statement die.

"His wife's a wreck," Shirley said. "The kid died. Little Bobby Koontz."

"Selma Koontz's boy?" Terry felt tears rushing to her eyes. Selma Koontz was one of the nicest people in Patterson. She'd do anything for anyone. "Poor Selma!"

"So this is it," Carol said, leaning back in the kitchen chair and folding her arms over her chest. "Either we're all in this together or Ralph says I'm to say goodbye. Because after today, I can't talk to any of you, or your kids, except on the phone."

"And that won't be for long," Shirley said gravely. "Already there are outages all over New England."

"Police and fire, too," Carol added. "Ralph says both are down to skeleton forces. No pun intended." She looked at her two friends. They looked back silently. All three realized the enormity of their situation, though none of them could even begin to imagine how their world was about to change. Terry looked out the window. She could see the two boys playing ball with Griz, their jackets flapping in the breeze, their happy shouts muffled by distance. What would their world soon be like, she wondered. So different from her childhood, safe and happy. She'd always had hordes of friends and games to play, places to go and things to do. She'd loved school and the life there. So had they, until now. Now they were going to be stuck home with her and Rob and Charlie, no one their age to play with, no school life to help them learn how to get along. She'd have to teach them their math and science, develop their tastes in literature. "My God," she said aloud. "How am I going to teach the kids what they need to learn?" Terry looked helplessly at Carol and Shirley.

"We're going to have to start our own school," Carol said. "Not right now. Not until...." she paused, "...not until things settle down."

"What about the Jamesons and the Curleys?" Shirley said, thinking about the neighbors between Carol and Terry. "Should we go see them? See if they want in?" Shirley looked doubtful. She didn't much care for Lisa Curley, and Ella Jameson was not very friendly. "Do we have enough food for them?" she added, wondering whether they too might have had the foresight to prepare and whether she wanted to share her stores if they hadn't.

The others were silent, thinking. Finally Terry said, "It'd be easier if we had this whole section of road." She was thinking that eventually they might have to barricade it somehow, to keep others out, to keep themselves safe.

"Ralph thought so too," Carol said. "He said that once things get bad, people might come looking. That article..." she trailed off.

"Nose Bartlett, damn him," Shirley hissed.

"Let's meet tomorrow," Terry said. "All of us. Kids too. Let's decide as a group."

Terry reached her hand out across the table. Carol looked at it oddly for a second, and then put her hand on top. Shirley slapped hers down last. The three women sat there for a second, their hands joined, listening to Michael and Chris laughing on their way to the house. Just before the back door opened, all three squeezed. "Deal," Carol said

"Deal," Shirley added.

"Deal," Terry finished.

36

Patterson, Monday, Early November

Rob and Charlie rose within minutes of each other, both without alarm clocks. Life on the farm adjusted its routine to the seasons, to the rising and setting of the sun and moon, to the coming and going of weather fronts. Dormant times, growing times, harvesting times. Now, in early November, harvest time was over. Apples were stored in the cellar or long ago sold at the local market. Hay was baled and stacked in the barn. Winter rye grass had already been planted. Chores at the farm evened out to preparing the land for winter, turning the fields under, repairing fencing, maintaining the barn and other outbuildings, and getting the farm machinery in shape for spring. It was time to go hunting, to put up some deer meat for the winter, smoking or drying it for later, when prey was scarce, the snow too deep.

This November morning was solemn and dark. Clouds hung low on the horizon, boding snow. The trees, leafless now but for a few oaks and the evergreens that dotted the perimeters of the pastures, swayed in the incessant wind. Dried leaves hurried about the ground, blown to the familiar places where they gathered every year in piles along the stone walls, against foundations, and beside the steps to the back porch. November is a sorrowful time, a time of loss and of endings, and Rob and Charlie felt it as they met in the kitchen. Charlie came in from his new room above the barn and Rob came down from upstairs, where the boys still slept. They sat down to the breakfast Terry made them, not saying much.

What was there to say in these times? The news was grim. Charlie had sat with them last night as they watched the six o'clock news and a Dateline special. Both were a litany of death tolls and power disruptions, mini-riots and hospital closings. Even the broadcasts themselves had been shaky, with segues into special reports that never appeared, the screen frequently going blank while someone at the network fumbled with switches, the anchormen looking exhausted and rumpled. Depressing stuff, all of it. The war on terrorism had all but petered out, at least as far as new reports were concerned. The terrorists were just as sick as everyone else. A few hardliners still continued to believe that America was the enemy, strapping themselves to bombs and blowing their body parts into the same bloody soup as the unfortunate others who happened to be nearby. Some had convinced themselves that the U.S. was responsible for the epidemic. Most fanatics, however, had switched causes and begun praying in large groups that gathered in Mecca, Jerusalem, Rome, or Calcutta, despite warnings that they were spreading the disease even more.

By 6:30, Rob and Charlie had already had two cups of coffee, so there was no excuse to procrastinate going out. They donned their coats and headed to the barn. Rob piled his chain saw, a can of gas/oil mix, and other equipment into the back of the pickup while Charlie milked their two cows. Before they left to cut firewood, they fed the chickens and let the livestock out to pasture. They left the egg gathering for the boys, who by now were just beginning to move about upstairs.

Minutes later they bumped along the cow pasture, avoiding the jutting New England rocks that cropped up everywhere as they headed toward the stream. It was cold in the truck, and both men had their jackets buttoned tight. Neither spoke, but Rob had switched on the radio, and now Charlie turned the dial, trying to find a station with some country music. "Where's that damn WINK," Charlie muttered, getting only static. Charlie rolled the dial past several newscasters, finally leaving the radio tuned to a talk show that neither wanted to hear. The stream ahead was the border between Rob's and Henry Jameson's land. Rob wanted to clear a sixty-foot section so that the cows and sheep could more easily get to water on hot summer days. This particular piece was just north of Rob's pond and, unlike the upper stream, was shallow, with a flat, sandy bottom, a good, safe place for calves with their mothers.

Rob brought the truck to a halt, and both men climbed reluctantly out of the protection of the cab into the chill November wind. Tree limbs groaned in the soughing wind, as if aching with arthritis. The stream had turned to an icy mush along the shoreline, in pockets between rocks and land, and among the still straight rushes. Within weeks that mush would harden to ice, growing thicker each day and extending to meet the other side by Christmas. Rob stood for a long moment beside the bank, studying the dark gray trees lining the water's edge. He pointed to a downed birch, its trunk lying in the water, its branches stripped by beavers. "Let's grab that before we leave," he said to Charlie. They turned back to the truck to pick up chain saws, gas can and leather gloves. Soon the area reverberated with the roar of saws on wood, their racket punctuated by the whoosh and earth-shaking thump of falling trees. Rob felled them; Charlie cut them into two-foot sections. They filled the pickup and then bumped back along the pasture with their first load, through the gate and into the barnyard, where they off-loaded the firewood in a jittery pile.

Rob walked into the house and saw the boys were putting on their jackets and boots. "You guys ready?" he asked, pleased to see them up and ready for work. Griz stood beside them, ready for action. He whined and he woofed, making sure everyone knew he was not going to be left behind. When Rob opened the door, he shot for the pickup, his tail pointed straight behind him, his head held low. He was up and into the truck in a heartbeat, standing with his paws on the sidebars as if he couldn't understand what was keeping everyone. Once in the truck, the boys shivering and bouncing hard against the steel floor of the truck bed, Rob headed back to the clearing. In his rearview mirror, he could see Griz staring back at him through the glass.

"Look at that," Charlie pointed. Rob had already noticed the black and white patches moving among the trees on the other side of the stream. "What's Jamesons' holsteins doing down here?" Charlie asked aloud, though he knew Rob wouldn't have any better answer than he would. Jamesons' land ended at the stream, but his cow pastures were way out beyond their log cabin house. This was forest, not intended for livestock.

"Must've broken down the fencing somewhere," Rob said. "You want to herd them back?" Rob and Henry Jameson were cordial neighbors, both having farmed this area their whole lives. And though the Jamesons were not what he would call close friends, they made a practice of cooperating with each other when they could, and this was just such a time. "We can cross over there at the narrows," Rob said, pointing to where the opposing banks were closest and a few large rocks made good stepping stones to the other side.

"Might as well," Charlie agreed. "Give me a chance to clear the sawdust out of my nose." Charlie had the look of old man winter; his hair, eyebrows, and even his eyelashes were thick with sawdust.

"If you don't look like a termite's mama," Rob guffawed, putting the truck in park and swinging the door open. "Let's go, boys," he called to Michael and Chris, who huddled shivering behind the cab. "We're going to do some cow herding."

Rob grabbed a length of rope, Charlie an old blanket. "Grab a couple of those switches from the pile over there," Rob told the boys, pointing to saplings lying in a heap where they'd been cutting. "We get across, spread out and send those suckers back home," Rob said, guiding the boys toward the crossing. Griz ran back and forth, his tail wagging as he tried to decide which way they were going so he could get there first. Charlie led the way, leaping dramatically from one rock to the next, steadying himself wildly, his arms making huge circles as if at any moment he might fall into the likes of Niagara Falls. Griz leaped past him, enjoying the fun. Michael followed, waiting at each rock for Charlie to finish his show, then following him. Chris jumped after his dad, and Rob held out his hand each time to steady him, since Chris had little of Michael's agility.

The holsteins looked suspiciously at the strangers and cautiously at their large dog. A few at the front began to turn, nosing those behind them to get moving. The men spread out on either side, with the boys and Griz in the middle, and soon the herd was quietly walking back toward Jamesons' barn and pastures, mooing at the arrogance of strangers but cooperating for lack of a better plan.

When they moved into the clearing, Rob pointed to the

broken fence and ragged electric line lying on the ground. "Wonder what scared them?" Rob called over to Charlie.

"Beats me," Charlie answered, running a little faster to keep the herd heading left toward the barn. He shook the old blanket, snapping it in the air. Griz began to dance left and right, hoping for a stampede. The herd obediently bore left.

"Michael, run ahead and ask Henry or Ella what they want to do with these vagrants," Rob ordered. "Don't spook 'em, though. Just cut right around Charlie and head up there." The roof of the Jamesons' log cabin was just visible over a long, rolling knoll of pastureland. Once Michael was far enough from the herd, he began loping toward it, skimming over the rough land with easy grace. Griz raced beside him. Rob, Charlie and Chris continued their slow pace behind the herd, which moved as if it had all day to get where it was going.

Far off in the direction Michael had run, they heard the Jamesons' dogs barking, carrying on as if hey were being invaded. They yowled, they hooted, their din carried lively in the wind. Rob listened for a dogfight, but heard only ruckus.

"Those labs are good watch dogs," Charlie mused. "Some day I'm going to get me a yellow one. Sweetest dogs there is." Charlie pulled a handkerchief from his back pocket and blew sawdust out of his nose.

"Not better than Griz," Chris corrected him. "Griz is smarter than any of 'em." He looked at Rob. "Tell Charlie what he did, Dad." He looked up at his father expectantly, but just as Rob began to regale Charlie with his latest Griz story, he spotted Michael and the dog at the top of the hill. Michael was running full out, this time clumsily; Griz ran beside him, trying to stay even with Michael's ragged path.

"Dad, Dad," Michael shouted over the wind. "Stop. Dad!" Behind him, frantically barking, ran the three Jameson dogs. Rob marked their progress down the hill, wondering what in heaven's name was the matter.

Michael slowed only when he could actually reach out to touch his father. His arm was extended, and Rob grabbed it and pulled him in. Despite his exertion, Michael's face was white, and he gasped between sobs. Tears filled his wide eyes, almost glassy with horror. "Dad," he cried, "Dad. Something's wrong up there. Mr. Jameson..." and he began sobbing again.

Rob hugged him and patted the boy tenderly on the back. "Here, here," he soothed, "it's okay. Slow down. Tell me what you saw." Between Michael's sobs, the best Rob and Charlie could gather was that Michael had run first to the house and, getting no answer, then to the barn. There he'd seen Mr. Jameson lying face up just inside the doors. Michael had called to him, but Mr. Jameson didn't answer. There was more. Something about dead chickens, pigs running around, and Mr. Jameson's pajamas. Rob didn't linger to put Michael's story together, for Henry clearly needed help. "Let's go," Rob said. Charlie was already twenty steps ahead of them.

As the four reached the top of the knoll overlooking the Jamesons' house and barns, Rob could see immediately that something very strange was going on. Several two-hundred-pound pigs wandered the front yard, rooting through Ella Jameson's flowerbeds, tilling up the ground with their snouts. Near the barn door was a destruction of feathers and blood. Getting closer, Rob saw that the back door of the house was wide open. Just then, a pig strolled out, stood briefly on the porch, and then picked her way down the steps to the yard.

"Michael, you and Chris take the road and run home. Tell Mom to call 911. Go!" Michael needed no persuading, but Chris lingered, reaching out for his father's hand, his eyes wide with fear. "Go, Chris. It's okay. We'll get the police out here." Rob pushed him gently. "Hurry now," he said. Chris took off after Michael, who by now had disappeared around the curve of the driveway, heading for home. With him ran Griz and the three labs, their tails wagging as if expecting something good was about to happen.

Rob watched Chris only long enough to make sure he would keep following his brother, and then he and Charlie headed down the hill to the barn. As they got closer, the havoc was obvious. The remains of Henry's chickens fluttered soundlessly about the dirt—blood-spattered feathers and wings. Nearby a pig slept, lifting her head as they approached to appraise them with one eye. At one nostril, the fluff of a feather flittered rhythmically as she inhaled and exhaled. Another, more curious pig rose and waddled toward them. Charlie stamped his foot, warning her with a loud "Eeeyah!" She stopped, diminished by his authority, then turned and waddled back to where she had been sleeping beside the Jamesons' pickup.

Rob and Charlie saw Henry just inside the doors. Sprawled in his flannel pajamas, Henry lay peacefully in the semi-darkness of the barn, his head resting on the hay-littered floor as if he were taking a quick nap. His eyes gazed up toward the rafters from which light filtered down in angular slits onto the stored hay bales. He was not breathing, and there was a blue cast to his skin.

"Henry?" Rob called softly, not expecting a response. "Henry, can you hear me?" Rob started to walk toward him, but Charlie pulled him back.

"Don't go near," Charlie whispered. "He's dead, that's

clear. Wait for the police." Rob almost pulled his arm away, but thought better of it. Even from the ten feet away that they stood, he could see that dried blood traced two meandering lines down the side of Henry's face, one from his mouth, the other from his nose. Other than that, he could see no wounds. Rob thought he was looking at a crime scene, but he puzzled over the pajamas and the animals. Who had let the animals out? And why?

"Let's take a look in the house," he said. "Ella's car is in the drive. She might be..." but Rob didn't finish his sentence. He and Charlie were both spooked. Rob felt an involuntary tremor that was not from the cold, and Charlie's breathing was shallow. They climbed the porch steps, passing Ella's two big rockers and her winter-empty flower boxes and stepped over a massacre of cereal and pasta boxes, coffee grounds, and assorted kitchen waste scattered from the front door clear down the hallway as far as they could see.

"What the hell?" Charlie worried. "Something bad's been done here, Rob." He started to walk inside, but Rob grabbed his arm.

"Better not," Rob said quietly. "We don't know what we've got here, but whatever it is, I don't think we should go walking through it." Rob turned to look back at the yard, biting his lip thoughtfully. "Let's look in the windows. See if we can see anything."

It didn't take long. Rob walked left toward the bedrooms while Charlie wandered right toward the kitchen. At the third window Rob looked into the Jamesons' master bedroom. In the gloom, he could see the king-sized bed, its comforter folded at the foot, the sheets neatly tucked into the sides. Ella Jameson lay on her back, her mouth agape, her hair spread across the pillow. Rob tapped repeatedly at the window calling, "Ella? Ella? It's Rob Grant, Ella." Then he stopped, realizing that she too was gone.

Charlie walked up beside him and looked in. "Jesum Crow," he whispered. "What the hell is this?" Charlie turned around as if he thought someone might be coming up behind him, but the yard and drive were empty. Far away, above the wind, Rob thought he heard a police siren. It was faint, then gone in the wind, and then back again, this time louder.

"They're coming," he said flatly, heading for the driveway.

Charlie followed, his hands on his hips. "What's she doing, dying in her bed and him in his pajamas out in the barn?" he asked. "The house is a destruction from the pigs. Don't make sense, Rob."

"I know," Rob agreed, watching the cruiser appear over the rise, its lights flashing. Behind it screamed the ambulance, and behind it another cruiser. The labs ran barking beside the noisy parade.

Jack Deitzel's cruiser pulled up next to Rob and Charlie, the window gliding down as the chief put the car in park. "Hear we've got trouble," Jack said, reaching over to grab a clipboard. He opened the door and swung his legs out on to the gravel. He shivered. "Jeez it's colder than a witch's tit." He pulled a thick plaid jacket out of the back seat and buttoned it up tight to his neck before hoisting his pants and holster up over his ample belly. Two paramedics descended from the ambulance and walked to the rear to remove the stretcher. Rob was struck by their surgical masks.

"I think they're beyond help," Rob said to Jack. "They're both dead, pretty sure."

"Hold on, boys," Jack called to the EMTs. "Let's go take a look." He looked at Rob. "Where're they at?"

Rob pointed to Ella's bedroom window. "She's in her bed. Henry's out in the barn."

"You go in?" Jack asked, his eyes narrowing as he took a step backward.

"Nope. Not sure we should," Rob explained.

"Well, damn smart, then," Deitzel exclaimed. "You know how many of these we've had in the last couple of days?" The chief's chin wobbled as he hoisted his pants again.

"There's more?" Charlie asked, astounded. "Like this?"

"Twenty to be exact," Deitzel replied. "We'll take a look, but my guess is Henry and Ella got the flu, just like the rest of them." He harrumphed, reaching into his jacket for a pen.

Just then Ryan Cary climbed out of his cruiser. The dispatcher had read out an address off of Blue Lake Road. "We got another, Jack," he said, walking up to the group. "The Mastersons. I better go follow up on that one."

Jack looked down at his feet and scratched his head. He sighed. "Yeah, okay. Gimme' a call," he said. Then, looking at Rob, "Where's Henry?"

A minute later, the five men stood at the doors to the barn, but no one stepped inside. "Sure looks like it," Deitzel said, walking to the other side of the doorway and looking in. "Looks like he died letting the animals out."

Rob couldn't contain his confusion. "What the hell, Jack? You're standing out here and deciding how he died? You haven't even looked close."

"Don't have to," Deitzel said, scratching his head again. "Don't want to neither." He grimaced and shook his head.

The paramedic spoke, his eyes shifting from Rob to Charlie. "These guys called yesterday. Both sick with the symptoms. But the hospital can't take anymore. None of the hospitals."

"Where've you been, Rob?" the chief asked. "They closed Almont two days ago. People calling in for an ambulance? There's no place to bring 'em." Deitzel sighed again. "What's worse, we gotta' leave the dead ones. The state will send some guys around to pick up the bodies soon's they get a chance. They've got special suits, you know. Those hazard things."

Rob looked back at Henry, lying cold and dead on the floor. "Seems wrong to leave him like this," Rob said. "What about his animals?"

"We'll get animal control out here. For now, they'll take care of themselves."

"Holsteins are down by the stream again, I bet," Charlie said to Rob. "Should we go round them up?"

"...And put them where?" Rob asked. "Can't go in the barn. Not now anyway."

"Leave 'em," Jack said. "Animal Control will take 'em or shoot 'em. These times, I don't expect we'll get any offers to care for them. Especially..." Jack nodded first to Henry's body and then at the house where Ella lay. "...Especially with this flu thing."

The paramedics turned, walking back to the ambulance. They talked quietly to each other as they climbed back into their vehicle. Deitzel kicked at a pile of bloody chicken feathers. "Henry probably figured the livestock was better off freed," he said. "Look at this mess. Dogs or pigs, the chickens didn't stand a chance." A lab sidled up to him, looking for attention. The chief paused a moment, looking down at the friendly animal. "Somebody don't feed these dogs, and we're all going to be chicken feathers." He reached down to rub the dog's head. Rob thought about how he'd sent Michael alone up over the knoll to the house, how the dogs had been there waiting. A chill ran down his spine. What if this was tomorrow or the next day? The dogs and pigs hungrier? And Michael alone, only twelve, against the pack of them. Suddenly he wanted to be home with his kids.

Jack walked back to his cruiser and removed a spray can from the front seat. Rob watched him paint a huge red X on the barn's siding, just left of the open doors. The Chief saw him gaping. "Got to, Rob," he said. "Marking any building with a body, so's no one goes in without a suit. Doing the house too, and the mailbox. I've about used this up," he said, shaking the can and then tossing it on the ground. He turned back to his cruiser for another.

"Let's go, Charlie," Rob said.

"Might as well," the chief said over his shoulder. "This here's a dying place."

With that he strode away, reaching for a new can in his car before heading for the Jamesons' front door.

37

Patterson, Tuesday, Early November

As she thought about it later, Terry couldn't decide what it was that first jolted her out of the deep sleep that had come on the heels of a terribly hard and wearing day. The day had begun, of course, just like every other day. She had awakened at first light, slipped her feet into her worn fuzzy blue slippers, tied her bathrobe, and headed downstairs to make breakfast for all her men. Rob liked eggs and bacon, and before long the sizzling smell had drawn him to the kitchen, dressed and ready to work. Minutes later, Charlie appeared from the garage, and Terry had thrown six eggs on the griddle and bread in the toaster while the men talked about what they'd need to take with them down to the stream. They finished quickly, grabbed their coats and hats, gloves, and a thermos of coffee, then disappeared out the back door.

Once they went on their way, she assembled the ingredients for the pumpkin bread and cookies she intended to serve that afternoon. They were going to create an alliance. Carol, her husband Ralph and their teenagers, Shirley and her kids, and if all went well, the two neighbors whose properties sat between them, the Curleys and the Jamesons, were going to join Charlie and her family in an alliance to weather the outbreak.

The idea of a group, especially one including her two best friends, gave Terry a new and profound sense of hope. They were going to make it through, she assured herself.

They had food, land and the wherewithal to grow crops. They had forests for hunting adjacent to their farmland. They had wood for heat, and once Rob and Charlie attached everything, a spring-fed well ready to send water down the hill to their house. Now they would have their friends to share the loneliness and help out if they needed help.

She hummed as she went about her baking, and when the boys awoke and came looking for breakfast, she'd tossed their eggs on the griddle and chattered happily about their preparations for winter. An hour or so later, when Charlie and Rob returned with the first load of firewood, she had the boys ready to work outside, Chris's hand-me-down long johns showing beige beneath his too short jeans.

After the boys left with Rob, she tried calling Doc. She thought maybe, just maybe, he might be willing to come wait out the emergency with them, for Doc was a widower with no children. In her heart, though, she knew she was wasting her time. Doc wouldn't leave his patients in the lurch, no matter what the dangers might be. When they'd said their goodbyes on the last day she worked, both had felt a finality. Putting the reality in words would have been too emotional for either of them, and so Doc had hugged her in his fatherly way and then pushed her away and said, "Get going. You have boys who need you." She had seen his eyes water just before he turned away, but she was also struggling to keep her own tears from coming, so she'd picked up her purse, turned, and closed the door behind her without uttering another word.

Doc's answering machine was full, she'd decided, for she was sure her message had gone unrecorded. The beeps just weren't right. She tried both his home and his office, and got the same response. She was about to try calling his next-door neighbor when Michael burst into the kitchen crying, "Call 911! Call 911!"

Terry's heart seemed to stop beating. Then it leapt into paroxysms that felt for an instant like a heart attack. She had the phone in her hand but couldn't move until Michael explained it was the Jamesons that needed help. Once she learned that Rob and Chris and Michael were okay, the beating evened out and she made the call. Then she sat down with the boys to extract the details of what they had seen.

She did not drive over to the Jamesons'. She had her hands full trying to assuage the boys' fears, trying to help them believe that they had nothing to fear without really knowing herself what had happened. Had they been murdered? Was Ella Jameson alive in the house? Could Henry have had a heart attack? A stroke? She thought she'd go out of her mind waiting for Rob and Charlie to return with answers, but she stayed put, not wanting to leave the boys.

When Rob and Charlie finally came bumping along the pasture road, the truck empty, she threw on her coat and ran outside to meet them. Rob's news was appalling, each bit more depressing then the last, like heavy stones piled one by one upon her shoulders. Rob didn't know what to do about the Jamesons' livestock. If Animal Control didn't get out there, who would take the dogs? Who would care for the house? But worst was the image of Henry Jameson lying on the barn floor in his pajamas while Ella lay tucked in her bed, her fingers holding evergreen sprigs. How long would they be left there? How had it all happened?

Rob told her the Jamesons had called for an ambulance yesterday, but none came. They were told the hospital was closed and that they'd have to make do on their own. She and Rob decided that Ella must have died first. Henry, that kind old man who loved his wife more than any living thing, probably sick himself, went out to cut her some sprigs and then tucked her into her bed like a small child going down for a nap.

Rob told her that Jack Deitzel thought Henry went out to the barn to let the animals loose and fell there. "He probably hoped they could fend for themselves, but if they couldn't, anything was better than being locked in without food or water to slowly starve," Rob said. "I'll bet a lot of farmers will do that. I sure would."

"Why didn't they call?" Terry asked, feeling guilty that she had been right next door while all this was happening. Rob didn't have to answer her question, because they both knew that the Jamesons had spared them by not calling. How could either Rob or Terry have done anything? And if they had, if one of them had gone over to administer aid, then their family would have been jeopardized, the very thing they were working so hard to avoid. Once Ella got sick, the Jamesons knew they were on their own. Life was going to be that way for everyone, Terry thought. With the hospital closed and no way to stop the dying once it got started, sick people's choices had been whittled down to one—curl up and wait to die.

That afternoon, as Rob and Charlie told their story at the meeting, Terry watched the faces of her friends darken with growing fear. The proximity of the flu to their own homes made them feel even more vulnerable. "I tried and tried to call Ella," Carol said sadly, "but no one answered. I almost went over..." and then her eyes glazed as she visualized herself wandering into Ella's house looking for them and stumbling upon Ella sick or dead. "I wonder when they died," she murmured. She had been able to reach Lisa Curley, though, and Lisa and her husband Paul were grateful to be asked. Lisa had not begun preparing early, as the other wives had, but she had spent the summer canning and had plenty to share and to trade if their dry goods grew lean. They had no kids, either. Paul was an experienced hunter and trapper, the assistant host of the town's annual game dinner and provider of such delicacies as bear, boar, and turtles. They would be an asset to the group even though Lisa hadn't spent her savings at BJ's as the others had.

When Rob and Charlie finished their story, the group was silent for several minutes. Carol and Ralph looked at each other, and then Ralph hesitantly asked, "Did Michael go near him?" Terry was quick to allay their fears. No, she told them. To make sure, she had questioned Michael closely. Of course, no one could ever be sure with a virus. She didn't know much more about this one than anyone else, but her nurse's training told her that it was very unlikely that Michael, standing ten to fifteen feet away in an open barn, with fresh cold air blowing through it all the night before, could possibly have contracted the virus. Same with Rob, Terry said, and she was going to be forever grateful that Charlie had stopped him from going near Henry's corpse, because she did know that viruses can live on for a time after the host has died. Charlie had straightened, looking proud.

While the meeting had been somber, it had also been productive. Later Terry went over and over in her head the agreements they had forged. They planned complete isolation if things got bad enough. For now, they planned careful forays into town whenever necessary. As long as stores remained open, they might as well save their resources until needed. Children were forbidden to go near the Jameson farm, and Terry knew that after hearing what they'd heard, none would. Classes would begin next week, with Carol taking care of math, Terry science, Shirley reading, and Lisa writing.

The men moved off into a separate group once the women began planning school and ways to keep the kids safe. They wanted to talk about hunting, planting, and protection, though they didn't think the latter was going to be much of an issue once they closed off the road. When that would be, they'd decide later. It was growing dark by the time everyone gathered up their coats to leave, calling the young people away from the TV and a rousing game of Hearts. After everyone left, Terry and Rob agreed that the meeting had been excellent. They had thought through a lot of possible problems and issues.

Despite the sense of accomplishment, an uneasy, sad mood had begun to descend on Terry. School for the kids did not diminish the image of neighbors lying dead in the eerie, dark cold down the road. After dinner she decided that she had to reach Doc. She wondered what was happening in Almont, if Doc was okay, what he was doing about their patients, if he'd heard any good news about medications or vaccines. She picked up the phone to try again and pressed Doc's number without listening for a dial tone. She put the cell phone to her ear, waited a minute for the familiar ring, and stood there for some time before realizing that the phone was dead. "Huh," she said, annoyed. Thinking maybe the battery needed charging, she picked up the wall phone in the kitchen and listened for a dial tone. Nothing. So it begins, she thought. "Rob," she called out, "the line's dead."

Once the boys were in bed, Terry and Rob wanted only to slip between clean flannel sheets and sleep. In the darkness, they said very little to each other. Rob began snoring almost immediately, and though Terry was sure she was too tense to fall asleep, it took only a couple of turns from left to right and back again to find the comfortable position that brought release. She didn't awaken as she often did to check the digital readout on the alarm or to go to the bathroom. Her sleep was beyond unconsciousness, in a place where troubles held no sway. So she did not know exactly what it was that woke her. Perhaps it was the odd red light slicing through the venetian blinds. Perhaps she heard the Jamesons' dogs barking, their strident voices carried clearly in the still dark night. Or perhaps she actually heard the bawling of frightened holsteins being loaded onto a truck by men with whips, themselves in a hurry to get back on the road and out of town. Did she hear the shot that killed one lab and sent the others fleeing into the woods? Although their window was open only a crack, could she have caught a whiff of the accelerant poured around the foundations of the house and barn? Or heard the whoosh of it igniting? Or perhaps it was the rumble of two huge trucks sending gravel flying in the Jamesons' driveway as they changed gears on the hill out to the main road. Whatever it was, Terry sat up fast, gasping, the blanket falling to her lap. Rob felt her thrashing immediately. "Whaa..." he said, half asleep.

"Rob," Terry whispered urgently. "Something's wrong. Look at the light." She threw her blanket aside and jumped out of bed, rushing to the window and yanking the blinds out of the way. "My God, Rob. Get up. It's a fire!" she cried in horror.

Rob rolled out of bed, kicking the sheets away from his feet and stumbling to where Terry held the blinds aloft. He took one look and muttered, "Jesus!" then ran to grab his pants and slide his bare feet into his loafers. "Jesus, Jesus, Jesus!" Rob roared, not able to dress fast enough. He ran down the hall, zipping his pants, his shirt flying out behind him as he raced down the stairs. Terry heard the back door slam as she grabbed her jeans, fighting to get her feet through the legs. She was out the back door minutes behind him, out in the yard where the red sky glowed from beyond the trees at Jamesons' farm. Smoke drifted toward her, its chemical odor gagging her. She thought about wind. Was it coming toward them? No, the air was still, thank God.

Rob had already called Charlie and was starting the pickup. "Get the kids up and drive to town," he yelled through the window. "Get the fire department out here." Rob's face contorted with fear and anguish. "We'll go over and see what we can do. Maybe we can hook up some hoses." Just then Charlie ran from the barn, carrying two spools of hosing and threw them in the back, trying to hold his pants closed at the same time. He looked at Terry with a helpless, spooked expression that she would always remember. It said, "What else could go wrong?"

Once she'd roused the boys and loaded them in her car, she drove a tire-bursting ride over backcountry roads toward 2A, praying all the while that no moose or deer would be along the side of the road, because she'd hit it for sure. Her knuckles were white on the steering wheel as she peered along both sides of the road while at the same time going too fast to stop without skidding.

She pulled up in front of the fire department, ordering the boys to stay put, and ran inside. A young trainee she didn't recognize told her both trucks were at another fire out by Blue Lake. He called Chief Garner on his radio, who told him they couldn't leave where they were, but to call Almont and Eaton to see if they had men and trucks to spare. Terry couldn't stand still while he fumbled with the mutual aid manual, looking for Almont's station number. When he did reach them, he heard that Almont was having two fires of its own, and Eaton, when finally reached, had its own problems. Terry had been pacing all this time, imagining the worst, that something terrible had happened to Rob or Charlie, that the fire was spreading toward their farm, that her house was aflame. And their barn. And their stores of food. "My God," she cried out at the trainee, who by now was leery of this wild-haired woman screaming at him, "help us! Get someone. Do something." When he just looked at her, shaking his head in frustration, she ran next door to the police station. Because of the flu, the police department had lost half its men. They were so stretched, they couldn't keep a man on duty by a dead phone. The office was empty, the lights on, but only the dispatcher's radio listened as two patrolmen shouted back and forth on their walkie-talkies. They were out at Blue Lake, the site of the other fire, and they were looking for the people who had started it.

Despite her shrill orders to stay in the car, Michael and Chris could stand the dark silence no longer. They had seen the flaming sky grow hotter as they flew past the Jameson farm, they knew their Dad and Charlie were there fighting it, and that their mother was nearly hysterical. Both had expected fire engines to roar from the oversized garage doors, their sirens wailing the minute she disappeared inside. When nothing happened while they squirmed and peered and fidgeted, both boys were out of the car in a flash. They found their mother standing paralyzed before the dispatcher's radio.

"I can't work this," she cried, her eyes filled with tears. "Help me, Michael. See if you can figure it out."

Both boys hurried to her side of the desk, wildly scanning the buttons and dials, trying to make sense of the radio. Chris picked up the microphone and pressed a small button on its side. "Testing, testing," he spoke into it, just as his principal, Mr. Stone, used to do.

"Who's that?" a voice barked out of the speakers. "Who's on our line?" Chris nearly dropped the microphone, but Terry quickly grabbed it and said, "This is Terry Grant. I'm at the station. We have a fire out at the Jameson farm. My husband needs help."

"Mrs. Grant?" a kinder voice replied. "This is Joey Grisholm. A fire you say? What's that address again?"

Terry blurted out the particulars, then explained about the Jamesons.

"We've got no more equipment, Mrs. Grant," Grisholm explained. "We've called in the Guard, but from what I'm told, we're so far down on the list we might as well forget it. But I'll head out now, Mrs. Grant. I'll do what I can."

Terry listened as Grisholm spoke with another officer, then she set down the microphone and put a hand on Chris' head. "Child, you are a wonder," she said, rubbing the velvet of his crew cut. "Let's go," she added, breaking into a run for the door.

The cruiser flew past them, making the turn into the Jameson farm almost on two wheels, its siren blaring. Terry and the boys sped behind it, bouncing over the Jamesons' gravel driveway until they reached Rob's pickup and Carol Green's SUV. Joey Grisholm climbed from the cruiser, glancing back at Terry and her boys as they emerged from their Honda. Rob and Charlie came to meet them, both men black with soot, their hair in pointed wisps, their shoulders sagging. She barely recognized Ralph following them; he was so blackened by smoke that only the whites of his eyes showed. A group of teenagers, Ralph and Carol's kids, hung back, talking among themselves and staring at what were now dying flames.

In the growing light of early dawn, Terry could see that part of the back wall of the house still stood, its windows gone. Small flames flickered among the upright studs; the floor still smoldered. The other three sides of the house were gone, consumed by flames. A few charred beams remained, fallen at ungainly angles, and some post supports as well, so that the floor plan of the house could almost be identified. Where the kitchen had been, the remains of a refrigerator, a stove, and a deep double sink stood buckled and bent, while the cabinets that had surrounded them had burnt to ashes. In the center of the kitchen stood one antique Windsor chair, its paint bubbled, its frame intact. Other than that, no furniture of any sort survived the conflagration. But leading up to the front porch, the steps were untouched, a stairway to nowhere.

Terry gulped to hold back the tears. A fierce, primitive, and helpless anger grew inside her. Who had done this? And why? When she looked to Rob and the others for answers, she saw despair in their faces. They looked and felt beaten. Chris reached up and took her hand, pulling her down so that she could hear his whispered question. "Are the animals dead?" he asked. His eyes were wide with dread. "Is that one of the dogs?" he asked, pointing toward the barn.

Terry looked where he pointed. Rob heard him and stepped closer, putting his big hand on Chris's frail shoulder. "Somebody shot him, Chris," Rob explained. "But I think the others made off into the woods." Rob gave Terry the eye above Chris's head.

"What about the cows and pigs?" Chris asked, looking up so quickly that he caught the glance between his parents.

"Gone. We don't know where. They weren't in the barn when we got here," Rob answered, glad that Chris wasn't going to see any more death.

"There's tire tracks over here," Joey Grisholm said,

kneeling down and playing his flashlight over the wide ruts made by a big truck's tires. "Looks to me like the livestock's been rustled." Everyone stared at the ground, shocked by the possibility that such a thing might have happened. Rustled? That only happened in the Old West. Then Ralph turned around, looked left and right, and finally walked behind the charred wall of the house. He called out, "Where's the tractor?" and a minute later, "Both their cars are gone!"

Then Rob, looking about too, shouted back, "His hay baler."

Terry pulled her jacket close around her and shivered, wanting only to be home in her own kitchen making breakfast. The burnt smell on her clothes and in her hair was repulsive. The first thing she would do when she got home would be to take a shower and wash her hair. Throw all their clothes in the washer. Get away from this place. Wash it away. Then she looked around at the destruction of the Jameson farm—the burnt buildings and grass, the detritus of the fire lying in lumps along what had been the house's fine oak floors, the remains of stalls for the animals stolen by thieves. The cars were probably headed for chop shops. But this was Patterson. Safe from crime. A good place where good people lived. How could these things be happening here?

She looked at young Joey Grisholm, one of a few now impotent officers of law and order left in Patterson. How could he ensure that justice was done? How could he and a few others prevent more of the same? Terry realized this was just the beginning. Whoever had done this, whoever had sneaked in while everyone slept and herded animals and valuables into trucks, whoever had set the place on fire to cover their tracks, they were going to be a fact of life with which she and Rob and her neighbors were not only going to have to learn to live, but were going to have to prepare to confront. In the growing light, she watched her quiet farmer husband and the other men as they wandered about the place in stunned silence, aghast at the destruction and sheer audacity of the thieves, and she wondered if they, or anyone, could possibly expect to prevail against such overwhelming odds.

38

Patterson, Friday, Early November

Taylor Farr drove Laura's car slowly along Richland Road toward 2A. He looked puzzled, but said nothing. Arnold sat in the passenger seat, gazing into the empty woods along his side of the road, a sheet of paper on his knee and a pencil in his hand. The two men had decided it was worth the risk to head into nearby Almont for some hardware supplies at Aubuchon's and Hunter's. The phone had been out since last night with no expectation that service would be restored soon. They couldn't call ahead, so the trip might be a waste. Arnold had it in his mind that they might need more PVC pipe and fittings, and he also hoped that one of the stores might have restocked those big 12-volt batteries after the first rush on them last week. Arnold could think of a hundred ways he might use those batteries, and also some wire if they could get it. He'd agitated and cajoled Taylor until Taylor finally said Arnold was giving him a headache. Arnold had smiled weakly, "Might be CVS still has some aspirin in stock. Be good to have some stockpiled since you're so sensitive."

Snow skittered at their windshield, though the road stayed merely damp. Taylor turned the wipers on low, looking over at Arnold as he gazed out the passenger window. Taylor had decided he liked this man, though he'd been doubtful at first, when Laura had wanted to include him and his wife. Arnold was older, and he hadn't kept in shape. He could do some physical work, but not for long and not anything too rigorous. Taylor would rather have partnered with someone his equal, someone who could share the load of what he expected might be a long and arduous winter. Arnold wasn't going to be able to do that. But Arnold had other strengths that Taylor had recognized might be even more useful.

Arnold was an inventor. His mind worked night and day on ways to do things better or faster or more cost-effectively. His house was rigged with gizmos he'd created for Ethel, ways to save on electricity; he'd even built his own power generator from an old Chevy engine. Arnold was smart, damn smart. Ever since they'd made their alliance, Arnold had been planning ways for them to survive the winter comfortably and ways to build a future if the worst happened. Arnold would have been welcomed out in Wyoming, Taylor realized, so who cared if he wasn't the fittest specimen in the world.

Arnold turned forward to scratch another item on the paper he held on his knee as Taylor drove past yet another mailbox with a mysterious red X spray-painted on it. "You'd think," Taylor observed, "that kids would have better things to do than vandalizing people's mailboxes."

Arnold looked up, surprised. "What?" he asked.

"The mailboxes. You see 'em? A bunch of them with red Xs?" Taylor replied, turning the long, slow curve that led downhill to Rte. 2A.

"Nope. Must've done it the last few nights," Arnold said. "Kids. You wonder where their brains are."

2A seemed abandoned. They rolled to the intersection and pulled right out onto the main highway without waiting. "Joe's closed," Arnold observed.

"So's the car dealer," Taylor said, pointing right. "Got the chains up across the entrance."

"This might be a wild goose chase," Arnold apologized. "Maybe everything's closed down." He looked up at the Rt. 2 overpass as their car rolled under and sighed. Then he pointed ahead. "Usually a cruiser here, catching speeders," he said, indicating a pull-off beside the road. "Caught me once doing sixty. Ethel was ripping when I told her. Sent our rates up $200."

They passed the high school, closed now until further notice. Just past it, two cruisers sat empty in front of the state police barracks. Just ahead, they saw a car at the Mobil station. "Someone's getting gas," Taylor announced. A tall woman with long blonde hair was filling her station wagon. She looked up, her face expressionless, as their car passed. "That's Lindsey Steinberg," Arnold said. "She paints the prettiest pictures you've ever seen. Trees, you know, and lakes, farms, beaches, stuff like that." But Arnold didn't wave either.

At Almont Memorial Hospital, someone had put large red sawhorses across the entrance. A poorly painted sign said, "Hospital Closed." The parking lot was nearly empty, but a few cars remained near the front door. "Never thought I'd see that," Arnold said, shaking his head sadly. "The hospital, you know?" He clicked his tongue and looked away.

"We've only passed two cars," Taylor observed. "You might be right about stuff being closed." He knew it was possible that everything had closed down by now, yet logic said otherwise. People had to work; people had to make money. As long as they could, families had to provide for their children. A place like Aubuchon's should be open, he reasoned, but the emptiness of the streets seemed to dispute that. He hoped they weren't wasting gas. He'd seen the hand-printed sign at the Mobil. Five bucks a gallon now.

Good old laws of supply and demand, though even that supply would surely give out soon. Truckers were moving the stuff, but along the coasts where the refineries were, the workforce had dwindled to a handful of men. Since shipping lines had been shut down, nothing was being imported. From what he'd heard on the news last night, places like Saudi Arabia and Kuwait had been devastated by the flu and they couldn't produce even a fraction of their usual output.

Down the final hill now into town, and Taylor noticed laundry hanging on the front porch of an old brown clapboard. In other times, such a display on the main street would have seemed tacky, but today, undershorts, T-shirts, and toddler jeans couldn't have been a more hopeful sign. At the bottom of the hill, he stopped for the stop sign even though not a car was in sight.

"Goodwill's open," Arnold said hopefully a moment later. They passed the new plaza where the American Legion boys had installed a fountain. The fountain was shut down, but the American flags, six or seven of them lining walkways, blew straight out in the wind. Taylor stopped for a WALK light, then realized that a teenage boy, so thin the pole nearly hid him, stood by the pole waiting to cross. He wore a surgical mask and a red knit cap pulled down nearly to his eyes. He couldn't help but look suspicious, all alone there on the empty main street. "We witnessing a robbery here?" Arnold asked, looking quickly about at the nearby stores. "This guy packing?" They watched the boy closely as he crossed in front of them, his low-slung jeans dragging behind his feet, the hems in tatters.

"If he's on the run, I'd hate to see him on the walk," Taylor replied. The boy slowed even more to peer at them myopically through the windshield, but he didn't stop. He headed down Bower Street, never turning back.

As they passed the Post Office, Arnold said, "Well I'll be damned."

"What?" Taylor asked.

"Wondered why I'm getting no mail," Arnold said. "Post Office is closed. You suppose I don't have to pay my bills? Can't pay 'em if I don't get 'em." Arnold smiled sardonically. "May be an up-side to this flu thing after all," he said.

"My experience is they'll shut off your power no matter what your excuse," Taylor smiled back. "'Spect they'll say you should've hand delivered it."

"How much longer you think we're going to have power?" Arnold asked.

"Till the first storm, or a truck hits a pole, or a downed limb," Taylor guessed. "They're holding out pretty good up here, I'd say. Better than down near New York. But we're on borrowed time's, my opinion."

"Yup," Arnold agreed. "Turn right up there."

The parking lot where Aubuchon shared mall space with a dry cleaners and a pool supplies store had more cars than they'd seen all day. "Wow," Taylor mused, "Five cars. A real traffic nightmare." Two were parked in front of Aubuchon's, and as Taylor pulled up closer, Arnold recognized two guys from Garrett's standing by the front door.

"Should we wait for them to go?" Arnold asked, turning to Taylor. "I'm not up to taking any chances."

"Let's drive by first," Taylor said. "Ask them what's what, but don't get out of the car." He guided their vehicle alongside the building, stopping to idle a good fifteen feet from the men at the door.

Arnold rolled his window down, greeting the men affably. "You boys got nothing better to do than stand outside in the cold?" he asked, smiling. Taylor kept his hand on the shift in case one began walking over. The two men made no effort to walk their way, and in fact, stepped back some, closer to the door. Still maintaining that distance, the bald one bent his knees a bit to see better into the Volvo. "That you, Arnold?" he asked.

"Sure is, Tommy," Arnold replied. "What's going on? Is the store open?"

"Yeah, but stay there till we're finished, will you?" Tommy asked. "We'll be just a minute or so." The men seemed hesitant, as if they'd run should Arnold get out of the car.

Taylor watched from the driver's seat. Clearly, they wanted to keep their distance as much as he did. But why were they outside the store?

Just then, a man in a surgical mask appeared at the glass door. He carried several items in a carton. A bag dangled from one hand. He set the packages down, fished in his pocket for his keys, unlocked the door from the inside and shoved the carton and bag outside with his foot. All the time, he held on to the bar handle of the door as if expecting the men to yank it open and burst inside. Instead, they bent, one picking up the carton, the other the bag. The guy with the carton turned to his friend, who peered inside it and extracted several bills and coins. Taylor figured that was their change. "Thanks, Frankie," Tommy yelled through the glass. Frankie raised a hand to wave "You're welcome," and re-locked the door. The men walked toward their car. As soon as Tommy put his carton in the back seat and opened his door, he yelled over to Arnold, "Okay, pal. We're done." With that, he slipped into the car, slammed the door, and turned the ignition key. He looked at Arnold as he backed up, but he didn't smile.

"Well if that don't beat all," Arnold said, his eyes wide. "Look what we've come to."

"They're being smart. So's that Frankie guy," Taylor nodded. They both looked back at the door. Frankie stood inside, waiting for them. They got out of the car and walked up to the glass. Frankie had pasted up a sign that read: "Make a list. Slip it under the door." Another read "Cash Only!" He watched them read, then pointed down, just in case they didn't know where under the door might be. Thick latex gloves covered his hands, the kind Arnold used to strip furniture. Arnold fumbled with his list. "Some's for Hunter's," he said aloud through the glass. But Frankie just nodded yes, yes, and waved the list under the door. "Some's for Hunter's," Arnold shouted in case Frankie didn't get it, then bending awkwardly he slipped the list under. Frankie reached for the list with a gloved hand. He picked it up, keeping his face a distance from the paper, then held it out and read. He made the OK sign, turned and headed toward the back of the store, holding the list away from his body.

"Jeez," Arnold said. "He think it's anthrax?"

"Worse," Taylor said.

They watched Frankie flit about the store, gathering what he had to fill Arnold's list, then going to the cash register and tallying the pile up. He looked up at them in the light by the counter and waved. The cash register chugged out the itemization and he took it in his hands to check it against the items piled on the counter. He looked up again and waved, then came forward, still holding Arnold's list away from himself. He held the register's printout up to the door for Arnold and Taylor to read through the glass.

"Seventy-four ninety," Arnold said, reaching into his back pocket for his wallet. He removed a fifty, a twenty, and a five, then held them up for Frankie to see. Frankie nodded vigorously. "Slide them under the door," he signaled. And Arnold did so. "This is not fun," Arnold groaned, straightening again. "My sciatica is killing me."

Frankie bent to take the money from the floor, then hurried back to the cash register. He piled what he could in two large paper bags, and the rest in another carton, then made two trips bringing the items to the front door. Between trips, he held up his hand to signal "Just wait another minute," but Taylor and Arnold weren't rushing him. He looked so hopeless there, trying to keep his store going despite locked doors and rubber gloves. Taylor felt sorry for the little gray man hurrying about under the fluorescent lights.

When he set the carton down, he pointed, "Change in the carton." Taylor nodded his head that he understood, and then Frankie made a motion with his hand for them to step back. He waited until they did, then, once again, took the keys from his pocket and unlocked the door. He watched them carefully as the door moved forward, then, as soon as he could get everything through the opening, he pulled the steel bar backward to speed the door's closing. "Thanks," he nodded, his eyes wide and sad.

"Thanks, Frankie," Arnold said turning toward the car with the two bags. But as he walked away, his back to Frankie, Arnold said under his breath, "This guy needs some people skills."

Taylor snorted, then opened the trunk. Arnold added the bags to the carton, and the two men climbed into the Volvo. "Something tells me a home delivery from Hunter's is unlikely," Arnold said, buckling his seat belt. "If Frankie has himself locked in there like that, my guess is no one's going to want to be delivering us some PVC."

But Arnold was wrong. Hunter's had a clerk taking orders

at the door, just like Frankie, and two fellows working out back loading people's orders. The place seemed far more accommodating, although when Arnold made the mistake of reaching for the door handle, the clerk grabbed the inside bar in a death grip. Arnold inquired about deliveries, shouting through the glass and exaggerating his lip movements like someone communicating with the deaf. Taylor folded his arms and smiled, watching quietly.

"PVC," Arnold shouted. "Two inch, twenty ten footers," and the clerk, from the inside yelled back, "Yes, okay, we deliver for twenty dollars," and then Arnold, "No, no, two inch, twenty ten footers," and then the clerk, "Ten feet of what?" Finally, Taylor walked back to the Volvo and brought Arnold's pad and pencil, handing it to him mid-shout. Arnold wrote out his request and held it up. The clerk read, moving his lips as he did so, then nodded his head and signaled them to wait while he wrote up a slip. When a few moments later he held it up, Arnold hissed, "Shit!" Taylor leaned forward to read what was wrong. "No, man," Arnold shouted, "Delivered. I said delivered!" Arnold had about had it with shopping through glass doors. The clerk pointed to Arnold's order, which did not say "Delivered." Arnold's face reddened with frustration. "Where'd you suppose we were gonna' carry 'em?" he cried angrily, pointing at the Volvo. "Fold 'em in the trunk?"

The clerk shrugged and shook his head, looking at Arnold with a smug and determined neutrality. Then he turned and ambled back to the cash register to re-calculate the order. He didn't look up, nor did he see Arnold tap his own head with his forefinger and growl, "Anybody there?"

"Getting a little testy, aren't you?" Taylor smirked, though he, too, had tired of dealing with merchants.

"How many clerks does it take to screw in a light bulb?"

Arnold began. But the clerk arrived at the door with his corrected merchandise slip, and Arnold forgot whatever riddle he had in mind as he leaned forward to read the total.

In the car again, Arnold directed Taylor the back way around Almont, through the Victory shopping lot. The supermarket was open, but only four cars were parked outside. They headed under the railroad overpass and up along Dwyer Street, where they slowed for a commotion ahead. A fire truck blocked the street and several firemen hurried about dousing the last flames of an apartment house that sat smoldering in ruins. The fire had clearly started along one side of the house, where now a gaping, charred mouth hissed smoke. The remains of a kitchen's white enamel cabinets smiled sooty teeth beneath two blackened windows on the second floor. The roof had collapsed inward, its beams seared by the flames below until they gave way beneath the layers of shingles above. A few neighbors solemnly watched the firemen go about their business from their windows, but no one stood outside in the cold except the handful of men holding hoses or chopping through the rubble. Arnold told Taylor to park. "I see Dan Fowler over there," he said. "I'm just curious."

Arnold pulled his coat tight about him as he walked over to the fireman, but he stopped several feet before reaching him. "How's it going?" Arnold asked. He hated the burnt smell wafting in the air, the sense of destruction, windows shattered by the heat, burnt boards looking like charred alligator hide, the scorched remnants of people's lives thrown about the lawn in soggy, stinking heaps.

"Arnold," Dan responded, turning. He looked for a moment at his friend, but his eyes were empty of warmth and he did not walk closer. "Poorly, I'd say."

"Big fire?" Arnold asked. "What happened?" Arnold placed his cold hands into the pockets of his jacket. He stamped his feet to keep the blood moving.

"Set, we think," Dan replied, not looking Arnold's way. "Seventh one this week." Dan moved the nozzle spray left, dousing an ember twenty feet away that suddenly flamed up. "We're down to less than half staff, and there are people burning the quarantines out." He said it matter-of-factly, as if such crimes had become commonplace.

Arnold's mouth fell open. He took a moment to assess this new information with horror. "Burning the quarantines out? You mean people sick with..."

But Dan interrupted. "Sick with, dead with, all the same. Minute the red X goes up, neighbors get scared, like the damn germs are going to fly fifty feet in through their living room windows. With them closed. In Goddamn November." Dan shook his head disgusted. "Tell you, Arnold, we've got a new world order here, and I don't much care for it. They're burning other places too, places where they can steal stuff." Dan walked back toward the truck. Arnold followed, but Dan held up his hand to stop. "Arnold, don't mind, but keep your distance, will you?"

Arnold halted, surprised that he was not surprised. "That's one way to get rid of the bodies," Arnold said grimly. "Can think of some better ways to treat people though." He looked at the ruin before him.

"Yeah? What?" Dan countered. "Least cooked germs can't kill you. People are afraid, so they destroy the enemy. Least they think so." Dan stopped a moment to observe the sky. "I've lost most of my relatives, Arnold. My cousin's family is moldering up on Crescent Street, and the state guys haven't come yet to pick up the bodies. I suspect I'll be hosing down their place pretty soon."

"Gonna' burn the whole town down," Arnold said. "Then what'll they have?"

Arnold looked angrily at the surrounding houses. He could see some faces in windows, a few curtains moving as people hid. People are what they are, he thought. They begin thinking that sick neighbors might spread the flu to them, they'll lash out to save themselves. Justify it later. Or maybe not. Maybe dream about it for the rest of their lives. Wake up at night trembling with dread. When it comes to being killed or killing first, people will choose survival every time.

"By the time someone comes in to let us know there's a fire," Dan said, "the house is already a goner. We've been lucky so far that the fires have been isolated, but get a wind like yesterday on a street like this, and the burners are going to become the burnees."

Just then a fireman working the rear of the building emerged from among the ruined shrubs. "Hey, Fowler, give me a hand here, will you?" he called, motioning Dan over.

"Gotta' go," Dan said. He lifted his arm as if to reach out to Arnold and pat him on the back. But they were too far apart. Instead he patted the air. "See you, pal," he said, striding away. He didn't look back.

Arnold turned toward the Volvo. He could see Taylor behind the glass, sitting with both hands on the steering wheel, assessing the situation. An unlikely friend, this cowboy, Arnold thought. How unlucky for him that he had to come visiting a girlfriend just when all this went down. Arnold wondered whether Taylor would stay or not. Why should he? He'd be far better off in Wyoming or Montana or wherever it was he had his little community. If Arnold had been free and young when this happened, no way he would have stayed in New England. What a shitty place to survive a pandemic, Arnold thought. People everywhere. Hardly any open spaces. No way to really isolate oneself, like out in the West, where neighbors lived twenty-five miles apart. But there was Ethel to consider. And what did he know of the West, anyhow. His kids might be okay living out in California, but New England was his home. There was no grander place, Arnold believed, freezing cold winters or not.

"Well, I know what the red Xs mean," Arnold said as he climbed into the car. Taylor waited. Arnold held out as long as he could. Taylor was already moving forward in first, still not asking. Then he said, "Means someone's sick or dead there," Arnold answered the unasked question. "Those red Xs along Loftis Street mean people there are dead. And the fire here? Dan says the neighbors burn a quarantined house, whether they're dead or not. They're afraid of the germs." Arnold leaned back against the seat, rolling his head back and forth to relieve the tension in his neck. He waited for Taylor to respond, but Taylor didn't. Instead, he continued stoically along 2A without saying a word.

"Life shits," Arnold said, closing his eyes. Behind his lids, he squeezed back tears.

39

Patterson, Friday, Early November

Rob, Ralph Green, Paul Curley, and Charlie had wasted no time barricading one end of their three miles of dirt road. On the Greens' end, the road connected to a paved backcountry road, most of it running through forestland and overgrown pastures. After several long curves and endless knolls, it ran into Rte. 2A. On Shirley's end, the dirt road wandered obscurely for miles through conservation lands.

They'd had a short meeting just after breakfast, the men standing around their pickups, their conversation sleepy and regretful. They all realized that once they dropped trees across the road, they were cutting themselves off from the rest of the world. That meant they couldn't go out either. Ralph tried to convince the group that dropping just one tree might be better in case they had to leave in an emergency, but Paul had resisted.

"Emergency to go where?" Paul asked. "The hospital's gone, the fire department can't muster enough men to save anything, the police department's down to one or two guys." Paul shook his head and shrugged, wanting to get on with the cutting.

"We might want something in Almont," Ralph said, annoyed. "Something none of us has thought of. We might run out of something too." Ralph glared at Paul, knowing that Paul and his wife had been included only because their property was situated on the same road and not because anyone particularly liked them.

Paul was not convinced. He folded his arms over his chest, his coffee still steaming in his hand, and met Ralph's gaze. "For now, if we need something, we'll walk down through Bear Den woods. It's better to slip in and out without attracting attention to ourselves in a pickup. Later, we can always cut a way out that we can hide. I'll scout one. " Paul knew those lands well, having hunted them in every season.

Rob agreed. "The whole point of barricading the road is to make it impossible for anyone to come nosing around. Sooner or later, the folks who survive the germ are going to run out of food. Or they may come looking for help. I don't want to have to shoot anyone, but we've all agreed that no one is going to be allowed in until we can be sure it's safe. That's months from now. Maybe years. Who knows?"

"Do we really plan to shoot on sight?" the older Green boy, David, asked, gulping. A gangling six-foot teenager, until that very moment he had visualized himself heading out within a week toward his friend Jack's house. Once things settled down, he'd go find out what friends were around. He thought they'd have fun hunting or hanging out in the woods. He couldn't imagine spending the rest of his days with just his siblings and all the Grant and Young kids or spending his time with a bunch of parents always telling him what to do and what not to.

And, of course, there was the matter of Cindy Lee, with whom things were just beginning to get interesting. He'd planned to ask Cindy to the Senior Prom that very week because it would warm things up between them even faster. If Cindy could be assured that he loved her, she could relax about their relationship. Cindy would trust him then. Cindy, beautiful Cindy of the silky, long blond hair, the sexiest girl he'd ever known.

"No, we're not going to shoot on sight, David," his father said to reassure him. "But if someone wanders in, past the barricade, even just to the barricade, we'll warn him to turn around and leave."

"Do we have to post guards?" Charlie asked.

"No point in an alliance like this if an outsider carries the germ in," Rob said, backing David's father. "We won't know for a long time whether a person is a carrier or not. Until we can be sure..." he trailed off, looking back at Ralph.

"We'll give him a warning," Ralph repeated, "but you've got to know, son, that this is serious stuff. We're talking about our lives here. *All* of our lives. That's the only way this will work."

David nodded his head and looked down, anxious to send their attention elsewhere and already thinking of ways to elude his family and seek out his pals. After that, he would head across town to where Cindy might at this very minute be looking out her bedroom window and thinking of him. A wave of warmth washed over him, and he consciously switched his thinking back to his buddy Jack to prevent betraying the excitement he felt just thinking about Cindy's kisses.

Soon the shrill whine of chain saws, broken intermittently by the "ka-thunk" of a tree falling, carried from one end of the road to the other. Once a tree was down, the younger boys, using hand saws, stripped the smaller branches for kindling and piled them beside the road in what they were now calling community piles. Anyone could take whatever was needed. As the piles grew huge, becoming tall mounds along the road, the sense of community grew and strengthened.

Soon the barrier consisted of three or four trees cut

from both sides of the road so that their tops and trunks criss-crossed, and atop them, several more trees cut from slightly farther back. The completed barricade stood as high as Rob's chin and wider than he was tall. They had created a fortress on the road, but as they stood back admiring it, they realized that it could only stop vehicles. People could easily walk around.

"We can't build the China Wall," Rob said, feeling disheartened. "All we can hope is that these deter folks. The ones who walk in are going to get in somehow anyway." He shoved his boot against one of the trunks to test its steadiness. Nothing moved.

"So that's it," Ralph said, gathering up his chain saw and gas can. "Come on, boys, we've got work to do." David and his younger brothers rose from the log they had been sitting on and followed their father to his pickup. Rob and Charlie climbed in theirs, with Michael and Chris in the back. The smell of chimney smoke hung in the icy air, sweet and as inviting as the pungent smell of dried brown leaves. They appraised the newly cut trunks, their stumps like dwarves' tables set up alongside the road. Rob took a deep breath, momentarily enjoying the clarity of the air, the thin gray of the sky. Were this any other time, he'd have been happy.

Back home, Terry sat in the gray light of the kitchen waiting for the truck to come back over the rise. She clasped a cup in both her hands, thinking that this cup of tea she'd just heated in the microwave would probably be the last she'd make that way for a very long time. The house was silent except for the ticking of her grandmother's clock and the soft clicking of the battery-driven kitchen wall clock. On a day like this, Terry would have turned on several lamps to warm the gray shadows filling every corner, but the power had snapped off only moments ago. The house seemed dawn-dark and inhospitable.

The TV had gone blank just after the speech, almost as if the power companies had held out as long as they could to accommodate Washington and then thrown in the towel as soon as the Vice President finished speaking. That had been a while ago. NBC had been broadcasting repeats of earlier shows for lack of an available host. Michael Lane's "Where in the World" had really become a mystery. No one knew where he was. Kristen Call and Arlene Corrie had reported in sick, and the producer's best solution was to replay a show from last week. Terry hadn't been paying much attention while she dusted and vacuumed, but she liked the background noise and, of course, she was hungry for news of the epidemic. Had it abated at all? Was it worse? So she kept the TV blaring just in case someone had something to report.

It was while she was on her knees polishing the brass legs of her coffee table that she heard the announcement that always preceded a Presidential broadcast. When she'd looked up, however, it was Vice President Springer on the screen. He stood in the Oval Office before the President's desk, and he had a script that he fingered nervously as he waited for the okay to begin speaking. Terry put down the Windex and sat back on her haunches to listen.

The speech had not been long. Springer apologized that the President could not deliver this report to the people, but circumstances were such that, for reasons of national security, he could not be there. Springer said that he was sorry that he had to give the American people the tragic news that "for all intents and purposes, the government can no longer carry on its usual business, nor can it provide the services to which you, the American people, are accustomed." Springer set down his papers and looked directly into the camera. "This is not just a national disaster," he said. "It is an international catastrophe of epic proportions. Leaders all over the world are today delivering or have already delivered much the same news to their own people." Springer ran his hand over his forehead to wipe away the perspiration.

Then he went on, detailing mortality rates, explaining why bodies had not been properly disposed of, why fires had been left to blaze out of control in crowded neighborhoods, why the hospitals had to close their doors. The essence of his speech, though he said it more eloquently, was that people were now on their own. He urged everyone to stay home. "Do no traveling. Do no socializing. Stay out of public places and do not go to public meetings," he warned. Finally, he apologized that the government and the world of science had failed the people in not being able to find a remedy quickly enough. "We are working night and day in labs everywhere—in Geneva, London, Hamburg, Atlanta— and I believe we will prevail. For now, however, I can only urge people to stay in their homes until the disease dies out." Springer looked grimly into the camera. "We expect the power grids to shut down sometime today. We do not have the manpower or the technology to provide the energy they need to continue. As with all blackouts, Americans in the northeast and northern plains will have to devise ways to keep themselves warm in the upcoming months. Many have already prepared themselves with woodstoves and generators; others will have to do the same. Additionally, when the power goes down, we will lose our means of communicating with each other. Those who can operate battery-driven ham radios will become the eyes and ears of national and international news. We will have to depend on them to disseminate information for the foreseeable future. Some radio stations may still be able to broadcast, but at this time we cannot tell you where on the dial you will be able to find them."

Springer went on a little longer, but in the end, his message was clear. Citizens were on their own. The government was impotent, and help did not exist except for that which Terry's own alliance could provide.

With that, the screen went blank. She had sat on the floor and stared at it, listening to the TV's dull, buzzing static until finally she had turned it off. Terry walked out to the kitchen, where she microwaved the tea now in her hand. It was just as she removed the cup from the turntable that a click startled her and the digital readout disappeared. In the ceiling fixture, the yellow glow was gone.

Terry glanced at the woodstove, cold, black, clean, and waiting for just this time, the time they had been expecting for days now. Rob had stacked kindling and short birch logs beside it. She knew that before long, maybe in another half hour, the chill would begin to creep along the glass faces of windows and in through the eaves and floorboards. Like a patient enemy, its time had come. She wondered what people in apartment buildings and houses without fireplaces were going to do today. How would they stay warm? Where would they go? If they survived the flu, would they be able to survive the winter? She looked out at the gray sky, brown pastures and gaunt trees. The world looked cold and forbidding, empty of promise. In the oak tree at the end of their herb garden, a slight movement caught Terry's eye. A lone crow danced across one of its limbs, its head ducking rhythmically. It called, "Caw, caw, caw," danced some more and then flew away. Terry walked over, opened the woodstove door and began the familiar task of firing it up.

Part Three

SURVIVAL

40

Patterson, Monday, Late November

In New England, Nature loves playing tricks. After a series of several achingly cold days, a bright sun broke in the eastern sky, boding warmth and with it some long needed cheer. Along the stream banks, the icy mush working its way toward the middle withdrew just slightly, its edges melting where the sun gleamed upon it. Even the air felt different, so that if one could forget that Thanksgiving was only three days away, one could almost believe spring had come. The air was crisp but not brittle, the kind of air that when breathed deeply cleanses lungs. Laura stepped outside, slowly inhaling and feeling herself immediately improved. The hostility of November had abated, if only for today, and Laura wanted to make use of the reprieve to learn how to shoot.

They had talked, of course, frequently and long about the possibilities facing them now that all the structures of government had collapsed and lay in ruins. They did not know what to expect. Taylor insisted they must be prepared for roving bands of city people looking to plunder their food stores. Arnold disagreed. He said that city folks had all the cities' resources to plunder and no reason to come out to the boondocks where they didn't know their way around a cow's ass.

Ethel had agreed with Arnold, saying, "Oh, no, we're too far out." She insisted they were safe, but Laura didn't think so. She worried about people not nearly as distant as Worcester or even Leominster. She worried about the families in Almont and over in Grayson, on the other side of Patterson, families with no land to grow things next spring, families that hadn't had the money to buy stores ahead, as she had, or some who had been just too shortsighted to think ahead. They would come looking, she figured; sooner or later she'd hear the humming of an engine and see a car slow as it glided past the house, its occupants dim shadows behind the glass as they peered out, looking for signs of life, something worth investigating. If later, when this thing subsided, they came peacefully, that would be one matter. But if they came to take by force, Laura had no qualms about standing up for herself and her group. On herb-gathering forays around the country, she'd faced down rattlers, eased herself around copperheads, seen bears and mountain lions at close range, and she'd done it unarmed. The human predator, however, lacked predictability or honor when it came to survival. Dealing with a human required preparations. She knew that her size was no help, and while her skills in Taekwondo were excellent, she didn't want to be within arm's or foot's reach of someone carrying the germ. What good would it do to subdue an enemy if it meant dying of the virus? No, the gun was essential to overpowering at a distance, and Laura planned to know how to use it.

Taylor was already next-door with Arnold, the two of them discussing the merits of guns most appropriate to teach a woman how to shoot. Ethel would have none of it. "I'm not going to kill anything!" she had insisted last night, her hands spread on her wide hips, and Arnold, beside her as they talked before the fire, had laughed at the thought. "She can't even kill a spider, Laura," he guffawed, slapping poor Ethel on the shoulder. Ethel winced and grew stormy.

"You smack me again, Arnold, and you're going to wish you were a spider."

But Laura wanted to learn. She saw herself helping to hunt. She imagined herself feeling safer should anything or anybody come snooping around. The last thing she wanted was to be helpless, and learning how to shoot would definitely improve her odds against that.

Laura saw Taylor hefting a shotgun, testing its weight and balance, while Arnold watched. "We think this one," Taylor said, and Laura walked over to look at it in the dim cellar gloom. "It's a shotgun," Taylor explained. "Good for thirty to eighty yards. You don't have to be a crack shot to hit your target, because the ammo sprays outward. It's not a single bullet, like a rifle. The buckshot comes flying out all at once. Your chances of hitting your target are better with this."

Laura took the gun from his hand and held it, feeling the pleasant heft of it, the cool metal and the smooth, lustrous wood of the stock. "This is nice," she enthused, not knowing whether it was or not, but already enjoying the new sense of power the gun afforded her.

"Watch me load it," Taylor said, reaching beside him into a box of buckshot shells. He inserted four small shells into the magazine and then, with the safety on, handed the gun to Laura. "You carry this," he said. He grabbed several boxes of shells and stuffed them into his jacket pocket, then turned to pick up his shotgun. Arnold lifted his own gun and the three turned to leave.

"Keep that gun pointed down, girl," Arnold instructed the minute he saw Laura's predictable mistake. He'd expected it and was waiting. Arnold loved telling Ethel what to do, but now he had a new victim. Arnold believed he was going to enjoy this day. Like all novices, Laura had carried the shotgun incorrectly, letting it point straight ahead at Taylor's back. "Never point a loaded gun at anyone. Keep it pointed up, over your shoulder like this," and Arnold demonstrated, "or down at the ground. Least if it goes off, the worst you'll hit is your own foot." Arnold snickered at the thought. Laura reddened, then put the gun up over her shoulder and followed Taylor out the door. "Hup, two, march," Arnold joked behind her, stamping his feet as if this were a parade.

They walked straight out behind their houses into the woods bordering Harvard Forest. The waning November sun felt surprisingly warm as it poured down upon them through the leafless trees. Laura began to sweat, realizing she should have worn something lighter that she could shed layer by layer. Behind her, Arnold huffed and puffed, trying to keep up with the pace Taylor set. Laura smiled at his discomfort, enjoying a mild revenge. "You need to stop for a minute, Arnold?" she asked loudly. Taylor turned around and she smiled knowingly at him.

"No, no, go on, go on," Arnold gasped, his boots crashing through the dead leaves and undergrowth loud enough to scare any game that might be in the area. His cheeks were red, and Taylor slowed, pretending to be tying his boot while Arnold caught his breath.

"How much farther?" Laura asked, thinking they'd gone quite deep into the woods already. She looked at her compass and broke a branch beside their path.

"Just up there," Taylor pointed. "Over the crest of that hill there's an open meadow I found. It'll be a good place to set up and you'll be shooting into the hill."

It was a beautiful place, Laura thought as they came over the rise and stopped to look. Even if the grasses were brown and dried, even if the trees overhanging it were bare, even if now neither birds nor butterflies flitted about, Laura thought this would be a wonderful refuge, a place to come for solace. Huge smooth rocks, flat on top, jutted out of the earth and encircled the area. Laura could see herself enjoying the sun here, maybe even taking a nap stretched out on one of them. She meant to take note on the way back, mark trees to guide her, because she knew she wanted to come back here later.

"So, Taylor," Arnold puffed, arriving seconds behind them. "Laura tells me you were a trained sniper in the army." Arnold stopped beside them, gazing about the meadow.

"Yup," Taylor replied.

"Were you good?" Arnold raised his gun, play-aiming across the meadow.

"Yup. Good enough."

Arnold sighted his rifle at imaginary game. "How good?" he asked.

"Accurate to a thousand or so yards," Taylor replied, wondering why Arnold was so interested. He, too, began sighting across the meadow. Laura realized this was some sort of male thing going on and leaned against the tree to watch.

"A thousand!" Arnold said, impressed. "You were damned good!

"There were better," Taylor said.

Just then Arnold froze, holding his finger on the trigger, his gun aimed across the meadow. "Tell me," he whispered. "Can you see that there woodchuck over by the big pine?"

"Yup," Taylor said, finding the target and freezing.

"Can you hit him in the eye?" Arnold asked, his eyebrows raised and a smile spreading across his face. He broke his stance and looked at Taylor.

"Which eye?" Taylor asked, dead serious, never moving.

Laura heard Arnold's little gasp. "The left one," he said, pushing matters.

The shot rang out instantly and across the meadow, Laura saw the round, brown body of what had been a perfectly happy woodchuck lift, somersault, and drop in the brown grass. Smoke drifted about the barrel of Taylor's rifle, but otherwise, all was still. Arnold stood on his toes, trying to see if the animal was dead, but he couldn't be sure.

"Well, I think I'll just go take a look," Arnold said ruefully. He began walking into the meadow.

"We'll start setting up," Taylor smiled, looking at Laura. "Got those cans I gave you?" Taylor spotted a fallen tree stump just off to the left. "We'll put them on that," he said pointing.

Laura wasn't listening. She watched Arnold as he grew closer to where she'd seen the woodchuck's somersault. He slowed, stepping tentatively as he got to within about ten feet of the spot. Then he hurried forward, bent and picked the thing up by the tail. He held it aloft, peering at the head. He stared at the slowly twirling corpse for what seemed long seconds, then Laura thought she heard him say, "Jeez," just before he turned and began walking toward them, the woodchuck dangling from his left hand. "Jeez," he said again, this time closer. "You did it, man," Arnold said, his eyes wide with amazement. Laura looked at the woodchuck as Arnold held it up. Its head dangled, and as it twirled in Arnold's hand, the left side of its face, just where the eye would have been, was gone. "Well, here's our supper," Arnold said, stuffing the animal into his canvas bag.

"Let's try from over there," Taylor said, ignoring Arnold as he pointed to a spot about fifty yards away. The five cans he'd set up stood waiting in the sunshine. They walked the distance, then turned. Taylor pulled out a small pair of earplugs, handing them to Laura. "Put these in; they'll protect your hearing." He took another pair for himself. Arnold put on the protections he used when mowing the lawn, giant red plastic earmuffs lined with rubber. He looked like an alien. Laura smiled at him.

"You put the butt end into that crook between your shoulder and your collar bone," Taylor instructed, stepping up behind her. She raised the butt, placing it against her shoulder. "No, not there. In between," he instructed, moving the butt closer in. "Now, hold the shaft with this hand," and he placed her hand farther out on the stock, "and put this hand here, with your finger on the trigger."

"Pull it in tight," Arnold added. "Otherwise the kick will knock you backwards and hurt your shoulder."

"Now lower your head so that you can see through the rear sight and then through the front sight." Laura did as she was told and both sights became one as they lined up. "What do you see in both sights?" Taylor asked.

"That pricker bush on the far side of the meadow, directly across from us," Laura answered.

"Well if you pull the trigger nice and easy, and you don't move or breathe, that's what you'll hit. Now sight the cans just like you did the bush." He waited while Laura found the cans in the gun sights. "Tell me when," he said quietly.

"Yeah, find a good position and hold still," Arnold interjected loudly. "You don't want to move when you pull the trigger. I hold my breath too."

Taylor squeezed Laura's elbow. "Just be still. Concentrate." He let go of her arm. "Do you feel it? Try to get your heart to slow down. Forget everything else but the can..."

"Yeah, you gotta' pay attention. Don't let anything

distract you." Arnold stopped when both Laura and Taylor stood straight and looked crossly at him. "Oh," he managed, "I guess you want me to be quiet." Arnold looked down at his boots and spit.

"Try again," Taylor coached. And Laura once again raised the gun and sighted. "Have you got the can?" Taylor asked. Laura murmured yes. "Now breathe deeply and hold. When you're perfectly still, pull the trigger back steadily, but slow." She did. The gun resounded, and her shoulder absorbed the kick easily. Two cans flew in the air.

"Hah!" Taylor laughed. "Damn good, girl!" He put his arm around her. Laura felt an incredible sense of pride, having hit her target and impressed Taylor.

Arnold said, "Beginner's luck, I bet. You say you never shot a gun before?" He wanted to hear that she had. The shot was just too good.

"Shall I try again?" Laura asked.

"Yup. This time, no coaching from me." He turned toward Arnold. "Or from Harpo here." Arnold got the message and stood quiet.

Laura raised the gun, sighting one of the remaining cans and finding a stance that she could hold steady. She took a deep breath and held. Ka-boom. The gun jumped against her shoulder, but she held tight. Another can flew in the air.

"What an eye you have!" Taylor grinned. "Most hunters couldn't do that." Taylor hugged her again, looking down at her with the proudest grin. "Best I stay on your good side," he whispered.

Arnold only stared. "Okay," he said, raising his rifle. "Let me get the next one." He sighted the can, drew in his breath, held, and shot. The rifle resounded, but nothing happened. The two remaining cans didn't even vibrate.

"Once more," Arnold said, once again taking aim. He shot, but only the tree bark just left of the two cans splintered in a small huff of dried sawdust. Arnold looked up, disgusted. "Damn," he said. "I'm out of practice."

"Let Laura try your gun," Taylor asked, thinking that when she missed, Arnold could save face. "A rifle's different, you know," he said to her. "You've got one bullet. If your aim isn't perfect, you hit nothing. Buckshot is sure to hit something when it sprays."

Laura reached for the offered rifle, jouncing it in her hand to get a sense of the difference between it and her gun. She looked at Arnold and Taylor, her jaw resolved. Then she lifted the rifle and once again began sighting. She ran her hand back and forth over the gunstock before finally resting her forefinger on the trigger guard and then wiggled the gun butt into her shoulder. She took her time. She heard Arnold sigh with impatience, but she paid no attention. She was in her head, focusing down onto the red Coke can fifty yards away. She breathed slowly, feeling her heart calm, and then finally she didn't breath at all. Her finger pulled ever so slowly on the trigger, back, back, and then the momentary resistance before the hammer slammed down and the butt kicked back into her shoulder. Almost soundless, so deep she had gone into herself. The can lifted and spun, tumbling backward behind the trunk, and it felt to Laura as if she had reached out an invisible arm and owned the can, forcing it to do her bidding. "Yes!" she said.

Both men stood silent. She looked up, expecting cheers. Taylor tried to hide the smile that he could not let Arnold see. Arnold's face drooped. "Well," he managed. "Good shot, Laura." He reached for his gun. "Guess I've got some work to do." But Arnold was not without sportsmanship.

Minutes later, as Laura tried Taylor's gun and Arnold practiced with his rifle while Taylor replaced the cans on the tree trunk between volleys, Arnold turned to her and said, "Not many women can shoot like that, girl. You're going to be one crack shot and a good hunter. But shooting something alive will be different."

After practicing for nearly an hour, the meadow smelled of gun smoke. The threesome decided to head deeper into the woods to find a Thanksgiving turkey. Taylor suggested they split up, with Arnold heading due east while they headed west. Arnold knew the woods better, but Laura had her compass, and Taylor knew how to explore forest without getting lost. They agreed that they'd meet back at the meadow before lunch.

Laura and Taylor soon came upon a stream and decided to follow it. "I think we must be into Johnsville by now," Laura said, pulling out a map. "Look, here's the stream, and this is where we started." She sat down on a rock, looking about. "What beautiful country," she said, resting the shotgun on her knees. Taylor sat down beside her. "You miss Wyoming?" Laura asked, tentatively.

"You forget I grew up in New England," Taylor said. "It took a long time to get used to Wyoming. There are a lot of dry brown hills out there. A lot of hostile land. But parts of it are as beautiful as here. Maybe more dramatic. Certainly wilder than here."

"Shhhhh," Laura cautioned, whispering. "Something's over there, beyond those bushes." She lifted her gun, taking aim.

Taylor put a hand on her arm. "Wait. Don't move." The two froze, listening intently. Several creatures were wandering about over there. Bushes rustled too far apart to be just one animal. As they grew closer, Laura could see the black backs of several birds, turkeys for sure, as they scratched and pecked at the dead grasses. A muffled gobble, gobble sound as one raised its head to look around. It did not see them, and the head disappeared. Laura could feel her quick breathing, and worked at focusing to calm her excitement. Both remained motionless. Taylor merely watched, waiting to signal her. The turkeys moved their way, busily scratching about for insects. Several young ones appeared, but Taylor whispered, "No, wait," and so Laura held, the gun becoming heavy in her grip. A large hen appeared, hustling about among the youngsters, then another, and finally a large male with its long and painfully red wattle.

If it caught the minute movement of Taylor's hand at Laura's elbow, it had no time to react. Laura felt the okay to shoot and pulled the trigger, catching herself from falling backward off the rock as the gun kicked back. Before them, the large male leapt into the air, its wings fighting to take flight while the others in its band rose squawking, the air trembling with the vibrations of their wings. The big male got about ten feet in the air, paused, and then flopped down, its wings still battling what its heart had already lost. Seconds later, it lay in a heap on the forest floor, its legs still moving, but its head limp on the grass.

Laura jumped off the rock and stood gasping. She had never taken the life of any animal and the momentary regret was painful. Taylor knew what she felt and he stood close beside her. "We won't kill what we won't eat, Laura," he said. "We need food and you've provided it. That tom will make a fine Thanksgiving dinner for all of us, and sandwiches for days." He put his arm over her shoulders.

"I know," she said. But in her heart the regret remained. Life eats life. She knew it, had always known it, but today she truly understood it for the first time. She walked over to the bird. "You know," she said, "primitive tribesmen had rituals for this, a way to thank the animal for giving its life so that they might live."

"I know."

"So that's what I'm doing right now," Laura said, holding out her hand to stop Taylor before he picked the bird up. She closed her eyes, still holding his arm and Taylor waited. In her head, Laura thanked God for her ability to shoot and for the bird, and the souls of all things. Then she let go so Taylor could bend to lift the bird.

"It's a beauty! Congratulations," he said. "What a feast we're going to have!" They both laughed. "Let's go home," he said. And in his use of "home," a great and wonderful sense of warmth spread through Laura, a real sense of thanksgiving.

It was on their way back, cutting a triangular leg northeastward toward the meadow where they planned to meet Arnold, that the unmistakable smell of death rose in front of them, a sickly, moist cloud of decay. Taylor slowed, holding his hand out behind him to warn Laura, who followed on his heels.

"What?" she said. "Phew." She peered around Taylor's shoulders and saw where the remains of something white and black lay ripped open and half-eaten. "What is that," she asked. "It looks like a dog."

"It is," Taylor answered. "Probably a small spaniel."

"A dog?" Laura asked, incredulous. "What happened to it? Look, it's got a collar." She felt immediate pain, not only for the pet but also for the owners who might be looking for it.

"I suspect we'll see more of this," Taylor said. "Probably other dogs. This one's almost too big for coyotes."

"You mean wild dogs?" she said, suddenly fearful and wary.

"I mean hungry dogs," Taylor replied. "Dogs whose owners have died."

The sudden realization that millions of dogs might now be ownerless sent chills down Laura's spine. "Good God, I never thought about that. They're going to become feral, all those sweet natured labs and shepherds. They're not going to just curl up and die with their masters, they're going to learn to hunt for themselves...or starve."

"They'll create packs. But the little ones, they're going to become the prey."

Laura thought about her old cocker spaniel, now long dead, being attacked by a pack of dogs. It wouldn't have stood a chance. "That won't be the end of it, will it," she said thoughtfully. "They'll move on to other animals..."

"...And people, when they can..."

"Good Lord," she said, seeing dogs in a whole new light.

"We don't go walking anymore without a gun," Taylor said. He hefted the canvas bag holding her turkey over his shoulder and said, "Let's go." Laura followed, looking this way and that as if the dog pack might suddenly attack out of nowhere. She held her gun firm and wondered whether, if the time came, she'd be able to hold steady facing a pack of growling, hungry, bloody-mouthed former pets. No matter how much she tried to imagine it, she could not.

41

Patterson, Wednesday, Early December

Arnold found Ethel curled in her bed, her shoulders heaving, the pillow wet with tears. He'd been outside splitting wood with Taylor, enjoying a growing sense of accomplishment as they watched their stack of firewood grow longer along the border of their two properties. In addition to the wood they had had delivered before the flu hit, Arnold figured that they had about fifty feet now, high as his chest, mostly oak and maple from the woods behind their houses. They had cut carefully, making the extra effort to transport logs from deeper in rather than clear-cutting trees close by. And they had set up the line far enough back on the property so that anyone who might pass by on the road wouldn't be apt to see their supply. Taylor and Arnold had talked quietly as they split and stacked and agreed that firewood robbers were unlikely, but it was better to be safe than sorry.

It had begun to snow just before lunchtime, big, furry white flakes that drifted lazily down to earth, in no hurry at all to cover the ground. This wasn't the first snow, but Arnold told Taylor that it was probably the first one that would matter. He'd been watching the heavy, dark clouds gathering in the west all morning, and the air had that unmistakable feel of a storm of substance on its way.

Still, they continued working. The flakes collected on Taylor's Stetson and his suede jacket, nestled in the lamb's wool of his collar and on the already stacked wood, outlining the logs in white. They landed, melted, and then dripped uncomfortable icy trickles down Arnold's neck where his collar was loose at his hairline. They caught in his bushy eyebrows and on the one lock of hair that hung down from his forehead beneath his red and black checked cap.

Arnold stopped to watch Taylor work, wishing he could keep up and hoping that Taylor would soon want to break for lunch, but Taylor showed no signs of fatigue and said nothing about food. Arnold's stomach growled as he looked around at the snow. On the hills beyond their houses, the pastures were turning white. Snow swirled in the light wind, the flakes sometimes pirouetting before landing on other flakes now lying two inches deep on the ground. He marked the snow with his boot. His toe came up covered. Arnold had loved snow ever since he was a boy, in the old days when snow covered the roads from December until April, before the DPW started spreading salt every time the sky even spritzed them with flakes. He loved the silence of snow, how it made all other sounds muffled and distant. Like hiding under a pillow, a big, fluffy, white pillow. December snow was great for tracking and hunting deer, and he liked how snow isolated families, made them close in on themselves before a fire, playing checkers or Monopoly when otherwise they would be too busy. His best memories were of snowy times when his children spread out on the carpet in their flannel pj's and furry slippers around some kind of game board while Ethel bustled about in the kitchen making soup. Well into his sixties, even when he knew that sooner or later he'd have to go out and shovel the stuff out of the driveway, Arnold savored school cancellations and the weathermen's excited predictions.

Taylor finally stopped, realizing he was working alone.

"You want to take a break?" he asked, leaning on his maul. He knew Arnold wasn't up to much more splitting. His face was beet red and his eyes looked smaller than usual. They had gotten a great deal done in the last few weeks, including the awesome pile of firewood they were stacking, and Taylor was beginning to feel as if things were under control, that he and Laura were prepared for a long winter. They'd enjoyed an excellent Thanksgiving, gorged themselves on Laura's turkey and Ethel's apple pie, and now it wouldn't be long before Christmas. The seasons were turning with some predictability, Taylor thought, and while January had yet to lay its icy grip on them, he could make himself think spring was not that far behind. Even in this snow.

When they finally broke for lunch, Arnold had stomped into the house, spreading snow all over the back hallway, hung his coat to dry over the pantry door, and looked for his lunch. "Where is that girl," he thought, annoyed that Ethel hadn't anticipated his arrival with some hot soup and tea. He had gone first to her sewing room, thinking she might have been so busy mending that she had forgotten him. The room was empty. He had arrived at their bedroom door exasperated and ready to berate her for dereliction of duty. Instead, he was shocked to find her crying like a little girl.

"You stub your toe or something?" Arnold asked feebly, knowing that Ethel didn't cry over such things. But she only snuffled. He walked into the room and sat down on their bed.

"We've got at least twenty cords of firewood," he said, hoping to change the subject.

"Goooooood," Ethel gurgled, her voice tremulous.

"We'll be warm for the winter," Arnold added, encouraged by her positive response. But his words had the opposite effect. Instead, Ethel wailed, her tears spouting anew.

"What did I say?" Arnold asked, befuddled. He ran the flat of his palm along Ethel's plump back, ending with a few pats. "Are you mad at me?"

"Nooooooo," Ethel wailed again. "I'm just so lonely," she added pathetically.

"Why are you lonely?" Arnold asked, confused. He thought they'd been fine, the four of them. Not that he didn't understand their circumstances or worry about his grown kids, far away and unreachable. Not that he didn't appreciate the severity of the world situation. He was just glad not to be going to work at Garrett's, happy for the first long vacation in his life. He felt...and he struggled for the right concept...he felt more manly than he'd been in a long time. He was hunting. Carrying a gun. He was cutting wood. He had become a pioneer, conquering the savage frontier. Before, he had been meek little Arnold, technician at Garrett's, quick to do the bidding of his bosses, whether he thought they were right or not. Now he was making decisions, ordering Ethel about, advising Laura and Taylor. For the first time, people actually cared about his ideas, so he'd begun using his brain again, figuring things out, finding ways to make life more livable for the four of them. He looked down at the hump his wife made under the blankets and thought her terribly ungrateful.

Whether Ethel appreciated Arnold's contributions or not made little difference. She was disconsolate. "I miss church. I miss my friends. It's just so...so.... isolated here," she whined. Her sobs accelerated.

"Oh, come on," Arnold chastised. "What have you got to be crying about? Would you rather be down in Almont rotting in one of those row houses? Rubbing elbows with the sick and the dying? For pete's sake, Ethel, get a grip. We're the lucky ones. We're surviving this thing!"

But Ethel was not to be consoled. "What good does it do to survive if all that's left is...is.... this?" she waved her hand and Arnold smarted, for she'd included him in the "this" she'd indicated.

"Well, by God, girl, I never before thought you was stupid. But I'm about to reassess..."

"Oh, go ahead and reassess all you want, Arnold Card. I don't care what you think. You're just so.... so..." but Ethel couldn't finish. Her sorrow welled up once again, choking off whatever it was she might have said. Instead, she shriveled in on herself, pulling the pillow to her face and wailing like a punished child.

Arnold could stand no more. He rose and stamped his feet as he strode to the door, then slammed it behind him without looking back. "Women!" he exploded, slamming a fist against the wall as he headed for the kitchen. Behind him, Ethel's wails increased in volume and tenacity, as if she meant to let him have it no matter how far away he got.

In the kitchen, Arnold stood by the window watching the snow accumulate on the road. It was coming down harder now; in the few minutes he'd been with Ethel, he bet another inch had fallen. He turned on the tap, watching the gravity-fed spring water they'd set up run smoothly from the faucet, filling a small pan with water for tea. He placed it atop the wood stove and returned to the window to wait for it to boil.

At times like this, Arnold made mental checklists. Had they provided for a ready supply of water? Check. Had they enough wood for heat and cooking? Check. Well, almost check. Did they have enough food for winter? Check. Had they planned for the future...for next winter's food? Check. Did they have enough candles? Check. But the one thing they didn't have, and this had been on Arnold's mind for some time, they didn't have a way of communicating. Arnold hungered for news. He had seen enough in Almont to know that when this was over, the world was going to be a very different place. Not only had the virus wiped out whole segments of the population, it had also ravaged the systems that supported and protected that population. He likened this new world to the old West, where people had to protect themselves because law officers were few and far between. His new friend Taylor looked like a modern-day Wyatt Earp. All those years of paying into Social Security, Arnold thought, shaking his head. Well, he reminded himself, they warned us that the fund would bottom out. Just not so soon. Just not this way. Now he and Ethel were on their own. He'd have to provide, and Arnold worried that perhaps he was too old to be able to do so. Without Taylor, they'd never have been able to hole up like this, and Arnold thanked his lucky stars that Laura had brought Taylor here just in time to save them all.

But what if things were resuming? What if controls were being repaired right now, as he stood there by the window? How could they know, way out here in the boondocks with no electricity or telephone? His battery radio produced nothing but static. No stations. No WPIX. Those systems had collapsed, but Arnold knew one thing for sure. Somewhere out there someone was broadcasting over a ham radio. Maybe even a lot of people. Just like the Vice President said, the ham radio operators were going to become the eyes and ears of the world. Arnold had always wanted to build one. He'd always meant to, but time and taking care of his place had always gotten in the way. Now that they were settling in for a long winter, he'd have lots of time, great spans of time. He and Ethel would be alone in this house for days on end. He blinked. That thought made him want to cry too.

The tea water had begun to boil, and Arnold brought the pan over to the counter where he had set a teabag in his cup. He poured the steaming water slowly, thinking about what it might take to build his own radio. It'd have to be battery-operated. That in itself was going to be a challenge. Arnold cursed himself for not having downloaded some instructions off the Internet the last time he thought about such a project. He'd always figured there would be more time. Now it was too late. He knew he had no reference books that would help. Despite buying probably fifty how-to books, Arnold had never bought a how-to on ham radios.

As he was jouncing the tea bag in his cup, encouraging the leaves to do their work, something caught his eye. He looked up, and there on the street he saw a black pickup approaching. It crept so slowly that it seemed hardly to move at all. Its windshield wipers flapped back and forth, its hood was white with snow, its headlamps iced with it. Arnold could see the back wheels fishtail, but it continued to move forward. He hadn't seen a vehicle on his street in weeks. The sight of it fascinated Arnold. A Ford, all-wheel drive, he thought. They ought to be able to move faster than that.

As the pickup came even with his house, Arnold looked harder, trying to make out who was inside. The snow swirled about so thick it was impossible to tell. Arnold leaned forward over the sink, pressing his nose to the glass. Looked like two or three people inside, Arnold thought, though he couldn't be sure. The truck was directly in front of the house now, rolling so slowly that he should have been able to see the eyes of the bearded man in the passenger seat who was staring at Arnold's sweet little cape, the smoke billowing from its chimney, the red siding looking warm and welcoming to passersby in the storm. But Arnold couldn't see through the swirling snow and the truck's fogged glass, nor did those studying his house notice the gray-haired man staring back at them from between Ethel's hanging plants in the kitchen window. The car moved on until only the taillights glowed in the snow, and then they too were gone.

Arnold picked up his teacup, taking a sip as he wondered who would be driving about in a storm like this and what they were doing out his way. He felt a mild apprehension, as if some secret had been exposed. In a way, Arnold wished he and Taylor could have blocked off the road so that no one could know they were there. But then they wouldn't have been able to get out either. Taylor had advised against it, saying a blocked road could handicap them in a number of ways, that he'd rather defend himself when threatened than protect himself from being threatened. The latter was just too hard.

"And," Taylor had added emphatically, "we don't know when we might have to venture out. We've got gas, and we've got a good siphon if we need more. Who knows where we might have to go to get something."

Arnold stood up straight. "That's it!" he thought. "I know where I can get instructions *and* the things I might need. All we have to do is go to the library!" The simplicity of this solution astounded him. They'd go tomorrow or the next day, as soon as the snow subsided. Taylor could get them there, and if Arnold was right, everything he needed would be available at Radio Shack. They'd find what they needed, and as soon as Arnold could build it, they'd be talking to the rest of the world. Maybe they could get word to their kids. They could find out what's what. They'd have contact. Ethel could talk with other people, maybe not feel so isolated and alone.

Arnold was so excited he nearly knocked his teacup off the counter as he reached for another cup to bring in to Ethel. He'd cheer the old girl up right now. He'd make her smile again.

42

Patterson, Wednesday, Early December

The snow had to be above his knees, Michael thought as he gazed out his bedroom window. He'd been reading the book his mother gave him, Where The Red Fern Grows, lying on his bed by the window to catch as much light as possible. Every day now after they helped their father with a few chores, both Michael and Chris endured home school at Carol Green's from nine till twelve, followed after lunch by the two-hour enforced reading periods that were his mother's idea to keep them learning. Michael had tried to argue his way out of it, saying school would start soon enough and probably last through the summer while they caught up. If they were going to miss their summer vacation, it was only fair that they be free now. But his mother was unmoved by his pleas.

"I'd like to think you're right, Michael, that all of this will soon be over and everyone will go back to school. But I don't think that's going to happen. I don't even know how many people are left here in Patterson. So in the meantime, it's my responsibility to keep you learning." Terry had folded her arms over her chest to emphasize her determination.

"But Mom," he'd argued, "if there aren't any schools left, then why bother? Why can't I help Dad? That's more important." Michael hoped this argument would win her over, especially the "help Dad" part, because now his father and Charlie seemed to be working extra hard to keep up with things.

"You're right," Terry agreed, nodding her head, "and your father and I expect you to help out. But that doesn't mean we're going to let you grow up ignorant. The neighbors and I have planned a curriculum for all of you, and you are going to school and you are going to read. That's that." When Michael's mother used that tone, he knew all was lost. And so for weeks now, every morning at quarter to nine he, Chris, and their mother walked down the road to the Greens' for "school house," as they'd come to call it.

The Greens' house was bigger than theirs. They had a living room and a family room, a huge dining room where books and papers could be spread out on the mahogany table, and a kitchen as large as their living room. Michael thought the Greens must be rich from the size of their house and from the fact that they had fireplaces everywhere. Mrs. Green had set up her card tables in each room for the kids to use as desks and she had been very teacherly in the way she organized their routine, so that within a day or two, going to the Greens' house no longer felt like fun; it felt like going to school. That is, except for the sweet smell of bread baking in their Dutch oven or of hot chocolate at break. That made it bearable.

His mother taught science, Mrs. Green math, Mrs. Young reading, and Mrs. Curley writing. The new teachers had been very serious about establishing each room as a classroom where nobody fooled around and no toys or games were allowed, but everyone headed to the cellar for pool as soon as Mrs. Green called break every day at ten-thirty. Michael wondered who was going to fall down the cellar steps first, because the pushing and shoving to get a stick meant that they all nearly tumbled down the stairs in one wild, struggling ball of arms and legs. No matter how many times Mrs. Green yelled at them, the same thing happened every day. As ten-thirty approached, they grew more and more restless, wriggling in the squeaky folding chairs, shuffling papers, sighing, stretching, and when the teacher wasn't looking, crossing their eyes at each other. Then the awaited words, "Okay, break time," and both boys and girls shot from their chairs as if they'd been launched from a rocket and raced for the cellar.

Michael smiled at the thought, for they all knew they were being naughty, and their mothers knew they were being naughty, and yet no one stopped it. Their mothers could have, of course, but somehow Michael felt they allowed this one infraction because they felt sorry for their kids. Michael had overheard them once when he was coming silently up the stairs to go to the bathroom during break. They were in the kitchen, taking a break themselves and talking. And he'd heard Mrs. Green say that she wished her children could have grown up when she did, when life was safer.

He'd heard his mother express her worry: "What are they growing up to? Now, I mean, with a world like this?" There'd been a silence, and Michael had hesitated on the stairs, his foot still in the air above the next step. He didn't like eavesdropping but he couldn't help himself. He eavesdropped when his parents were downstairs in the kitchen, long after they thought the kids were asleep. And he listened out in the barn, when Charlie and his dad were making plans. And he listened when anyone was on the phone, even Chris. He just couldn't help himself, even though he knew such behavior was not fitting a man. Certainly he was sure his dad never eavesdropped. Or his mom. Or even Charlie. So as he stood there in the shadows, he felt guilty, but he still stood there.

"I'm afraid it's going to be a ruthless new world," Lisa

Curley said. "Maybe a kind of survival of the fittest sort of thing. We've got no police to protect us, at least not that I know of. And after they burned the Jamesons, well...I'm just really scared is all."

"I'm not sure I can survive in a ruthless world," Shirley said. "I've had enough troubles. I don't think I can handle more." Michael knew Shirley was referring to her divorce, the way her husband had left her nearly penniless and disappeared somewhere across the country. Michael had been prying then too, when Shirley had spent many mornings crying in his mom's kitchen.

"What's the alternative?" his mother asked. "You just can't roll over and give up. You have to go on, no matter what." His mother's voice was stern. Michael knew that tone well.

"Why?" was Shirley's response, and it made Michael frightened. Why? He thought. People are asking why go on? Are things that bad? And for the first time, Michael sensed the void. The nothing. It was if he had run pell-mell into a wall and had all the air knocked out of him. His chest actually ached, even though he took a deep breath and straightened his back. He set his foot down on the step and leaned against the wall, looking at the cobwebs over the cellar door, where Mrs. Green had missed them. Why go on?

"Because no one promised us anything. No one said our lives were going to be safe. But we're surviving, Shirley. We're going on despite the odds. And we've saved our kids, who are going to survive us and make a new world. A better world than we've given them." Michael listened intently, feeling somehow assured by his mother's passion.

Mrs. Green added, "We've made it this far, we're going to make it through. Who knows? Maybe life will be better out the other side. Simpler. Kinder. Who says it has to be ruthless?"

"And we have each other," his mother added. "We're a community."

"One for all, and all for one!" Mrs. Green reminded them.

Again there was a short silence. Michael felt it was time to make himself known, so he stomped up the last three stairs and burst into the kitchen, pretending he was out of breath. All of the women straightened when he entered, but he pretended not to notice and headed directly for his coat and the outhouse.

The re-entry of the outhouse into their lives was one thing he didn't like about the new world order. Michael missed the comfort of a warm tiled bathroom and steam on the mirror. He definitely did not like running outside every time he had to go. In fact, he'd learned that at night his bedroom window afforded him an easy way to avoid such necessities, letting the ground outside absorb all traces of what would certainly earn him a punishment if his mother found out. Of course, now that it was snowing, he'd have to be more careful. His mother might just notice yellow snow and put two and two together. He leaned forward, looking down at the ground through his window.

Watching the snow accumulate, Michael felt excited. His reading period was nearly over and once his mother called him, he and Chris were going out to build a fort in the snow. There was surely enough snow by now. They'd build their fort on the hill up past the barn where the wind created high drifts each winter. The fort would be a cool place to get away from his parents and Charlie, if only for a while, now that they weren't allowed to go to their tree house. His dad said going into the woods was just too dangerous without a gun. He feared packs of hungry dogs ever since his talk with the Police Chief. But Michael felt a strong need to get away, out of his parents' range of influence.

Griz slept soundly on the floor beside Michael's bed. Every so often, he let out a little "woof" and his back legs jerked. Sometimes, for a minute, he'd breathe hard. Other times, Michael could tell his eyes were moving erratically underneath his lids. Michael called these his wild dog dreams and wondered what Griz was doing in them. He was their mystery dog, come out of nowhere, and claimed by no one, yet perfectly housetrained and well mannered. He knew tricks, too, like getting his dad's slippers and carrying his metal dog dish around in his mouth when it was suppertime, a beggar pleading for a handout. The first time he did that, his mother couldn't believe it. "That dog is smart!" she said, her hands on her hips. He was an endless ball-fetcher and ruthless rabbit chaser, but he knew enough to leave their chickens alone and he never chased the other livestock. He had passed all his dad's and mom's little tests with flying colors and been accepted into their family as one of them.

Though Griz stuck by his father most of the time, he had taken to being with Michael the rest, especially during the afternoon reading periods. Michael figured Griz pretended to protect him, when really, this was Griz's chance to sleep undisturbed for two hours. Michael smiled just looking at him. Griz was going to love it out there in the snow. He had the coat for a snow dog, thick, long, and silky. They would make snowballs and throw them and laugh while Griz tried to fetch them. But first, he had to do his time. He looked back at his novel, not reading the words.

"How many pages?" his mother asked from the door, having just missed catching him daydreaming.

Michael looked up, relieved. "Maybe twenty," he fibbed. "I didn't pay attention."

Terry moved into the room, watching the snow falling outside. "Isn't it beautiful out there?" she asked. "I love snow. Well, I especially love the first snow."

"Chris and I want to make a fort on the hill," Michael said. "Can we go now?"

Terry had been just about to sit down on Michael's bed for a chat. She'd hoped he might want to talk to her about all the things going on, discuss his fears or whatever he was feeling. She worried so about both of them, penned up like this, though schoolhouse at least gave them some outlet, some opportunity to be with other kids. "Oh," she said quickly. "Okay. Make sure you put on your snow pants." She rumpled his hair and watched him as he slid off his bed and hurried away.

Michael and Chris waddled up the hill, bundled in layers of clothing and snowsuits, boots, mittens, and hats. Terry had stood guard by the door, inspecting each of them before she would let them by. Only Griz was able to slip out uninspected, and now he ran ahead of them, leaping through the chest deep snow. Michael called him and threw a snowball, and Griz took off after it, sending snow flying behind him. When he reached the spot where he thought it had landed, he dipped his nose into the snow, sniffing it out. When he couldn't find it, he began plowing, tunneling around in a fruitless attempt to find something that looked like a ball. When that didn't work, he began digging, his back legs spread wide and his front paws attacking the snow and sending it flying out behind him. Chris and Michael laughed, knowing that the ball had long ago been pulverized. And when Griz lifted his snow-encrusted face to see what they were laughing at, they laughed even more. "The abominable snowman!" Chris cried. "Run!"

They reached the top of the hill and looked down at their farm, nestled neatly in the snow. Smoke rose from the chimney, and they saw Charlie and their father walking from the barn to the house for their mid-afternoon break. Michael was struck by how far away and small they looked. As if out of a story, he thought, a story about someone else's life, not mine. But Chris pulled at his sleeve. "Come on, Michael," he said. "Let's get going."

They decided to roll huge snowballs to a spot just left of a giant oak tree. That way, the tree could act as one of the fort's side supports and tomorrow they could bring up a hammer and some slats to nail steps up its side. They'd have a lookout that way, and maybe they could climb as high as the first branch, which sent a sturdy arm out from the trunk about twelve feet above them. They worked industriously, rolling ball after ball to the foundation they'd marked until they had outlined the fort's base with two-foot snowballs. Michael had just finished putting the last one in place when he looked over at Chris, who had plopped down in the snow. Griz was nuzzling him, his face wet, snow and ice sticking to his whiskers. "Let's finish tomorrow," Chris said.

Michael knew his brother was tired. He sat down a few feet away, looking back at the farm again. Then he lay back in the snow and made a snow angel. Chris liked that idea, and began doing the same, though Griz used his prone position to begin licking Chris' face with his hot, red tongue. "Yuck!" Chris yelled, laughing. "Yuck ! Yuck!" he cried out again, but by now, Griz was upon him, ready to wrestle. Chris could do little, because the dog was as large as he and probably heavier. Michael watched, smiling at the comedy of it, happy for the first time in a long time. "Let's go see if our tree house is okay," he said, struggling upright.

Griz immediately jumped off Chris, dancing about in readiness.

"Dad said no going into the woods," Chris said. He looked down at their house. "Dad would be mad." But Chris' eyes said, "Let's go." They had not been to the tree house since the Jamesons' fire.

"Dad's back in the barn, " Michael said. "I saw them a while ago."

"They're milking then?" Chris knew this meant they wouldn't be coming out for some time. "Maybe if we just go and come back quickly," he added, already turned and walking toward the woods.

Their father had helped them build the tree house only this past summer. They'd been clearing a pasture along the tree line, and he had asked them if they'd like him to help them build it, and of course, Chris had not been able to stop jumping up and down with excitement. Now, it was their castle in the sky, accessible by a stout set of steps that ascended the great oak into an eight by eight room. It even had a tarpaper roof so that on rainy days, they could play cards and drink soda, eat bags of Cheetos and read comics all afternoon without getting wet. It was a cherished place, a place they thought about all the time and had missed since their dad's ultimatum. It wasn't all that far away, just a few minutes walk into the woods. Their father was busy in the barn. He'd never know. And the boys could no longer resist its call. They disappeared into the trees.

The tree house was only over the next knoll, they were sure, when Griz, who had been walking quietly ahead of them, suddenly stopped and began to growl, a low, grating growl that continued without his taking a breath. The boys froze, their eyes darting wildly about to see what Griz saw, then back to Griz, whose hackles stood straight up in ragged points along his back. His growling continued and his head followed something left and right that they couldn't see in the falling snow. Griz's tail stood straight out behind him, rigid with intensity.

Both boys backed up without looking, terrified. Chris was holding Michael's arm, and Michael could hear his shredded breathing, the growing rasp as Chris' throat began to close on him.

Griz leapt forward three pronounced steps, his front feet wide apart, his growling louder and angry. Then he pounced over the other way, the same defensive dance, his paws parted, hind end crouched, ready to spring. His ears stood erect, moving like radar antennae to capture sounds the boys couldn't hear and his head turned back and forth, watching through the snow something moving out there, behind the trees.

Chris saw the first one. He clutched Michael's arm, gasping, and when Michael looked in the direction Chris indicated, he saw the black eyes of a Doberman staring at him. The dog peered from beside a tree, almost indistinguishable from the trunk. The dog's teeth were bared. Then it moved sideways in an arc. Michael could see it clearer now, for the dog had worked its way around, closer to him and Chris. Suddenly the dog became two dogs, as another one, a dark, slightly smaller dog passed it, looking directly at the boys. Griz followed the dogs' movements intently, leaping to place himself between them and the boys. Michael stood fascinated, watching Griz now from the side, his white fangs long and terrible. The dogs were trying to get at him and Chris, he knew for sure from the way they tried to move around Griz. But Griz wouldn't allow it. Always, he placed himself between the dogs and them. The boys backed up farther.

Growling, the Doberman stalked them, back and forth, so that the dark dog and the Doberman crisscrossed each other. They were looking for a weak spot, a place to attack. Griz shot forward, then stood. Michael saw the smaller dog retreat a few steps, but the Doberman held its ground, snarling.

"Should we run?" Chris asked, gasping. Michael had only to look at him to know that doing so would be fruitless. His face was white, his breathing erratic. Chris would fall within minutes. They could never outrun these dogs.

"No. But move backward. Step by step. Slowly."

The boys inched backward, watching the wild dogs every second. Griz held his ground, focused on the Doberman, who paced warily, watching him. Suddenly, something in the Doberman's movement changed. He was getting ready to spring, Michael was sure, and his snarls came faster. It had come so close now that Michael could see the spittle around its muzzle and the hunger in its eyes. A fearless killer, Michael thought, his heart pounding. The other dog held back, growling but unwilling to move forward. The three raged at each other, a snarling chorus.

Suddenly Griz sprang forward, his charge down and close to the ground. The Doberman sprang forward, and for a minute it was difficult in the flying snow to see which was which. The Doberman, its white teeth bared, pounced. Their two bodies collided, each seeking to clamp the other's throat in its snapping jaws. Their growls were ferocious, loud and continuous as they wrestled in the snow, their legs throwing out powdery sprays, rolling, struggling, snarling as each tried to get a death hold on the other's throat.

"Go, Chris," Michael urged, pushing his brother away. "Get home." But Chris was as paralyzed as Michael, fascinated by the life and death struggle they were witnessing. Both boys knew instinctively that if Griz lost this battle, they would be next, that the dogs had come for them, and that only Griz stood in their way.

Suddenly blood spattered on the snow, then spurted in wild paint strokes. The Doberman fell to the ground on its back, its eyes wide, its legs pumping wildly as it tried to regain a foothold. Griz, above it, held fast onto its throat, thrashing his head left and right, his teeth ripping at the Doberman's flesh. Griz's growling continued, but the Doberman became suddenly still. Its forepaws hung at odd angles.

Griz lifted his head, his muzzle bloody, to look at the boys. Despite the violence, Michael thought he saw there a kind of sorrow. Then Griz leapt off the Doberman and ran for the trees where the dark dog, admitting defeat, ran yelping away. Griz only followed for a few feet, then turned, walking back to where the two boys stood traumatized at the sight of the dead dog and the blood-soaked fur of their own pet.

"Good boy," Michael managed, bending to pet him gingerly, yet at the same time horrified by the blood.

"Good boy," Chris added, petting him on his rear. "Is he hurt, Michael?" Chris asked, pointing to blood on Griz's haunch.

"I don't know. Let's get out of here. We'll check at the fort."

They watched Griz walk heroically ahead of them, looking for him to favor a leg, but nothing seemed out of order. At the fort, they threw a few snowballs, knowing that Griz would dive into the snow after them. Each time, his face came up cleaner. And then they used the snow to wash his fur, rubbing it with their mittens to wash all the blood away.

"Yuck," Chris said, shivering. "This is gross." He looked at his mittens, rubbing them with snow. "Blood smells weird."

"How does he look?" Michael asked, appraising Griz.

"Like a dog," Chris answered, smiling timidly, his shuddering finally over.

"We can't tell Mom or Dad," Michael said. "They can't know."

"But they should know how Griz saved us," Chris begged. "He saved us, Michael. He should get steak for dinner."

"They can't know. If you tell, we'll be in big trouble for going to the tree house."

"Won't Dad find the Doberman?" Chris asked, quaking at the memory of the dead dog, its throat ripped open, lying in the stained snow.

"Who knows," Michael said. "Maybe. Maybe not. Even if he finds it, he won't know what happened. And the snow will cover it. Maybe even before morning. Promise, Chris. We can't tell."

The two boys looked down at Griz sitting in the snow, his tail making snow angels behind him.

"You see any more blood?" Michael asked, inspecting him.

"Nope," said Chris.

"Then let's go home," Michael said.

The two boys headed down the hill. Griz ran out in front, leaping through the drifts. Down below, smoke billowed from their chimney, a gray streak in the darkening sky. They could see their father and Charlie emerging from the barn, their chores done for the night. Chris began to run.

43

Patterson, Mid-December

As Christmas approached, Arnold became more and more insistent that he and Taylor use some of their gas to go into Almont. "Look," Taylor argued, "why take a chance now? Maybe later, February or March. Maybe then we can go in with a measure of safety. We go now, we know that people are still sick there. It hasn't been long enough."

"When's long enough, man?" Arnold wheedled. "Maybe it's already over. How would we know, stuck out here with no news. Maybe they're giving shots right now at the VFW, people lining up for vaccinations. Maybe the bank's already foreclosing on my mortgage for lack of payment. How would we know?"

Taylor usually walked away during these assaults, but this morning, Arnold sensed he was weakening. "Look," he said, "we need a source of communication and I can build a battery-powered ham radio. I just know it. All I need are some instructions and the parts."

Taylor did not want to go anywhere, but he knew his friends out in Wyoming had a ham radio. He wondered how they were. He knew they were probably worried about him too. The more Arnold worked on him, the more his curiosity grew. So he capitulated. "All right," he said helplessly. "We'll go. Get your gun, though. And the siphon. We only have a quarter tank in your pickup."

The unplowed roads were treacherous, but the sun had melted the snow cover enough to distinguish the road from the fields beside it. Their snow tires cut easily through the foot or so still remaining, though occasionally the back fishtailed and braking had to be a cautious process to keep from sliding. Arnold was glad to be away from home. He sat in the passenger seat, his hands between his knees, and stared about at the white fields and trees bent with snow. "Pretty, isn't it?" he said.

"Yup," said Taylor, enjoying the change of scenery himself. "See that house up there?" Taylor asked.

Arnold looked ahead.

"Bet they have cars in the garage," Taylor mused.

"Bet you're right. Bet most houses do," Arnold replied, knowing Taylor was compiling a list of sources they could use come spring. "No smoke, either." Arnold added. They knew what that meant.

"We'll get some gas in Almont," Taylor said. "There'll be cars along the streets. Let's save these closer places for later, come spring when we have to start planting."

"The time is going to come..." began Arnold, drifting off as he thought about how the supply of cars to siphon would quickly diminish in a year or so. Well, he thought, maybe more. It depends on how many people were surviving as they were.

They crawled down the long hill into Almont. Taylor kept the truck in first gear to avoid braking and held both hands on the wheel. "You see what I see?" he asked, looking over at Arnold.

"I see 'em," Arnold replied. He'd been watching the wavering lines in the snow ever since they hit 2A, not saying anything because he knew that's what Taylor worried about. Cars had been through here. Looked like trucks too, from the size of some of the tracks. Not a lot, but some. On both sides of the road. Taylor had wanted their existence to stay secret if at all possible. "Others see us driving around, they're going to know we've got food," Taylor said. Now they had made their own tracks in the snow, tracks that could easily be followed if someone decided to do so. Arnold felt a bit guilty that he'd been so insistent. Still, he knew he was right. They had to have the radio. Once they did, they could make better decisions., know when things were safe and where things were being done to put life back together. "The library is right there," Arnold pointed. "Maybe pull around the back."

"There are foot tracks there," Taylor pointed as he pulled into the side drive. Arnold saw the broken snow and followed the line as it ran along the side of the brick building. "Probably dogs," he said.

A few seconds later he and Taylor were surprised to see three boys standing on the ramp leading up to the back door of the library. They were smoking cigarettes, leaning over the rail, their faces red with the cold. All three straightened up when the truck appeared, their dark eyes peering to see who was driving.

"Recognize any of them?" Taylor asked.

"Nope," said Arnold. "Maybe the big kid. I'm not sure."

Butch Jones flicked his cigarette into the snow and put his meaty hands on his hips. "Who're they?" he said, straightening so that his wide chest inflated. Beneath his open jacket, a dirty white sweatshirt hung past his hips.

Another boy answered stupidly, "I dunno'," not realizing Butch didn't care. He looked down at the pile of books they had dropped from the ramp into the bed of the pickup backed up to it. "Not cops, for sure," he added, knowing that the force had been decimated by the bird flu.

Taylor parked next to their truck. "What are you boys doing?" Arnold asked, climbing down. The big pile of books in the pickup was hidden from his view as he walked forward. "What are you boys doing here?" he asked again.

"What's it to you?" Butch answered. He stood a good foot taller than Arnold and wasn't about to back down just because Arnold was an adult. Butch nursed a lively dislike of adults, especially the ones who tried to boss him around. He had learned the sneer and swagger his father had so skillfully mastered, and he prepared to use it on Arnold.

"What's it to me?" Arnold said, and then, before he could finish, he saw the stolen books. "What are you doing with those books? You boys don't look the reading type."

Butch leered. He pulled up his jeans and loosened his arms in his jacket. His friends snickered. In the truck cab, Taylor faced straight forward, while he reached his right arm backward, slipping his rifle from the rack behind him.

"Firewood," Butch sneered. "Burns gooooooood," he added, stretching the word to sound enthusiastic. The other two laughed again, a chorus of sniggers.

"You're burning books?" Arnold gulped. He couldn't believe their stupidity. He imagined the book he wanted being somewhere in the pile they'd made, his hopes of a ham radio captive in their dirty hands. "You idiots can't go cut down some trees if you want wood?"

"Books burn better," Butch replied, taking his pack of cigarettes from his pocket and lighting one. "Great kindling." He spread his legs at the top of the ramp, clearly intending to block Arnold from coming closer. The other boys lounged against the railing, enjoying the scene. Following Butch's lead, they lit up too.

Arnold paused only a second to consider his next action. As he stepped on the ramp, He looked up at the threesome. He had never been so mad in his whole life. Burning books. Goddamned idiots were going to send the civilization's knowledge up in flames. Who knew what they'd need to find in those books? Not just ham radio instructions. They'd need it all, every bit of how-to the library had collected and then some. And not just the how-to stuff. What about philosophy? What about literature? What would they read on those long winter days ahead if the books were reduced to cinders?

Now Butch stepped forward down the ramp, his hands holding both rails, creating a mountainous obstacle. He had that smile on his face that his friends knew meant fun ahead. Butch was going to beat someone else to a bloody pulp for amusement. He'd done it so many times that they knew every move. The stand. The stretch. The block. The challenge. Butch had never made it to middle school; they had barely made it themselves. But Butch lived on their street and so after school the boys' little gang had terrorized summerhouses for years. Now, of course, things had changed. They no longer had to worry about property owners or even the police. Only Butch's father, that monster who periodically felt the need to assert his domination over Butch by pounding him with his fists. They stayed clear of him. They did whatever Pitbull and his buddies told them to do, because it was in their interests to do so. Pitbull had warehouses full of stuff from all over the county. He'd been a junkyard dog before the bird flu, but now he was a major retailer. Anyone who needed anything was soon going to have to go through Pitbull and the boys. They wanted to be on his right side. Pitbull didn't mind seeing them beat an adversary bloody. He and his boys were doing far worse whenever the opportunity afforded itself. They were terrorizing every small pocket of survivors from Fitchburg to Greenfield.

"Get out of my way, young man," Arnold ordered, now within three feet of Butch.

Butch smiled, his eyes narrow slits above bulbous red cheeks. He shifted, spreading his legs even wider, leaning forward in anticipation. "Who's making me?" he asked, waiting for Arnold to come just a step or two closer so he could deck him. Butch's anger boiled. Another adult trying to tell him what to do. This one was going to be sorry.

"I'm making you," Taylor said calmly, standing beside the pickup, his door open. He walked toward them, his rifle pointing down at the ground. "You boys get on over to Aubuchon's and find yourselves a saw. Looks like you could use a little exercise there, big fella'." Taylor smiled, the lines beside his eyes crinkling. He strolled forward toward Butch's pickup.

Neither Butch nor his friends had noticed this tall man emerge from the pickup, but something about him made them hesitate. "Yeah, big guy, carrying a gun," Butch managed, wishing he could reach his gun in the truck.

"You boys come down off that ramp, now," Taylor said quietly, refusing to take the bait. "Get on your way." He was standing by their pickup now, looking inside. He opened their door.

"Hey!" Butch spit. "Get outta' my truck!"

"What's this I'm finding?" Taylor smiled, lifting Butch's pistol from the front seat. "You old enough to be carrying a gun?"

"I do what I want," Butch growled. He'd passed Arnold on the ramp now, heading down toward his father's pickup. His friends followed, uncertain what else to do.

Taylor twirled the pistol. "Say," he teased, "a Colt .38. Not a bad gun for target practice. That what you're using it for?" Taylor looked at Butch sternly, raising his rifle to point it at Butch, who stopped about five feet from him. "I don't think you're old enough to be carrying this thing, and

I don't think you ought to be destroying public property either," Taylor said.

"Free country, asshole," Butch replied. "The librarian's dead. Ain't nobody left who reads."

"I read," Arnold said from above them on the ramp. "So do most people with brains." Butch gave him a threatening look, then turned back to Taylor. "I tell my dad about you two, and there'll be two less readers," he hissed, staring hard at Taylor as if to memorize his face.

"That so?" Taylor pretended to muse. He was surprised, actually, at the venom he felt coming from this boy/man who stood almost as tall as he and who surely weighed more. When he'd worked in New York, he'd run into a few tough guys on the street, young boys with ugly hearts and a score to settle with the world. He knew the studied arrogance, the stances meant to intimidate. He could see in the boy's dark eyes the void where compassion should be, the empty, convictionless, guilt-free stare of a killer and wondered if the boy had already crossed that line or if he was just working up to it. "Well, I'll tell you, boy," and he emphasized boy because he intended to embarrass him in front of his friends, "I think your daddy and I might have a talk someday. But until then, I'd like to see you put those books back in the library. Won't take you long, if you work together. Just pile them up inside where they won't get wet. How's that sound?" Taylor smiled again but Butch saw the rifle rising to waist level.

"Like shit," Butch said. "I'm not putting them back."

Taylor had expected that answer. The revolver, which he held pointed down in his other hand, suddenly exploded, the bullet slamming into the snow just right of Butch's left foot. The boy jumped, fear collapsing his stance like rubber gone soft. "Jesus Christ," he shouted, not sure whether he still had a foot. The other boys gaped, their mouths wide. They had never seen Butch taken off guard like this and it undid them.

"Come on, Butch," one said. "Let's do what the man says." He walked toward the bed of the pickup and began climbing up.

"Yeah," the other said, dodging around Taylor as if he thought his foot might be next.

Butch glared at Taylor. "You're gonna' be sorry, asshole," he hissed. But he walked partway up the ramp and leaned over the rail. "Start handing them up," he said.

At the top of the ramp, Arnold looked down at Taylor and smiled. He might not have been so tough himself, but he was the cowboy's sidekick, and he loved the feeling. On the other hand, Arnold knew that Taylor was not going to be happy about what had happened. Now they had enemies. Not just the boys, but also, if the boy was telling the truth, his father. And they weren't going to be able to steal back home without leaving their tracks in the snow, either. So the situation had changed. Bird flu was only one thing they had to worry about.

Arnold supervised the stacking of books beside the librarian's desk, making sure that the boys didn't just throw the books inside, while outside, Taylor saw to it that the truck was emptied. When they had finished, Taylor told the boys they could go.

"Gimme' my gun," Butch said, holding out his hand.

"I don't think so," Taylor said. "I think I'll just hold on to it. Boy your age shouldn't be needing a pistol."

Butch climbed into the driver's seat and turned the key in the ignition. "You ain't heard the last of me," he growled.

"Gee, where have I read that line before?" Taylor asked,

pretending to search his memory. "See, if you read, you'd know that's not original." He snickered at his own joke, watching the truck pull forward. Butch tried to leave rubber, a noisy show he'd learned from his dad, but his back wheels just spun in the snow. He had to try again, this time slowly, cautiously, just the way Taylor liked it.

Inside Arnold fussed about like an old woman, furious at the condition of the library. Whole shelves had been tipped over, books swept onto the floor in piles. A few bookcases had been tipped over and lay atop the books. The wooden tables were gone, probably used for firewood, and the librarian's desk drawers had been emptied, their contents spilled on to the floor, before being removed as well. The card catalogue's 3x5 cards lay there as well, those drawers having shared the fate of the others. The antique framed painting of Josiah Landry that hung above the fireplace in the main room now sported a red moustache and fangs. One corner had been ripped with a knife and hung in tatters. Everywhere was desecration and destruction.

"How am I going to find the book?" Arnold whimpered, walking in circles about piles of books. He dropped to the floor as he peered at titles in one large pile. "It may not even be here anymore."

"Use your head," Taylor said, having quietly walked up the ramp and inside. "If it is, where would it be? What section?"

Arnold sat back on the floor, feeling the cold working its way up from the boards into his hips and hands. "Well, let's see," he thought out loud. "It's electronics, so it'd be....." he looked around, then rose, walking around the piles and bending to pick up books. He seemed lost in thought. Taylor stayed by the door, occasionally looking out to be sure Butch didn't return. He half expected it. He thought it quite possible that a kid like Butch really did have a father he might not want to tangle with. Not that he would back down from a fight if someone pushed him. He hadn't been a college champ in the ring for nothing. Taylor was as good with his fists as he was with his gun, but he didn't pick fights or go looking for them. On the contrary, he hated confrontations. So he hoped he wouldn't hear the crunch of tires on snow before Arnold found what he was looking for and they could be gone.

He looked over at Arnold. It was funny how that old guy walked right up to Butch as if he didn't have a scared bone in his body. Taylor smiled, thinking how courage came in strange packages, and once again was glad that he and Laura had decided to team up with Arnold. Then again, and his smile faded, it was Arnold's pestering that had gotten them into this fracas. He wanted to think this would be the end of it, that they'd drive on home and the fat kid would never know where they went. He'd be careful when they pulled out onto the street and drove home, watch to see if anyone followed them. No sense in leaving a trail, either. They'd make a few detours.

"Got it!" Arnold yipped, standing straight and waving a book back and forth. He hurried toward the librarian's desk and set it down, opening to the table of contents and running his finger down the chapter list. Taylor stayed by the door, looking outside frequently while Arnold read. Then Arnold took a pencil out of his coat pocket and began writing a list on some scrap paper he picked up off the floor. The man was too fastidious, Taylor thought, afraid that at any moment he might hear someone coming. But Arnold took his time, reading some more, erasing some items, looking out the window while he pondered, then writing down more items.

"Arnold!" Taylor snapped.

"Huh?" Arnold looked up startled. He was in his own world, building the radio in his mind.

"Can you get a move on?" Taylor asked, waving him forward.

"Ah....." and Arnold looked back down at the book. "Well......" He began reading again.

"Arnold!" Taylor said, this time louder. "Can we get going?"

Arnold looked at him as if for the first time. "Going? Oh, yes, of course," Arnold said, somewhat addled by Taylor's tone. He picked up the book, inserting the paper in it, put the pencil in his pocket and looked around. "Damn shame, those kids," he said, clucking. "They sure have made a mess here."

"I'd like to be gone before they come back," Taylor urged. "Lest I have to shoot one of them."

"Ah, they're just kids," Arnold said naively. "Just tough old farm boys without much sense." He passed Taylor at the door. "By the way, we have to drive to Grayson."

Taylor's face went slack. "How did I know that," he said, sighing.

"I dunno'," Arnold replied, missing the point.

They pulled out of the library driveway, looking both ways for signs of the black pickup Butch drove. Cars were scattered along the main street, snow a foot deep surrounding them and on their roofs and hoods. Taylor turned off the ignition of Arnold's pickup and said, "Wait here and keep your eyes peeled."

He took the gas can and siphon from the back, walked through the snow to the nearest car, a Jeep Cherokee, pried open the flap on the gas tank with his pocket knife, unscrewed the cap and inserted the siphon tube. Once he'd squeezed the bulb enough times to get the gas running into the can, Taylor stood looking at the windows above, half expecting someone in the apartments there to look out a window and shout "Thief!" He expected at the least to see a curtain move just slightly to betray watchers from above, but unless he missed it, nothing lived up there. He wondered how many people were alive in the town, for the buildings' stony silence felt absolute as a graveyard.

When the siphon ran dry, he moved to the next car, this time an old Ford, repeating the same process until the gas can nearly overflowed. He put the cap back on the Ford, thinking he might return for the rest of its gas at some later time, then screwed the gas can top tight, put it in the back of the pickup, secured it with a bungee cord, and hopped back into the driver's seat. Arnold jumped when the door opened, not having seen Taylor coming. His pencil was in his hand and he had scribbled notes all over the paper he'd taken from the library. "Good to know I have an alert back-up," Taylor said.

"You know, right now, during the current sunspot conditions, we'll be able to talk to people anywhere in the world on just a few watts? During daylight, that is." Arnold was speaking aloud, but he wasn't paying Taylor the slightest attention. "We'll work in the 28-Mhz band. That's the 10-meter band if you divide 300 by the frequency."

"Where is the store in Grayson?" Taylor asked, climbing slowly on to Route 2. He stayed in the tracks already made in the snow. The snow had been packed down in wide ruts by previous drivers, and it was impossible to tell how many cars or trucks had driven through. Taylor felt he was driving on tracks rather than a road.

"It's a good thing I learned Morse code in Scouts," Arnold said. "Says here sometimes those signals get through when voice transmissions can't."

"Arnold," Taylor said softly, looking over at his friend.

"I wonder if Radio Shack has any hand-held radios. Maybe I wouldn't have to build anything if it does."

"Arnold," Taylor said, this time louder.

"Maybe they're too short range. I think I want to build the old tube-type short-wave receiver. It may not be cutting edge, but it won't be dependent on satellites."

"So it's Radio Shack you want?" Taylor had reached the point of exasperation. "Arnold? Radio Shack?" he nearly shouted.

"What are you shouting for?" Arnold asked, shocked out of his train of thought. He looked at Taylor, annoyed. "My hearing is fine. Radio Shack. That's what I said."

He was returning to his reading before Taylor managed to ask, "Where, Arnold? Where is Radio Shack?"

"Well, right here at this exit. See? Twenty-three? Right here. Don't miss it." Arnold sat up straight, pointing to the exit as they passed it.

Taylor had to push the brakes harder than he wanted to. The car began to skid, ready to do a 180, but he turned into the skid and righted it.. When the car came to a stop, Taylor sat back in his seat and took a deep breath. Arnold looked at him. "Going a little fast, were we?" he said, smiling. "When you back up, go down the exit and follow the rotary until you see 68 North."

For a minute, Taylor remained silent, staring at Arnold. He steadied his breathing. "What?" Arnold said. Still Taylor stared, thinking Arnold the doggondest pain in the ass he'd ever had to work with. "You're wasting gas," Arnold added.

Radio Shack was easy. The front door was locked, but the back stood wide open. The store had already been stripped of its batteries and other devices people thought might be of use. Fortunately, the items Arnold sought were there in ready supply; panicked raiders weren't thinking about building ham radios. Arnold took a small shopping basket and wandered the store, piling in the things he needed and checking off his list as if he were doing grocery shopping. "I'll bet they'll have more of these in the back," Arnold said. "Did you bring your flashlight?"

Taylor reached into the wide pocket of his suede coat and produced a short black flashlight. He handed it to Arnold, who disappeared into the stockroom. While he waited, Taylor stood in the front window, once again searching the street and the window for signs of life. There were none.

"Okay, that's it," Arnold announced cheerfully, handing Taylor his flashlight. He had exchanged his shopping basket for a large carton, which was now filled with smaller boxes and packages.

"You got a house big enough for all that?" Taylor asked sarcastically.

"Got a cellar big enough," Arnold replied. "And a good reason to stay out of Ethel's way." He smiled meekly. "Give me a hand?"

44

Patterson, Late December

In two more days his family was going to try to pretend its way through Christmas—put on fake smiles, give each other little homemade gifts not worth the space they took up, work all day to prepare a holiday feast, and sing carols to the accompaniment of his guitar. His mother had been enforcing hour-long practices for him every day now since Thanksgiving, oooohing and aaaahing about the importance of tradition and of keeping up the faith. What faith, David thought to himself, though he didn't dare ask it. His mother had a way of going ballistic during such religious lapses. If he asked for it, their Sunday Bible readings would extend into Monday. Sunday mornings were bad enough. David thought the whole thing a useless exercise in view of the fact that any God who killed off most of the world with one virus didn't deserve worship. If David had any faith before the Bangkok flu, it was gone now.

So was any joy he'd ever felt. David was bored out of his mind. He'd said so to his father, and his father had given him additional chores. He'd said so to his mother and she had begun prying into his private thoughts, worried about his mental health. He'd said so to his brother, and he'd suggested they play more Monopoly. His sister had just rolled her eyes and said, "You're always bored. Get a life."

Well, that's what he intended to do when he slipped away from the farm, ostensibly to go hunting. At least they let him do that. He was good with a rifle and getting to be a pretty good woodsman, so no one worried when he put on his boots, ski jacket, backpack, and hat, took the rifle out of the gun closet, his dad's pistol off the high shelf, and trotted off into the snow. He'd already brought home turkey, raccoon, and one doe, and he told everyone he'd set his sights on more game for Christmas. So when he left his house in the gray dawn, silently closing the kitchen door behind him, no one stirred to raise himself up in bed, wondering what he'd just heard. They all knew he was leaving before breakfast, and they all hoped that he'd bag something really special for Christmas.

David did not like lying. In fact, until the Bangkok thing, he'd been a pretty straightforward kid. Well, straightforward enough. Some things were nobody's business and his lust for Cindi Lee was one of them. His mother had inklings, he thought. She'd wheedled him many times about the girls in school. Did he know a lot of them? Were any of them especially nice? Did he have any special friendships? On and on. He'd fielded her questions, giving her as much as necessary for her to let up, but no more. She'd go ballistic if she really knew what he was thinking, let alone what he had been doing with Cindi Lee. She would probably have prevented him from seeing her if she had known what they did on Saturday nights, parked out on that dirt road or during their trysts beneath the bleachers at school. No, David had no intention of telling Mom any of that.

He'd learned that a lie, once begun, spawned other lies. It was hard for David to remember the stories he'd made up and keep his facts straight. Especially when there was so little else to distract his folks. They had no social life. They had no church choir or Bible studies, no Women's Benevolent, no Masons. Except for the Grants, Mrs.

Young, and the Curleys, they had nothing but David, his brother and his sister to think about. They wanted details. Always details. Where did you go? What did you see? What about the deer tracks up near the Grants' pond? Any sign of geese left? It was like a checklist of observations they wanted from him every time he returned.

In the beginning, David hadn't minded. He'd filled them in on what he saw, where he saw tracks, signs of wild dogs, and so on. He told the truth gladly, offering up clues to wildlife he'd found and guesses where he might next be more successful. In fact, he'd liked being the center of attention at the dinner table, the fire roaring behind him and warming his back while they congratulated him on the delicious venison they were eating. He'd set the precedent, telling stories with such drama that they all hung on his every word.

So when a week ago, he'd been reluctant to entertain them with more, having come home empty handed after being gone all day, they poked and pried, trying to extract from him what he'd seen. In doing so, they'd forced him to make up stuff out of thin air. Because David hadn't been hunting at all.

It had all started when David decided he could easily walk the ten miles from Whitney Road north to the end of Richland Road near the Almont line and back in one day. If he left early enough, he'd still have time to see Cindi Lee. She had been looming in his dreams, disturbing his sleep, and flavoring his daytime moments with such unnerving frequency that David thought he might actually be possessed. Cindi Lee's sweet, heart-shaped face, Cindi Lee's dancing blue eyes, Cindi Lee's platinum hair hanging in coils over her shoulders and back were only the topmost part of the visions David daily had to quash to keep his sanity. He just had to see her. He didn't care if he was risking his life to do so; he had to find out whether Cindi's family had survived. He believed that her existence could make the next months bearable. They could meet in the woods. They'd find an abandoned spot. They could make love and no one would be the wiser. Just the thought of unsupervised time alone with Cindi created in David such rushes of passion that he found himself almost frightened by the effect they had on his helpless body.

He had told his family that the next morning he intended to hunt. His father had been peeved because, he said, he could use some help in the barn. But his mother had prevailed. "Christmas is coming soon. It'd be nice to have another turkey." And that was that. His mother's desire to cook one and his family's desire to eat one had swayed his father. "Okay," he'd said. "But be back by milking time."

David had left at first light, but he had been ready since midnight, tossing and turning under a ton of comforters, his nose icy, his pillows like cold drafts. He couldn't wait to get moving, to be on his way. Cindi danced before him in the darkness, beckoning him with glistening, pouting red lips. He sighed. He groaned. He turned on his left side. He turned on his right. He watched the window for the first crack of light, and when it finally arrived, he was up and out of the house within minutes.

He'd carried his compass and the map of Patterson, just in case. But David was not worried about getting lost. He just didn't want to waste any of the precious time he might have once he reached Cindi's. He didn't really know what he was going to do when he got there. Would he knock? Would he throw stones at her window? He decided he'd wait to see. All would depend on how long it took to make the trek. He figured about four hours, but he wasn't sure.

He saw things along the way that, had he more time, he

would have investigated. Just past Sanders Corner, near the reservoir, he came upon the bloody remains of a deer, most of it eaten, its stomach disemboweled and lying frozen on the snow. The tracks around it were so many that it was impossible to tell whether dogs or coyotes had brought it down. They'd left its head intact, so that as David stared down at it, the doe gazed back through a dull eye, its expression inscrutable. He didn't linger. The sight wasn't pretty, although David had seen many deer shot while hunting with his father and had, in fact, butchered his first deer while his father sat on a stump and watched. "You kill something," he said, "you prepare it as well. That way you learn to respect the life you've taken."

Farther on, he'd come upon another bloody scene, this time a cow and its calf. David shook his head, sorry for them. Milkers were in no way prepared for the new life they faced. They were too stupid, too slow, and too docile to be suddenly thrust out on their own in a wilderness. He wondered how many other cows were wandering the woods, probably starving, easy prey for any predator big enough to take them on.

When he reached Route 2, David decided he was far enough from home to safely walk along Hope Avenue. He knew it would intersect with Brimley Road sooner or later, and had he stayed on it, he would have reached Cindi's house in another hour. But along the way, David had heard the rumble of a truck coming behind him and decided to cut into the woods. It wasn't as if David was afraid of whoever might be driving. But he was wary. They'd heard trucks the night of the Jamesons' fire, and look how that had turned out. Who would be driving a big eighteen-wheeler around here? No point in having contact with someone who might have the flu. So he cut into a copse of pines just off the road and stood hidden while he waited for the truck to pass.

It came over the hill a minute later, moving slowly. A shiny, new, black International pulling a fifty-three foot long trailer behind it. Its wheels crushed the snow in front of it as it growled its way forward. David wondered why it moved so slowly and hoped that the passengers didn't notice the tracks he'd made cutting off the road and leading right up to where he now stood, hidden by a group of scruffy pines. He stood absolutely still, his rifle finger poised on the trigger.

As the truck came up even with him, he could see three men in the front, big guys, from the way each one's shoulders melded with the others'. And then his heart nearly stopped when the truck's air brakes squealed and it halted just past the place he'd cut off the road. The driver put the truck in neutral, the engine idling, and for a minute, David thought they'd caught him. Especially when the passenger door opened wide and a giant of a man with a long, black ponytail climbed down out of the cab.

"Fucking cold out here," he snarled, looking about him before walking directly into the woods. David didn't dare even turn his head to see where the guy was going. How would he explain himself, hiding there among the trees like some trapped rabbit? And who were these guys, anyway? They looked mean. David listened as the man crunched through the snow, stopping about forty feet in.

"Hurry up, will ya'?" someone yelled from inside the cab.

"Geez, it's cold," the other yelled, reaching out a long arm to pull the door closed. It slammed with a thunk.

The guy in the woods fumbled around in the snow, and David heard him mutter, "Can't even take a decent shit," before the snow began crunching again as he walked back to the truck. He opened the door and someone inside said something David couldn't hear. The big guy growled, "Shut your fucking mouth and get moving. It's just a few miles up this road." He climbed inside and the truck sighed as the driver put it in gear.

Its wheels began to turn slowly in the snow. David waited while it gained momentum and headed north, not even breathing until the taillights disappeared around a long curve. His legs trembled and his heart raced, both at the same time. He had been standing so stiff in the snow that when he finally moved, he felt old and arthritic. He looked at the road, wishing he could just follow it, but he didn't dare. Those guys were going somewhere up ahead, he thought, and he most assuredly did not want to run into them. He would cut northeast for a few miles and circle around the point where Hope intersected with Rimley. He looked at his watch. Only 8 a.m. He had plenty of time to be home before four.

He crossed the south end of Rimley Road by nine o'clock and continued north in a loop up , over and back to Rimley past the intersection. He kept to the woods, although at times as he walked through snowy pastures and fields, he was in the open. Wherever he could, he stayed along the wood line, hoping he would not be seen. And when the pastures ended in forest, he used his compass to go now northwest, intending to cut south eventually. A light snow drifted in the air, its flakes large and airy. David knew it would be wise to head home, for without weather forecasts, he had no idea if the snow would accumulate or peter out. But he could not turn back, not after having come this far. He was close. He could almost see Cindi Lee's face breaking into a wide smile as soon as she saw him. He could almost feel her warmth and that sweet, perfumed smell of her hair. He had to go on.

The tree line broke at the top of the hill. From it, swooping downward, a long, snowy hill descended to a blue clapboard house and barn. David stood under a thick pine stand, knowing that this was Cindi's house and that in all probability, Cindi was not there. The unbroken snow meant that no one had been in or out of either the front or side door. No smoke rose from the chimney. The family cars looked like igloos.

David's heart sank. It seemed impossible to believe that beautiful, sexy Cindi Lee could be gone...dead, he corrected, trying to be realistic. Knowing he shouldn't, David began the long slip and slide down the hill to the house, hoping as he did that someone inside would see him coming, would come to the door or shout or appear on the porch, hands on hips. But nothing moved. Not a curtain nor a blind. No door opened. When he rapped on the side door, his glove removed so that he could use his class ring against the glass, no voices emanated from within. Nor did any footsteps hurry to answer the strange caller outside.

David waited, stamping his feet in the cold. He rapped again, this time harder and more impatiently. Still nothing. He tried the doorknob, but it would not turn. The door was locked.

David stepped down off the porch. As much as he wanted to rap against every window until he roused someone, he feared what he might see inside. What if they were all still there? What would he see? Shriveled corpses? Skeletons? David shivered at the thought. As much as he wanted to know, he didn't want to know. If he left now, he could always believe that Cindi's family had gone away. Maybe they'd found some place safe from the flu. Maybe someday he'd see Cindi again, all healthy and beautiful. Someday when this was all over. At least, if he left immediately, he could hope, whereas if he started looking in windows, he might see something too horrible to forget. He knew he was afraid, but at the same time, being afraid to see unspeakable images might be the best thing. Whatever lay inside couldn't be changed. If they were there, he could do nothing for any of them. It was best, he thought, to head home, leaving things as they were. He looked back one last time, then turned toward the hill and retraced his way through the broken snow.

45

Patterson, Mid-Janurary

"I've been thinking," Arnold said, looking up from his venison steak.

"God help me," Taylor said, slicing his meat faster as if to erase Arnold's voice. "I can't take any more confrontations with townies."

"Taylor," Laura smiled. "Shame on you."

"You don't have to go with him on these jaunts," Taylor said to her between chews. "Last time he nearly got us shot." Taylor sounded perturbed, but with the eye Arnold couldn't see, he winked.

"This is right up your alley," Arnold continued, unaffected by his friend's reluctance.

"Okay," Taylor replied. "What have you got in mind?" He leaned back in his chair, ready to hear Arnold's next screwy idea. Ever since they'd returned with ham radio supplies, Arnold had spent his days down in the cellar. Ethel claimed he was avoiding her, but Arnold assured everyone he was making progress and that he would make more if she'd leave him alone. In truth, while he was down there, he was also percolating new projects. Yesterday, he'd talked seriously at dinner of building a generator. Who knew what today's project would be.

"I'm thinking we ought to do some cattle rustling." Arnold set down his fork and knife and nodded his head smugly to accentuate the importance of his statement.

Taylor snorted. "Cow rustling's punishable, Arnold. Out

where I come from rustlers've been known to get hanged." Taylor laid his western twang on thick. Laura and Ethel smiled, glancing at each other as if they all knew a secret Arnold didn't.

Arnold didn't care if they were amused. He was earnestly forming an idea that might make their lives a whole lot more livable. "Laugh if you want, but we've seen their tracks out there in the woods. They aren't deer tracks. They're cow tracks, you said so yourself," Arnold replied, looking at Taylor. "You said farmers are probably letting their livestock free before they die, and that even if the wild dogs were eating some, there are still plenty wandering around out there barely surviving on pines and whatever they can nose up from under the snow. Now, didn't you say that, Taylor?" He picked up his fork again and stabbed a piece of meat.

Taylor felt the stab as if it had been his own flesh. He decided to take Arnold seriously. "That's true, Arnold. But you've got no barn, no hay, no fences, no nothing. What are you going to do with any cattle we might rustle? We can't keep them in your cellar."

"Certainly not!" Ethel harrumphed.

"Who says we have to?" Arnold asked rhetorically. "Don't we know there's farms around here with dead people minding them?" Arnold's eyes were wide with exasperation. What he never understood was how slow others were to grasp things. Didn't they think? Weren't things as obvious to them as they were to him?

Taylor sat back in his chair, the possibilities a white flash in his mind. Of course, he thought, of course there are. "You thinking we're due for an inheritance?"

"Call it what you will," Arnold said. "Right now nobody dead is going to mind our using his farm for our own purposes. Maybe later, if the heirs ever come looking, but certainly not now."

"You mean round up the cattle and deposit them in somebody's barn?" Ethel asked, just now getting the idea.

"Try to keep up, girlie," Arnold answered. "Of course that's what I mean." Arnold reached out and patted her hand. Ethel used hers to slap him once, good and hard. "Don't be smart with me, Arnold Card, or it's you who'll be sleeping in a barn."

"You know, Arnold, I think you've got something." Taylor leaned forward, his forearms on the table. "We scout out a good farm nearby, and maybe the herd isn't too far away. Bet the barn's full of hay and even some decent grain."

"What the critters haven't eaten," Arnold said, excited by Taylor's sudden enthusiasm.

"What about water," Laura asked. "Don't they drink gallons?"

"We'll figure that out," Arnold said, waving her concern away. "Maybe they've got an old well, or like us, a gravity feed line, or a nearby pond. We'll find a way."

Taylor was already thinking about the farms they'd passed on their way to and from home. Most had looked deserted. No smoke. No wheel ruts in the snow. No activity whatsoever. "Let's take a ride first thing tomorrow, Arnold," he said. "Assess the possibilities."

At sunrise, Taylor and Arnold filled the pickup's tank from several of the gas cans they now took with them on every ride. They had become expert at finding abandoned cars and trucks from which to siphon gas and had established a routine that included stopping to refill the cans whenever they spotted a likely source. The pickup was already warm as they headed along Old Stagecoach Road toward some of the outlying farms where Arnold knew he had seen several small herds of cattle. "I didn't know too many of these guys," Arnold apologized as they drove. "Working at Garrett's, we didn't socialize much with the farmers. I knew some of their names and I saw plenty of them at church. Ethel knows...knew...the wives better than I did their husbands, with church stuff and all. That Ethel, she knows...practically everyone in town." Arnold leaned back in his seat and sighed deeply.

"How long have you two been married?" Taylor asked, passing the time as the pickup moved slowly along the snow-filled road.

"Since we were kids," Arnold answered. "Went to school together. Graduated together. Got married as soon as I got a job." Arnold ran his right forearm across the passenger window to remove condensation and leaned forward to stare out.

"You never went to college?" Taylor asked, stunned. "I figured you for an engineer."

"Would have been, maybe," Arnold mused. "My family was dirt poor. My dad died when I was five."

"How did your mother manage?"

"She worked up at the Walkin estate, cleaning, cooking, till the day she died. Slow down just up there," Arnold pointed, "See that cut-off?"

They took a right onto what could be a dirt road or a driveway. Taylor peered ahead, wondering which, because no farmhouse was in sight. Over a short knoll, however, they could see a farmhouse sitting low in a snowy valley, its old barn leaning somewhat westward about two hundred feet off to the right. "These people have the weirdest cows," Arnold said. "Purple. They're purple. Damnedest things."

"Devons," Taylor said. "If they're purple, they're Devons. Best kind of stock we could find. We're lucky if they're Devons."

Arnold turned toward Taylor, his eyes bright. "How so?"

"Don't need grain for 'em," Taylor responded. "They'll eat hay out in the pastures and fatten up just fine. Anything else, we're going to have to locate grain for them." He slowed the pickup to a stop and sat looking down into the valley. "No smoke," he said. They both sat watching.

"Suppose we drive up and take a look around," Arnold said. "They may be just holing up like us."

"No tracks," Taylor said.

"What?"

"No tracks from the house to the barn," Taylor said, pointing his finger back and forth between the house and barn. "If they're there, there'd be tracks."

Arnold gazed down at the unbroken snow. "Well," he said finally, "let's take a look."

Taylor put the pickup in gear and pressed the gas pedal. They moved slowly forward, watching for signs of life at the windows or doors of the house. They saw nothing. "How shall we do this?" Taylor asked.

"I'll get out and knock on the door," Arnold replied, unbuckling his seat belt. As soon as the truck came to a halt, he slid down into the snow, leaving his door wide open, and walked resolutely to the front door. Taylor watched as he rang the doorbell, waited, rang again, and then banged the brass knocker impatiently. If anyone was within, they had to hear the summons. Finally, Arnold turned back to Taylor, raising his hands in question. Taylor turned off the engine, put his pistol into his jacket pocket, and stepped down into the snow. The two men looked hesitantly around, unsure what to do next.

"Let's try the back door," Taylor said finally.

Crunching through the snow as they walked around to the side, Taylor pointed to the barn doors. They weren't completely closed, so that an opening about four feet wide remained. Neither man commented. Instead, Arnold rapped on the backdoor. "Try the handle," Taylor murmured.

Arnold turned the knob, which gave easily. "Open," he said, looking back at Taylor.

"Call inside," Taylor suggested.

Arnold opened the door slightly, sticking only his head inside. "Hello?" he called.

After several more hellos, he pulled his head back out. "I don't want to go looking," he said. Arnold was pretty sure what they'd find inside, for even in the frozen kitchen, he noticed a faint odor that he'd smelled before.

Taylor nodded, clenching his jaw. "Let's take a look in the barn."

As they approached the barn, Taylor pointed again, this time to the broken snow behind the barn, an arc with about a twenty-foot radius that they had not seen from the knoll. "Must be a back door," Taylor said. He removed his pistol from his pocket, keeping the barrel pointed down.

Near the door, both men stopped short. Something inside made a noise. "What's that," Arnold whispered, grabbing Taylor's sleeve. If Taylor had not been startled himself, the fear in Arnold's eyes would have been comical. But he knew that whatever lurked there could be dangerous—coyotes, wolves, wild dogs, possibly even a mountain lion. The two stood silently, craning their heads, wishing they could see through wood. Something grumbled, a deep, gurgling sound. It did it again. Then all was quiet. Taylor walked forward, his gun at the ready, while Arnold followed a step or two behind.

Taylor stood just behind the open door, his back to it, and motioned Arnold to come alongside. Then, when Arnold was in place, he slowly rotated into the opening, his gun pointed up, peering into the darkness. Something scuttled in the hay. Then a great thrashing about in the darkness sent Taylor rotating back outside, breathing hard. Arnold's eyes were wide with fear. "What the hell is it?" Arnold whispered. Taylor merely shook his head. Now they heard hooves running frantically about inside. Taylor swung back in, his gun pointed. He cursed the time it took for his eyes to adjust to the darkness, and just as they began to see shapes, he saw movement near the rear door. Things were abandoning the barn, running outside. He stepped farther inside and stood alone in the darkness, searching the gray lighted nooks and crannies and the loft above for further signs of life.

Arnold's head appeared sideways at the door as he leaned in to see what was going on. "Taylor?" he murmured.

"Pigs," Taylor said, staring at the knot of pink butts moving about just outside the door.

"Taylor?" Arnold whispered. "You there?"

"Come on in," Taylor said. "We've got hogs living here." His eyes roamed the barn's walls, seeing better now in the dim light the bales of hay stacked in the loft above.

Arnold stepped up beside him, his own eyes slowly adjusting. "Take a look in the side stalls there," he said, pointing. "I think I see grain bags." Taylor moved toward where Arnold pointed.

"You're right," he said. "Maybe twenty or so. At least it's something." They moved to the next stall, looking in. "Pigs got to these," Arnold said, looking at the ripped bags and the trampled grain spread about the floor. "Too bad they left the door open."

"Maybe they meant to," Taylor said.

"No cows, though," Arnold said, disappointed. "You suppose we'll find 'em?"

"They left before the snow, that's for sure," Taylor said. "These pigs decided to stay on, but the Devons wandered off." He walked to the rear door, causing a sensation among the seven or eight Yorkshires, annoyed at the intruders. They moved away from the door, eyeing the barn with their beady eyes, snuffling and grunting among themselves. Their pink hides looked naked in the snow. They stomped, their heads lowered, assessing the intruders.

"They look pretty good," Arnold said. "Been gorging themselves on grain."

"And drinking snow," Taylor said, watching a big sow shoveling some into her mouth. She shook her head, snow catching on the hair of her chin like a white goatee.

Arnold sniffed deeply, his hands on his hips. "Can you smell bacon cooking?" he smiled. He whiffed the air again. "Suppose we can round up some eggs as well?"

"Doubt it," Taylor said. "But we're not going to find those Devons standing here. Let's leave these guys doing what they've been doing and head out that way. My guess is that they wandered off through their own pasture."

"Let's pull down a bale of hay," Arnold suggested. "If they're out there, they ought to be pretty glad to get their chops on real food. We can strap some to our backs."

After a long search, Taylor spotted tracks that began in a small stand of pines and wandered further south to another stand. All the branches up to six feet above the ground had been ravaged. "Cows," Taylor said.

"Not deer?"

"Nope. Look at the hoof prints. Too big for deer. If these cows are eating pines, they're desperate." He pointed to the disturbed ground. "See how they've worked their way down into the snow? Looking for anything worth eating down there. If we find them, they're going to be pretty skinny."

They followed easily then, Taylor guessing that maybe a dozen or more had trampled the snow in their quest for food. It was Arnold who first saw the dead heifer, half covered by a white blanket, its eyes milky, its legs rigid. "Poor thing," Arnold said. "Look at those ribs."

"We'll be lucky if we don't find them all dead," Taylor said quietly.

By late morning fluffy snowflakes began drifting down, almost one at a time, and to the west, the darkening clouds hung heavy over the tree line. Neither man spoke about the weather, both understanding that tracks are easily covered in a matter of a few new inches, but Arnold was growing more uneasy by the minute. He puffed. He sighed. He stopped regularly to look around, so that frequently Taylor had to look back and wait for him to catch up. By noon they had discovered two other corpses, both frozen rigid in the snow, each of them plundered by other animals hungry for meat. "Dogs?" Arnold had questioned.

Taylor looked down at the ripped innards, at the flesh torn off about the thighs, at the red-brown snow where blood had drained and frozen. "Think so," he said, walking to the edge of the despoiled snow surrounding the cow. "See here," he said, pointing at the single prints outside the worried circle around the cow. "Paw prints. Maybe two or three dogs. It's hard to tell."

"They bring her down?" Arnold asked. "She could have starved first."

"Or maybe both at the same time," Taylor suggested.

"Wonder which is worse," Arnold mused, then shivered.

It was in that quiet moment that they both heard mooing. Taylor stood up straight, removing his hat and shaking the collected snow from its brim. "Let's go," he said.

Not fifty yards farther, just over a small rise and then down into a ravine thick with pine, they saw them. "Maybe ten?" Taylor whispered as they stood looking down.

"Can't tell. But they're purple, for sure," Arnold answered excitedly.

"I'll circle around left. You go right. See if we can herd them back."

"No, you circle around, and I'll begin laying a track of hay. My guess is that they're too hungry to be rowdy," Arnold replied.

"You think they're going to walk right up to you?" Taylor smiled.

"I do," Arnold nodded, pulling a handful of hay from the stack tied to his back, and then holding it out. "I'm irresistible."

Taylor took about five anxious minutes to work his way down the ravine in the slippery snow, circling wide around the herd. They knew he was there, but except for a few snorts and low moos, a bit of stomping, and some careful assessment, the herd did not respond. Above, Arnold dropped three small piles of hay, each about ten feet farther back the way they'd come. "Just enough to get you started," he said softly. Then he pulled an armful from his back and held it ready.

Seconds later he heard them crunching through the snow on their way back up the ravine towards him. They weren't moving fast, he thought, and that's good. They're not panicking. He heard Taylor urging them on. "Eeeawwww," Taylor spoke in a normal voice. A head appeared, then several, as the cattle reached the summit. The leaders recognized hay and fell upon it, relishing mouthfuls, working their jaws back and forth. The followers, having missed getting any of the first pile, moved forward to the second, and then the third. Within minutes, they surrounded Arnold, nudging him with their wet noses, working their way behind him to rip more hay from that strapped to his back. "Girls, girls," Arnold giggled. "There ain't enough of me to go around."

"I dunno', Arnold," Taylor snickered. "They sure think you're pretty."

With Taylor behind and Arnold ahead until his supply ran out, then switching, with Taylor leading, parceling out his supply as he walked, the herd made its way back along the trail. The cows moved slowly, lacking the energy to hurry, and stopped frequently to lick the snow clear of fallen hay. By now, swirling snow had begun filling the tracks Taylor and Arnold had created and making it impossible to see more than fifty feet ahead. Still, the men couldn't have been happier. The farm was ahead, they had rustled their cows, and, as Arnold put it, "The good Lord had thrown in some bacon to boot."

46

Patterson, Late January

They had all braced for the last two weeks of January, predictably the coldest it got in Patterson, and colder by far than any of the towns around. Something about Patterson's altitude kept it cooler in the summer by as much as six degrees, and in the winter frigid when it was just cold everywhere else. Icicles no longer dripped from the sun-heated asphalt shingles; instead they grinned like glassy fangs. The snow no longer crunched underfoot; it cracked a sharp, shattering reproach. No matter how many layers of clothing were worn outside, the numbing cold penetrated every tiny opening with icy fingers. January made everyone feel vulnerable.

Terry awoke feeling sick to her stomach and at first could not figure out why. She twisted under the covers, pulling the comforter closer under her chin to shut out the cold. Light was just beginning to define the edges of the window and the stretch of floorboards beside it. She could feel Rob's weight behind her on the mattress and hear the gentle rhythm of his breathing. She turned over, watching him sleep while the nausea subsided. How lucky she felt to have married this man, despite his tendency to assume all would be okay. If a husband had to have a fault, she was glad this was his, for his optimism soothed her. If any wife was ever qualified to do the worrying to make up for it, Terry was the one. She worried all the time. She worried about whether the gravity feed water line would freeze.

She worried that they didn't have enough firewood. She worried that next year they would not have enough food. That some disaster would destroy their planned harvest. It was all she could do to keep herself calm, but Rob could calm her. Thank God for him.

Again, she felt a wave of nausea. This time, she had to move fast. She threw on her bathrobe, shoved her feet into slippers, and raced down the hallway and stairs to the kitchen, to lean over the sink. Sour, disgusting, agonizing, the contents of her stomach dribbled onto the stainless steel and into the drain filter, where it sat in a sorry yellow puddle. Terry turned on the tap. The icy water spit and spurted before beginning to run fluidly, and Terry stood watching the bilious yellow slime thin and disappear down the drain. "Damn!" she thought to herself.

Behind her Rob appeared in the kitchen doorframe. "Ter?" he asked, bewildered. "You okay?"

Terry didn't turn around immediately. Instead, she looked out at the frozen snow. "I guess," she said. "You okay?" She almost hoped Rob would say no, because that would mean that something they ate might not have been quite right. That something she'd served had disagreed with them.

"Fine," Rob said. "Maybe you have a touch of something."

"Yeah, probably," she agreed, unconvinced. Terry knew this feeling, but she didn't want to admit it, even to herself. "I think I'll go lie down for a little," she said, turning now to look at her husband. "I still feel a bit queasy."

"I'll get an early start on the cows," Rob said, stoking the woodstove. The embers chittered as he tossed two small logs upon them and then glowed orange. "Get some more rest. We'll take care of ourselves." He stood straight, reaching out to hug her before she slipped outside to the outhouse.

Back under the cold covers, Terry shivered, trying to keep her eyes closed against the growing light. But she couldn't sleep. The reality of her situation stunned her. How had it happened? She had been so careful once she ran out of birth control pills. She, of all people, should have known better. A nurse, for pete's sake. And here she was, pregnant again, in a world with no doctors, no hospitals, no health care system, no nothing. What was she doing anyway, bringing a child into this frontier life to face hardships the likes of which only her distant forebears had experienced. It was hard enough imagining a future for poor Michael and Chris, a life for them to look forward to. What was it going to be for them? Work that was only going to grow harder as they had to rely more and more on the fruits of their own labor, as supplies of things dwindled in their pantry, as the world of down jackets and other store bought clothing disappeared. And now a newborn, a tiny, fragile thing facing freezing winters and summers of fieldwork.

Tears welled up under Terry's closed lids and spilled out onto her face. Instead of wiping them, she let them run across the bridge of her nose and the side of her face onto her chilled wet pillow. She savored for a moment a memory of how warm and snuggly her bed used to be, in the days when the oil burner sent boiling hot water through the baseboard radiators. She yearned for just a few minutes of such peaceful luxury and let the quiet sobs of what she knew was her own self-pity overtake her.

But not for long. Within a few minutes, she heard the muffled sounds of Michael and Chris talking in their room, something they did now that life had changed. Instead of rising and rushing to and fro to be outside in time for the school bus, mornings for them had become a little more leisurely. They liked to lie in bed and talk while hugging their covers tight around them, postponing as long as they could the need to leap from their beds, throw on some clothes, and beeline it for the outhouse. Their reluctance to rise had brought them closer, Terry thought. She loved hearing the give and take of their conversation, muffled, sometimes punctuated with a word or two that she could understand. She found herself alert, striving to know what her boys were talking about, what they thought about, what they did when she and Rob were busy doing parent things. Terry relished their camaraderie, for they were good brothers to each other, seldom fighting, seldom teasing, and almost always supportive of each other, just as she had always hoped they'd be.

Her nausea had subsided, with only a minor queasiness remaining. Nothing to keep her in bed, she decided, throwing the covers off again and slipping her feet back into her furry slippers. She rose, walked to the window, and shivered. How she hated January.

In late January, nightfall came early, long before supper. The temperature dropped thirty degrees once the sun had gone down, and the wind blew while bare trees groaned their frozen complaints, their branches chattering. In the safety of their houses, underneath piles of blankets that barely provided enough warmth, insomniacs watched the pale yellow moon make its way across the snowy fields and felt rising within them the bitter taste of fear. January nights made sleeping elusive and thinking relentless.

Rob lay on his back in bed, preparing himself to go downstairs to stoke the woodstove. His wool socks were already on, and under the covers he wiggled his toes to increase his circulation. He pulled a cold hand under the covers, waiting for his body to warm it. His face was still cold, and the pillow where he moved his head was colder. It was time to get up, no question, so he sighed and slid his legs quietly from beneath the covers. Beside him, Terry whimpered.

From their bedroom window Rob could look out over his fields. He had made a habit of doing this, even before, especially before the flu, because Charlie wasn't sleeping above the garage then. A midnight check of his property made good sense. It could forestall trouble, he always believed. And so, on rising Rob opened the blinds, despite the cold air now penetrating his long johns, and let his eyes roam the pastures.

How different his land looked in the winter moonlight, Rob thought. Like the old negatives his mother had kept for extra prints. What was dark, the sky, should be light. What was light, the land, should be dark. Only the dime-sized moon sitting high in the sky above and, oh yes, the stars, presented themselves properly. Rob sighed. His world had become a negative. Nothing was as it should be. However were they going to survive this, he wondered. Could he provide for and protect Terry and the boys now that they had been plunged a hundred years back in time, with no electricity, no stores to buy what they needed, no government to structure their lives, no society at all except for the three other families in their fragile alliance? Could they possibly do it? And would the life they now faced be worth the struggle?

Rob had never thought of himself as especially strong. Oh, yes, he did the man thing. He provided, with Terry's help. And he was physically strong. But compared to the Spartan life of the pioneers, a modern day farmer had it easy. Wasn't that a laugh? Calling modern-day farming easy? It was one of the hardest jobs in the world, a job with the worst prospects, yet only now, having lost it, did he appreciate how good he'd had it. What he wouldn't give now to go turn on the lights in the kitchen, to fry eggs on the stove, to feel the luxury of warm water running out of the faucets. A hot shower, my God, a hot shower, he thought. What I wouldn't give to soap up under the steaming spray of my shower.

The wind had died, and the trees stood rigid in the cold. Rob threw on his bathrobe and padded downstairs to the soft glow of the woodstove's dying embers. Hearing his steps, Griz left the boys' room and followed him, whining hello and looking concerned. Rob stoked the fire and watched the flames crawl over the dry wood. Griz leaned against him, his head at Rob's thigh. The heat was a comfort, and he lingered, his bathrobe growing warm about him. They'd have to plan carefully, he knew. Among them, they'd have to employ their lands to grow the bulk of the food they'd need to survive next winter. They'd probably have to make some adjustments in their land use, changes for the good of the alliance. He'd have to talk to Ralph soon about what those changes should be. They'd always been able to buy what they didn't grow, and sell what they did grow to buy what they needed. Now, they had no money. They had to grow everything among themselves. While they might soon be able to venture out for the things they needed, clothes and the like, they weren't going to find food anywhere. Of that, he was sure.

Rob looked at his watch, wondering how long its battery would keep it running. Like everything else, he thought, its days were numbered. Then he turned and crept silently back up the stairs. In his bedroom, the pale light coming in through the blinds laid bright lines across their bed, lines that angled and arched where he'd tossed his cover back and then crept up over Terry's hip as she lay sleeping on her side. Griz followed him as he walked to the window to close the slats.

It was as he raised his hand to the rod that he sensed something moving. Something at the barn, along its left side. The movement almost escaped him. But then Rob craned forward, using his right hand to pull the metal slats down at eye level. No, all was still. Perhaps it was nothing, he thought, still peering out, running his gaze around the perimeter of the barn, and then outward in every direction. Nothing. Yet Griz had begun a low, slow growl, his ears pricked though he could see nothing outside. Rob figured Griz for a false alarm and almost let go of the slats, but just then he sensed movement again. He grabbed the drawstring and raised the blind, his forehead knocking the bottom section as he leaned into the icy window glass.

"Rob?" Terry asked sleepily, flipping over toward him.

"Shhhhhh," Rob said, not moving. Griz continued to growl.

Terry jumped from her bed and hurried to the window. "What?" she whispered.

"Look there," Rob pointed, thought he didn't have to. Terry immediately saw one dog become two and then four or five, all of them prowling the barn's outer walls, sniffing at the foundation and between the boards. One of them was hard at work scratching at a narrow opening where an old board had rotted away. Rob saw that they were trying to get in and he knew why. Inside the barn their livestock waited nervously, easy prey for hungry dogs.

"Hold Griz!" he ordered, unwilling to set the dog against the pack. Terry struggled with Griz's collar while the dog strained against her, anxious to attack whatever was out there. Rob was down the stairs in seconds, grabbed his rifle and was out the door without stopping for jacket or boots. He ran pell-mell into the snow, slipping immediately on the icy crust and catching his balance only through sheer will.

The dogs had already heard Griz barking inside the house. They heard the back door open and slam and saw Rob instantly. Their ears went up, their noses sniffed the air. They growled, their hackles rose, but they didn't charge him, although his flesh must have smelled as good as anything in the barn. They weren't yet feral enough to charge a man. They knew about men, having only recently had their own masters, having been cared for and fed by them. They padded around, unsure about this two-footed creature that for centuries had meant absolute power to them. His interference could cost them their dinner, and they were hungry, having found little in the surrounding woods to sustain them. Their leader, a German Shepherd of massive proportions, stepped forward in a symbolic gesture, his fangs bared, his growl intense and deep. The other dogs stood near him, indecisive as they watched Rob flailing his arms.

As soon as he could, Rob raised his rifle, took aim and shot directly into their midst. The rifle resounded, and one of the dogs yelped, its hind legs collapsing on the snow. The others, frightened, raced across the adjacent field and over the hill without looking back. Within seconds, they had disappeared.

Rob strode toward the wounded dog. Behind him, he heard Charlie running across the snow. They reached the agonized animal together and looked down at the bloodied snow where he twisted about. Rob pointed his rifle at the dog's head and pulled the trigger. The bullet burst through the dog's jaw just below his ear, making only a tiny hole that barely bled. Its body convulsed and then relaxed on the icy crust.

"Shit," said Charlie. "They're getting braver, aren't they?" He nosed the dog with the barrel of his rifle. It did not move.

"I believe this might be a Jameson dog," Rob said. He walked the few feet to the barn wall and began inspecting it, running the point of his rifle along the boards. "See here?" he said, calling Charlie over. "They were working this old board to make themselves an opening."

Charlie kneeled in the snow, inserting his arm into the hole. "They were almost there," he said, shocked. "I don't want to think of what we'd find in the morning if you hadn't woken up."

"I almost missed them. If Griz hadn't begun growling..."

"That's a damn good dog you've got there," Charlie said. "But he's going to wake the whole road if you don't let him out."

Rob had been so focused, he had stopped hearing Griz, whose wild barking had never ceased. He turned toward the house and waved to Terry, who he assumed was still upstairs watching from their bedroom window. Instead, the back door burst open and Griz sprinted across the ice toward them, his growl rumbling deep in his throat as he approached the dead lab. He skidded to a stop and sniffed the still animal, then picked up the scent of the other dogs and began running in the direction of their escape. Rob called him back, but it was only when Griz reached the knoll that he stopped, looked off in the moonlight, and then, reluctantly turned back toward the barn where Rob and Charlie stood watching him.

"Tomorrow we better fix these weak spots," Charlie said.

Rob patted Griz. "And I think maybe we ought to set Griz up inside. We'll make him a nice bed, so he won't be too brokenhearted not to be sleeping with the kids."

"The good old days are over for you, boy," Charlie laughed, bending to play wrestle with the excited dog. Griz licked his face, his tail wagging.

"The good old days are over for all of us," Rob said, grimacing. "Leave that fella' there in the snow till morning, Charlie. We need to get some sleep."

47

Atlanta, Mid-February

Lester Savant awoke to near darkness, rubbing his eyes and stretching. His back had cramped on him for the umpteenth time since he'd been stuck in these Spartan quarters. Parker's ultimatum: "Stay here until you find a cure" had been issued two months ago, fifty-nine days to be exact, and he'd been sleeping on a cot designed to cause paralysis ever since.

He'd complained, of course. So had several others. The rickety Government Issue metal beds sagged in the center so that one could only sleep holding on to the sides. And the six-inch foam mattress pads did nothing to cushion the body from the center bar, which was a torture in itself. Parker finally agreed to requisition better ones, but by the time the agency had done the paperwork, transport companies were no longer transporting and furniture stores were no longer open for business.

Not that any of them had been allowed out to see for themselves. They heard this word of mouth, from Parker. The order had been clear: Stay until you find a cure. Truly, no one was holding a gun to their heads. It was still a free country, what was left of it. And while guns did exist on the premises, held by guards also living there who monitored the perimeters and insured no one, absolutely no one, came inside, they hadn't actually been threatened or imprisoned. But if you left, you left for good. Parker made that clear. You could not return or change your mind later.

And when a few of the staff had opted out, mostly fathers and mothers of young children, no one had blamed them. They'd only watched thoughtfully as the others gathered up their belongings and said goodbye.

The rest of them had not seen their families for two months now, nor talked to them since the phones went out. They had no idea whether their husbands or wives, parents or children were still alive. The mood at the CDC was grim and guilt-ridden. The remaining staff could not be sure whether they had reason to grieve or not, but they were grieving anyhow.

When materials were delivered, back in the early days of the outbreak, they were left in holding areas, their outsides sprayed with disinfectant, and only after considerable precautions, opened and delivered to the labs where they were needed. Now, Savant had no idea what was out there. He had to depend on the communications that still existed, and that was through the sole Government Issue ham radio now installed in the lobby. There Washington and Parker kept each other informed. Each day, Parker had to report the same thing: "Some progress, we think, but nothing definitive." Savant avoided Parker in the mornings because he knew what making that report did to Parker's mood. The man barked at everyone who had the misfortune to be within twenty feet of him as he was on his way to and from the lobby. He looked like a bear, growled like a bear, and only a fool got in a bear's way.

Late morning wasn't much better, but the degree of ferocity moderated. Parker became hopeful as he walked through the various hallways, their glass walls shielding the labs where they all worked. He'd pick up the wall phone and ring inside, and someone would answer on the other side of the glass and give his or her report on their progress.

A few things were really hopeful. Mary Steers thought she was making progress with increasing B-cell adaptability to the mutations of the virus. And Mark Harris, a relative youngster recruited from the Level Two labs, thought they might be able to utilize killer T-cells to attack the virus. He'd had some promising results at Tuesday's meeting.

Still, Lester's theory was that no vaccine was going to work on the spectrum of mutations this virus had already demonstrated. That was the problem. Mutations always made this year's flu vaccine ineffective for the next generation of viruses. This virus was so intense and fast-moving that it mutated many times within one victim, much like AIDS. Lester believed, however, that some people out there were surviving exposure because of an anomaly in their systems that somehow counteracted the virus on the cellular level. He wanted to test those people. He believed that if they could round up enough of them, they might find the answer to immunity.

The problem, of course, was so complex that Parker would have none of it. He had made that clear at the last meeting. First of all, people had civil rights. The government couldn't just go round up those believed to have survived exposure and drag them kicking and screaming to the facility, lock them up, and stick them with needles just because Savant had a hunch. Hunch. Parker said the word with such disdain in his tone that Lester had squirmed, looking down at his lap while the other scientists at the table looked at the walls. Worse, once they had them for guinea pigs, Parker reminded everyone, the next step would be to infect them to be sure the subjects actually were immune. That, he stressed, would be nothing short of murder if it didn't work.

Third, Parker didn't want anyone from the outside

introduced to the inside. He feared exposing his teams to potential infection. Working in the labs with cultures handled "by the book" was one thing, but human beings were too unpredictable. The team could work with monkeys and pigs or any other animal the CDC had at its disposal, but they weren't going to work with humans. It would take just one incident, and the world's last line of defense, and he pointed at them, could be decimated in a matter of days.

"But what if there is something in their RNA that prevents the virus from invading their systems?" Lester had queried. "Couldn't we make some progress using stem cells?"

"Stem cells!" Parker made "stem cells" sound like expletives. They weren't going there, that was clear. And while Mary had given Lester a sorrowful look and several others had apologized quietly to him after the meeting, no one dared support him during the exchange. Not against Parker. He might as well be God.

So the days dragged on. Lester rose with the sun and fell dead asleep when his body would no longer function—usually well after 10 p.m. The others did the same. They were a devoted lot, that's for sure. But then, of course, a lot was at stake. What good would it do to find a cure too late for the world to utilize? And if they didn't find a cure, how long could any of them stand being quarantined at headquarters? Right now, they all knew from the reports Parker recounted after his morning sessions with Washington, the statistics couldn't be more dire. The cities had borne the brunt of the epidemic. Where people could not get away from other people, their chances of survival, unless they were miraculously immune, were zero. Zero. Lester thought about the absolute nature of zero. A conceptual impossibility, but there it was. Right now, every high-rise in every city was believed stacked with moldering corpses, their bodies' own bacteria reducing them to puddles and bones. Concrete ghost cities, not just LA, New York, Chicago, but also Paris, London, Moscow, Beijing. Smaller cities had fared no better, and even the suburban towns had succumbed. Those people depended on transport of goods for every bodily need—their heat, their water, and their food. Those systems had completely disintegrated over a month ago.

The survivors, the ones he believed had some form of immunity, had done one of two things: they'd either stayed put, living by raiding condos and apartments for supplies, or they'd migrated to rural areas and found shelter and supplies in houses they came upon along the road. The government's theory was that pockets of people were surviving in these latter areas by isolating themselves, and their life expectancies were good as long as they avoided contact with outsiders. No one knew how long it would take for the pandemic to die. Like the Spanish flu in 1917, a virus could seem to go dormant for a time and then, like an irritable dragon, flare up again a year or two later and devour the ones it had missed on its first go-round.

Lester swung his feet off the cot and stood, very slowly straightening himself and then leaning backward to relieve the screaming muscles in his lower back. He rolled his head on his shoulders, then leaned forward, his hands on the edge of the cot, and stretched his Achilles tendons, first one leg, then the other. It was agony. What a pain it was, growing old, Lester thought. Then he realized he should be glad he was around to grow arthritic. Billions of people weren't ever going to be so lucky.

By 7:00 a.m., Lester was suited up and in his lab. He'd

made himself coffee in the staff kitchen, eaten his usual cereal with Coffeemate, a not quite totally disgusting adaptation to a shortage of milk, and a roll made by Clarice, the one cook who volunteered to stay on when the others went home two months ago. They had an unlimited supply of NASA's prepackaged space food, of course, but that was being saved until the last. Clarice had stockpiled beef and ham, butter and vegetables, in the freezer. Unlike most of the world functioning without electricity, they had their own generators. Parker had seen to that, even if he did neglect decent bedding.

He worked steadily from 7:15 on, inspecting the cultures neatly placed along the long stainless steel counter and detailing the changes he observed in his lab notebook. Except for the sound of air being pumped into his Chemturion suit, he had grown accustomed to silence. So when the alarms sounded just after 9:30, Lester almost dropped the culture he had just been inspecting. In the labs, scientists looked up from their work, scalpels in hand, and held their breath. Everyone knew the alarm meant that one of them had been exposed. They had talked, worried, and had nightmares about this happening as the weeks passed, knowing that sooner or later it would happen and praying that their dread virus would be conquered before it did. They knew the pressure to find a vaccine or cure had affected their minds and bodies in all the wrong ways: they were working an unhealthy number of hours, they felt Parker's disappointment every time he looked in on their labs, they knew people were dying by the thousands with every passing minute. They were constantly distracted by worries about their own families. Working constantly without taking a weekend break to get their minds off the problem had over time made them frenzied, anxious, and depressed. Now the accident or mistake they dreaded had happened. In every lab scientists stopped their work to gaze through the glass and wonder who was going to the slammer.

At the CDC, as at many biohazard facilities, the slammer was an isolation room for people suspected of contracting a deadly virus. Even if the victim survived the exposure to the virus, he still had to survive thirty days of solitary confinement, enough to make even the mentally sound partially deranged. Everyone knew what was happening at this moment. The lab had been locked tight and the scientist was now undergoing a disinfectant shower while guards suited up to remove him to a wheeled, environmentally-sealed crate that then would be rolled into the slammer. Once the victim was safely inside and the guards were safely outside, a remote device would unlock the door of the crate and the victim could emerge into a larger cage where for the next month he would be treated as a biohazard threat.

If he lived that long.

Lester closed his notebook, left the lab, and began his own disinfecting procedure. Fifteen minutes later, he emerged showered and clean, and hurried to the cafeteria, where he knew the facts of the event were already being discussed and the identity of the scientist already known. The bustle in the cafeteria was loud and anxious, most of the team already there with their version of the rumors. Jack Whitehall had been in the lab next door when it happened. He held forth, describing the sudden lockdown, the guards rushing past his window, Parker hurrying on their heels. It was the young guy, the Level Two kid, Harris. Somehow, his air tube had been sliced without his realizing it. On a corner or something. Whitehall clearly did not know, "But that's what you get letting a Level Two novice into a Level Four lab. He only discovered it by accident, a tiny rent in the tubing, but he'd been breathing it, for God's sake," Whitehall groaned. "Breathing it!"

Lester sat down on the edge of the small circle of scientists feeling sick to his stomach. Poor kid, he thought. Lester could predict with certainty how the next days would play out. Constant rumors. The kid pricked, prodded, tested, observed, his every itch and tingle recorded. Then the inevitable sore throat, the tickle that exacerbates into a hacking cough. The lungs filling with thickening fluid, the cough exploding as a moist viral cloud, leaving Harris gasping for air. Damn, Lester thought. Damn this thing!

Lester was the first to see Parker enter the cafeteria. His face was angry red, his eyes icy. He stood momentarily in the doorway, waiting for the jabbering knot of men and women to notice his presence. Lester, sitting where he was, saw how quickly the knot loosened, the voices stilled, while Parker stood watching them. Within seconds, only the generator hummed in the distance. Parker stepped into the room.

"Obviously, you all know who it is and what happened. If you don't, it was Mark Harris. A ripped air hose. He's now under quarantine." Parker looked around the room, making eye contact with each of them. "We need you, every one of you. I know you're tired and fed up and frustrated, but you can't let your guard down. If you're tired, book out of your labs and take a rest. I can't emphasize enough the importance of knowing your own limits. Each of us wants the same thing, and it's easy to fool ourselves that we're not getting sloppy when we're tired. But that's when accidents like Harris's happen. You know it and I know it. I'm not going to try to con you by saying 'We're doing everything we can for Harris' because you know we don't know what to do. But we'll make him as comfortable as we can. Any of you want to talk to him, you can use the intercom phone. That's it, people." Parker turned and disappeared into the hallway. The group's response was a low murmur. Then, like antibodies flowing into the bloodstream, the team dispersed into the surrounding hallways.

48

Patterson, Mid-February

The February meeting began just after Sunday worship at the Greens' house, a planning session they had anticipated since the first of the year. When farms lie dormant under mounds of snow and outside thermometers sink to their lowest temperatures, farmers are already envisioning verdant fields of produce and planning ways to make this year's crops more abundant than last year's. January is thinking time. February is preparation. March thaw and mud begin the new season. This meeting was important for the four families. They knew that next fall they could not go to BJ's or Victory or Super Stop and Shop and load up on food and supplies. They were going to have to do it all themselves—grow it, grind it, and can it. Whatever they forgot or failed to do at the meeting could make a difference to all of them for the next year.

Furthermore, they had to plan for enough of everything. Terry, Carol, Lisa and Shirley had taken inventories nearly every week since the men had barricaded the road. They had watched their ample supplies of flour, pasta, sugar, tomato sauce, canned ham, tuna, sausage, canned vegetables, jars of peanut butter, jelly, pickles, and boxes of crackers, cereal and cookies diminishing faster than they had ever thought possible. They would have enough to last until harvest time, but only if they were careful.

Carol had even placed a lock on her pantry door. Her friends laughed when they saw it, but they also knew that hungry teenage boys, and Carol had two of them and a girl as well, could ravage a food supply and feel guilt only after their stomachs were full. "I'm not starving them," Carol maintained, embarrassed when Shirley asked about the lock, "but those boys forget there's five of us living here, not just two!"

Terry soothed Carol's injured pride. "You have anymore of those padlocks, Carol?" she asked. "I might just put one on my sewing room door. I've got cookie thieves raiding it, I don't know when, and pretty soon desserts are going to be a thing of the past." She looked sternly at Michael and Chris, who were trying to fade around the corner.

Rob had chaired the meeting. Something about his nature, perhaps the kindness of his character or the calming effect his demeanor had on people made him the natural choice. Charlie was a hired hand. Ralph Green had a tendency to get edgy, to say things without thinking first. Bob Curley's arrogance and his wife's criticisms had made them the least popular from the start, included only because their property sat between the Greens' and the Grants'. The others had agreed it would be too hard to exclude Lisa and Bob, especially if they wanted to close off the road, but the Curleys' voice or power at any of the meetings remained minimal. A few times, Shirley or Carol had spoken to Terry of their annoyance at things Lisa or Bob had said to one of them or their kids. And a few times at meetings, a tentative spark would fly that all of them quickly extinguished because they knew, above all else, that among themselves they had to maintain peace if they were to survive at all.

The meeting had to be choreographed carefully. Rob and Ralph had met days before to discuss their needs and decide who was best suited to be responsible for achieving them. While their farms were similar, they had developed them differently. The Greens, for example, had a small herd of sheep that Ralph thought should be increased. "They produce wool," Ralph said. Rob had asked what Ralph would do with it, now that he couldn't just send it off to a buyer. "You see Carol spending her days spinning?" Rob asked gently. Ralph had almost taken offense, but then the image of all four women spinning wool to knit or weave into clothing became just too absurd. "I suppose we'll have a better chance of finding clothes we need at J.C.Penney's."

"Designer stuff, too," Rob had smiled.

"We're going to have to go out sometime soon, you know," Ralph said.

"Yup, pretty soon," Rob agreed. "For seeds and fertilizer. And I need some spark plugs. And we're going to have to figure out how to replenish our gas tanks. I'm not looking forward to pulling a plow on my shoulders."

While their parents discussed their plans and laid out who would do what with which field, David Green studied the graceful lines of Ellen Young's shoulders. She sat directly in front of him, her long, dark hair cascading over the back of the Greens' dining room chair. David had known Ellen Young his whole life. They had played together as children, raced their bikes along the road between their houses, waited at the same bus stop for school, and waved to each other at dances and sports events. But David's friends were not Ellen's friends and the two seldom crossed paths at the spontaneous gatherings or planned parties David attended, parties that he guessed were wilder than Ellen or her friends might like. But in the last few months, isolated as they were and both in the same "class" at his mom's school, David's appreciation for Ellen's intelligence and wit had blossomed. He liked her smile, the way she cocked her head when she asked a question, the way her eyes sparkled when they discussed books or laughed about their mistakes on their geometry homework. And he hadn't noticed before how much she had changed in the past years, so that instead of the wiry stalk she had been, she'd softened and reshaped into beautiful curves.

Last week, when she had scored higher on their English test, David had put his arm around her shoulder in a friendly, congratulatory hug. He was surprised by a sudden surge of electricity that he knew she felt as well. She'd turned to him, her eyes gone soft. And since then, they'd begun finding every reason they could to brush hands or lean close or smile at each other.

The adults had been discussing Rob's confrontation with wild dogs and the dangers of hunting alone when Ralph gestured toward his oldest son. "David?" Ralph said, annoyed that his son had not been listening. "David?"

"David!" his brother whispered, punching him in the arm.

"What can you tell us?" His father waited for an answer. David, suddenly aware that all eyes were on him, had no idea what to say. What were they talking about? What were they asking him? He felt his face grow hot.

"About what, Dad?"

"About your difficulty finding deer. And what about the wild dogs? Have you seen any?"

"I've seen some dead ones. None alive."

Ellen turned, smiling her radiant smile at him. His face burned.

"You all know about the attack on our barn," Rob said. "But Charlie also saw a pack last week." Charlie suddenly sat straighter, but said nothing.

"Tell them," Rob urged. Ellen had turned forward again, and David, embarrassed, sank in his chair.

"Bout five miles south. I flushed a doe. Brought her down easy, with one shot." Charlie shrugged, remembering. "I had severed the legs and all. Packed the thighs, and was just cutting out the filets when I heard something behind me. Some things, I should say. There were about five of them, moving about behind the trees, trotting to and fro. I think they were getting ready to attack."

Michael sat up straight, looking for Chris. Across the room, Chris looked back. Chris had wanted to tell what he knew, ever since the attack on the barn, but he'd promised. Michael would kill him if he blabbed.

"What'd you do?" Ralph Green asked, concerned that his own son so frequently hunted alone. They'd been anxious about dogs from the start. They had no idea how many pet dogs lived in Massachusetts, but they knew that the largest ones were going to become feral in no time at all, forming hunting packs that could become a menace to their livestock and to themselves. Rob had ordered his boys to stay within sight of the house and forbidden them to enter the woods alone. And all the men now carried a pistol when working outside, and both a pistol and rifle when hunting. Charlie had suggested that dogs were as good as raccoon for eating, but no one had begun salivating at the thought of roasting one. It would be a while, they all agreed, and only if the wildlife was depleted. Of course, Rob had said, the dogs are going to help that happen sooner.

Charlie took a pronounced swallow. He did not like public speaking. It made him nervous, and now all these people were staring at him, waiting for details. "I shot one. Well, I shot at one. I thought I scared them off, you know, after that."

Everyone waited for Charlie to continue. Michael and Chris were riveted. Charlie sighed and adjusted his sweatshirt. His discomfort was obvious to all of them. David tapped the leg of Ellen's chair. She giggled softly, her shoulders shaking.

"Go on, Charlie," Ralph said gently.

"Well, once I finished packing up the deer parts in my knapsack, I left the remains. You know. And I figured that would be the last of it. That they'd clean up what was left and leave me alone." Charlie rubbed his chin and looked down at his knees. "I took my time heading back, but about a mile from the farm, I realized I was being followed."

Michael sat rigid in his chair. He knew exactly where Charlie had been at the time. Right near their tree house. His eyes were wide, remembering their own close call. Only now there were more dogs, not just two. Griz could never have stood up against a whole pack. He shivered and looked over at Chris, who was now standing.

"I don't know whether they were after the meat I carried, or me. But I think they'd have been glad for both," Charlie said. "They were quiet. Tracking me, you know. I'd look back and only see the occasional flick of a tail or dot of a nose behind the trees. They were stalking me."

"Why didn't you shoot?" Ralph asked.

"Well, I did. Twice I shot out at them. Where they were and all. But that didn't stop them. Every time I got going, there they were behind me again."

"You mean they weren't afraid of the gun?" Paul Curley was astounded. He'd seen them, or others like them, but he'd never been stalked.

"I mean they'd hide when I stopped and keep coming when I moved is all," Charlie said. "But I'll tell you, I was glad to be close to home by that time. I wasn't carrying that much ammunition."

The room was silent as everyone digested this new

information. Terry, sitting near Chris, reached out and pulled him onto her lap. He gulped visibly.

"I think we'd all better take extra precautions," Rob said. "You all know that Griz sleeps in the barn now. Charlie and I hunt together, and you all better double up too."

"You hear that, David?" Ralph Green said. "That's it for going out alone."

With that, several men stood and the women hurried to the kitchen to set out refreshments. Chris and Michael huddled together in the front hallway, whispering their shared worries while David lingered in his chair, waiting to see where Ellen would go. Instead of standing, however, Ellen turned back toward him. "I don't suppose it would be too dangerous to take a walk, would it?" she asked, her eyes dancing. "If we don't go into the trees?"

"I'll get my rifle," David said. "You're safe with me."

49

Atlanta, Mid-February

"Why isn't he showing any symptoms?" Parker wondered, staring through the glass.

Lester, beside him, shrugged. "It's only been forty-eight hours. Perhaps the incubation of this particular variation is longer."

"Perhaps he wasn't infected at all," Parker said, rubbing his chin. "He had no idea when the tube ruptured."

"Maybe he's immune."

"Oh, for God's sake, Lester, let it go."

"It makes sense."

"Forget it, I'm telling you." Parker turned without saying goodbye and strode away.

Lester stood watching the sleeping Harris, both anxious to notice anything out of the ordinary and worried that he would. Ever since Mark Harris had been rushed to the slammer four days ago, Lester had spent every spare minute at this spot. It was a glass wall that looked in on a small room about the size of a motel room at the Holiday Inn but one furnished far less attractively. Harris had a reading chair, a desk, a small dining table about thirty-six inches in diameter, a closet kitchen, and a bed. He also had a bathroom, where only a camera watched him, and he could draw the blinds on the glass wall if he wanted privacy. Even then, cameras installed at ceiling height monitored his every move. Harris didn't seem to care what people saw. He was only too glad for the human contact.

He seemed so young to Lester. Not a wrinkle crossed his forehead, and even in sleep, his face didn't sag. Too young to die this way, Lester thought, then thought of the billions of others even younger who were already dead. This was his first experience with the virus attacking someone he knew. He had read the reports and he had seen the corpses in Bangkok. He knew what to expect. Yet he dreaded seeing a colleague go down with it.

Lester couldn't decide which could be worse—being infected and dying quickly or being exposed yet immune, because if he was immune, he would become a guinea pig. Lester was becoming convinced that it was the latter. Mark had been exposed and he was going to survive without getting sick at all. He had not shown a single symptom. Oh, yes, a slightly elevated temperature that lasted for about twenty-four hours. Then nothing. No sore throat. No cough. No difficulties breathing. He had worked diligently at his laptop, continuing his research as best he could. His pleas to return to his lab, have it sealed off and let him just stay there, had gone unanswered by Parker. They all knew that was an absurdity, for Parker did everything by the book, and allowing a potential spreader outside the slammer was not in the book.

So if he didn't die from his exposure, what then? Were they going to keep him inside the required thirty days and then just let him return to work in his lab? Pretend that he hadn't actually survived a virus that appeared to kill 100% of the time? Would Parker be bullheaded enough to let that happen? And if he, Lester, could persuade Parker to use Mark as a guinea pig, to re-expose him so that they could actually be sure he was immune, could he live with himself if he was wrong and Harris died because of his stupid idea?

And if he did nothing, what then?

Harris stretched and rolled over, dragging his blanket with him. Lester looked at the back of his head now. He wondered what Mark would think if he knew what Lester wanted to do. They'd become friends since Mark's exposure, mostly because Lester stood so long each day at the glass wall, talking into the phone to Mark on the other side. At first Lester had been cheery, trying to calm the young man's fears. By the second day, Lester began bringing books and videos he thought Mark might enjoy during his stay in Motel CDC. They'd gotten a little more personal, something foreign to both of them, and they talked about their surprisingly similar histories. Both had grown up in the rural South, Lester in Georgia, Mark in Arkansas. Coming from dirt-poor families, both had been outsiders because they read ravenously and outstripped every student in their schools. Both got scholarships and found their niche in college science labs, surrounded by beakers and petri dishes and others equally interested in the worlds they discovered through their microscopes. They both lived for science. They had grown up a generation apart, and their experiences had taught them that nothing much changes when it comes to tolerance for those who are different, especially those who are smarter.

Lester really liked this young man. His humility, for one thing, was astonishing, considering the awards and achievements Lester knew filled his resume. And his ability to stay centered, calm in the face of his mortality, had won Lester's admiration. He wondered whether, in the same position, he could demonstrate equal equanimity.

So, as Lester watched he wondered how he was going to propose his idea to Mark. How long he should wait before broaching the topic, how he should begin. And most of all, he wondered what Mark's reaction might be, if having survived one exposure to the world's most deadly virus, Mark would consider him a raving lunatic to propose doing it again.

50

Patterson, Early March

Laura Block had returned to her own house to spend some time alone. It was one thing to conserve on firewood by spending most of her time at Ethel's, especially when the men were working at the new farm, hunting, or reconnoitering the countryside. She and Ethel got along just fine almost all of the time. Unable to re-charge her laptop, Laura had taken to handwriting a journal sitting at Arnold's desk in the little office he had tucked away behind the laundry room. She kept busy there while Ethel quilted or cooked. Sometimes though, she needed her space, and this was one of those times. Ethel had decided to take a nap, so Laura headed home, stoked up her own woodstove, and sat down to read by the front window, reveling in the luxury of being alone.

It was probably an hour or so later that she thought she heard Arnold's pickup coming up the road and leaned closer to the glass to catch a glimpse of it as it turned into the Cards' driveway. If she was right, she'd hurry to the bathroom, comb her hair, and dab on a little rouge before Taylor arrived. Who knew what might happen next? Things were going so well, and in spite of the scarcity of a social life or a variety of things to do, they were happy.

It was with a little leap of the heart, then, that she pressed her cheek to the icy glass. For months now, the only sounds on the road had been those of the Cards' pickup coming and going. As the vehicle approached, it never crossed Laura's mind that the grillwork wouldn't be that of the familiar Ford, its bumper dented from a confrontation with a snow-covered rock. She was so used to seeing Arnold's little blue pickup that it took her a minute to realize that this was a big black Durango. When she did realize it, she jumped from her chair, her book falling to the floor.

Laura hurried to the kitchen window, which faced the Cards' house. She could see only the tail end of the black pickup. Nothing of Ethel's front door or whoever was knocking on it, but what she saw in the back yard was Ethel, in her worn plaid coat, bent over a pile of logs. She seemed unaware that anyone had arrived, perhaps because she had her scarf wrapped tightly around her head to keep out the cold.

Then Laura saw a man edging his way along the front of Ethel's house, peeking in the windows. Laura felt panicky. She wanted to raise the window and yell to Ethel, but that would alert the man to her presence. She wanted to run outside and ask the man who he was and what he wanted, but something about his furtiveness and stealth gave her pause. And of course, always the worry about contact. What if he was a carrier?

Laura tore through the laundry room toward her own back door, grabbing as she ran the rifle that Taylor kept cleaned and loaded inside the cold pantry. They had made a pact to fully isolate themselves, and the man working his way around Ethel's house was a stranger. If she had to scare him off with the rifle, she would do so. Their lives hung in the balance. She would hang back, she thought, creep carefully through the snow along the back of her own house and wait to see what the man intended. If she had to, she'd step out into full view. He'd see her rifle and know she meant business. That was her plan as she slowly opened the storm door and slipped outside.

By the time she inched her way along the back of the house, the man had reached the back of Ethel's and spotted Ethel, her back to him. Ethel wasn't taking a nap after all. She was loading firewood on her sled. Laura watched him stop abruptly, considering his next move. Clearly, he wasn't a friend or he would have called to her, making her aware of his presence. Instead, he seemed to be peeking around the house, looking for something or someone to appear. And then he raised his arm, pointing at Ethel as she bent to pick up the rope of the sled on which she'd carefully piled wood.

In an instant, two things happened. Another man appeared in the back yard, having come around the far side of the house, and Ethel turned, astonished to see two strangers, stood still, holding onto the sled rope, her mouth open. The two men started to walk toward her.

"Please stay back," Ethel managed, her voice trembling. She held up her hand like a traffic cop, and both men snorted at the same time.

"You telling us what to do?" the big man ridiculed. "You and who else?"

"Me!" Laura announced, stepping forward now, keeping her rifle pointed down.

The two men and Ethel turned toward her at once. Laura couldn't see the relief on Ethel's face, her attention focused instead on the big man with the long black ponytail. Even from a distance, Laura felt the hard glint of his eyes as he stared at her. He changed direction, now, walking slowly toward her.

"Well, my, my," he oozed, and the other man snickered, walking beside him toward her. "Lookie, lookie, Buzz!

What a pretty sight." Laura raised her rifle barrel to waist level without thinking. She bristled at the malice in his voice.

"Stop right there," she said, her voice calm. She was strangely unafraid, despite his leering glare. She had dealt with creeps before and had learned Taekwondo to even the playing field. As she studied the big guy, the leader, she thought that in a gym she could probably flatten him easily. He was big, but he was soft. He had a beer gut; she could see it hanging over his belt inside his open jacket. And she bet herself that she was twice as fast as he and three times smarter. But there were two of them, and she didn't want them close enough to touch.

When he continued toward her, now not thirty feet away, she raised the rifle and held him in her sights. "I said stop," she repeated, steadying the barrel.

Buzz hesitated, unsure what to do. He didn't like having a rifle pointed at him, whether the woman could shoot or not. He looked at the big man, who, sensing his hesitation, said, "She ain't gonna' shoot, Buzzie, my boy. She probably don't even know how." He continued forward to prove his words.

Laura lowered her sights to a point in the snow directly ahead of his boots, took a slow breath, and pulled the trigger. The shot resounded, but not until after the snow five inches from the tip of the man's boot exploded in a white spray.

"Shit, Bull," the small man yelled, jumping backward and slipping in the snow. He struggled to keep his balance.

The big man stopped short, assessing the situation. Laura raised the gun sights to his chest and held steady. "We want you gone. Now. Come any closer, and I'll put one through your belly." She did not move.

"Come on, Bull," the other man pleaded. "She means business."

"We got no fight with you, lady," Pitbull said, raising his hands to show his innocent intentions.

"Then what are you doing here?" she asked.

"We're looking for a cowboy and his sidekick," Pitbull said. "Drives a blue pickup."

Laura experienced a momentary tremor. She hoped he was too far away to see it. "Don't know any cowboys," Laura lied. "I drive a Volvo." She remained frozen in position, but prayed that Ethel would remain silent. She wanted desperately to look over at her, but did not dare.

"We tracked him this way a few weeks ago," Pitbull said, not believing Laura for a minute. "Had new snow then." He paused, waiting to see what her answer would be.

"You tracked the wrong car, then," Laura said, unable to think of anything better. "Now it's time to move on." She cocked the trigger to emphasize her intentions.

Pitbull stood a moment considering his options. He didn't like backing down from anything, but this witch could shoot. No point pushing things when there was always later, when he could come prepared. With friends.

"Well, if you see these guys," Pitbull said slowly, "tell the cowboy I don't like him messing with my boy. I ain't got time now to keep looking, but sooner or later, we have a score to settle." He lowered his hands slowly, to indicate he wasn't going to try anything sudden.

"I've already told you, mister. I don't know any cowboys," Laura said.

"Yeah," he said sarcastically. "I heard you." Pitbull turned to the little guy. "Let's go, Buzzie boy," he said, as if inviting him out for a ride.

Laura kept the two men in her sights as they headed

toward the front of Ethel's house, then walked along the side of her own house to be sure both climbed in the truck. She watched it back out of the driveway, turn, and head back toward town before finally lowering the barrel.

The minute she did, she began trembling uncontrollably, her heart pounding. Would she really have shot a man? She wondered. But she already knew the answer. She had stayed calm throughout the confrontation because her resolve to protect Ethel and herself was unshakeable. Yes, she would have shot him dead if she had to. That was just the way things were now. And she was a survivor.

Once she was sure they were gone, she remembered Ethel out in the backyard. Laura crunched her way through the snow to the back of the house, looking left and right across the yard. The sled remained where Ethel had dropped the rope, but where was she?

"Ethel?" Laura called.

"Is it safe?" a wee voice cried from behind the woodpile. Laura watched a red scarf rising, then Ethel's frightened face below it, then the shoulders of her plaid coat. "Are they gone?"

"They are," Laura said, but she knew she had not seen the last of them.

51

Atlanta, Early March

"No, I feel fine," Mark Harris insisted through the wall phone. "But two weeks by myself in this room is going to make me crazy, Lester."

"Try to think positively," Lester smiled. "You've outlived an accident that probably would have killed any of us."

"There's some doubt, you know," Mark said, almost sadly.

"I know. But the chances are good that you were exposed and lived to tell the tale."

"We both know what that means," Mark said. "If I'm immune, that is."

"Yup," Lester said, eyeing him and nodding his head.

"The initial blood tests seem to corroborate your theory, pal."

"Yup," Lester said again.

"So what next? You want to expose me and see if I can do it twice?" Mark looked at Lester through lowered lids. He knew that if Lester were wrong, he could be agreeing to his own death. But he also knew that if Lester was right, he could be the key to a vaccine or a cure. Something about his genetic makeup just might be different enough to thwart the Bangkok virus, and if that was true, they might be able to find a way to make others immune too.

"I think you know," Lester said. "You'd inhale the mist first. As if someone sneezed on you."

"And then if I lived through that?"

"More tests. Probably an injection."

"I think you're right. I bet I was exposed, because when I think back to that time in the lab, the only thing that could have hooked my tube enough to cut it was that stainless steel edge. I should have sanded it down weeks ago, but I didn't have time. And I had been at that lab table for about an hour before I discovered the tear."

"But what if I'm not. Right, that is." Lester liked this young man. As the weeks had passed, visiting him every day, Lester had begun to wish that he'd had a son like Mark. "Suppose by some circumstance we haven't considered you weren't exposed, and you're not immune?"

Mark considered, walking to and fro on his end of the phone line. "I guess if you look at it statistically, you know, weigh the two downsides, then it's me, one guy *maybe* lost against the sure bet that millions more will be lost if we do nothing." He looked at Lester, his eyes sad. "Doesn't sound like much of a dilemma, does it?"

"I suppose not," Lester said, himself sick with the thought that he might be wrong. "Unless you're the one guy.

52

Patterson, Early March

Arnold sat back in his swivel chair, glorying in the sound of human voices from afar. For the first time in months, he was listening to someone other than Ethel, God help him, or Taylor or Laura. Though he couldn't understand the speaker and didn't even know what language he was speaking, someone out there was broadcasting something, and whatever it was, Arnold was overjoyed to hear it.

He had been working steadily on the radio for the last two days, much to Ethel's annoyance, who after the visit from somebody named Bull was terrified of going out to the woodpile and who now watched constantly from the front window for pickups that did not come. She wanted Arnold to sit with her, an absurdity, of course, for while Arnold loved Ethel completely, the old girl could certainly get on his nerves.

Not that he wasn't worried about the confrontation Laura and Ethel had had with this guy. He knew the reference to "his son" meant that set of hoodlums at the library. He knew also that a father who would come calling when his son got chastised for burning books was nobody he'd like to know and certainly nobody he'd like to fight. At least, not without Taylor for backup.

Although he did not sit with Ethel by the front window, downstairs he kept his guns cleaned, loaded, and ready for what he had built up in his mind to be the Gunfight at the OK Corral. He was nervous about it. He figured the Bull would surely be back. He just didn't know when, but he wasn't going to sit listening to Ethel yammering on and on about the state of the dust on her tabletops when he could be doing something useful like building his own battery-operated ham radio.

Now he had done that. He couldn't transmit yet, but he could listen. And now that he could listen, he'd find people speaking English and maybe have some important news for the rest of them at dinner. He turned the dials and recognized French from someone with a sharp, nasal voice. He turned again and caught a few words of English before static blew the guy away. He turned some more, and suddenly, clear as glass, he heard someone with what he guessed was a mid-western drawl twanging on with someone else about the weather. The *weather* for God's sake!! The world had collapsed and all they could talk about was the *weather*?

How he longed to interrupt them. Break in and say "Hey! I'm here! Who are you?" But that would come tomorrow or the next day, as soon as he could work out that part of the diagram and connect his mike. Until then, the weather would have to do.

He turned the dial again. This time a man was explaining that he and his family had moved into someone's estate on the Madden River, wherever that was, and that others who had survived had joined them in a communal living arrangement. He reported that of a town numbering over ten thousand, they guessed that less than a thousand were still alive, most of them doing the same thing as his group, moving in together to share resources.

The other guy seemed pretty interested in the particulars. How did they dare interact with others they weren't sure about, he asked. And the fellow replied that they used the gatekeeper's cottage as a kind of Ellis Island where people had to stay at least thirty days before being allowed in. There weren't that many asking, he added, but they'd admitted three families over the four months they'd been there, people that someone inside already knew and vouched for.

Had they turned anyone away, the other one asked. The first fellow said yes, they had to. Arnold could tell from the way he lowered his voice that he felt bad about it. He went on to explain that some of the riff-raff in their town, the ones who didn't work, one a drunk, another two or three known druggies, they'd had maybe six total he said, came sniffing around in the early days, once the food in the grocery stores ran out. But they'd sent them packing, he said. "Had to," he added sadly. "We can't have any malingerers out here come spring. We've got major planting to do if we plan to eat next winter."

Arnold caught his breath. What about next year, he thought. What are we going to do? I'm no farmer and Taylor isn't either.

When the other guy inquired about their planting plans, clearly another farmer from the confident sound of his voice, Arnold grabbed his pencil and pad and began writing as fast as he could. He could barely keep up with their chatter about the ins and outs of planting certain crops at certain times, but he did his best, and when they signed off, a good fifteen minutes later, Arnold had a list that looked pretty workable. That was going to be dinner conversation. And after that, if Taylor was as ignorant as he was about farming, Arnold was going to propose another trip to the library. He could see Taylor's face when he brought it up, for Taylor sometimes got annoyed with him, he knew. Arnold smiled. "Too bad. I'm always right," he thought smugly.

For now though, Arnold intended to continue listening to whatever news was out there while Taylor did the chores at the farm and Ethel chewed her fingernails watching the road. Someone ought to know the state of the nation. Was the government still intact? Did we still have a President? Arnold was dying to know and he intended to keep trying until Ethel called him for dinner, when he would appear like a prophet out of the old times and wow them with divinations. He could already see his wife's wide eyes and slackened jaw, Taylor's shrewd stare and Laura's beaming smile as he made his pronouncements and proposals, and he savored the moment in advance. Arnold had finally come into his own. After a boyhood fraught with the jibes of other boys and countless schoolyard humiliations, after years of working for bosses who claimed his ideas as their own and kept him down in the lower ranks, his intelligence was finally being confirmed.

He turned the dial again. This time more static...more static...a distant voice blurred by static...and then again, clear as if the man was sitting right next to him, someone reading announcements. This was not a conversation. Someone was broadcasting what sounded like official news. Arnold dropped his pencil and leaned forward over his workbench, riveted. He had found Washington's wave band. The announcer droned on and on, his voice grave, but to the overjoyed Arnold, nothing could have been more exciting. The government still existed. Even if fragmented, it existed. The President was still alive, as were several of his advisors. The army had been decimated, but enough of it still remained to be called an army, though from what Arnold gathered, no enemy outside U.S. borders mounted much of a threat. If terrorists still existed, they didn't have much to terrorize. They had gone on to more important things, like trying to survive themselves. No reports of bombings or beheadings, not one in the last three months, he learned. Well, Arnold thought, it takes a pandemic to put things in perspective.

The announcer went on to national news. Reported outbreaks of the Bangkok virus were diminishing by the day. The virus had swept the planet, and now, having done its worst, it seemed to have died out. That didn't mean citizens should let down their guard, the announcer stressed. Pandemics have a way of reasserting themselves. For now, however, officials from all over were indicating a slowing of outbreaks. "It is believed," the announcer stated matter-of-factly, "that over one billion in the U.S. and over four billion world-wide have perished since the onset of the virus. The infrastructure of the nation, though tenuous, has not collapsed and plans are being made to restore services as soon as possible. In the meantime, survivors have found ways to exist without the support of the government, a strategy necessary at the present time. To aid them," he went on, "this station will broadcast help and advice, including hour-long instructional programs for those interested in planting, hunting, and gathering edible foods."

He went on to detail the schedule of the instructional programs, and Arnold jotted down times that he thought all of them should tune in. Ethel already knew how to can, Taylor knew plenty about raising cattle, and Laura might just as well be the instructor on edible plants, he smiled. But the tutorials on what, when, and where to plant were going to be essential, because while winter was now drawing to a close, they had to be prepared to get crops going at the optimal time. There'd be no second chances. New England summers could be "iffy" and they were always too short.

Tomatoes and corn took a long time to grow and ripen, and they couldn't be hurried by anxious or starving farmers. Worse, plant diseases and predators could ruin a harvest unless you knew what you were doing. Arnold knew that he didn't know, because he'd never learned.

Finally, the announcer explained the means by which government was getting its information and assessing loss of lives. Heat-imaging cameras installed on military planes were photographing areas laid out on a national grid. Aircraft were canvassing the country, looking for pockets of population on the ground below. "You who are in these pockets are the future of our country," the announcer continued. "You are the survivors who will be re-building the U.S. and restoring our way of life. The government needs to know where you are so that it will be able to furnish vaccines, medicines, and other emergency aid as soon as possible. For now, we can only gather information. We are all on our own," the announcer said. "God bless us all."

Arnold sat back in his chair thinking about planes. Had one passed that he hadn't noticed. Was help on the way? Or was this just hogwash from the political establishment? He'd have to pay more attention to the sky, he decided. Those planes fly so high that he could easily miss them. And he had to tell the rest of them—Taylor, Laura, and Ethel—to be vigilant. He'd like to think that someone knew where they were.

53

Patterson, Early March

Knowing it was Sunday, Rob asked Charlie if he'd mind finishing up whatever needed doing. "I think it's time my wife and boys took a little break," he said, tossing a bale of hay down from the loft. Below, Charlie lifted the bale and set it by the doors to the cow bay.

"You go ahead. Looks to be a nice afternoon," he said without turning.

"Just a hike," Rob said, knowing that the boys would jump for joy at the thought. More importantly, Rob hoped a walk would lift Terry's spirits. She'd been unusually solemn since January, when she'd realized she was pregnant, and despite Rob's joy at the news, her mood had not changed. Even Michael and Chris couldn't convince her that a new brother or sister was just what they wanted. So now that the weather was more accommodating, the sun warmer and the days a bit longer, Rob hoped a hike would do them all good. Hikes had been their mainstay just about every weekend before the virus, and he'd missed them. "We'll be back by dark."

It was only eleven o'clock when the four of them headed up the hill toward the forestlands that lay beyond. They left Griz behind, despite his pleading whines and sorrowful looks, because Rob didn't want to chance an encounter with wild dogs in which Griz might be an obstacle to a clear shot. Rob carried his shotgun and stuck his pistol in his coat pocket. Not quite the kind of peaceful walk we're used to, he thought as he checked his ammunition. He'd never felt the need to take a shotgun before, although he'd always carried a pistol in deep woods just in case he had to scare off some wildlife.

"Which way?" he asked Terry, who was still reserved.

"Let's walk toward town," she said. "I'd just like to see it. Know everything's still there, the church and all."

"It's a long hike, there and back," Rob warned. Actually, he wanted to see the old church too. It had withstood two centuries of blizzards and hurricanes, tornados and floods, while sitting just off the green, a reminder of the original settlers' purposes there. The church was now Congregational, and though Rob and Terry were Catholics, members of the Almont church, they felt a kinship with this white clapboard place of worship. Boy Scout meetings were held there, public dinners, fund raisers, and all manner of other non-sectarian activities.

Beyond that, something about the sanctuary, perhaps the ancient pews or the simplicity of the altar, made Rob feel a connection with his own ancestors, that he was just another in a long line of people, his father, his grandfather before him, his sons and someday their sons after, each taking a brief turn at life. Rob found such thoughts comforting. They made the problems he faced bearable, the work he had to do reasonable. No more, no less than everyone who had gone before. And when thoughts of death overwhelmed him on those nights when he lay worrying while Terry slept, he found relief in the conviction that his was only a minute part being played out in time and space, so minuscule that neither his birth nor his eventual death was anything more than a momentary flash in one of an infinity of universes.

Rob had been right. The walk was demanding. As the

family made its way along trails and dirt roads, cutting across empty pastures and through thick stands of pine, the boys raced ahead, calling back to their parents to hurry up. Rob held Terry's hand, and when the boys were out of earshot, he spoke of how happy he was to be expecting another child. "I've always wanted a big family," he declared, clasping her shoulder and hugging her close.

Terry smiled, but her expression betrayed her doubts. "This shouldn't have happened, Rob," she said. "It's a bad time. What future will a child have now? And no doctors, Rob. What if the baby gets sick? What will we do?"

Rob knew Terry's fears were well-founded. While Michael had been an extremely healthy baby, Rob remembered how many times Chris had wakened with a high temperature or the croup, how often they had been up all night monitoring his temperature or trying to soothe him, how many times Terry had called Doc Strong for advice. It was with these thoughts in mind that Rob stopped suddenly. Terry stopped too, looked up at him, afraid that he had heard or somehow sensed danger. She pulled her earmuffs off to listen and turned, following his gaze toward the cemetery that lay on the last turn before town. Michael and Chris, who had waited for their parents to catch up, stopped also, struck by the expression on their father's face.

"Listen," Rob said, holding his hand up, fingers spread wide.

Nothing.

"What, Dad?" Chris pleaded, worried that his father sensed some danger. He pulled his cap off, turning his head like a radar antenna to catch sound.

"Shhhhh!" Rob said. In that instant when he had slipped most inside himself, worrying about the new baby, he heard music. He was sure of it. Music! He hadn't heard music for months, and suddenly he was certain he heard music. A violin. An organ.

Everyone stood stock-still, afraid to move a toe lest the crunching snow block the sounds Rob heard. They waited.

Then, as if their total attention was required, faintly, as if floating on the air itself, it was there, and they all heard it. Music. Coming from somewhere close. Beautiful, sorrowful.

Terry knew it immediately. How Great Thou Art. "The church!" she said excitedly. Someone was playing music in the church. Without waiting, Terry began running up the road. Rob and the boys followed, though Rob was trying to decide whether or not it was wise to go there or not. Had it been long enough? They had their alliance pact. Should they risk exposure? Could they go in without danger?

Terry ran unafraid. Whoever played there had also survived, and perhaps they had news. And there was music! Terry yearned for it, longed to sit and listen to music. It was as if she had awakened suddenly ravenous after a long, deep sleep. She'd had no idea how much she'd missed hearing music until this very moment when the sounds of it wafted lightly on the air like the smell of lavender or fresh baked bread. She craved more. She had to go listen to the music.

Terry rushed up the granite steps to the front doors, expecting them to swing wide open with a crescendo of sound, but try as she might, none of the doors gave. They were locked tight. Because of her fervent yanking and rattling, those inside had stopped playing, waiting fearfully for someone to burst through. By the time Terry gave up on the doors, Rob and the boys had caught up and now all four sought the side door that led into the church vestry and up to the sanctuary. They made no effort to hide the clatter of their footsteps as they climbed the worn wooden stairs, but stopped as they reached the door and realized that the music had ceased.

Terry was the first to make a move, slowly opening the heavy oak door and peering shyly around it. Inside, a short woman with close-cropped steel gray hair stared at her. Her mouth hung open and Terry could tell from her expression that she was frightened.

"It's okay," Terry said, reassuringly. "We heard the music and had to come." As if that was enough reason to jeopardize everything, Terry realized.

"Please stay back," the woman said, her eyes beseeching. A young girl set down her violin, saying nothing.

"We won't come near you," Terry said, putting her hand on Chris' head. "We were just taking a walk. The music sounded so beautiful…" she trailed off.

"I know you," the woman said, her tone softening.

"I know you too," Terry said. "You're Lily Fenn. You're playing the antique organ. I heard you once."

"We come to practice," she said. "There's more of us… just not today."

Rob now appeared beside Terry. Lily Fenn smiled. "Hello, Rob," she said. "It's so good to see others are…"

"I know. Same here, Lily," he said. "How many do you know of?" he asked, hoping for good news.

"Most everyone's gone," she said, not changing her expression. "We've got a small group here in town, mostly along the Benton Road. Maybe twenty."

"We've got four families. Maybe seventeen."

"There are others," she said. "We've seen them drive by."

"You know who?" Rob asked.

"I think Jack Patterson and his family are still out at their farm. But most of the houses are..." and she couldn't say it..."we haven't seen any smoke."

"What news do you have? Anything?" Terry asked.

"Nothing. We're just riding this out. Like you."

Michael had pushed his way through his parents and now began to walk into the sanctuary. "Please," Lily warned, holding up her hand. "We're just afraid. You understand."

Rob grabbed the back of Michael's jacket. "Hey, pal. Hold back, okay?"

"Could we just sit in the back and listen," Terry asked, her voice pleading.

The woman looked at the girl beside her. They reached an unspoken agreement and she nodded her head. "We're almost done here, but you're welcome to listen."

Terry and Rob led the boys to the rear of the sanctuary and sat the last pew. Terry pulled her coat tight around her, for the chill in the church seemed dank after the afternoon sun outside. She soon forgot the cold as the music began again. The two at the front readjusted their seats and score sheets, agreed on a place to start, and then in no time at all, the reverent chords of Be Not Afraid caught her up. Terry found herself thinking about the silent child within, its limbs now distinguishing themselves, its body curled, knees bent, its umbilicus attached to her blood source, a lifeline bonding them forever in a chain stretching backward through centuries of hardships and achievements, loves and losses. How could she have possibly doubted the wisdom of its coming? The world would need her children to make a new world and more than ever before the pandemic, she and Rob would play a greater part in the shape and substance of that world. Before, their little family had little or no influence on the course of things, but now they would, whether they wanted to or not. Perhaps, she thought, rubbing the small mound of her belly, a mound so small no one in the alliance had yet guessed a living child was growing there, my children can help to make it a better one.

For Rob, sitting with one arm across the back of the pew, the other across his wife's shoulders, a simple peace loosened his shoulder muscles, softened the wrinkles in his brow, slackened his jaw and lowered his eyelids, so that when Chris looked up at him, he thought his father had fallen asleep. But then he could see the movement of his father's eyes beneath the lids, as if his father was gazing about the church in his mind's eye, fully awake. And truly, that is exactly what Rob was doing in the darkness behind his lowered lids. He was imagining a time when his kind first experienced religious bliss, the wonder of expanding out of one's finite body into an infinite universe. He felt grateful for being alive, for his family's health, for all that still survived, and he savored the hope that spread from his heart down through his finger tips and, beyond them, into the warm skin of Terry's neck and along the smooth patina of ancient oiled wood where his other hand rested. The music swelled and softened, its fluid notes reverent and beautiful. Rob hadn't realized its loss until this very minute, when its return to his life so easily swept him up into joy.

Michael and Chris sat quietly, recognizing that this moment was significant to both their parents, although they could never have said why. They watched their mother and saw beneath her lowered lashes the hint of tears. They watched their father's face smooth, the usual lines and crevices disappearing so that he somehow looked younger than they were used to. They gazed about the church,

480 Joan J. Johnson and William E. Rose

wondering why the statues of the Virgin Mary and Christ on the cross weren't in this church as they were in theirs, they watched the back of Lily Fenn's head and the movement of her arms as her hands swept the keys, and they studied the serene face of the teenage girl whose name they did not know, the way her long neck arched left over the violin as her right hand moved the bow over the strings.

When they finished, Lily Fenn straightened the sheet music in front of her, and the young girl bent to pack her violin in its case. No one said anything, for what was there really to say? Terry stood reluctantly, patting Michael's shoulder and smiling wanly down at Chris. "Let's go, boys," she whispered.

"Thanks, Lily," Rob said. "May we come again?"

Lily turned then, smiling shyly. "We don't always know when we're going to find the time to practice, Rob," she said apologetically. "There seems to be so much to do. But we try to get here on Sunday afternoons and most of the time, we make it."

"No promises expected," Rob said, grateful for her willingness to let them share her music.

"Thanks, Lily," Terry added, tapping both Michael and Chris on their shoulders to remind them to be polite.

"Thanks, Mrs. Fenn," they said quietly.

"You're very welcome, boys," she said in that tone adults use when they know they are training youngsters to use the courtesy expected of them.

"I'm really glad to see you're all right," Rob said. "And your husband?" he asked tentatively.

"Yes."

"And your son's family?"

"Yes, they are too." Rob felt her reluctance to divulge more, understood and accepted it. In this new world order, one had to be careful. Survival depended upon it.

54

Patterson, April

For several weeks now that the ham radio was functioning, Ethel, Laura, and Taylor pulled Ethel's old kitchen chairs around Arnold's radio table and tuned in to the world. Evening had quickly become the focus of their lives, something hungered for more than their evening meal. News that there were people out there surviving in small clusters like their own had given them more hope than they'd dared to feel all winter. Hearing that the government was at work putting itself back together allowed them to believe that someday, maybe not soon, but someday life would return to normal.

"You wait," Arnold had insisted. "The minute they get up and going, they'll be voting in a penalty for missing the April 15th deadline. Won't matter that none of us got W-2s."

"Oh, Arnold," Ethel exclaimed. "Wouldn't you rather have taxes than no government at all?"

"No," Arnold said flatly. "We're doing just fine by ourselves. Don't need to be supporting a bunch of fatheads in Washington."

"You're hopeless," Ethel sighed, crossing her legs and adjusting her sweater.

"Shhhhh," said Laura, catching something about a vaccine. They all leaned forward. The news was hopeful and ominous at the same time. Reports that a vaccine had been created down at the CDC for the most recent strains of the virus were followed by the obstacles that had yet to be overcome. The most important one, of course, was that the virus mutated so quickly there were no assurances that by the time the vaccine was manufactured it would still be useful. A new strain could make the vaccine obsolete even before it reached the public, what there was left of it. Manufacturing was another problem, for the pharmaceutical companies were limping along on skeleton staffs just like everyone else. It would be months before a production line could be up and running. Several antiviral drugs had been ordered before the outbreak, drugs aimed at preventing viral replication, but not enough of them. The U.S. had been slow to place orders, and by the time authorities realized more were needed, the U.S. was in line behind other countries that had placed their orders earlier. Some experts even questioned whether the drugs would be effective against the avian flu, because the course of its infection was so fast. Distribution was the third great problem. Washington was toying with the idea of helicopter drops where communities existed, because air, rail, and highway transportation systems were all but defunct.

"Listen to those guys making a big deal out of every problem," Arnold huffed. "The roads haven't ever been better for travel. They're just worried about missing out on tolls."

"Arnold!" Ethel hissed.

"Think we could try reaching Wyoming again?" Taylor asked, tired of Arnold's banter.

Arnold continued turning the dial. Now that he could actually broadcast, he found it hard not to stop at every voice and initiate a conversation. Already he had made a few pals, one a Georgia cracker who was still fighting the Civil War despite the fact that the South was worse off now than it was after General Lee. As he rolled the dial, he named people he could already identify by voice, and when he broadcast, some people already knew him. This especially pleased Arnold, whose self-importance had been growing by the day with each new invention, so much so that Ethel had told Laura she could hardly stand it anymore. "He thinks he can order me around. Me, of all things. That man is in for a come-uppance."

Laura had only smiled, knowing from experience never to get between a husband and his wife. Ethel was as proud of Arnold as she was annoyed with him. And if anyone ever dared to say something against him, that person would have to face her wrath forever. "He had a bad time of it, you know," Ethel confided at one time. "His mother dumped him in an orphanage during the war and left him there. He never knew his father. And then the nuns at the orphanage didn't cotton to a wiseacre who knew more than most of them by the time he was ten. The knuckles in his right hand? You ever notice them? All enlarged? That's from raps with the ruler whenever he acted smart. Poor Arnold. His whole life people have been putting him down."

Laura wasn't surprised. She had seen other boys like Arnold face the same kind of derision, stuck in classes with kids who took months to learn what they understood in minutes, forced to chew a subject to death until everyone was ready to swallow instead of being encouraged to eat up whatever was out there as fast as they could. By the time the school system was through with them, they'd already starved to death. And in the meantime, they'd had to take the ridicule of slow kids and even some slow teachers who feared them. Her dear old friend from high school, Evan Brandt, had been like Arnold, only unlike him, Evan Brandt had given up his senior year and hung himself. Perhaps that's why Laura found Arnold so endearing. He was an older, wiser version of Evan.

From what the group around the radio could gather, people had survived all over the world, all of them in small pockets. The more rural the community, the more people who had made it. Tales of the cities were another thing entirely. Those that didn't die of the flu died of starvation or were murdered by those who thought they had food. Some had frozen to death in one of the worst January freezes on record. The cities were places to avoid, most agreed, for disease was probably still festering there, despite what the CDC maintained. Arnold scoffed at that, saying that once a body died, the disease lost its host and died too. He'd listened to some doctors talking back and forth only yesterday. Ethel wasn't so sure, and Laura and Taylor knew very little about biology, so Arnold stood alone in his certainty.

"How many in Patterson, you think?" Arnold offered up for discussion. He and Taylor were the only ones who had ventured off their street and, though they had seen a few people, neither of them had any idea how many others were hidden away on other back roads.

"What would you say to a Sunday ride, old girl?" Arnold asked, turning full around to pat Ethel's knee. She didn't have to answer, nor did Laura, for at the mention of a ride, they brightened like lamps. Ethel nearly knocked her chair backwards as she stood up. "A ride?" she enthused. "Go for a ride, Laura?" she said, turning to her friend.

The following morning, they were up and ready with the sun.

"Do we have to carry guns?" Ethel chided the minute she saw Arnold come from the cellar with his shotgun and pistol. "For pete's sake, Arnold, you expecting Indians?" She put her hands on her hips in protest.

"You want to be out there unarmed if we meet up with your pony-tail friend?" Arnold reminded her.

Her face clouded. "You think he's out there waiting, Arnold?"

"You want to be unarmed if he is?" Arnold was enjoying her dismay.

Ethel sighed. "You can sure wreck a beautiful day, Arnold Card."

The sun was especially warm as they walked to the car. "Happens every year," Ethel said. "Come late April, we get a warm spell. Might as well be July." She breathed deeply, savoring the smell of growing things. "Look at my tulips," she pointed, her smile wide. "Aren't they the most beautiful things you've ever seen."

"Enjoy 'em now, girlie, before the blackflies come. This heat will have them swarming before the week is out." Arnold whacked Ethel on the rear before he sped ahead to Laura's Volvo. He opened the back door and bowed. "Madame?" he called, "your chariot awaits."

Ethel giggled like a girl and hurried forward, leaving Laura to admire the flowers. Taylor watched her through the driver's open window, his arm on the steering wheel, thinking her more beautiful than any woman ought to be. When she turned, she caught him gazing at her. She smiled and he winked.

They headed for 2A, looking at the bright blue sky, the budding trees, the greening bushes along the road. "Slow down, Taylor," Ethel said. "We're coming to my friend Nettie's house."

Taylor stepped lightly on the brake, forcing the car into a slow glide. He could see the mailbox ahead and a driveway beyond it, but he had to pass a line of tall pines that blocked their view of Nettie's yard. As they drew even with the pines, Ethel leaned forward in her seat, craning to see if anyone was about. Taylor stopped the car.

Nettie's yard was thick with dead leaves left over from the fall, dew glistening in the morning sun. Grass and weeds had begun growing up through them, untended. Nettie's car sat in the driveway, blackening leaves caught in its bumper and against the windshield wipers. A rear tire had gone flat. When Ethel looked at the house, she gasped. The front windows along the bottom floor were broken, and in one of them, a scraggly white curtain had caught on the broken glass. It hung half in, half out of the window. "Oh," Ethel sighed. "Oh."

Arnold put his arm around his wife's shoulders. "Don't look like she made it," Arnold said softly, hugging his wife to him.

"Look at the flowers," she said, pointing. "She loved her flowers. See?"

On the far side of the house, Nettie's garden was blooming, despite the ragged piles of unraked leaves covering the ground. Hyacinths, daffodils, and tulips had fought their way stubbornly to the surface and were unfolding yellows and reds, purples and pinks, in waving banners of color, while beside them, Nettie's house had begun a slow decay. All four of the people in the car saw it, the contrast of life and death there on Nettie's lawn and their silence attested to the sorrow they felt for Nettie, for Ethel, for themselves, and for all people, living and dead.

Everywhere it was the same. Empty houses, unkempt lawns, spring flowers. House after house on their way to the main road stared stoically back at them through broken windows. "Who did this?" Ethel whimpered. "Why would someone break their windows?" No one had an answer for her. The sheer stupidity of the destruction made no sense at all.

When they reached 2A, they saw their first car. A man and woman stared at them, trying to see if the Volvo's occupants were people they knew. Ethel recognized the woman. "That's Mary Sawyer," she cried, lowering her window and leaning out to wave. "Mary!" she yelled. "Mary, it's me. Ethel!" The woman in the other car leaned toward the driver, waving. Her husband gave them a quick smile and slowed, but did not stop. Nor did Taylor. But inside, Ethel was jubilant. "Mary Sawyer made it!" she enthused. "Mary's okay!"

Arnold patted Ethel on the shoulder. "Quiet down, girlie. We know. We know."

They saw others. Some people were walking along the main street in Almont, family groups that stayed close together. Taylor slowed again to give Arnold and Ethel a closer look. "That's Albert's son," Arnold stated. "Him and his kids."

"I wonder if Albert made it," Ethel asked. "Stop, will you Taylor?"

Taylor pulled alongside the walking group. Immediately the man grabbed his kids, herding them back closer to the building. He looked at the car, and then his eyes focused on Arnold, who by now had lowered the window and was leaning out.

"Hi there, Junior," Arnold chirped. "How's your dad?"

The young man squinted at Arnold. Without moving closer to the car, he said, "My dad passed in December. Mom too."

Arnold paused, sighing. "I'm sorry to hear that, Junior. The rest of you okay?"

The young man looked at the group gathered around him and hugged the small girl closest to his thigh. "We're all fine," he said. "The wife's at home. We thought we'd just get out and see..." he shook his head, "...how things are."

"Any news?" Arnold asked.

Junior didn't seem to know much more than the rest of them about who or how many people they both knew had survived. "We've been kind of isolated out there…" Junior explained. "This is the first time we've ventured into town."

"I know," Arnold said. "Same here. Doesn't look like many stores have anything left to sell," Arnold said, eyeing the row of stores with broken windows.

"Scavengers," Junior said. "But the Agway's open."

"It is?" said Arnold, turning to glance at Taylor. They'd been planning a trip there to look for seeds. "You got any money on you, Taylor?" he asked, hopefully.

"You'll need a lot," said Junior. "Guy there's charging triple."

"Price gouging."

"Stealing's what it is," Junior replied. "Guy doesn't even own the stuff. He just took it over."

"Don't say," Arnold responded thoughtfully. "Selling what's not his to sell?"

"Who's to say these days, Mr. Card," Junior said, shaking his head.

"That's so," Arnold agreed. "Well, I think we might meander over there, Junior. Was good seeing you."

"Same here," Junior smiled, turning to walk on.

"Bye, Junior," Ethel called from the other side of the car. But Junior had already begun herding his children along the walk. He merely turned and nodded.

Taylor had put the car in park while Arnold talked with Junior and had twisted around, his arm on the back of Laura's seat. "I've got some money on me," Taylor said. "We ought to be able to get some starter seeds."

"I just happened to bring my list," Arnold announced,

awaiting a compliment. When no one responded, he began searching his pockets, fighting all the while with the seat belt. "These damn things are a pain in the..."

"Arnold!" Ethel admonished. "Watch your language."

"Well they are," he grunted, trying to lift his body enough that his right hand could slide into his pocket. He extracted the paper and began reading. "Cucumbers. Peas. Lettuce..."

By the time they reached the Agway, Arnold had already begun discussing the merits of particular planting arrangements. Taylor pulled up to the gray building and looked about. Two pickups sat in the lot, and one of them was the black pickup they all knew. "You noticing?" Taylor asked, his head indicating the direction Arnold should look.

Arnold stopped talking as soon as he saw it. "Looks kind of familiar, don't it?"

Laura recognized it too. "That's the one I saw!" she said, craning.

"As came to our house?" Ethel cried. "That Bull guy?"

"Same one," Arnold said, opening his door.

"Arnold," Ethel whined, "You can't go in there. That's the guy."

"I know girlie, but we need seeds. Can't spend our lives hiding."

Taylor had already climbed out and slipped his pistol into his belt, beneath his jacket. "Maybe you two had better wait in the car," he said, leaning in to look at Laura. Without saying anything aloud, he indicated the rifle he'd left beside her. Laura nodded, looking worried.

Both women watched as the two men strode purposefully through the door, neither of them looking back. Laura heard Ethel whispering to herself, a sound so tiny that it could have been the air seeping in through the cracked window. "Oh dear, oh dear, oh me..." Ethel repeated, working her lips, her eyes narrowed and pale in her wrinkled face.

As Taylor stepped inside, he quickly surveyed the store, looking for the man Laura had described. Arnold strode in beside him and stopped, looking about as well. A thin man with a beak of a nose was standing behind the counter, his face a study in obstinacy. On the other side of the counter, one of two men leaned forward while the other stood, his arms across his chest. From the looks of it, both were angry and Taylor realized that he had come upon a confrontation of some sort. The man with the nose looked up as they entered, and Taylor watched his Adam's apple jump as he swallowed. Then he looked back at the man leaning on the counter who continued speaking to him as if he had no idea anyone had entered.

"You can't be serious, Nose," he hissed. "That's highway robbery, and you know it."

"That's the deal," Nose said quietly. "I don't make policy. I'm just glad to have a job, Rob. You don't like it, you take it up with Bull."

"Where is he?" the other man asked, looking back to where Taylor and Arnold stood quietly in the doorway.

"He's out somewhere," Nose said "Took the eighteen-wheeler. I don't know when he'll be back."

Taylor glanced at Arnold, then began walking about the store, which was filled to capacity with all sorts of tools and other farming supplies stacked so close that both had to be careful as they negotiated the aisles. While they browsed, they listened intently to the conversation at the counter.

"Dammit, Nose, I need those seeds, and I can see bags of 'em piled out there in the shed twenty deep. I don't know where he got all those supplies, but you and I both know that this place and this stuff weren't his to begin with. Sam Moss owned the Agway, and he never once had stock like this."

"Moss is dead."

"That doesn't make a bit of difference. One thing's for sure, he didn't make Bull Jones a beneficiary, so Bull's got no right to be taking over here."

Nose Bartlett could see that Rob Grant was getting angrier by the minute, and he relished the fact. If there was anyone Nose Bartlett despised, it was this high school football star whom everybody had cheered Saturday after Saturday throughout his entire high school career. While Nose ran around the sidelines gathering facts for the school paper, Rob had been out there like some Ty Young hero, a magnet for everyone's attention. Especially Terry Shaw, who to this day Nose could still see cheering from the stands, her camel-hair coat open in the fall sunshine, her long hair cascading about her shoulders. Terry Shaw, the love of his life, had never even seen him staring up at her as she waved the school banner and shouted the school cheer with the rest of the fans. And now here was Rob Grant, hat in hand, begging for a better deal on seeds, a deal he wasn't going to get as long as Nose Bartlett was at the register.

"That's the deal. Five thousand cash or you sign this 'in kind' contract for forty percent of your crop. Otherwise, take it up with Bull." Nose loved saying that: "Take it up with Bull." He'd seen the look of resignation cross the faces of at least fifteen farmers in the last few weeks, farmers who came in preparing to pay the same prices they had last spring only to find that Bull had a corner on the market and that he was going to price gouge them or sign them into a level of debt they could never get out from under. Pitbull Jones was running things now. He'd spent the winter robbing every facility within fifty miles. He had warehouses and barns full of equipment and supplies, a band of tough guys with guns who would stop at nothing to get their booty, and Nose had been smart enough to ingratiate himself into running the store.

Out of the corner of his eye, Nose sensed that the small guy had stopped browsing and was now standing just off to the side of Rob and his friend Ralph Green. He recognized the older man, but he had no idea from where. His eyes darted about the tops of other aisles, looking for the tall, lanky fellow who'd entered at the same time. He was over in the garden section, piling up seed packets. Obviously, he wasn't a farmer or he'd be buying fifty or hundred pound bags.

"I'm not paying your prices," Ralph Green said.

"Your choice," Nose smiled.

Taylor strode up to the counter, setting down a basket with the seed packets he'd gathered. Now Nose had four men looking at him, and he wished that Bull and the boys would pull into the parking lot. Not that these men were violent types. Nose wasn't afraid they'd hurt him, but they might do something rash, like take what they needed without paying. Nose could see that idea cross the minds of literally every farmer who'd been by. But each had decided better. Bull Jones had a reputation that preceded the flu. No one liked crossing him, even when he ran the junkyard, and they had the police and the courts to back them up then. So the rest had resigned themselves to signing the ledger book, knowing full well that they were going to be working all summer to make Bull rich and maybe, just maybe, grow enough food to get them through the winter.

When the little guy spoke, Nose almost thought he wasn't hearing right. "Ain't signing no ledger book,

Bartlett," the old man said quietly. "We're taking what we need, and we'll pay you a fair price when and if the bank re-opens. If not, we'll provide you with a fair percentage of our produce—five percent, maybe."

Rob and Ralph both turned, surprised at the little man's tone but delighted that he'd taken the initiative. They'd both been thinking the same thing. Taylor, on the other hand, wanted to smack him in the head. Arnold was at it again.

Nose consciously controlled his gulp. "You can't do that," he said.

"I can and I will," Arnold said. "I've lived here nearly my whole life, and I'm not putting up with some asshole thinking he's going to take over my town and run things. This here's stolen property. You know it and I know it. But I'm willing to pay a fair price just so's I don't have to go out and steal it myself. "

Nose was at a loss for words. He might have expected Grant or Green to pull something like this, but the old twerp looked harmless. How would it look to Bull if later Bull went out to retrieve his stuff and found an old man had been able to intimidate his clerk? Nose slowly began to run his hand along the counter to the spot below which he had stored a gun. He'd show this guy.

"I wouldn't do that," Taylor said, his hand ready at his side. Something in the man's eyes scared Nose; the hairs on the back of his neck prickled and his hand froze where it was on the counter. He had never seen the guy before, that he knew for sure. No one wore cowboy hats around here, but the guy looked dangerous. Nose was outnumbered four to one.

"You boys want to rob this place, you're going to have to deal with Bull Jones. I don't want no trouble." Inside, Nose seethed.

Rob Grant looked at Ralph, then back at Nose. "I'm going to make a list of everything I take. Come fall, we'll do the same thing. A fair percentage. If Bull wants to discuss this further, he knows where I live."

"You got paper?" Arnold asked.

Nose reached behind him for a pad and pencil.

"We need one too," Ralph said, reaching his hand out.

Nose turned again, grabbing another pad and handing it to Ralph. "You guys are going to be sorry for this," he said, hating the fact that his voice sounded so small.

"Maybe so," Arnold replied. "But you goddamned well ought to be ashamed of yourself for being part of this operation, Bartlett. What kind of man beats a man who's down?" Arnold's fury showed on his face, which was red with anger.

Nose started to speak but thought better of it. He could feel his face flush and his heart race. How he wished his phone still worked so that he could call Bull in from the road and watch him pound these guys into horsemeat. He'd have to do the next best thing, which was to follow them out to the sheds and itemize the stuff they took. He knew he was going to take shit from Bull when he got back. Bull was going to berate him, blame him for being a wimp not to stand up to these guys. Nose worried that Bull might even tell him to get lost. Then what would he do? He had no way to earn a living. He was no farmer who could raise his own food. He hated physical labor. He hated sweating.

Rob Grant followed Arnold out the door, glancing up at the Volvo parked just outside the door. An older woman with glasses rolled down the window. "Rob Grant," Ethel called. "I'm so glad you're okay!"

Rob recognized the woman, though he could not recall her name. His confusion showed on his face. "It's Ethel.

Ethel Card," she called, now leaning her head out the window.

"Mrs. Card," Rob repeated dumbly, a half smile on his face. He stood in the lot, not wanting to go too near the car.

"I know your wife Terry," she said, realizing the young man did not really know her. "And you're our selectman."

It was strange to hear his public office mentioned when government no longer existed. Like a reminder of old duties. "Yes ma'am," he said. "Was selectman." He emphasized the was.

"Well?" Ethel asked.

"Well what?" Rob asked politely, not knowing what the woman wanted.

"Is Terry okay? And the kids?"

"Oh," Rob said. "Yes, ma'am. Doing as fine as can be expected."

"You tell her I said hello, will you?" Ethel asked, sitting back in her seat and dismissing Rob by speaking to Laura. "I'm so glad that girl's okay," she said to Laura, who had turned around in her seat. "You remember I introduced you?"

Laura was not sure, for Ethel had introduced her to a lot of people, but she nodded yes just the same.

"On the road? We were walking?"

Then Laura realized who this man must be. His wife was the woman in BJ's, the one who was behind her in line that day. The one she guessed was storing up just like she was. And she smiled.

Meanwhile, the rest of the men walked about the shed locating the bags of seed they needed. Ralph called to Rob, "Bring the truck around, will you?"

While he waited, he watched Arnold and Taylor pulling

down the supplies they needed. "You guys are going to need more than a Volvo to carry that stuff home."

"Yeah. We should have brought the pickup. But the girls needed an outing," Arnold explained. "I'm Arnold Card, from out on Old Stagecoach Road." He reached out his hand but then withdrew it immediately, realizing that handshakes were no longer polite.

Ralph nodded, smiling. "We'd be pleased to drop it off for you, Mr. Card. I don't think you'll want to be coming back here soon." Now his smile was ear to ear, his eyes twinkling. "Don't think Nose Bartlett likes you much."

"Don't much care what that parrot face thinks," Arnold said matter-of-factly. "There's always guys who want to make a buck off someone else's misery."

"That's so," Ralph said.

Rob had now backed the big truck up to the shed and jumped down. "Okay, let's get at it." His urgency was apparent, but he took a minute to appraise Arnold. "I'm glad you spoke up," he said. *Sometimes courage comes in small packages,* he thought. *Small old packages.*

"We're going to drop some supplies off for them," Ralph said, watching as Taylor hefted a hundred pound burlap bag onto his shoulder.

"Let's load up and get out of here," Rob said, looking back at the entrance to the lot. "I don't much relish a fight today."

Nose had come up behind them, his clipboard at the ready. Though he trembled with anger, he managed to sound matter-of-fact. "Today or tomorrow, you're going to get one."

55

Patterson, April

Carol Green walked out to the kitchen to add wood to the stove. While the days were considerably warmer now, Spring was a frivolous season, full of tricks and teases. Yesterday, the temperature had risen to eighty degrees. Today it was only forty-five. Yesterday, she had flung open every window to let in the warm fresh air. Today she was once again stoking the wood stove. She stood, watching the hot flames lick the new logs, rubbing her hands together and listening to the classes being conducted in the other rooms. She could hear Terry talking about Antigone, and Shirley working with the younger kids on Oliver Twist. Lisa was too far away to hear, working with the youngest ones. Her own little class was taking a test—David and Ellen both struggling to keep their minds on geometry while they fought the desire to touch each other. She could almost feel the magnetic tension whenever she stood near them. She smiled. Her son was madly in love, and despite all reason, she couldn't be happier. What seemed like a lifetime ago, she had worried about his crush on that girl across town, that boy-crazy one. Now he had fallen for Ellen Young, and she couldn't imagine a more fitting match. She and Shirley both knew they'd better keep their eyes on the two of them; they didn't want something unforeseen happening when both David and Ellen were still so young. But, Carol thought to herself, this is a different, new world her children would now have to face, and she hoped David would face it with Ellen.

She turned to look out the kitchen window, surprised to see Griz in her yard. Rob liked Griz to stay home now that feral dogs had become such a menace. Once Terry and the kids were safely deposited at schoolhouse, Rob and Griz walked home, the dog on a lead, Rob shouldering his shotgun. Griz was not on a lead and school had started an hour ago, so Carol knew Griz had come back on his own and she knew why. Lady, their sheep dog, was in heat.

Carol leaned against the counter, amused. Lady had pushed the barn door open just enough to stick her nose through. The shiny black nub looked like a licorice sucker. Griz was dancing about on the dirt outside, attempting to tease her out. He whined, he pranced, he ran about in circles, each time returning to touch his nose to Lady's. When she'd extend enough of her muzzle, he'd lick her around the dewlaps like he was kissing her. Lady would allow him just so much of that and she'd withdraw her head, leaving poor Griz to whine some more and scratch at the heavy door. Carol could not understand why Griz didn't slip inside the barn. He was such a massive dog, he could have done so with only a little maneuvering. But he didn't. In frustration, instead he'd pretend to be sniffing at things about the yard, his tail erect, all the time glancing back at the door to see if Lady had changed her mind. Usually by then, Lady was curious where he'd gone, and the black nose would once again protrude, sniffing the air for him.

This was entertainment too good to miss. Carol poured some hot water into a teacup and stood at the window, agitating the bag in her cup. By the time she was ready to take a sip, Griz seemed to have disappeared. She leaned forward to the glass, looking both ways, but she couldn't see him. Lady was curious as well. She stuck her head completely out, peering left and right just as Carol had. Lady sniffed the air. Carol thought she could read disappointment on Lady's face, then chided herself for attributing human emotions to dogs. Still, Lady's demeanor seemed anxious. She pushed through the barn door into the full sunlight and stood looking. Then she began following Griz's scent, which must have been confusing, for he'd danced about in front of the door so many times that Lady's tracking circled around and over itself several times. She had her nose to the ground, though, and she was determined. As her circles grew wider, Carol had to lean forward again to watch her. Then Lady disappeared around the side of the house.

Carol shrugged, disappointed. When she saw them again, they were in the field to the left of the barn. They were running together, as if racing, but when one stopped, the other did too. She saw Griz playfully raise a paw to Lady's face, pushing her nose down. Lady shook him off and rose up on her hind legs, both paws aloft, then she twisted and ran some more, this time back toward the house.

Griz was on her trail immediately, catching up quickly and nipping at her forelegs as she ran, impeding her gait. Lady stopped again, this time twisting and running the other way while Griz continued his pursuit. Back and forth for what seemed ages to Carol, their coats glistening in the sun, panting, tongues lolling as they courted each other. Sometimes Lady stood, facing the far trees, her rear legs rigid, while Griz sniffed and licked about her tail. But just as he was about to mount her, she'd break stance once again and run, leaving poor Griz confused and frustrated. When he'd catch up, she'd do the same thing, as if teasing him.

Carol wondered how long this was going to go on and looked at her watch to check the time. The kids had another ten minutes before their test was over. Soon she was going to have to go back into the dining room. She saw Lady running up the hill toward the tree line, Griz at her side. "Darn," she thought. After all that, the dogs were going into the woods and she was going to miss the climax. She smiled at her pun and at what a dirty old lady she could be, then worried a bit about what might be in the woods. Would Lady's scent attract the wild dogs? She watched for several minutes, well aware of time passing and wondering whether she should do anything.

Just then, Ralph emerged from the barn. Carol walked to the back door, then outside to where he stood in the yard. "Better call Lady," she said, "She's up there in the woods with Griz." She stretched her arm to point.

Ralph put his two fingers into his mouth and whistled, a long, urgent call. Nothing. "What's going on?" Ralph asked, surprised at Lady's disobedience.

"I think we might be having some puppies," Carol smiled, happy at the thought.

56

Patterson, Late May

Butch Jones drove his father's black pickup along Lincoln Hill Road, an open bottle of Jack Daniels leaning against his hip. Dobie Maxwell sat in the passenger seat, his arm out the window, his chinless profile facing forward. Butch hated the way Dobie's mouth hung open. Between that and his heavy eyelids always hanging half closed, Dobie looked like a lizard. Butch laughed out loud.

"What?" Dobie asked, turning, his jaw slack.

"You're a jerk!" Butch said, his fat hands gripping the steering wheel.

"What?" Dobie asked again.

"You look like those dragon things," Butch snorted, reaching down to grab the bottle and taking a swig with one hand while the other steered.

Dobie looked hurt, but he only shrugged. "Ain't so perfect yourself," he muttered under his breath.

"What?" Butch asked, turning toward him and pretending to be angry. He deliberately steered right so that the pickup veered toward the side of the road. Butch kept his head turned toward Dobie, as if he didn't realize they were about to have an accident. Dobie saw the tree line looming in front of them.

"Butch!" he cried. "Watch out!"

"What?" Butch asked, mimicking Dobie. Then he laughed and righted the vehicle, steering back on to the road. "Dumb ass," he said, taking another swig.

Dobie shrugged, trying to loosen his shoulders. Butch was a pain in the ass, and Dobie hated when Butch had nothing better to do than concentrate his malice on him. Sometimes Dobie nursed thoughts of revenge, like someone blowing Butch to smithereens or Butch's father smashing him just once a little too hard or Butch slamming into a telephone pole, as long as Dobie wasn't in the truck with him. In fact, Dobie thought about Butch meeting his end just about all the time now that they were always together. He wished Bull would team him up with one of the other guys instead of always sticking him with his sorry son. An ape of a kid and mean as hell. Dobie would get rid of him himself, except then he'd have Bull to deal with. And that would not be good. Oh no, that would not be good at all. Dobie knew when he had a good thing going. Teaming up with Bull Jones was the smartest thing he'd ever done. They'd robbed every facility that had anything valuable in it within a twenty-five mile radius. They'd stockpiled stuff in barns and warehouses from Leominster to Greenfield, stuff people were going to need now that winter was over and planting season was in full swing. They were going to be rich off those stupid farmers. Let them sweat out there in the fields, hoeing and raking, weeding and watering. Hah! Not for him. Not for Dobie Maxwell. He was going to grow fat on their labor.

"What's your Dad want us to do out there?" Dobie asked. They were on their way out to the Grant farm, he knew that much. But he didn't know what for.

"Just looking. Find how they're getting in and out, for one. Pop says they've got a roadblock. Wants us to figure out how they get in and out."

"Nothing else?"

"Nope. The old man says 'Let 'em plant the seeds and

grow the stuff.' He'll come to collect just before they harvest it."

"Ain't he taking a chance then? What if they won't cooperate?"

"Then he'll take the stuff." Butch turned to Dobie, his wide smile showing crooked teeth.

Dobie snorted. "Wouldn't that be a lesson? Do all that work and just when you're about to reap your rewards, poof, it's leaving on trucks!" He laughed, enjoying the irony.

Butch took another swig, and the pickup veered again as he did. "I got a better plan," he said, nodding.

"What?" Dobie asked, watching the trees flying by.

"Let 'em harvest the stuff, you know? Put it all up in the barns and on their shelves. Do the whole job and think they're sitting pretty?"

"Yeah?" Dobie knew where he was going and liked the idea.

"Then come some night with gas cans..."

"Yeah..." Dobie enthused. "Burn 'em out. Houses, barns, and all."

"Wouldn't that be a pretty sight? What a bonfire!"

"Yeah!" Dobie seconded. "We could toast marshmallows!"

Butch slowed the pickup as they turned left. The barricade was just ahead, sitting high across the road and down some into the bushes. Neither side looked promising.

"They've got some other way out," Dobie said, stating the obvious. "They're not coming out this way."

"Got to get out somewhere."

"Let's go around, see what they've got on the other end."

"How much land you think they've got between 'em?"

"Old man says nearly a thousand. Maybe not that much, but close."

"Jeez," said Dobie. "You think they're planning to farm all that?" Dobie was thinking about how much work that would be. Nothing he'd want.

"Naw," Butch said, "Look how much is woods."

The pickup sped along, then cut right onto another road.

"Suppose you didn't burn 'em out," Dobie mused. "Suppose they woke up one morning and found themselves surrounded. Suppose we just took everything? 'Stead of burning it."

"Eat it," Butch laughed.

"Leave 'em high and dry. Take their preserves right off the shelves?"

"I'd laugh all winter!" Butch liked this idea.

"We could still burn 'em out..."

"Yeah, after...."

Butch slowed the pickup, realizing they had circled the entire area without finding an entrance.

"Sheee..it!" Butch said.

"So let's circle around again. I saw a couple of places where maybe they could be driving in."

This time Butch took his time, scanning the side of the road carefully for signs of tire tracks or other clues that might reveal the opening the alliance was using. "Sneaky bastards," he said, pausing to look into the woods.

"We'll find it," Dobie said, sitting forward and resting his arms on the dashboard.

They took their time, stopping frequently to peer about. Once Butch ordered Dobie out of the truck when he thought an open area looked promising. Dobie jumped down the embankment and took his time to pee before coming back. "Naw," he said. "No way. There's a bunch of huge rocks in there."

As they climbed a slow, winding hill, Dobie spotted a chimney off in the distance. "Whose place is that?" he asked.

"How should I know," Butch growled, frustrated and bored by their fruitless search. "Let's park and cut down through the woods. Take a look."

"Walk?" asked Dobie, shocked at the thought.

"No, skate, asshole. How do ya' think?" Butch heaved his big belly past the steering wheel as he pushed the cab door open. "Bring your gun," he said, slipping his into his belt. Dobie climbed out the other side, swearing under his breath. He had on his new Nikes, compliments of Dick's Sports, and he really didn't want them wrecked so soon.

Together, the two slipped, slid, and tripped their way down the long slope into the woods. "Keep your eyes peeled," Butch said.

"What for?" Dobie asked, too loud.

"For whatever," Butch growled again. "Dogs, maybe."

"Bears?"

"Could be."

"Yeah? You think?" Dobie looked around doubtfully. The only hunting Dobie had ever done was mailboxes and windows, targets that didn't move.

They worked their way slowly through the woods toward open pastureland, where they stopped to survey the farm below them. "Shit, will you look at that," Dobie said, pointing. In the yard beyond the house, a bunch of kids were playing basketball. Boys, some not much younger than Butch. He craned to see who they were.

There were six of them and their shouts carried in the bright air as one or the other made a basket.

"Let's cut down over there," Butch said, his eyes narrowing. "I think I know who one of them is." Butch's mouth had hardened into a straight line. He certainly did know who one was, and the littler one too. Butch felt anger inflating like a balloon, filling his entire chest cavity.

They took their time, cutting back into the woods and over, following the tree line down closer to the farmyard. "Would you look at that!" Dobie whispered loudly. He had spotted Ellen playing badminton with two younger girls. Butch's eyes flicked about, then settled on the lithe girl, her dark hair flying as she raced back and forth. Both boys' mouths hung open as they watched her, each thinking his own thoughts. Just then David came around the side of the house, calling to her. She left the girls to play by themselves and disappeared back the way he had come.

"Let's get closer," Butch said.

Dobie worried. "Someone might spot us."

But Butch was already moving through the trees. Dobie followed reluctantly, then squatted beside him.

Butch glared down at the kids throwing hoops. "Michael Grant," he said, relishing the words in his mouth. "And his pissant brother." Butch's face was a study. Dobie watched him watching the kids and wondered why he was so interested. But he didn't say anything. Something about the way Butch stared, his chin jutting forward, his eyes squinting, made Dobie silent. Sometimes it was best to be quiet around Butch, unless you wanted his hammy fist in your face. He'd seen it before and learned to be careful when Butch got that way. One thing Dobie knew for sure was that Michael Grant was someone Butch hated, and that was all he had to know.

57

Atlanta, Late May

Lester stood in the hall, watching Mark through the glass, jostled by others gathered there to witness an important moment. Parker stood beside him, smelling of aftershave, his perfect suit unwrinkled despite their lack of services, his hair perfectly trimmed despite the lack of adequate barbering facilities on compound grounds. Parker growled, his opposition to this process audible. He had fought Lester from the beginning, and now, standing there watching one of his own administering a lethal poison into his own system, Parker raged that he had been put in this moral no-win situation. Despite his many faults, Parker cared about his people and could make no excuse to sacrifice a single one of them, no matter how high the stakes. Yet here they were, watching Harris flick the hypodermic needle several times before he jabbed it into his own arm.

Parker had been over-ruled. Not by his people but by Washington. Once Mark had been exposed to the virus, Lester had taken it upon himself to discover the reason for his survival. It didn't make sense, Lester had insisted. The avian flu hadn't harmed Harris at all. No fever. No chills. No coughing. Nothing. While his blood test had shown the presence of H5N1a immediately after the exposure, within hours the virus had disappeared. Destroyed, they guessed, by Mark's own immune-system. How had that happened, they had all wondered, discussing the topic everywhere they congregated. Lester had reported the exposure, Mark's survival, and his own theories, compelled by his conscience to hide nothing from the government. Washington had responded exactly as he'd dreaded: "Go forward. If Harris is willing, stop at nothing."

So began full-scale testing of Mark's blood and vital organs, his DNA, the usual approaches. It was Lester who finally figured it out. He had spent every free hour talking through the intercom with Mark. When he wasn't in his own lab experimenting, he was at the glass wall, intercom in hand. While everyone was waiting for Mark to die, he and Lester talked a lot, reminiscing and learning about each other. It was Lester who found the clue to Mark's immuno-response. Mark had forgotten the time when he was six and unable to go to school because he was sick with the flu bug a lot of people got back home in Luckless, Arkansas, where only a few people had toilets and even fewer had phones. Something evil had passed, the townspeople had said, a plague or the devil. Luckless folks, Lester had learned, were dirt farmers without any education. Most had a few pigs, a couple of cows, and a flock of chickens for laying and eating. But that year, the year that Mark now vaguely remembered, people got spooked. Their chickens got sick for no good reason, and many farmers lost all of them. Worse, it was a bad year for flu. Mark remembered that he'd lost his grandparents that winter, and a couple of school friends. He slept in the same bed with several brothers and sisters, and soon the whole family was ill. "It was so bad," he remembered, "that Mom was too sick to cook. We all just kind of dragged ourselves out to the kitchen and ate what we could find. And my father, he slept in the barn because he was too weak to walk back and forth from the house."

And there it was. Lester shook his head, sick with the

sudden realization that the avian flu had recombined with human flu long ago, when Mark was a boy. Whatever the strain was, most had survived it. Luckless wasn't even a dot on the map, so no one had ever heard of or cared about the outbreak there. Because of its isolation in the mountains, the virus had not spread beyond the little town. The flu had its go-round and then disappeared, leaving Luckless less populated but fortunate to have survived. Mark's antibodies were the proof that he was immune to the avian flu because he had contracted the illness in a less lethal form years ago and had survived it. He carried a human antibody to an avian disease. Even with new recombinations, Mark had the antibody necessary to fight back, because he was immune to any avian strain. It followed that other survivors of the Luckless flu were probably still alive. All the CDC had to do was find them and use them, Harris included, to produce a vaccine that would protect people from avian illness. It was daunting. But it was doable.

58

Patterson, August

"Sheeeeeeee....it," Pitbull hissed, stretched out on the ground in the darkness. Beside him, Butch crawled forward for a better look. "What the hell are they doing down there?" Bull wondered aloud.

"Looks like a party," Butch said, gazing down at the campfire blazing orange in the darkness, at the candlelit paper bags on every table, but mostly at the couples dancing to the sound of a fiddle coming from somewhere at the edge of light. Butch's mouth hung open. It looked pretty, really pretty, all those lights in the darkness, all those people dancing. He watched as the music slowed, then paused. People began rearranging themselves, grabbing others and forming two straight lines. It looked like men on one side, women on the other, except for the kids arranged every whichway. And then the music began again and they were all dancing together, couples skipping their way between the two lines and back, then around again, ending their part at the other end. As soon as they finished, the pattern began all over again with the next couple. Laughter carried on the night air, drifted above the music and up to the men hiding on the hill.

"Well, ain't it just our luck to pick tonight," Bull growled. "Goddamned people should be sleeping by now."

Behind them, they heard the bushes crackling and the grunts of Dobie Maxwell and Nose Bartlett as they struggled forward with their gas can. "Put it down, boys," Bull ordered. "Can't use it tonight."

The men did as they were told, glad to be freed from the burden they had been struggling with since they left the pickup parked at the side of the road. They had cut through the woods from Lovell Lane, a path Nose and Dobie had determined was the shortest route into the Grant farm, the easiest of all the alliance farms to reach on foot. Nose and Dobie had spent days reconnoitering the area, trying to find a quick in and out route, one no one would expect and one not guarded by barking dogs. They'd spent days a few weeks ago trying to figure out how the alliance was getting around the barricade they'd made at the end of their road. They knew there had to be some way that Butch and Dobie had missed and they'd had plenty of pressure to get the job done. Pitbull had already lost his temper and nearly smashed Butch's head permanently flat against the warehouse door. He'd assigned Nose to the job, swigging on his Jack Daniels and snorting that maybe Nose could nose it out better with that nose of his. "Hah, hah," Nose had thought, "fat asshole thinks he's funny."

"Maybe you can do a better job on that than you did minding my store," Bull had added, his eyes a warning that this might be Nose's last chance to prove he had some value.

Butch had stood behind him, wiping the blood spurting from his head on the shirt he had removed for that purpose, his face purple with anger. He kept looking at the blood each time he wiped, as if he couldn't believe what he was seeing. Nose wondered why, for Butch had more scars from Pitbull's rage than he could count. That blood couldn't have been anything new. The kid didn't look up. He just kept wiping the blood away as if he didn't know what it was. "Working on one cylinder," Nose thought. "Stupider than a stone."

So Nose and Dobie had taken up the task of getting them in undiscovered. Nose wondered how Butch and Dobie could have missed the bent bushes he spotted hiding the narrow track into the undergrowth. The bushes had been intertwined with gray rope so that they could be pulled aside when cars went in and out, then released to hide any tire marks. Pine needles and rocks hid the tracks as they wound deeper into the woods, then straightened when they hit the pasture road leading directly into the Green farm. They had left the pickup back on the road, deciding not to risk someone hearing a car engine. But when they got close, they saw they had another problem. The alliance guys had set up all kinds of booby traps to alert them to trespassers. Trip-wires attached to saplings laden with bells. Nose had almost tripped over one himself, and when he stopped dead short, grabbing stupid Dobie before he stumbled into it, he'd looked around and spotted six or seven of the easy ones just waiting for them. Nose had pointed to them, nodding to Dobie, whose lizard eyes had followed his finger without moving his head. They stood there in the silent woods for several minutes, assessing the situation. Nose knew that if he could spot six, there were certainly many more he couldn't see. In fact, he wondered whether they had blindly set any of them off already, further back, and whether the alliance men were already heading out to confront them. So they'd backed up carefully, trying not to panic when they heard a dog barking, the sound growing closer with every step they took. By the time they reached the pickup, both of them were frantic to get in and throw the truck in reverse, which they did. Dobie had swerved his way out of there in reverse going fifty miles an hour, and a couple of times Nose was sure the idiot was going to slam into a tree before they made it to the road. But they did make it, and later, they reported to Pitbull that while they'd been successful finding the road, sneaking in from the main road was the safest way to get in without giving notice, even though it was longer and more arduous. There were just too many booby traps.

After setting down the gas can, Nose and Dobie found their way over to the place Bull and his son lay. They all scanned the partyers for particular people. Nose was looking for Terry and was shocked when, finally spying her in a gaggle of women setting out the food, he realized that she was pregnant. She looked happy and let her head fall back with laughter. Nose felt the bile churn in his stomach.

Butch checked each of the kids, looking for two in particular that he meant to pulverize as soon as he had the chance. He had to look hard, though, for Michael had grown two inches since last year, and Chris was at the bandstand, amazed that the fiddler could get so many sounds out of his small instrument.

Pitbull checked out the men, especially the tall guy, Rob Grant, who he remembered seeing around town hall a few times when he was fighting to enlarge his junkyard. Grant was one of those damn goody-goodies always worrying about zoning regulations and whether the junkyard would be a bother to his neighbors. Pitbull snickered. "What neighbors?" he smiled, for they were long gone, just like almost everybody else. He did a head count of the adult males there, getting to six before he lost track. He'd thought that the alliance farmers were just a couple of guys. Three, they'd figured, since they knew Jameson was dead. They'd taken the Jameson livestock and equipment on one of their first forays back when the flu had just started. So if there were others there, the alliance must have expanded, something Bull was not happy to see. He could control individual farmer families that came in begging for seeds or grain or equipment or fuel, control them easily. All he had to do was lean over the counter and glare at them, flex his muscle a little, get up close and personal, and they backed down. Those pussies didn't want trouble. They'd back away from a fight as long as they could. Bull already half-owned everything they were going to grow this summer. He was already putting up stores in the barns he'd acquired, barns on vacant farms stretching nearly to Leominster. Bull didn't need money to be rich or powerful. Pretty soon he'd own everything, including the manure-boots those boys walked in. Why, pretty soon, he'd even own them.

So alliances could be dangerous. They had to be broken up before they expanded. Bull had about fifteen guys, not including wimpy Nose Bartlett, guys who could pick those farmers up by their overalls and hang 'em on a hay hook. Most of them were pretty good shots as well, at least good when they weren't drinking. In the beginning, before he figured out a better way to survive, he'd been hunting with a few of them. They'd had some pretty good old times out there in the woods, shooting at everything that moved. They'd killed probably thirty dogs in an afternoon back then before the snows came and Bull decided he'd rather sit by the woodstove and swill his Jack Daniels than wander around in the snow freezing his ass off.

The best way to break up an alliance is by example. Bull knew that instinctively, and he also knew that the best example is the most powerful one, the one that's daring to show some backbone. Bull could have chosen to go after the little guy, the old one Nose told him started the revolt at the counter. He already had a score to settle with him and his friend the cowboy, and not just for his son's sake. Who cared about him? But for his name's sake. He wanted the sound of his name, Pitbull Jones, to set people to trembling whenever they heard it. The woman, the good shot, he'd take her out too, after he'd shown her the best time of her life. But first, he wanted at the alliance. That's what they'd called it when they signed the list of things they took. Alliance Farms they'd called it. He didn't know whether the word of their little uprising had spread or not. He figured it had. There were too many people down there to be just alliance farmers. And if the word spread, others would begin thinking that they might be able to stand up to him. If that happened, Bull knew he'd have trouble. His fifteen guys would stop at nothing, but fifteen was no match for what Bull figured was several hundred farmers and their families stretched out across his territory. The best thing he had going was that most of them had no idea the others existed. They'd isolated themselves so well, they'd lost touch with the rest of the world.

Still, if this group dancing down there was any example, they were beginning to associate now that they knew the flu had died out. They were feeling safer, so it was time for old Bull to show them they had something else to worry about, and it wasn't a germ. His eyes narrowed as he watched Rob Grant stroll around like a cock in the hen house. Grant was the one to get. What happened to him would become a lesson for everyone else. Old Bull was going to show them who was boss.

Dobie Maxwell lay on the ground watching the tall girl dressed in pink. He'd seen her before, when he came with Butch, when they first found a good way in. Ever since then, he could think of nothing else. He kept waking up nights in a hot sweat thinking about her. He found himself dreaming of her all the time, his arms wrapped around his pillow. Dobie had already decided that when they came with the trucks, the first thing he was going to do was take that chick out behind the barn and show her what's what. Dobie hunkered down on the grass, feeling the cool of it, pretending she was beneath him. He watched her and that kid, the tall one who had summoned her the other time. They were walking around together, their arms joined.

"How many they got," Pitbull hissed, nudging Nose.

"Got to be twenty or more," Nose guessed.

"Shit," Bull said, striking Nose hard in the side. "I can guess that. How many exactly? Count them."

Nose groaned from the pain splitting his ribs, but began counting. Bull was right that there were too many down there to be just the Alliance Farm guys and the other group with the old guy. Terry had arranged for a party, driving out to Lily Fenn's place, and asking them to come. She'd grown quite friendly with them once she began attending their practice sessions, curling up in the pew and listening dreamily to the music she so loved. So Lily had offered her musicians as their contribution, and their music for dancing as well. The whole idea had caught fire among the alliance people, the kids making special decorations out of anything they could find, including some of their old toys, the women sorting out linens and dishes and cooking all kinds of food. The men's contribution was to butcher a pig and built a pit for roasting, and up on the hill where Bull and his boys lay, the sweet smell of pork rose in the air.

Arnold Card sat at a rickety folding table, surrounded by people who had stopped to listen to his latest news. Arnold had become the eyes and ears for all of them, his nightly conversations with other ham radio operators the source of national and international news. Arnold was in the midst of explaining how a state militia was in the offing, how the interim governor down in Boston was calling for volunteers to register for a training program to begin soon. The militia would be set up in state police barracks all over Massachusetts to aid in maintaining law and order wherever they were needed. Arnold was thinking he might even volunteer, he said, leaning back in his chair. He did not expect the back legs of his folding chair to sink into the lawn, and when they did, his chair would have catapulted him backward had David not been standing near enough to catch him.

"Easy there, Mr. Card," David had said, smiling.

"You're too old for militias," Ethel said, putting her hand on Arnold's, relieved that he hadn't fallen.

"I'm as spry as ever," Arnold insisted. "Why not help out if I'm needed?" Arnold's eyes were bright as he looked around the table.

"How are they paying people?" Ralph Green asked, knowing money wasn't much of a bartering tool these days.

"Necessities," Arnold replied. "Gasoline, oil, stuff the government has in reserve."

"We've got that now," Taylor said. "With your new contraption, we'll be able to pump all we need from the tanks at gas stations."

"That's not going to last forever," Arnold said. "As soon as others figure out how to do it, they'll all be drawing from the same well."

The men at the table nodded, estimating in their heads how much gas and diesel they'd already used just working the fields.

"The government will think of something," Ethel said, her eyes bright.

"The government's as lame as we are," Ralph said .

"The government is lame period," Arnold said. "They're all meeting down in Washington trying to figure out how to justify their jobs when there's hardly anyone left to govern. Any bills they pass will be to protect themselves."

"Oh, Arnold," Ethel chided. "You're so negative."

"If negative's true, then that's a blessing," Arnold pronounced, looking around the table for support.

"What else have you heard?" David asked.

"Any news of a vaccine yet?" Ralph added.

"Last I heard they're still working on it." Arnold was in his element now, for whenever he had time, he spent it learning what he could about viruses. The cellar was filled with books he'd borrowed from the library, signing a card for every one even though the librarian was long dead. He studied deep into the night, and every chance he got, he was down there talking with other "hammies," soaking up whatever they knew as well. "The best way to protect ourselves is exactly what we're doing, giving each other elbow room, avoiding anyone who's sick."

"Flu season is not far off," Ethel said, her voice tremulous as she realized that with winter's approach, the same thing could happen all over again. As she looked around the table, she could see that others had been thinking the same thing. They nodded, their faces glum.

"What are the chances, Arnold?" Ralph Green asked.

"The Spanish flu came back a couple of years later. Worse the second time around." Arnold knew that news would not be welcome.

"Worse!" Ralph exclaimed. "How could it be worse?"

"I think this time things are different. That flu did only moderate damage the first time. This one…" Arnold's voice dropped off. "This one…" He was thinking of all the guys at Garrett's, friends he'd had his whole working life. He was thinking about his kids, his grandchildren, wondering whether they had survived or if they too had succumbed.

"Enough of this sad talk," Ethel said, rising and brushing the crumbs from her lap. "I want to hear more fiddling."

The people still seated glanced at each other, realizing that Ethel was right. There wasn't much they could do beyond what they'd already done. Somehow they'd survived the unspeakable. Somehow they'd been spared. What point was there in living fearful, when the path of a killer virus was incomprehensible and inescapable. They'd just do their best. They'd just take their precautions. They had gotten through one year. It was up to God whether they would live through another.

Ralph Green turned in his seat, looking for Carol. "Well, if it's time for dancing, I'd best go find my wife." Ralph rose. Rob Grant and Paul Curley followed. David and Ellen moved on to another table. Arnold, sitting alone now, leaned forward over the table, folding his hands while he looked up at the starry sky.

Above them, Pitbull slapped at mosquitoes, swearing. "Let's get the hell out of here, boys," he said. "These Goddamned bugs are going to eat me alive before those idiots finally go to bed."

The underbrush rustled beneath them as all four crawled backward from the knoll, then stood. "What do you want to do with the gas?" Nose asked, realizing that he might have to drag the big can all the way back to the truck.

Dobie grimaced. "That thing's heavy as hell, Bull."

Bull looked at both of them disgustedly, then peered about the darkness while he thought. "We'll take it back a little way, hide it in some pines, then cover it with branches. Maybe this is a good thing. Next time we come, we'll bring another can. Maybe two or three. The more I think about it, the more I see the value in burning them out. Not just the fields or the barn. The whole damn place. A really big fire. One the rest of these asshole farmers can see for miles around."

"Yeah," Butch enthused, looking back. "The whole sky lit up." He smiled at Dobie.

"Yeah," Nose said, glad he didn't have to carry any more heavy loads.

"Yeah," Dobie said, thinking a big fire would allow him plenty of time with the girl. They'd all come, surprising everyone, and in the fracas, he'd find the time, no, he'd *make* the time to drag her off for their own little party. Dobie scratched himself and smiled. "Yeah, he said. "Great idea, Bull."

59

Atlanta, Early September

General Caine stood at least a foot taller than Parker as the two strolled toward the conference room. His helicopter had arrived only minutes before, heard before seen in the brilliant September sun. Almost everyone had turned out for his arrival, holding their ears against the copter's roar and squinting to protect their eyes from the sun and the dirt kicked up by its swirling blades.

It had been an exciting time at the CDC. First there had been Harris's survival and the follow-up testing. Then Washington had sent the military to Arkansas and rounded up half the town of Luckless for guinea pigs, all of them volunteers unscathed by the pandemic. Then had come the pharmaceutical people who took the information and cultures they were given back to their facilities. Aided by National Guard volunteers, doses of vaccine were already being produced. It would take a while, of course, because full-scale operations were impossible. Even with the National Guard deployed to the factories, production was understaffed and undersupervised. Too many people had died to make it possible to run operations at anywhere near normal pace. But at this point, with the promise of a defense against the virus that could enable life to once again return to normal, optimism was uncontainable. Everyone at the CDC knew why the General had arrived and not one of them could wait to hear what he had to say.

Parker, of course, called the meeting to order. While

in the halls the hubbub made normal conversation impossible, once they all had taken their seats in the large conference room, conversation ceased in deference to Parker. Nothing had changed on that front. Every one of them knew that it was Lester Savant's persistence and courage to stand against Parker that had led to a vaccine capable of stopping the pandemic should it resurface. They all knew that a pandemic could disappear and then reappear with a vengeance. The Spanish flu had done that. But this time, they believed that the Luckless strain, now called H_5N_1b because it provided avian immunity, an immunity much like that of the wild ducks and geese who carried it without becoming ill themselves, would protect them against the characteristic mutations so elusive in their earlier unsuccessful vaccines. People might now get the flu, but their immune systems would be capable of fighting the avian aspects of the virus. People might still die of the flu, but only as they would have died with any of the other viruses that continually wreak havoc every flu season: the at-risk population of senior citizens and infants and those with already compromised immune systems from other diseases such as cancer or AIDS. Statistically a low mortality rate, no matter how awful the aches and pains, chills and fevers that accompany any flu. While viruses coming out of the jungles and off the prairies and new viruses originating from yet to be discovered sources still loomed deadly and indomitable, at least this one, so much more deadly because of its ability to leap from host to host in the coughs and sneezes of its infected victims, at least this one had been defeated.

"And now I give you General Caine," Parker said. He nodded his head and then sat down in a chair to the right of the General.

"Okay, folks. The first thing I want to do is congratulate you." The General let his eyes scan first one side of the long conference table and then the other. "Because of you, it's the U.S. that has stopped this disease in its tracks. Because of you, vaccines are now being flown to every country in the world for their facilities to replicate. In our own country, we've begun preparations to drop the stuff wherever we know people are still alive. Our guesstimates indicate that within the next two to three months, we will be able to insure that every U.S. citizen is inoculated. We've done it, folks," the General said, smiling widely, "we've stopped this bastard and some day soon, maybe not this year or next, but soon, life as we knew it is going to resume. And it's because of you," the General reiterated, turning to Parker as he did so.

"You know, I'm used to fighting wars. I've seen combat on three continents. I've been shot at, bombed, even gassed once, and I can't count on all my fingers and toes how many times I've come this close to dying," he said, holding up two fingers nearly pressed together. "But never have I faced a more terrifying enemy than this one. I've seen war-ravaged countries, but never a country so ravaged as my own country has been this year. We don't even know the half of it. We have no idea whether the U.S. has lost millions or billions. We haven't a clue because we can't even tally the dead. We haven't the people to do it. Or the stomach. How many dead are out there, we haven't a clue. I've witnessed the deaths of family members and friends and not been able to do a thing about it."

The General paused, gaining control of his emotions by pressing the back of his chair with his huge hands. Then he went on. "My own wife and two of my grandchildren were lost this past year, and all of my Army training, all of my arms and technology were powerless to help. You've been cloistered here. You haven't seen. Many of you have no idea whether or not your families are still alive. After today, I suppose you will. You'll be able to leave and go look for them. I've seen it out there. The government exists, but it can barely function for lack of skilled people or supplies. Transportation is a joke. The roads aren't too bad, but there are places it isn't safe to drive because the people have become lawless and desperate. It's going to be a long time before we can establish law and order. When the structure breaks down, there are those who..." He looked up, shaking his head sadly. "There are those who take advantage. It's going to be a while before we can set things right. We've got the military, of course, what's left of it, and the Guard. We need everyone we've got just to begin the rebuilding process. So the good people out there are on their own. They'll have to protect themselves. I suspect we'll see more death before it's over."

Those assembled at the table could see the General trying to regain his composure. He looked embattled and tired, despite the good news he brought. Watching him and imagining all that he'd seen, they understood. Each of them considered the horrors they might yet face, now that they could leave to find their families, or what might be left of their families.

The General took a deep breath. "The President sent me down here to thank you. I've got some medals he wants awarded. To you, Mark Harris," he said, heading behind the people seated at the table to the place where Harris sat. He put his hand on the young man's shoulder. "For courage. And you, Lester Savant," and he put his hand on the shoulder of the older man next to Harris. "For the brilliance of your theories, for your perseverance and for your courage." He patted Lester's shoulder while the room broke into wild applause, for everyone knew that it was Lester more than any of them who had found the vaccine. Lester and Mark.

Parker rose, both hands examining the edge of the conference table as if searching for something stuck there, while those assembled clapped. He bit his lower lip and nodded solemnly. Then he looked up. Everyone waited to see what he would do next, whether he'd be annoyed after having fought Lester tooth and nail over using human guinea pigs. "Don't forget obstinacy," he said, slowly breaking into a thin smile and raising his own hands to clap. The rest of the scientists rose, laughing for the first time in months. "Hear, hear," many sang out. "Hear, hear, the General said, clapping. Lester, leaning back in his chair, raised a hand to quiet them, but they would have none of it until finally things began to quiet and one by one, they sat down.

"How long before the vaccine is distributed?" someone asked.

"We've had the grid for some time. Enough time to plan. Where we have contact, and I might add that there are ham radio operators all over the country, we'll locate doctors and nurses and set up drop points. Some places we can reach by truck, and when we can, that will be the preferred method. Where we have no contact, we've done heat imaging to find those living in clusters. The drops will include instructions that any layperson can follow. We'll get the stuff out. That's our job now."

"You said we'd be able to go home..." a middle-aged man said, tentatively raising his hand.

"It's true," the General said. "You're free to go. You'll have to work out the logistics, because gas is at a premium and you can't get very far on a single tank. But yes, you're free to head out…this morning if you'd like…and face what you've got to face out there. I warn you, it's not going to be easy. I suspect many of you are going to find what I found when I finally got home…" The general paused. "My best wishes go with you."

When the General sat down, Parker rose once more. "There's nothing more to say, my friends. You've got as much time as you need to do what you need to do. We'll be waiting here for your return. Good luck and God bless."

Within minutes, the room cleared. Parker accompanied the General to his helicopter, standing alone on the tarmac to wave good-bye. His jacket caught the wind, billowing behind him as the copter rose. But no one was there to notice. They were all getting ready to go home.

60

Patterson, Late September

By late September, cold nights have already turned a few of the trees orange and gold, a teaser for the heraldry only a few weeks away. Nighttime temperatures can drop temptingly close to freezing, especially when the moon is full in a cloudless sky. Morning mists drift above shallow ponds and lakes, their waters re-warmed each day by the sun. September mornings are full of promise, energizing, beckoning one to come work or play outside. Often the days heat up to feel like midsummer. Some call it Indian summer.

On the Grant farm, fieldwork had slowed somewhat, allowing the children to resume their studies at the Greens' schoolhouse. This morning, however, Terry Grant did not go with Michael and Chris, because she was in the last days of her pregnancy and needed rest. She'd been canning and laying up preserves for months, standing long hours on her feet. The work had taken its toll, and now as she looked down over a huge belly at her swollen ankles, she felt sweaty and over-ripe, a melon about to burst.

Terry stood by the sink, looking out at the lawn. Rob and Charlie were working the cornfield. She could hear the low mumble of the tractor and an occasional shout, and could see the dust drifting in the sultry air. Griz was out there with them, having grown tired of his new role as father of nine puppies that insisted on jumping all over him whenever he appeared at the Green farm. She wondered how he was going to take to the arrival of two of his puppies in another week, or how she would either, for the last thing she needed now, with the baby due any minute, was to housetrain the things. On cue, the child inside thrashed her with an arm or foot, as if to say "Let me out!"

Terry rubbed her distended stomach, smiling. A perfect day, she thought. Warm, sunny, sweet. A beautiful day for a swim. Terry had enjoyed the luxury of their pond all summer, using it to bathe and wash her hair, bringing the boys down nearly every night to do the same. Keeping clean in the summer was so much easier than in the winter, when water had to be heated on the woodstove and mixed with cold water in the tub, never more than a few inches to sit in, not that one wanted to sit very long in their drafty bathroom. She shivered to think of what they'd been through the past winter, the way the cold found its way everywhere, no matter how much wood they piled in the stove. Cold had a way of seeping in through every crack, of turning the outside walls and windows to ice that vied with the warm air inside for dominance. And now, with fall here, icy days were not far behind. That was the sorrow of September. For all its beauty and promise, it was the last really warm month before winter.

Terry wiped her forehead and began washing the dishes in the sink, letting the cold spring water rinse them clean before she placed them in the drainer. A hummingbird hovered at the window box outside, sipping nectar from the impatiens she had planted there. She watched the tiny thing with wonder, awed by how so minute a creature could survive all of the obstacles and dangers of its environment. Hummingbirds, like little dogs, could be fierce, standing up to potential attackers with deceptive courage. They were mere morsels to their predators. "Like us," Terry thought.

"Mere morsels in the universe." With all the billions of people who had died this past year, not one other thing had changed. The hummingbirds still sipped their nectar. The trees still blossomed, turned green, and now gold. The seasons changed, so that once again they were back at the beginning. Fall. Just like last year.

Only last year Doc was alive and she worked as a nurse and the boys went to a real school and...and...Terry felt sorrow welling up in her, but instead of letting it take hold, she took a deep breath and hardened herself. "And what?" she thought. She knew she had almost lapsed into the familiar "Life was so much better then" thinking, and she didn't want to go there. Life was good now, too, she had to remind herself. Maybe harder. Maybe more dangerous. Maybe more tentative. But still good. The baby she was about to bear might face a tougher world, but tougher by whose standards? At least it was a world with room in it. The simpler life made many of the old dangers obsolete— the things parents had worried about before, the violence of movies and TV, the sex and pornography, the drugs, the gangs, internet predators, all of that was gone. Her children could grow up uncontaminated by the filth generated by greed in the old society. They could make a better life for their children, Terry hoped, now that they'd begun to learn how.

Terry looked up at the sun, figuring that everyone would be coming in soon, anxious for lunch. She had perhaps an hour before Rob and Charlie would arrive, hot from the fields, and Michael and Chris, electric with the joy of release from their studies. Everything was ready for them. All she had to do was let the bread cool and slice it. There were several things she could get done in that short time, but Terry had no heart for work. What she really wanted to do while everyone else was engaged was bathe in the pond, really lather up and relax in the sunshine. How many more days would she have for this before the water grew uncomfortably cold and the air too brisk? She decided to go, bending uncomfortably over the kitchen table to leave a note for Rob. She'd be back at lunch, she said.

She grabbed a towel, soap, and shampoo and hurried off across the lawn, past the barn, and down a gradual slope that led into the woods between their farm and the Jamesons' land. Picking her way carefully along the path she and her family had worn during the summer, Terry sang softly to herself.

When Rob came back early, annoyed that the tractor was not idling properly, he stopped at the kitchen door with his tool box before heading back out to the barn. He'd left Charlie bundling stalks for forage out in the west fields, figuring he could do a little engine maintenance before the kids came home from school. Surprised when Terry didn't answer his calls, he opened the screen door and went in.

When he read Terry's note, Rob swore under his breath. Wasn't it just like Terry to wander off by herself despite the wild dogs. Darn foolish, Rob thought. What he loved so much about his wife was sometimes the thing that made him most angry—the fact that she had too much courage. It had gotten her into trouble enough times that she should have learned by now, but she hadn't. She was always trying to do things a woman shouldn't or taking chances without being cautious about possible dangers. Rob set down his toolbox and wrote on the note that he was going to the pond to make sure Terry was okay. Charlie and the kids could take care of themselves.

With Griz beside him, his shotgun in hand, Rob hurried across the yard, following Terry's path down the long slope and into the woods. The trees were alive with birds, especially jays that protested his coming with raucous caws. Chipmunks scurried in the underbrush, their sharp chirrups warning others. The woods were beautiful this time of year, especially when the sun hit the upper leaves of the trees, creating a translucent gold and orange canopy against the blue sky. On the ground leaves were gathering in bright clusters of green and gold, not enough of them yet to create piles but certainly enough to pepper the ground with color. Rob forced himself not to slow down, despite his desire just to sit and look about.

Before he reached the pond, he heard Terry singing "Amazing Grace". The woods near the pond were silent, as if listening. Rob stopped, loving the sound of Terry's voice. In church, he proudly stood beside her, holding one side of the hymnal while she held the other. He loved the lightness of her singing, the lilt, the tremolo when she held a note. Rob stepped forward a few trees until his view of the pond opened up, then stood quietly in the shadows.

The pond shown like diamonds in the September sun, every ripple catching light in myriad sparkles that seemed to dance upon the surface. Near the shore closest to him, Terry stood hip deep in the water, her body a shadow against the blinding light. She was washing her hair, her arms raised high as she massaged the lather, singing up to the sky. Rob could make out the shape of her breasts, already heavy in preparation for the child to come, and below them, the great mound of her belly before it disappeared beneath the surface. He was so dazzled by the brilliance of the water and by the beauty of his pregnant wife that for a moment he could barely breathe. Then Terry squatted beneath the surface, submerging her hair in the water to rinse it. A moment later, she stood again, shaking her head so that droplets of water sprayed out in sparkling white crystals about her. He took a deep breath, sighed, and leaned against the tree, not wishing to disturb his wife, not wanting this moment to end.

For Rob, the past year had made him question his faith and all the other things that he had once believed about nature and mankind. But what had never been in doubt was his love for Terry and his boys. They had shouldered their new hardships with such acceptance that sometimes Rob almost burst with pride. Terry's foresightedness, her perseverance, her purposeful plans and preparations, but most of all her determination to remain positive had given Rob the strength he needed to make it through. He had spent many nights pacing the floor, watching worriedly from the windows, or tossing restlessly beneath the quilts, but when he felt the greatest despair, all he had to do was think about Terry, Michael, and Chris, and the thought of them always gave him hope. Even with a new baby coming, he was no longer afraid. He had learned over the past months that family and friends were everything one needed to survive, that their love and support made it all possible.

Terry stopped singing. He glanced about, wondering what had distracted her, but could see nothing around the pond's shores that might have been the cause. Still, he took his shotgun off his shoulder, his finger on the trigger, and stood straight again.

In the water, Terry let out a small "Ohhhh," her hands on her belly. She stood still for a moment as she felt a warm gush of water between her legs flowing into the cool water of the pond. "Ohhhh," Terry said again, realizing what had just happened. She turned immediately and struggled back to shore, the water sloshing around her legs. When she emerged, she bent immediately to throw on the long shirt she had brought with her. As she did so, Rob stepped forward into the light, so that once the shirt was over her head, it was as if he had appeared by magic.

"Rob!" Terry said, overjoyed that he was there. "Get me home! My water just broke!"

61

Patterson, Late September

Ellen and David sat silently on the ground just outside the Grants' back door, listening to the sounds upstairs. Charlie had summoned everyone at the schoolhouse with the announcement that the baby was coming and that the women were needed. The entire contingent came running behind the car Charlie drove to pick up Carol, Lisa, and Shirley, stopping only when they reached the house. Now the children were out back, running about the lawn in a loose game of soccer while Rob and Charlie paced the kitchen and upstairs Carol, Lisa and Shirley encouraged Terry to breathe. Ellen winced every time she heard the moans. "My God," she whispered to David, who hugged her close.

"Let's go for a walk," David suggested, hoping to allay Ellen's fears by distracting her. "Look how the leaves are turning. A walk will do you good."

The young couple no sooner reached the end of the Grants' lawn than the boys running about with the soccer ball stopped their game. Michael was dying to see how their tree house had fared all these months. The boys still were not allowed to go alone and both Rob and Charlie had been too busy to accompany them. "Can we come?" Michael called to David, who slowed and turned.

David looked down at Ellen, who nodded her head. "Sure," he called back, turning to walk again. Within seconds, a noisy horde of young people surrounded them, racing up the hill, knocking each other down and wrestling in the grass, calling to one another. David put his arm around Ellen's shoulder. "So much for a peaceful walk."

"They're fun," Ellen said, watching her own two brothers in the midst of the melee. "Look at Eddie," she said, nodding in his direction. Eddie lay on the ground, challenging the rest of them to a roll-race down the hill. His face was so full of joy that Ellen couldn't help but smile herself. "They're so happy."

"So are we," David said, hugging her again.

"So are we," Ellen repeated.

The group slowly made its way up the long hill, intermittently breaking into noisy piles of boys and girls that went this way and that in spontaneous games and challenges that ended as quickly as they began. Only Ellen and David held to their course, and soon they disappeared into the trees, with the others on their trail. Once into the woods, however, Michael asked if they could go see the tree house.

"What tree house?" Bobbie asked, excited at the thought.

"Come on," Chris said, waving them forward. "I'll show you."

"Don't get too far ahead," David cautioned. "You have to stay within our sight." He looked down at Ellen and smiled.

Chris and Michael could barely make themselves walk, so anxious were they to climb that familiar ladder up the tree and into their old clubhouse. "Wait till you see it," Michael confided to Bobbie. "It's sooooo cool."

A moment later, Naomi cried out, "Ewwwwww! Look! What's that?" She stood pointing to something just off the path.

Michael knew immediately what she must have seen and ran back, afraid the Doberman might still be staring at the sky, its teeth bared. Instead, its skeleton was barely visible in the undergrowth, its graying leg bones scattered about. Its rib cage, however, lay almost exactly where they had left the dead dog that snowy day. Michael gave Chris a sharp look, warning him to be quiet. Chris looked worriedly up at David as he and Ellen drew closer.

"Looks like a dog," David said. "A pretty big one."

"What happened to it?" Naomi asked.

"Could have starved," Michael lied.

"Yeah," Chris said. "My dad said a lot of the dogs people owned weren't good enough hunters to make it through the winter." He looked at Michael, smug with the quality of his deception.

"The big dogs killed most of the little dogs," Johnnie Green said.

"This was a big dog, though," Ellen said.

"A bigger one must've got it," Johnnie replied.

"Or something else. Maybe a hunter? Coyotes? Even a bear?"

Naomi had been silent all this time, fascinated at the sight of the skeleton. She picked up a stick to prod the bones, turning one in the weeds. "Let's look for more!" she said. "See who can find another one!" She bent down for one closer look and then stood, her eyes wide with enthusiasm.

Bobbie started walking purposefully along the path, scanning the bushes and undergrowth to his left, poking at ferns with a broken branch. The rest followed, spreading out on both sides of the path while Ellen and David continued along it. The undergrowth was alive with the rustle of their footsteps as the young people scurried about like overgrown chipmunks, peering around and beneath anything that might hide another skeleton. Everyone was suddenly intent, their tomfoolery forgotten.

"Hey, what's this?" Bobbie called, barely visible in a copse of scrawny pines.

"What's what?" Michael called from the other side of the path, ready to run if he'd really found something.

"Does your Dad store gas up here?" Bobbie asked. "There's like five or six big cans of it."

Michael knew something didn't add up. Why would his father store gas up here? His father almost never came up here anymore, and he kept whatever gas he'd siphoned from abandoned cars in the farm tank down by the driveway. The others began walking over to look. "Can't be gas," he said, following.

David guided Ellen toward the group now pushing their way into the pines. By the time he got there, Bobbie was already unscrewing the top of one can. He bent to peer inside and, seeing the liquid within glisten as it caught the light, said, "This one's full." He sniffed. "It's gas all right."

Eddie had already opened the cap on another. "This one too."

Johnnie opened the third and sniffed, jostling the can back and forth. "Same here."

David's puzzled frown worried Michael, who muttered, "My dad didn't put these here." A nervous awareness spread among them. Immediately they all began looking around, as if expecting something to jump out at them. But the woods were golden and silent.

"How long have they been here, do you think," David asked.

"Move one of them," Ellen suggested. "See if the ground is bare."

David rolled one on its bottom just far enough to expose the ground below. "It's not. These were only put here recently."

"Why?" Naomi asked.

"See these weeds? They're the same as what you're standing on. They wouldn't be if the cans had been here a long time."

"They wouldn't have been able to grow," Ellen explained, putting her hand on Naomi's head.

David looked about, trying to figure things out. Finally he shook his head. "Let's put everything back the same," he said, rolling the can back to its original position. "I think we ought to go tell your dad."

The tree house forgotten, the group abandoned the pines, checking first to make sure they left no telltale signs of their presence. David and Ellen followed the stampede along the path back home, walking slowly despite their own interest in the find. By the time they emerged from the woods, the children were already nearing the barn below, their shouts carried on the wind. They could see Charlie and Rob Grant emerge from the back door, quickly surrounded by young people all talking at once, many pointing back up toward them. Charlie had his hands on his hips as he looked up at David and Ellen approaching.

By the time the young couple reached the Grants' back door, the children had already run out of things to say and begun repeating themselves. Rob and Charlie looked up. "Go get your father, will you, David?" Rob asked. "Take the car."

"Paul Curley too," Charlie added. "He might be able to track something."

David squeezed Ellen's hand and took the keys from Rob. As he jumped into the car, the group was already dispersing, the children to renew their soccer game, Charlie hurrying back to his room over the garage, and Rob and Ellen into the house. David felt a rising sense of panic as he put the car in reverse, turned it, and headed down the Grants' long driveway out onto the road. Someone had been there, up in the hills overlooking all of their farms. Someone had stockpiled gas up there, and it hadn't taken David but a minute to infer the reason. Someone had plans to set a fire. A big fire.

By the time David had explained things to his father and gotten him and Paul Curley back to the Grants' farm, Rob and Charlie were pacing the yard, their shotguns on their shoulders. They all headed back up the long hill and into the woods, David pointing the way. For the first time, David heard about the confrontation with Nose Bartlett down at the Agway. "But Nose Bartlett isn't the type of guy to do this," David said. "I know him from football. He covered our games. He's just a wimpy guy." David could not imagine Nose Bartlett posing a threat to anyone.

"Nose works for Bull Jones," Ralph Green explained to his son.

"Who's that?" David asked.

"A bad ass," Charlie replied. "Bet you know his son, though. Butch."

Oh yes, David thought. Oh yes, everyone in town knows Butch Jones. "That kid's been driving one of his father's junks since he was ten, always challenging somebody to a drag race." David didn't disclose the fact that he had raced Butch several times and that the last time, that idiot Jones had almost gotten him killed. He'd kept him trapped in the left lane, slowing and speeding up every time David tried to get back over into his own lane. When they hit the long curve before Downer's Crossing, a car coming at them had to veer off the road to let them pass. It had been the closest call of David's life, and the experience had quickly soured him on road racing, especially with the likes of Butch Jones. When they had pulled up at the next intersection, David had jumped out of the car, furious, just as Butch emerged laughing and swilling a pint of Jack Daniels. "Scared the shit out of you!" Butch had roared. A kid in the rear seat opened his window, yelling, "Yo, Green, betcha wet your pants on that one!" slurring his words in the darkness.

"You're an idiot," David had said. "I just hope whoever was driving that car is okay."

"Well, pussy, go back and see. Unless you want to race me again."

"Not you, asshole," David had said. He'd stormed back to his car, making a U-turn, then left rubber on the road as he headed back. When he approached Downer's Crossing, he had been instantly relieved to find nothing there, no car wrapped around a tree nor upside down in the underbrush. Only skid marks that stopped in the sand just where he'd seen the car pull off the road. The driver had managed to pull the car to a stop instead of catapulting into the woods. As he stood there in the darkness that night, David had sworn "never again" and he'd meant it.

"I have no doubt in my mind that Bull Jones is up to something," Ralph Green said. "Bull can't afford to have farmers standing up to him like we did. He's got to show the rest of them what happens if they refuse to sign his little contracts. We didn't and he's got to make us pay. Nothing else makes any sense."

By now the men had reached the pine stand, and the minute David pulled some of the lower branches aside, they stood staring as if they expected the gas cans to get up and walk. Finally, Paul Curley turned, scanning the area for clues. "Looks like they came in from over there," he said, pointing. "They must be parking out on the Brooks Village Road. That's quite a hike with loaded gas cans."

"So they're probably bringing a few in at a time?" Ralph asked.

"Maybe they came intending to use them and didn't." Rob pushed his cap back to scratch his head.

"You mean they changed their minds?" David asked.

"Could be. Maybe they just decided to leave them rather than bring them back to their trucks."

By now, Paul Curley had wandered out of sight, following the trampled underbrush looking for clues. He reappeared saying, "It looks to me like they've been here several times. There's several paths they've taken in, but only three lead to this spot, and two go directly to that knoll overlooking your house, Rob. And one of those comes here. My guess is they came twice, the second time with gas. They left the gas here, then came a couple more times with additional gas."

"So they're getting ready to set a big fire," Rob said, shaking his head. "Good God, how am I going to protect all this land from some guys intent on burning it?" Rob looked down at the gas cans.

"We're going to stop them," Ralph said. "Surprise is on our side. They think they're going to surprise us, but we're going to be ready for them."

Rob looked up then, his face determined, and took a deep breath. "How many do you think they have?"

"No way to know," Ralph said. "But we've got the five of us, and we can call upon Farr and Card. That's seven. Maybe the Benton Road people might help. We can ask."

"Then let's get a move on. If they're coming, we're going to be ready for them," Charlie said.

Paul stepped forward. "I want to track them out to where they park their cars. We need to know that. Let's meet back at your house. You guys drive out and get Farr and Card and stop by the Fenn place." He looked at his watch. "It's already 1:30."

"In an hour, then," Rob said, turning. He wondered as he hurried with the rest down the long hill toward the barn what he was going to do if Terry was still lying upstairs in labor. They wouldn't be able to move her, not just then. Not until the baby was born. He felt nauseated, thinking about his fields and buildings going up in flames, about the battle that would erupt if Pitbull intended to burn him out, about his wife and children being right there if a gun battle did break out. Rob looked up at the sky, wishing he could take solace from a prayer, but there was no time to stop, and maybe, he thought, no one was listening.

62

Patterson, Late September

Terry Grant heard the first cars arriving through a cloud of pain and growing exhaustion. For some reason, this child about to be born was taking its time. Shirley, Carol, and Lisa fidgeted about her, putting compresses on her head, adjusting the sheets, encouraging her, and when she'd think the baby was ready to descend, her labor pains would cease. It had been over an hour since the last pain, and Terry was growing more and more concerned that she might have a problem. She tried to take comfort in the fact that the two boys had delivered normally, without any real need for a doctor or a hospital. Of course, Dr. Graham had overseen their delivery at Almont Memorial. She had been safely monitored throughout her labor. Emergency equipment was at the ready if anything went wrong. And more important, she'd had excellent pre-natal care. Nothing that happened was a surprise.

Now she was facing an entirely different situation. No doctor had looked at Terry at any point in her pregnancy. She was a nurse, of course. She had been pretty certain that the fetus inside was developing quite normally. Certainly, it was active enough. And she hadn't shown any worrisome symptoms, no exceptional swelling or bloating, no excess gain of weight, and hardly any tiredness except for the last few days. She had felt good, really good, only just this morning. That's why she went for a swim in the first place—because she felt so good.

But what now? What if the baby was not in the proper position? What if the umbilical cord was twisted around its neck? What if? What if? A thousand things could go wrong, that she knew, and as she looked at her friends, none of whom had any medical training, she knew the best qualified midwife was the one having the baby. If something was wrong, both she and the child could easily die. It happened all the time in the old days when the number one killer of young women was childbirth. While this was the twenty-first century, it might as well be the old days, because there was no hospital to go to, and as far as she knew, no doctor to deliver her child. Whatever happened was going to depend on good fortune and a smooth delivery. And the longer this labor went on, the less likely it was that the delivery was going to be smooth.

Shirley stood at the window watching two cars appear over the rise and head slowly down to the house, parking directly beneath her in the yard. "Here comes Ralph and David, and they've got Taylor and Arnold in the car behind them."

Carol hurried to the window to watch the men below. They were already out of their trucks and talking in a small group. The back door swung open and Rob and Charlie came out of the kitchen below, anxious to thank Taylor and Arnold for coming. Taylor was at the rear of Arnold's pickup, removing a couple of shotguns, and he turned as Rob approached him and smiled.

"What's happening?" Terry asked, trying to rise a bit on her elbows.

"Lie back," Lisa cautioned. "It's just all the guys arriving."

Rob had come upstairs as soon as he returned from the woods and quietly told them what they had found and what they were going to do. The three women had been amazingly calm, advising him not to worry about Terry, insisting that he go make preparations instead. They'd take care of things up here and when the time came, deal with the children. "Go on, Rob," Carol had said, gently pushing him out of the room. "We're fine. Really."

While Shirley watched the activity below, Carol noticed a new dust cloud billowing up on the other side of the knoll. "Who else is coming?" she wondered aloud, and Shirley shrugged. "They told Lily Fenn's people," she said, her eyes watching the tip of the knoll, waiting to see who might appear there. Seconds later, her mouth fell open as first a new blue pickup, then two or three older ones, then a long line of assorted cars and SUVs slowly rose up over the hill and headed down the long driveway. "My God!" she said. "Who are all those people?"

"What?" Terry called from the bed. She began to swing her legs over the edge, but stopped abruptly, her arm clutching her belly. "Ouch!"

"Lie back down," Lisa ordered, pushing her gently backward.

Shirley opened the window and leaned out. "Who are they?" she called down as she pointed.

Ralph looked up. "Don't know, but the front truck belongs to Elijah Fenn."

Shirley could see that the men below were as perplexed as she was, most of them standing with their arms crossed on their chests or hands on their hips. No one below was saying anything.

As Elijah pulled his pickup to a stop in front of them and stepped out, the other vehicles began parking in a line beside him. Elijah looked at Rob and smiled. "Seems a lot of people don't mind helping you, Rob."

Rob recognized a number of farmers as they emerged from their cars, people he had long ago imagined dead. Jack Patterson was one, Hammie Wilson another. He was an old grizzled fellow, wiry and sharp, who ran the organic farm near the Eaton line. He had been Rob's father's friend their whole lives. As he looked from man to man walking from their cars, Rob had to fight back the lump in his throat. They were coming to help him. He wasn't alone. He'd never been alone.

"There must be fifteen men down there," Carol said. "There's Leo Waters. And Carmine DeSantis. I wonder if Estella is still alive."

"Look," Shirley said pointing. "There's Gary Peters." Shirley's gaze softened as she watched.

"Ah, Shirley," Carol teased. "I knew you were smitten." Carol had encouraged Gary Peters to ask her friend out whenever she saw him, but he'd been too shy to call Shirley, afraid she'd refuse.

"Am not," Shirley protested, purposely looking elsewhere.

"I'll be darned," Carol whispered to Shirley. "Rufus Lincoln and his brother Bill." She watched as the two tall black men, identical twins, joined the group. "If Marianne is alive, we sure could use her. I'm going to run downstairs." She poked Shirley, signaling her to be quiet. She didn't want Terry to know how worried she was or to get her hopes up for a doctor if Marianne was dead.

"What?" Terry called from the bed. "Who else?" But then the pains began anew, and Lisa insisted, "Come on, Terry. Breathe." Having never had children herself, Lisa had no clue how to use natural childbirth techniques other than what she'd seen on TV dramas, but she was doing her best.

When the last of the men had joined the group, Rob led everyone into the house just as Carol reached the kitchen. Their greetings were warm but grave, for everyone knew the gravity of the situation. Taking on Pitbull Jones was something not one of them wanted to face, yet each knew that it had to be done or life in Patterson would be unbearable. The man had terrorized all of them, and now he was planning on destroying the one group that stood up to him. If they didn't fight back now, together, they never would. And each of them knew too that it might be a long time before law and order would be restored. It might never be the same. So they had to fight for it themselves and risk getting injured or killed. Better that than dying a slow death with Pitbull Jones squeezing them dry.

Carol pulled Rufus aside as the men filed into the Grant living room, some of them picking up chairs from the dining room on their way. "Rob's wife is upstairs in labor," she said. "I'm worried that something's wrong. Do you think Marianne would come help?"

"Can you go get her?" Rufus asked, pulling his car keys back out of his pocket. "She'll come." Then he ducked slightly to pass under the doorway into the living room.

Carol hurried back up the stairs, stopping just outside of Terry's bedroom to signal Shirley to come into the hallway. Shirley saw her and came immediately. "I'm going for Marianne," Carol whispered.

"I hear you out there," Terry called weakly. "What's going on?"

"I'll be back as soon as I can," Carol said, grabbing Shirley's forearm for a second and pushing her toward the bedroom. "I'll be all right. Don't worry."

By the time she passed the living room on her way outside, the men were already listening to Rob, Ralph, Paul and Charlie explaining what they had found and where, and what they thought might happen next. She didn't have time to stop, however, for getting Marianne Lincoln was more important. She was in Rufus's Jeep within seconds, stopping only to glance at the children playing tag football out in the field behind Rob's barn. She saw Ellen perched on the fence with David, supervising as they'd been asked to do and keeping the kids out of the way. She looked quickly for her younger son, Johnnie, and saw him and her daughter running wildly after Michael Grant, whom no one could catch. Carol rammed the shift lever into drive and sped along the gravel driveway, sending up her own plume of dust as she disappeared over the knoll toward their secret exit.

63

Patterson, Late September

By dusk, the plans were in place. The Grants' living room had been turned into a men's dormitory, the furniture pushed aside to all the walls, and sleeping bags laid like checker squares across the entire expanse of the floor. The kitchen had become an armory of guns, ammunition, flares, axes, hammers, and chains. Even two bows stood against the kitchen sink, their quivers tossed on the drain board. The men, however, were still preparing things outside, some of them along the perimeters of the hay and cornfields, some in and around the barn, others in the woods above. For a group that had no plans at 3:00 p.m., they seemed well prepared as the sun sank in the west. Their cars had all been driven over to the Young, Green, and Curley farms, separated and hidden. The Grant yard looked normal, except for the fact that Rob's tractor sat outside, placed strategically with his haying truck as a blind near the other field. The young children were with Ethel Card and Ellen at Shirley Young's house, safe from gunfire if things turned violent. Marianne Lincoln was still upstairs, finally seeing the baby's head appear. She hoped the delivery would soon be over. Carol had taken over as breathing coach while Shirley and Laura Block worked downstairs making sandwiches for dinner amidst guns and ammunition boxes. No one laughed or gossiped; any discussion was dead serious and focused on one thing.

No one was sure that this night would bring the

confrontation. They had no way to know how many more cans of gas Pitbull would want in his hiding place before initiating the attack. Perhaps he was planning on building a larger cache, then attacking later in the week or even next week, right before final hay mowing. But Paul Curley and Arnold both agreed that this was the optimal night, if Pitbull had any sense at all. Not only was the moon a mere slit in the sky, but banks of clouds had been building all day. Arnold said that Pitbull already knew where the gas was going to be spread because he'd probably been up on the hill himself, laying out his plans. He'd want to get his men and the gas down the long hill without chancing being seen by anyone in the house—a near impossibility if the moon were bright. "No," Arnold insisted, "he's going to want darkness. The element of surprise. My guess is he plans to wake all of you up to a raging fire. Then he can take his enjoyment out of watching you run helplessly about trying to put it out."

"I think he's going to do more than that," Taylor said. "Rob's barn is loaded with feed. So's his silo. Even the house is fully stocked with goods. I think he intends to take it."

"Maybe so," Arnold nodded. "But if he's planning that, he's also planning for a fight. He knows Rob and Charlie aren't going to give up easily."

"That never stopped Bull Jones," Charlie said. "He lives for fights."

"Then we've got to be ready to stop them before they reach the barn and the house. We've got wide open hay fields, cow pastures, a corn field over on the right, and this huge yard area. We want to stop them out in the open, where we can surround them and hopefully surprise them into giving up. We don't want them getting in close enough to do damage."

"But he'll probably have already spread the gas along the back perimeters by the time he approaches the barn and house," Rob said, thinking of how much hay and corn out there could go up in flames.

"Water don't light with matches," Arnold said.

The other men looked at him, confused. "First thing we do is replace the gas with water. The smell and some residual traces of gas will fool them. They'll be irrigating your fields for you Rob." Taylor smiled as he looked at the men's faces. They weren't used to the way Arnold's mind worked.

"They'll probably bring more with them, though," another farmer said.

"Nothing we can do about that but shoot the guy carrying it," Arnold said. No one liked the image of a man bursting into flames, even one of Pitbull's men. They paused as everyone considered his own mortality.

"We need sentries," Arnold added. "If we're wrong and they don't come tonight, you boys have got to go home until tomorrow night. Can't do much work without a good night's sleep."

"I say we put someone out on the back road to spot them as soon as they arrive," Jim Patterson said.

"What's he going to do? Shoot up a flare?" another responded.

"We'll do like the Indians. Set up runners," Rob said.

No one relished that idea either, for while they were all strong farm men, none of them were fast. "Who's going to do the running?" Rufus asked doubtfully.

"I say we put me out at the road with one of the young boys," Arnold said. "David or that Michael of yours, Rob. That kid's fast as the wind. The minute they arrive, I send him off. Maybe have someone half-way in to run the second leg."

"Where are you in all this?" Ralph asked.

"I'm waiting for those good old boys to head into the woods. Then I'm flattening their tires so they can't make a run for it once they see they've got more than they bargained for. When I'm done, I come in from the rear."

"Can the alert come fast enough for us to rush out and position ourselves before any of them arrive?"

"Don't know," Rob said, not liking the idea of his boy being involved.

"Let's time it," Arnold said, pulling out his pocket watch. "I'll take Michael and David out. Michael and I will go all the way to the road, note the time, and then practice his run. I'll follow, walking like men carrying gas and guns through the dark. Let's see what the time difference is. You guys have to be in position before I reach the knoll up there, because even if it's dark, we can't take a chance of some movement alerting them to the trap. Our best chance is the element of surprise."

They'd practiced the run, and Rob had been proud of the way Michael stepped up to this dangerous job. When the men had called him over, Michael had seemed so little. They all towered over him. He'd looked up at his father, a bit doubtful, but as his job was explained to him, Michael had straightened as if growing before them, his jaw set, his eyes eager. "Yes. I can do that," he had said, looking again at Rob. Rob had thought his heart would burst for the second time that day, he was so proud of the young boy he'd raised. He was also glad that Terry didn't know anything about it, for she would never agree to Michael's participation. Rob wouldn't have either, but he knew also that Michael was the fastest runner among them. He'd always been incredibly quick, but a summer of work and of growing had given him long muscular legs and a sure-footedness that not even

David could equal. The alliance needed Michael. They needed the extra time Michael could give them to position themselves. Michael could make the difference between success and failure. David could be ready near the barn to awaken everyone inside the house.

Arnold and Michael had taken their sandwiches and fruit with them just before dusk, intending to eat later, when they had established their positions. After the second practice run, they figured they could give the men sleeping in the house at least an eight minute head start to their positions before Pitbull's men arrived at the knoll. Michael would have to run through the darkness without his flashlight for the first three of those minutes, getting far enough ahead of the enemy before he could turn it on. After that, he could keep it on as he made his way out of the woods and down the hill to the barn where David was waiting. Michael would then go to the house and stay with the women.

By 11:30, everything was ready. Most of the men were already asleep in the living room. One or two still sat talking quietly at the kitchen table, where a single candle burned. Just in case Pitbull thought to send a spy ahead, though an unlikely possibility, Rob had closed the blinds in every room. Now he paced about downstairs, picking his way around sleeping bags and other paraphernalia, listening to the men in the kitchen and to his wife's muffled cries upstairs. Twice he climbed the stairs, standing at their bedroom door shyly waiting for Doc Lincoln to nod an okay to enter. This time, no one paid any attention at all when he appeared, for the baby was finally ready to emerge.

"Push," Marianne Lincoln said. "Come on, Terry, push." His wife's groans had grown weaker with every passing hour. As he looked at her, Rob panicked at the sight of her worn face and her hair wet with sweat. He was beside her in an instant.

"Come on, honey," he said, kissing her forehead as he took her hand from Shirley. "This is it, babe. Push!"

And then, with a whoosh of relief and new excitement, Doc Lincoln was suddenly holding a wet and bloody child, already howling, its tiny fists knotted, its legs splayed. "A girl!" she proclaimed as Carol rushed forward with a blanket and carried the baby over to a bureau they had cleared. Shirley and Carol began cleaning the infant, but Rob was far more interested in tending to his wife. "God, I love you, babe," he whispered as he kissed her forehead repeatedly.

Terry closed her eyes in relief and exhaustion. "Is she okay?" she asked, though her head was already falling to the side.

"She's beautiful," Carol said, bringing her over for Terry to hold.

"When can we move them?" Rob asked Doc Lincoln. As interested as he was in the peanut face and curly brown hair of the tiny child now mewling in Terry's arms, other things took precedence, and the most important was getting the women off the second floor and into the cellar where no stray bullet could find them. Rob feared that a gunfight out in the fields and yard might send bullets flying through the windows and walls of the house. He didn't want his wife and new baby in danger.

"Go downstairs now and get it ready," Doc Lincoln said. "Give us twenty minutes, and we'll be ready to move."

Rob kissed Terry one last time and quietly tiptoed down the two flights of stairs to where Laura and Lisa were preparing the bed set up there hours ago, before the men went to sleep. "A few minutes," was all he said, and then back he climbed, trying to deal with emotions that ranged from joy to pride to anger to terror. What if Pitbull set the house on fire, he thought. Would the women be able to get out? And if he could change anything, it was that his new baby would have chosen another day to come so that Terry could be with Chris, over at Shirley's house, safe and far from the bullets that he knew without a doubt would be flying if Pitbull came tonight. His only hope was that Pitbull wasn't coming. One more day could make a huge difference in their preparations, including getting Terry and the rest of the women out of harm's way. One more day, he asked God, after they'd brought Terry and the baby down and closed the cellar door. One more day, he repeated. as he stretched out in his chair, his feet up on the ottoman, the afghan Terry had knitted spread over him, his feet icy where they protruded at the far end. One more day was the last thing Rob was thinking before he fell asleep.

64

Patterson, Late September

"Easy boy," Arnold whispered close to Michael's ear. "Don't say anything."

Michael fought to awaken from the deep sleep he'd been enjoying. Hours of watching the darkening sky, worrying whether he'd be able to do his share and give his dad and the others enough time to be ready for Pitbull, had kept him awake way past his usual bedtime. As he and Arnold had lain on the ground in their sleeping bags, hidden by bushes, Michael had been so keenly aware of the slightest sounds that he'd decided the woods came alive at night as soon as people went to sleep. The bushes rustled, things fluttered and skittered about, he even thought he could hear snakes slithering. He was glad Arnold was right beside him. "Would a poisonous snake want to get warm inside my bag?" Michael had asked, earnest and frightened.

"Ain't no poisonous snakes in Central Massachusetts," Arnold had replied, his tone certain. "You've got nothing to worry about here, Michael," Arnold added. Then Michael heard him slap his cheek. "'Cept the damn mosquitoes," Arnold hissed. "Why didn't I bring some Off with me?" He slapped again. "Aren't they biting you, boy?" Arnold had said, sitting up.

"Nope," Michael replied, but to make sure, he snuggled down farther into his sleeping bag, leaving only his nose, eyes, and forehead exposed. It was after that, feeling protected, that Michael had finally fallen asleep to the

irregular slaps and curses of Arnold battling battalions of
mosquitoes intent, he claimed, on "sucking the last of his
juices dry." How long ago that had been, Michael had no
idea. But now, with Arnold's face close to his, the smell
of the old man uncomfortably close to his nose, Michael
opened his eyes wide.

"Slide out of your bag, boy. They're coming."

Arnold was already standing by the time Michael
unzipped his bag and stood trembling in the darkness.
"This is it," Arnold said, holding Michael's arm for just a
second to be sure. They could see car lights coming slowly
toward them through the pine branches, and hear the slow,
winding sounds of engines climbing the hill to the place
where Paul Curley said they had been parking each time
they came. The headlights lit the air, growing brighter
as the cars approached. "Just wait 'til we're sure," Arnold
whispered. "No sense waking everyone unless this is really
it."

Michael's instinct was to set off running. He felt his
skin jumping, all his hairs on alert, but Arnold held fast
to his arm. "Got your flashlight?" he said, and Michael,
embarrassed, bent to feel around his bag for it.

"Yup," he said, relieved that it was where it was supposed
to be.

As soon as Arnold saw the third car come up over the
rise, he felt certain this could be no coincidence, nobody
driving home somewhere Arnold didn't know about. When
the first car slowed, pulling up silently along the side of
the road, Arnold released his grip on Michael's arm and
whispered, "Run!"

Michael took off in a flash, racing through the darkness
and trying to remember each detail of the first part of the
trail. It was far more difficult than he had imagined, trying

to move fast in almost complete darkness, trying not to run headlong into a tree or trip over a protruding root or stone. They'd practiced the first three minutes five or six times once he and Arnold had set up their sleeping bags and eaten their dinner. Even as it began to grow dark, Arnold had insisted that they go over and over the first part of the trail, the first three dark minutes before he could avail himself of the light he carried in his hand. So he knew what to expect. He just couldn't be sure he was exactly where he thought he was, and if he was wrong, if he fell or if he got lost, or if he couldn't make it in time, Michael knew his dad could be taken by surprise, and if that happened, it would all be his fault.

Meanwhile, Arnold hunkered down in the bushes, trying to remain perfectly still. Six vehicles pulled to a stop along the side of the road, their drivers turning off headlights and ignitions before opening their doors and climbing out.

"Shit, it's dark up here," one of the men said.

"Quiet!" someone ordered.

"They can't hear us two miles away, Bull," someone else said.

"Get those cans out and shut your mouth," Bull ordered. Arnold strained to see movement in the darkness. A couple of guys had on light shirts or sweatshirts and he could see their upper bodies moving as if without legs. The rest were invisible, though as they walked about, their footsteps in the rustling leaves sounded like many men. Then someone turned on his flashlight, and Arnold could see pairs of legs moving around the pickups parked not twenty feet from him. Another flashlight went on, then others. "Okay, boys. We got everything?"

"Yeah," someone else said, and when Bull's flashlight rose to the guy's face, Arnold recognized the kid he had seen at the library.

"Let's go," Bull said, his flashlight swiveling, the light running lightly over Arnold in the pine stand before flitting about the woods and the trail on which Michael had only minutes before disappeared. Arnold remained frozen in the darkness, his heart beating wildly. Those bozos thought they were going to get the best of a bunch of farm boys, did they? Well, they were in for a big surprise. Arnold only wished he could be there to see their faces when suddenly they were surrounded with determined farmers with guns. Hah! Arnold thought. But he didn't move, not even for several minutes after the men had left. He had to be sure they hadn't left a sentry to guard the cars and he had to be sure they were far enough gone not to hear him moving in the leaves. In his hand, he held the ice pick he had sharpened just before leaving the Grant farm. He felt the tip of it prick his finger and smiled. He had some surprises of his own for Pitbull Jones and as soon as he could safely move out of the pines, he intended to do his own kind of damage.

He started with the last pickup, moving from wheel to wheel, standing each time to hear the whoosh of air, to be sure enough pressure escaped to flatten the tire. Sometimes the self-sealing tires hampered an immediate flat, and Arnold had to plunge the pick in several times to get the job done. He knew he didn't have to do all four tires on each vehicle, but he wanted to. He had enough time, for he knew he couldn't head into the woods until he heard the ruckus of guns or saw flames or, most unlikely, someone came to get him because Bull Jones gave up without a fight. He didn't count on the last one. What he wouldn't have minded at all was to see these blackguards come running back for a hasty escape only to find themselves stranded. The thought was just too delicious not to really mess up their tires, so Arnold moved about slowly, puncturing, standing, sometimes re-puncturing, then moving on to the next vehicle. He'd increase his pace, he figured, as soon as he heard something. In the darkness he listened for shots, but knew that it would take the men a while to get themselves positioned, pour their watery gas on the fields, and suddenly discover themselves surrounded. No need to rush. He'd speed up his work as soon as he heard some telltale sound.

Bull Jones and his men moved slowly along the path they had created in their many trips to the back of the Grant farm, their flashlights aimed at the ground. No one said anything. Four men carried two additional gas containers. They frequently grunted with effort and annoyance, and every so often someone swore as he tripped or stumbled on rock outcroppings and tree roots. Nose Bartlett shouldered the shotgun Bull had forced him to carry, though Nose had no intention of using it unless he had to. Personally, Nose would have given just about anything to have been excluded from this foray. He was worried and scared. The last thing Nose wanted was to participate in a gun battle, especially with his rudimentary skills as a shooter. He doubted he could hit anyone, even though Bull said that a shotgun always hit something. Worse, Nose didn't like violence, especially violence that might include him. Even violence enacted on others was repugnant. Nose had his limits. Smearing people, price gouging, spying, even stalking were acceptable, even enjoyable pastimes, but Nose feared blood and he wasn't a killer. As he followed behind the first group, he fought a growing panic that gripped his chest, making it hard to breathe. What the hell was he doing out here, he thought. How did he get himself into this mess? But of course, he knew. Bull Jones had offered him a job and some safety to repay him for the article he had written condemning Rob Grant. For the third or fourth time, Grant and the zoning board had denied Jones an additional junkyard permit because the one he had was such a eyesore. That was years ago, before Grant was Selectman. Nose always took every opportunity to undermine Grant, and he seized upon the board's refusal as just another example of petty bureaucracy and people minding other people's business. The article had worked in his favor. Jones remembered his one "friend" in town and consequently, when Nose came begging, was willing to pay him back. Nose had made it through the winter as comfortably as anyone, with plenty of food and few worries because of Bull. And he'd never minded the jobs Bull gave him until now.

He looked at Pitbull's back, a huge shadow in the darkness, and at the light fluttering across the ground as the men ahead of him moved forward. His mind was racing. How could he get out of this? He couldn't just say no. He had to think of a way to go back without arousing suspicion. What could he say he needed? And then it hit him. Suppose he just dropped back. Suppose he just bent down to tie his shoe, let the ones behind him pass, and then headed back to the trucks. He could wait there safely. Listen to the shooting, if there was any. Watch the fiery blaze light the night sky. Then, when he knew it was safe, hustle back there. Pretend he'd hurt his leg trying to catch up. He'd think of something those blockheads would accept.

Without agonizing another second, Nose bent to his knees, making it clear he was tying his shoe by aiming the flashlight at his foot. Other men stepped around him, looking down momentarily to see what he was doing on the ground. No one stopped to wait for him. He lingered, listening as their footsteps continued through the underbrush, continuing to fiddle nervously with the laces. While he did, he considered alternatives. He could play it safe and continue on behind them. Just catch up and go along with things. But he was too scared. Nose had a strong fear of dying. He could stay here and wait, but if things turned out badly, he could be captured. The safety of the pickup seemed so much smarter. He could smell the leather seats. He could feel the warmth of the cab. He would have the steering wheel and keys in his hands and a headstart if he needed it. No, the cab was the place to be. He felt almost instant relief once he'd made up his mind.

As soon as the last patch of flashlight disappeared, Nose stood and looked about. Then, hoisting his shotgun and flashing his light backward the way he had come, Nose began picking his way through the woods toward the road. He was careful and completely silent, afraid that the slightest noise might somehow give him away. At any minute, someone might suddenly bellow, "Hey, where's Bartlett?" Bull would surely send someone back after him. He looked back cautiously, almost expecting to see light dancing on the trees. But the woods were black and silent. He kept walking, trying to be as quiet as possible, so that as he grew closer to the road, he became aware of a strange sound ahead of him. He stopped, turning off his flashlight to listen. He had no idea what could be making the strange plunking sound, but he knew the trucks were just ahead over the next rise. Whatever it was, it was near them.

Carefully, setting one foot down at a time, his shotgun pointed, Nose made his way toward the road. His legs shook with fear and his hand trembled as he held the shotgun. He could barely breathe. The noise continued, but now Nose could see, almost invisible in the darkness, a figure appear above the bed of the second pickup. It popped up from behind the truck so fast that Nose almost fired. He realized that whoever it was hadn't seen him, for the figure moved along the side of the pickup. He heard the sound of air escaping, and at the front of the pickup the fellow disappeared. The same pattern repeated. Something plunking, then air, then the fellow stood up. Nose realized the guy was letting air out of the tires. Who? And why was he even here?

There could only be one explanation. Rob Grant knew they were coming and was ready for them. Bull Jones was walking into a trap, and if he tried to get away, this guy who was fixing things so that no truck was going anywhere'd foil him. A wave of nausea washed over Nose. He'd almost been with them, down there in the fields by the barn, out in the open. He would have been shot or captured. He'd narrowly escaped. He gulped. And then he began to consider a whole new set of options. If he got out of here fast, no one would ever be the wiser. He could claim he had no idea what Bull Jones was up to. All he had to do was disappear. Now. No one had seen him, no one knew he was there. But he had to get away fast and without being recognized.

The figure popped up once again and was not only coming around to his side of the vehicles but was heading for the first pickup. If the other trucks were already disabled and he let this guy flatten its tires, he'd have no way to escape. He had to do something and do it fast. He had to stop the guy, get past him into the truck and get out of there. But if the guy recognized him, he was a goner. Unless. Nose's finger tightened on the trigger as he realized he couldn't leave the guy alive.

Nose raised his shotgun and took aim as the man stepped out from between the first and second cars. Nose spread his legs for greater stability and sighted. Something, a branch or twig, snapped beneath his foot as he did so. Arnold heard it and stopped dead short. He looked helplessly into the darkness, the pick in his hands, doing a quick inventory. Where was his rifle? In the pines? Leaning against the last truck? Why hadn't he thought to keep it with him? His eyes narrowed as he peered, seeing nothing. But he knew someone was there. Could he make a run for it? Duck behind the pickup? Arnold had no time to consider possibilities. The barrel of Nose's shotgun flashed before the sound of the gun ripped through the night air. Arnold saw the flash, stunned, then dropped the pick. He put a hand out to steady himself on the hood of the truck and moaned out loud. Nose tightened his finger on the trigger, unsure whether he had hit his target or not. He watched as the man teetered, wrapping his other arm around his waist, still looking into darkness for some clue as to what had just happened. Then his knees buckled and he slumped to the ground.

Nose waited to see if he moved. What a lucky shot, he thought, wondering how in God's name he had hit his mark. When the fellow didn't move, Nose inched forward, emerging from the woods on tiptoe. Behind him, he heard gunfire, but he didn't stop to listen. He jumped into the first pickup, turned the key, and waited only long enough for the engine to catch before flooring the gas pedal. He heard the tires spraying sand on the truck behind him and the siren-squeal of his tires leaving rubber on the asphalt.

The pickup swerved and fishtailed, leaving behind a cloud of dust that billowed up around and over Arnold's body, silent in the red glare of the truck's rear lights. Nose no longer cared who was behind him. He'd shot a man and betrayed Bull Jones, and he wasn't going to stay around to wait for everyone to find out. Nose Bartlett was leaving town.

65

Patterson, Late September

Bull Jones had lingered on the knoll overlooking the Grant farm long enough to wave his men this way and that before heading down the hill along the pasture fence toward the barn. Everyone knew where they were going and what to do when they got there, for they'd laid it all out days ago, sitting around the pot-bellied stove in Bull's new house. Last month, Bull had decided he'd avoided going into "dead houses" long enough. He wanted better quarters, quarters fitting a leader, and so, before the weather became cold, Bull had outfitted his men with layers of Tyvek and heavy rubber gloves, given them scuba gear for breathing, and sent them in to clear out the remains of any of the rich bastard Larsens still rotting there. The work had turned out to be easy, for the last Larsen had buried his wife and two children before climbing into his king-size bed to succumb. Bull's men had merely rolled up his skeletal remains and bacterial muck, tied the mattress with rope, and sent it out through Larsens' sliding door, across his deck, and down onto the waiting pickup. They threw his bedroom furniture on top, followed by the oriental carpet to cover the load, and then mopped the walls and floors with Lysol. Bull moved in as soon as they finished, and had ensconced himself there with great pride of ownership. The Larsens' family room had quickly become Bull's new meeting room, and there he'd assigned each of his men specific tasks, pointing to the hand-drawn map he'd made like the General he had become.

As soon as they reached the knoll, all flashlights were turned off, so as Bull moved along the fence, he stepped carefully, frequently looking about the darkness in the directions he knew he'd sent his men. The plan was simple. The men at the back were at this moment dousing gasoline in a line along Grant's corn and hayfields. He and the four men carrying gas cans behind him intended to hide near the front of the house and wait. Once Bull was sure everyone was assembled in their proper places, he would wave the flashlight in the air, a signal to the men at the rear to light their fires. Bull figured it would take several minutes for the size of the blaze to waken the family sleeping inside, but once they did wake up, Bull figured they'd all come running like crazed ants to douse the fields or beat the flames down with brooms and blankets. They'd all run out, Bull was sure, and someone might even be sent as a messenger to the other alliance farmers, but once they had evacuated the house, Bull and his group would set both the house and barn on fire. He imagined with a smile the look on Grant's face when he turned from the fields, shocked to see his house and barn being devoured as well. Bull didn't want any of the Grants to die from his fire, but what would happen to them as winter descended was their own fault for defying him. They'd starve, for sure. The rest of the farmers now harvesting the last of their crops would hear of Rob Grant's misfortune and show up, hats in hand, their trucks loaded with bounty for Bull and his men. The plan was perfect and easy, and Bull couldn't wait to flash his light and watch the fun begin.

They were about sixty feet from the barn when Nose Bartlett's shot resounded across the fields and valleys. In the silence, it sounded more like a cannon than a shotgun. Bull froze, wondering what had happened, and turned, wondering whether one of his men had tripped over his own damn-fool gun. Then all hell broke loose. The men dousing the rear of the fields closest to the woods had no idea who was shooting, but they ducked and began searching the underbrush for a rock or log to get behind. The alliance men, already hidden in the trees along the wood line and behind strategically placed obstacles, thought someone had spotted them and began shooting into the woods and at the places where they had last seen Bull's men moving. Bull's men shot back, not sure at first what they were shooting at. One of them lit the gasoline he had just poured along the fence line only to discover from the small fire that did flame up that the gas wasn't doing what it was supposed to do. Something was wrong with it. Seeing a flame burning brightly near the hay field, the men who had doused the cornfield tried lighting their gasoline only to find the same thing happening. All of this while bright flashes of gunfire were popping everywhere.

"Shit," cursed Bull, bending low and running toward the barn. "Come on, get those cans to the house."

Over the flashing gunfire, Bull heard Rob Grant shout, "It's over, Jones! Put down your guns." Bull was not about to give up that easily. It wasn't over, it was just different. He dropped to the ground and began shooting in the direction of the voice. One, two, three rifle shots. He crawled closer to the barn, inching his way into the deepest black shadows along the foundation.

"They've made us, Pop," he heard Butch cry from behind him.

"Move those fucking cans along the ground, asshole," he yelled over the pounding gunfire. He didn't bother to look back, just kept moving on his belly, pushing forward.

Out in the fields, the gunfire was relentless. The small

fires had begun to catch, spreading outward and growing brighter. A couple of farmers tried using their jackets to smother the flames, but Bull's men used the light to take aim and shoot. One farmer went down with a shout, and two others appeared out of nowhere to pull him back into the safety of darkness. By now, with the element of surprise gone, Bull's men had figured out where the shots were coming from and had found places to lie low behind stumps, fence posts, and rocks. Bullets flew through the darkness, criss-crossing each other, most often hitting other stumps, fence posts, rocks, and the tractor that Rob Grant had placed there as a blind. Periodically, someone shouted or cursed, hit by a bullet or scared by one that landed too close. The din was enormous.

Still Bull kept crawling forward, passing the barn and heading for the house. He had no idea why burning Grant's house was so important to him. Perhaps it was a trophy, the fact that the man would have no place to live. Perhaps he just couldn't let go of his original goal, despite the change in circumstances. Whatever the reason, Bull stood up just past the barn, calling backward to his son and Dobie Maxwell to get a move on. He made a safe run to some bushes and then alongside the house foundation, and only when he felt safe enough to take a breath did he realize that Butch and Dobie were not behind him. "Fuck!" he cursed, peeking around the side of the house. But all he could see were the flashes of gunfire and a hayfield now half engulfed in flames. The sight so cheered him that he lingered, trying to make out what was what and where his men might be. He couldn't see Butch and he swore at his misfortune to have borne such an idiot for a son.

Butch had followed his father to the edge of the barn, but when he got there, he didn't have the stomach for making a run through the Grants' open yard toward the house, especially dragging a gas can. Instead, Butch decided he could do more good from inside the barn. He could set himself up in the loft, a perfect place to make some good shots. And safer too, Butch knew, not relishing all the gunfire. Then, when his father's men took control, he could pour the gas around the inside and light it. The sagging wooden structure would explode in flame. He turned left, crawling along the face of the barn toward the doors, which were slightly ajar, pushed the gas can inside and threw himself to the floor, where he looked around before moving.

It was only then that he heard a low growl. Butch knew the sound of an angry dog when he heard it and stood, fumbling his way backward against the door. He heard the sound of a chain being yanked and he heard something else. A "Shhhhhh! Griz!" A kid's voice from deep inside the recesses of the barn. He knew immediately that the dog couldn't attack because of the chain and that Michael Grant was most certainly hiding there.

"That you, Pussy?" he said aloud, hoping that he was right.

The dog continued growling, pulling against its chain, but no one replied.

"Hey, Grant, you hiding, you little pussy, afraid to come out?" Butch's confidence grew every time the dog threw himself against the chain. He had located their position, back about thirty feet and off to the left. He could make out bales of hay, but no actual figure.

"Come on out, Grant, or I'm gonna' spray your corner with bullets," Butch ordered. He cocked his rifle. "Not so brave without your little brother to bite me, are you," he said.

Michael Grant gulped. His father had told him to stay in the house, down in the cellar with his mom, but Michael had run across the yard to the barn as soon as the men piled out to their positions. He was worried about Griz tied in the barn and terrified that something might happen to his father. He couldn't hide down in the cellar knowing that danger was outside, so he'd disobeyed, and now he was in for it. "Don't shoot," Michael said, standing. Beside him, Griz fought his chain, leaping forward and growling.

"Come out of the darkness then," Butch said, his rifle pointed, his finger on the trigger. Butch felt the old anger boiling, the humiliation of having that turd of a kid stand up to him on the bus. His eyes narrowed, sensing the possibilities for revenge.

Michael stepped forward and sideways, away from Griz who was by now frantic to get loose. "I'm coming," he said slowly, walking forward into the dim light from the window above. He stopped, looking at Butch, peering to see better. He tried not to shake.

"Step closer," Butch said, for the first time realizing he wanted to shoot. For a second, just a second, he considered the consequences. No one knew he was in here. Any shot from outside could have burst through and hit the kid. This is something he could do without fear of punishment. In the chaos of gunfire outside, no one would ever know. His father would be proud.

Michael Grant did as he was told, while behind him he could hear the constant clash of chain links as Griz leapt against his restraints. Griz's growls were ferocious, but each time he yanked at the chain, he choked. Furious at the pain in his throat, he increased his thrusts until finally, in a moment of sheer release, a link gave way and Griz flew forward toward the voice, past Michael and up, into the air, his fangs bared.

Shocked out of his focus, Butch saw the dog coming. Just in time he turned the barrel away from Michael and shot directly into the chest of the dog now leaping at him. Mid-air, Griz seemed to pause, his front paws limp at his chin, his rear legs still in the final stretch of his spring. Michael saw the pause, saw the momentum of his flight suddenly cease, saw Butch get ready to take another shot, and ran at the boy, his "Noooooo!" a scream in the darkness. He was on him in a minute, his fists pummeling Butch in a rage that stunned the bigger boy, who for a minute, did nothing but back up. Butch struggled to free himself without dropping his rifle, helplessly using one hand to push Michael off. But Michael was punching him, repeatedly slamming his fist into Butch's eye while he held tight to Butch's neck.

"Get the fuck off me," Butch managed. But Michael was relentless. Finally, Butch dropped his rifle and used both hands to grab Michael by the throat. He squeezed, while Michael's feet, hanging in mid-air, slammed him time and again. And then, in a blinding flash, one of Michael's feet caught him hard in the groin and Butch, crippled with pain, released Michael and dropped him as he doubled over. Butch saw blue flashes exploding in his head. The rush of fury at Michael became a rush of pain focused between his legs. He groaned, watching helplessly as Michael, his feet once again on the ground, grabbed Butch's rifle and stepped backward, pointing it at Butch.

Michael could have shot him right then and there, but Michael wasn't interested in killing Butch Jones. He looked down at his dog, whose breathing had become a tortured wheeze, and dropped to the ground. "Griz," he cried, still holding the rifle pointed at Butch. "Easy boy, I'll get you help," Michael sobbed, patting the dying dog gently on the head. He tried desperately to wipe the water from his eyes, his vision blurred.

Butch saw that he had one instant of Michael's inattention to slip through the doors and outside, and he didn't hesitate. Before Michael could wipe his eyes and look away from his dog, Butch had disappeared. He cut left, around the back of the barn, avoiding the melee in the field, then ran down the Grants' driveway toward the road. He figured he'd circle around, find his way back to his pickup and wait there for his father. What else could he do? He'd left the gas in the barn. He had no gun. His eye was swelling closed. The pain behind it was excruciating. Butch knew when it was time to retreat, and he took it.

66

Patterson, Late September

Dobie Maxwell wasn't going to waste his time following Butch's old man to the front of the house once he saw that his buddy cut left, the gas can bouncing along the ground beside him. Dobie figured Butch was going to set the barn on fire and he needed time to find the girl before someone else got to the house with more gas. Dobie had been fantasizing about this night since the first time he had seen Ellen, tossing and turning in his bed with dreams that thrilled him beyond mortal pleasure. He planned on grabbing her, dragging her out the front of the house and across the road, far from the shooting. Dobie envisioned this act countless times, seeing himself pointing his rifle and ordering her to come with him, pushing her out the door, and then taking his time with her once he got her into some woods. When the surprise shooting started, for a moment Dobie had been crestfallen, thinking his hopes shattered, but after a few minutes, he got hold of himself. Bull's men were shooting up a storm, probably picking those stupid farmers off one by one, the back field was already on fire, and Butch was going to light the barn up. He had time to grab her and get away.

Dobie moved carefully along the side of the house, keeping in the flickering shadows that the walls afforded. He could see the side door just ahead of him, and as he reached his arm along the wall, feeling for the handle, his excitement had him breathing hard. The knob turned, and

Dobie slunk sideways, pulling the door open only enough to slip his rangy body inside. He stopped, still holding the doorframe, listening for a sound detectable over the gunshots and men shouting without. He heard a clock ticking near his head, probably a wall clock. His head swiveled, sniffing smells. But he heard nothing else.

Dobie peered about the kitchen, trying to make sense of its layout. His gaze followed the counters along the wall to where they ended, then dropped, running along the floor. There was a door there, and beneath it, the merest slit of light. Bonanza! Dobie thought. She's hiding in the cellar. No way out but the way he was coming in. Dobie smiled, setting down his rifle on the kitchen table and pulling a pistol from his belt.

"Pretty girl," he called softly. Dobie didn't bother to tiptoe now. He wanted the girl below him in the cellar to hear his footsteps. He imagined her excitement, hearing someone calling her. He imagined her helpless fright as he slowly opened the cellar door. "Pretty girl," he called louder, reaching for the doorknob. He smiled as the door creaked and the candle lighting the cellar was extinguished. The stairs became a black hole. "Pretty girl," he called again, his voice resounding in the empty stairwell. Dobie switched on his flashlight, then put one foot down on the top step. He flashed the light about the base of the cellar steps, delighted to hear some rustling there, visualizing her and the other women huddling together in the darkness, visualizing the girl looking up at the light, paralyzed with fear. Oh my, oh my, he thought.. This is going to be fun.

In the cellar, Terry huddled on the floor, cradling her peacefully sleeping newborn. Beside her Carol, her arms wrapped around her friend, tried to control her breathing, which was coming in tiny gasps. On the other side of

Terry, Lisa squeezed tightly into the corner made by the bed frame against the wall. Doc Lincoln lay curled on the floor in front of them, her back to the stairs. Beneath the stairwell, Laura Block hid under hastily-piled ski jackets, her rifle gripped in her trembling hands.

"Come out, come out, wherever you are," Dobie called, moving down three steps and bending to flash his light across the cellar floor. The light played along the base of the shelves of preserves Terry had worked so hard to finish before the baby came. It moved to several old toys, a tricycle and a child's walker. It moved along the other wall to several cartons of clothing and then to the legs of Rob's work bench upon which a hammer, a battery operated drill/screwdriver, and two rolls of duct tape sat in ordered readiness. Then it moved to the bed. Dobie was perplexed by the sight of it, a bed in the cellar. Certainly the women didn't intend to sleep through the attack. But clearly someone had been sleeping there. He let his light play across the tossed pillows. The sheets were rumpled. The quilt had been thrown back and lay doubled across the far side. And then he heard the tiniest of moans. Carol had not been able to stop herself. She saw the light on the bed, saw it linger there, and was certain that whoever was calling from the stairs had seen her. Instantly Dobie ran the light over the quilt again, and then he saw what he had missed before. Only the tips of their heads showed above the tossed quilt. It looked like two of them, but it could be three. Foolish women, hiding behind a bed, as if he couldn't find them there. "Pretty girl," he called again. "I see you there." Dobie smiled as one woman tried to duck lower.

"I've come for you," Dobie said, stepping down again, as if the girl there would know who he was and why he had come. In his mind, Dobie almost believed that she had been waiting, that she had lingered outside those weeks ago just so that he would notice her, that she wanted him to come for her.

Silence. But Dobie could sense movement among them as they hunkered lower against the wall. Dobie remained still, but his eyes darted about the lower expanse. He sniffed the air, picking up musk and the slight hint of perfume. His tongue flicked out, wetting his upper lip. Dobie ran the light around the rest of the cellar, leaving the frightened women in darkness. He wanted to be sure they were the only ones in the cellar, just in case. Then he descended three more steps, so that now he was almost to the bottom. He stood straight, carefully scrutinizing the cellar one last time. Then he played his light again on the bed behind which he believed Ellen hid.

"Time to come out now," he said. When no one moved, he said it again, the second time louder and with more authority. When still no one moved, his tone became cross and indignant. "Come out now," he ordered. Still nothing.

Dobie descended the last two steps, letting his boots fall heavily on the wooden planks. He wanted to punctuate his intentions, scare the women a little more. "Oh, you're a teaser," he said, his voice coy. When he reached concrete, he paused, once again checking the interior of the cellar. He saw the pile of clothing under the steps, all the jackets and parkas tossed in a heap. If he'd looked a little more closely, he might have questioned such sloppiness, but sloppiness was a way of life for Dobie Maxwell. He'd grown up in chaos and he continued to live that way. Dobie only glanced at the heap, his excitement palpable. He wanted to see the girl. See her face. Look into her frightened eyes. Touch her.

"Okay, now. No sense in hiding. I know you're there,"

Dobie said, walking purposefully toward the bed, his gun pointed. When he sensed a sudden movement, it confused him because it came from two places. Behind the bed, Carol pressed her body in front of Terry's in order to protect her weak friend and the baby. Lisa began to rise, one hand on the edge of the bed as she struggled to straighten. Dobie saw Lisa and his brow knitted in confusion. This wasn't the girl. He peered, looking to see who else hid behind the bed, momentarily ignoring the other sound, the one of nylon sliding upon nylon as Laura slipped quietly from beneath the heap of jackets, rose, and in two steps, pressed the barrel of her rifle into the back of Dobie's head.

Dobie froze. He could feel the cold steel against the bone at the base of his skull. His eyes darted about, his pupils black saucers, but he didn't try to turn his head. "Drop your gun," Laura said.

Dobie hesitated, weighing his chances against a woman. She probably couldn't shoot. She was probably just bluffing. He could turn quickly and grab the rifle barrel. Overtake her easily. But while Dobie weighed options, Lisa Curley reached under a pillow and pulled out the pistol Paul had left with her. Taking it in both hands, she pointed it at him, her finger on the trigger.

"Don't even think about it," Laura said, seeing Lisa now ready with her gun. "You can die right now, or you can give up. We don't care which you choose. Either drop your gun or I'm going to blow that bony head off your shoulders." Even Laura was surprised at the evenness of her voice, how resolute she sounded. More surprising was how confident she felt. Her body trembled. She focused on just one thing. Laura knew she would kill this intruder rather than let him harm anyone.

Dobie took a deep breath, his eyes narrowed slits. Then

he lowered the hand holding the pistol and let it drop. The gun thudded on the concrete. "Move five steps to your right," Laura said. Dobie did as he was told. "Turn, facing the workbench," Laura said. Once Dobie was positioned, Laura moved behind him and bent to pick up his gun. "Now down on the floor," she said.

When Dobie didn't move, Laura jabbed him with her rifle barrel. "Lie down!" she ordered.

"Ow," Dobie cried, reaching for the back of his head.

"Down!" Laura reiterated. Dobie dropped to his knees, then to all fours, slowly spreading himself out on the concrete.

"I'll get the tape," Lisa said, moving toward the workbench. As she did so, Carol and Doc Lincoln rose, then took the baby from Terry. Terry struggled to her feet, sighing.

"Get back into bed, sweetie," Doc Lincoln said, helping Terry settle herself comfortably and handing her the still sleeping infant.

"Put your hands behind your back," Laura ordered, once again pressing the barrel to the back of Dobie's head. When he complied, Lisa wrapped his hands and then his feet with duct tape.

"You're gonna' be sorry for this," Dobie said vengefully. "Bull Jones is out there burning your place down and your sorry husbands are dropping like flies," he lied. Dobie had no idea who was winning outside, for the muffled sounds of gunfire had not once ceased since he came in the house. Dobie was not looking forward to having Bull Jones discover him wrapped like a mummy by a bunch of women. The concrete was cold, and he shifted to lift his stomach off of it. Laura jabbed him again.

"Fuck! That hurts," Dobie cried out, wriggling along the floor.

"Tape his ugly mouth, too," Laura suggested.

Lisa immediately straddled Dobie's back. "Gladly," she answered, reaching in front of Dobie's face with a strip of tape. "Hold still or I'll tape your nose too," she said. In a second, Dobie tasted tape glue on his tongue, but he remained still as Lisa wrapped him three times around.

"*Errrr onna eeeeee orry,*" he growled. Lisa, relishing her task, began wrapping his legs with more tape. Then back to his hands, where she reinforced her work.

Dobie lay on the concrete looking more like a silver worm than a man. His fury at this humiliation burned in his chest. He tried to roll over onto his side, and Laura watched him struggle, letting him make himself more comfortable. Lisa pulled up a chair and sat, pointing her pistol at him and smiling. "Which one of us is the pretty girl?" she asked, her eyes dancing.

Dobie looked at Laura, at Lisa, then threw his head backward to look over at Carol, Doc Lincoln and Terry. He cursed. The girl wasn't even here. All this for nothing, he thought.. Dobie Maxwell rolled back over on his stomach. "*Unn uv ouuu,*" he growled as he stared at the concrete floor.

67

Patterson, Late September

Pitbull Jones moved stealthily along the front of the Grant house, avoiding the light from the blazing field to the west. He was listening intently to the shouts of men, trying to discern who was shouting and what they were saying. The gunfire from the western field had petered out but for an occasional pop and as he peered around the side of the building, he could see the black shadows of men pushing other men, who held their arms aloft. What he couldn't be sure of was who had given up. Had his men? Or the farmers? In front of the fiery fields there was no way to tell who was who, because the figures were mere outlines in black. What he could see is that the men with their hands in the air numbered only three, while the men with guns had to be eight or nine. The entire group, however, was making its way toward the house, which made Bull think that his men were the ones captured.

In the gray light of dawn, Bull ran along the front of the house to get a look at the cornfield. Small pockets of flames still burned, but the fire there had either been put down or burned out. He heard someone shout, "Put your hands in the air," an unfamiliar voice, and saw one of his guys, Booze Lockhart, struggle to stand, his vast belly nearly upending him before his legs got far enough under him to straighten. No chance of mistaking Booze; no one else Bull knew had a belly his size. So that was four. Bull wondered where the rest of his men were. He'd come in with sixteen. Where were the other twelve?

The shooting had ceased. Men were out in the hay field shoveling dirt on the burning hay, some beating it with shovels and maybe, from the looks of it, even blankets. While it still looked like a dangerous fire, it wasn't moving toward the house anymore. The breeze had shifted east, toward the already burned cornfield.

Bull wondered where his idiot son was. He and Dobie had been behind Bull as he had headed toward the house, but then, they had disappeared. Probably run off, Bull figured, too scared to fight. Bull looked around, considering the best route for his escape. He could cut up the driveway and be hidden by the house, then cut into the orchard and out to the road. As far as he could judge, this might be the only route, for there was no way to go east or west without being seen, and south would lead him right into the men coming his way. Bull made a quick decision, and scooted as fast as his legs would carry him toward the orchard, his rifle in his hand.

Taylor Farr had seen to the round up of men and was heading for the house to tell Laura and the rest of the women that it was over when he glimpsed Bull's fleeing figure. Taylor knew immediately that it was Bull Jones. It had to be. In the growing light, he could just about make out the black ponytail and the huge frame Laura had so carefully described that day back in March. Taylor immediately changed course, breaking into a run after him.

Bull knew someone was coming almost without looking back over his shoulder. When he did snatch a peek, he saw it was only one guy. Bull smiled. No way was one guy going to capture him. Not Bull Jones. He was too wily for that. The guy had to be half the pasture behind him. No way could he hit him from there. Bull increased his pace, feeling his heart pounding with effort, watching the ground ahead of him for holes or stumps, anything that might trip him. He knew once he got to the orchard that he would have the safety of trees to hide behind. He'd have to keep moving, of course, for those other guys would come running once they heard gunfire. But he'd knock off whoever was pursuing him before any of the others even knew what was going on. Only another forty, maybe fifty feet and he'd be past the first tree.

Taylor knew why Bull was heading for the trees and knew also that once he got there, he'd hide behind one of them and take his best shot. But there was no way to wait for the others. He'd get away for sure. Taylor shouted, "Stop where you are, Jones!" into the wind, but Bull merely looked over his shoulder and kept running. Taylor shot a warning into the sky, still running, but Bull only increased his speed. He wasn't going to give up. "Stop, Jones, or I'll shoot!" Taylor shouted, but Jones continued his rush for the woods.

Taylor stopped, sighted, and shot, purposely aiming for Bull's legs. For a moment, Bull thought he'd run into a stick or something, so sharp was the pain in his leg. Then he heard the shot and knew he'd been hit. He tried to run, but the flash of pain from his calf sent agonizing arrows clear up to his jaw. When he stepped forward again, his leg collapsed, and Bull nearly tumbled to the ground. He clenched his teeth, shouting his swears at the disinterested dawn, then aimed his rifle at the oncoming figure and pulled the trigger.

Taylor knew the man wasn't going to give up. He guessed Bull couldn't run any farther when he saw him stumble. He knew Jones was going to shoot even before Jones did. He was already zigging left by the time Bull pulled the trigger, then zagging right immediately thereafter. Bull saw his evasions, saw the man coming despite his second and even his third shot. Enraged, Bull snarled and aimed again.

Taylor yelled, "Give it up or else," just before Bull pulled the trigger for the last time. His response was a clear "no". Taylor dropped to one knee, sighted, this time for the man's chest, pulled the trigger, and watched the big man take the hit.

Bull was in the middle of a curse when he felt the impact. His eyes widened in surprise, his jaw clenched, he grimaced, and his hand flew up to his chest. He staggered, stunned, felt the wet blood there and whispered "What?" as if surprised. "Fuckerrrrrr!" he screamed to the dawn. Then, like a tumbling statue, Bull fell forward still holding his rifle. He landed face first with a thud, then lay still in the frosted grass.

Taylor stood cautiously, not really expecting Bull to move but careful just the same. He watched the still figure for any sign of life, then walked toward him, his rifle at the ready. He walked slowly, thinking all the while what a shame it was that all men could not learn to live peacefully with their neighbors. By the time he reached Bull, heavy with sadness, Bull had already been dead for over a minute.

68

Patterson, Late September

Rob hurried ahead of the others, rushing into the house to check on the women and to tell them that it was over. No one could have been more surprised than he to find Dobie Maxwell packaged in duct tape on the cellar floor while Lisa Curley sat cross-legged on her chair, a pistol pointing directly at Dobie's back. When he heard the story of Dobie's capture, Rob felt faint at his foolish oversight. Why hadn't he thought to keep one man at the back door to guard the house? He quaked at the thought of what could have happened had it not been for the quick thinking of the women and resolved that as soon as Terry was well enough, he would teach her to shoot.

It took several minutes for the story to be told in all of its parts, and for Rob to tell the women what had happened outside. Almost immediately, Ralph appeared and Paul Curley, and more and more details emerged about the battle. Laura Block raced up the stairs, looking for Taylor, with Doc Lincoln right behind her, anxious to see her husband's face. It was when Rob was about to suggest they send Michael to Shirley's that he realized he hadn't seen him. "Where's Michael?" he asked.

"Isn't he with you?" Terry's eyes went wide with fear. "Rob, I didn't know he was supposed to..." but she didn't finish. She was horrified to realize that she had not thought about Michael, had never wondered where he'd gone.

"I sent him to the cellar. I didn't look to make sure he went."

In the sudden silence, everyone feared the worst. Rob hurried up the stairs, calling Michael as he went, hoping that the boy had hidden somewhere else in the house. He flew through every room without finding him. But Michael was not to be found. Outside, Rob stood in the yard shouting for Michael. The men being tied up scowled and looked away. Rob asked the farmers if anyone had seen his son, but none of them had. Then he thought of the barn and Griz.

Rob stood in the doorway, searching the cavernous interior for signs of his son. By now, the light was strong enough for him to make out Michael sitting cross-legged, cradling Griz's head in his lap. The child sobbed when he looked up, his face red and bloated. "He's dead, Dad," Michael cried. "He saved my life."

Rob walked silently the few feet to where his son sat, seeing on the floor in front of the still dog the telltale pool of blackening blood. Griz's tongue hung lifeless from his mouth. His eyes dimly stared at nothing. Michael gently stroked his head. "Butch shot him," he said as his father sat down beside him on the floor. "He was going to shoot me, and Griz broke free." Michael sobbed again, wiping his eyes with a dirty hand.

Rob wrapped an arm around his son's shoulders and pulled him closer. "Easy, son," Rob murmured. "It's okay to cry. He was a great dog."

"He saved me twice," Michael blurted. "Once against wild dogs up in the woods. Me and Chris." Michael sniveled, the tears pouring down his cheeks.

"You never told me that," Rob said, surprised.

"We were afraid. We weren't supposed to be in the woods."

"Chris too?" Rob asked, stunned at this disclosure.

"He killed a Doberman," Michael said.

If parents knew what their children never told them, Rob thought, they'd never let them outside. He looked down at Griz, grateful for the dog's sacrifice. "Now I know why he just appeared like he did," he said quietly.

Michael looked up at his father. "Why?"

"Well think about it, Michael. He came out of nowhere, right?"

Michael nodded.

"And he saved you boys. You, twice, right?"

"You're going to say he was sent here purposely," Michael replied. "That God sent him."

"Why else?" Rob answered. "Couldn't have been a coincidence, could it?"

"Like a guardian angel?"

"Well? What else?" Rob said.

"But Dad, why did Butch have to shoot him? Why did his dad come to burn us out?" Michael's face agonized, all twisted and hurt.

"I think God puts bad men on earth to help good men learn to work together," Rob said, thinking about the past months, how his family had survived by working as a part of the alliance, how all the other farmers had appeared to help him protect his farm from Bull Jones, risking their lives to stop him. "When good men join forces, they can prevail. But sometimes they forget that. Sometimes they get all caught up in themselves, forgetting that we're all kin. Then a flu comes along, or a Bull Jones, and they either learn to cooperate or they perish. God gives them that choice."

"Is Bull Jones dead?" Michael asked.

"Yes," Rob said.

"Did you get Butch?" Michael's voice was hopeful.

"I don't think so. At least, I didn't see him."

"He got away." Michael's voice went flat.

"I don't think we'll be seeing that boy around these parts ever again," Rob said to reassure his son.

Michael looked down at Griz. He touched the silky fur that still stood thick and luxurious around his ruff. He wrapped his cold fingers in it, feeling beneath the fur the still warm neck of his beautiful dog. He swallowed hard, hating how his head ached and the muscles in his back throbbed. Butch got away. He knew it just as he knew that the battle outside was probably not the last he'd see in his lifetime. If what his father said was true, there'd be other Bull Joneses and other Butches. That's how life is. Nothing ever ended with one big battle.

"Come on," Rob said. "Let's go tell your mother you're all right. And you just might want to say hello to your new sister."

"A girl?" Michael smiled. "A little sister?"

Rob stood, helping Michael to slip gently from beneath Griz while carefully lowering the dog's head to the floor. Michael stood, looking down. His tears had dried. "We'll bury him later. The right way," Rob said.

"Can we bring the pups home, do you think? So they can be there?" Michael looked pleadingly up at his father.

"I think that would be fine," Rob said, taking his son's shoulder and turning him toward the door. "I think Griz would like that."

69

Patterson, Late September

Taylor Farr walked back from the apple orchard, his arm around Laura's shoulder. Their eyes were on the ground as they walked, seemingly worlds away from the carnage strewn about the Grant farm. Others stamped out the last of the flames in the cornfield and still others stood before the barn discussing what to do with three prisoners and no jail. When Rob and Michael emerged, they looked up surprised, then grew quiet when they saw the look Rob gave them. "Go tell your mother you're okay," Rob said. "Then you and David drive up to the Young place and let them know it's over. If anyone wants to come back here, tell them to wait a while. We have some cleaning up to do."

Michael disappeared into the house quickly, while David, filthy with soot, fished around in his pocket for car keys. He couldn't wait to hold Ellen and tell her all was well, but as he gazed about, waiting for Michael to reappear, he felt sorry for Mr. Grant. He had lost the last cutting of hay and half a cornfield. Enough to make a big difference in his winter supplies and put Mr. Grant in debt to his neighbors. The closest fields looked like war zones, some of them still smoking in places and black as pitch. The smell of burnt vegetation lingered in the air. Had David not been so exhausted, he would have liked to get the tractor and turn the fields under, just to cover everything with soil. But they couldn't do that until all the bodies had been removed. David didn't know how many lay out there, but he had seen several as he walked in from the rear of the hay field. Two had most assuredly been Bull's men. David had never seen either of them before. But he thought another one was a farmer from across town, and he knew the alliance must have suffered other casualties. They would get to that soon, the locating, the counting, and the burying. David shivered in the early morning cold, glad the worst was over, but sorry it had to have happened in the first place. He didn't think that he had killed anyone, but he couldn't be sure. When he had returned from the back field, he had been instructed to cut left and wait behind the tractor for the men in the house to join him. He had done as he was told, leaving Michael to sprint the last distance from field to house. Michael was so fast David doubted he could have kept up anyway.

Within minutes, three men had come running through the dark, leaping into the space behind the tractor so fast that they'd almost landed on him. David had guessed the men meant to protect him, for they'd pushed him into the middle where he could only get a shot lying down and aiming through the underbelly of the Grants' International. He'd tried to do his share, but not once did he see a man go down from his bullets. Secretly, he was glad.

Mr. Fenn rubbed his bearded chin. "What say we gather the dead?"

The other men nodded, pawing the ground with their boots or spitting off to the side of the assembled circle. They adjusted their caps. They hoisted their pants. David could tell none of them looked forward to the task and was glad that he had been sent on another errand. Just then Michael pushed open the kitchen door and called, "All set, David."

After they left, Rob asked how many were dead. "I counted nine out in the field," Ralph answered.

"That include any of ours?"

"No," another said.

"How many of ours?" Rob questioned.

Mr. Fenn said two, and paused to swallow. "My brother and a fellow from over in Almont." The group sighed, knowing the agony their friend felt. "I've got him ready to load on my truck," he continued. "I'll bring him home."

"I guess we better gather up Bull's boys," another suggested, looking away as he spoke. "Can't leave 'em out there to rot."

"What do we do with them?" another asked.

"Bury 'em, I guess. What else? No sheriff to come get them. No funeral home. Not even any coffins."

"Those boys have families?"

"Suppose so."

"We gonna' bury them without telling them?"

"Got a better suggestion?"

Everyone looked at Rob for leadership. It was his land, after all. "Suppose we take the tractor down to the far meadow, over by the Jameson land," Rob said pointing. "Suppose we dig nine graves and put them in. The ones we know, we can put a marker on. Then if a family comes looking, they can dig them up."

"Sounds like a plan," Ralph said, nodding. "My guess is no one will come looking. But just in case..."

"I'll take Jake Marks back to Almont," Bill Lincoln said. "I know his family."

"Then let's get moving," Paul said. "I'm about dead on my feet."

As the men finished planning what to do, Taylor left Laura at the kitchen door and headed over to the assembled group. Before he reached them, however, he stopped dead short. "Where's Arnold?" he asked.

The rest of the men looked round, suddenly realizing that no one had seen Arnold. Some scanned the fields, hoping he had lingered out there to smother fires.

"Maybe inside?" one asked.

"I haven't seen him," another added.

Taylor's eyes narrowed with concern. "Did anyone? At any time?"

Rob ran to the kitchen door shouting Arnold's name, and when he didn't respond, disappeared into the kitchen to ask the women.

When he came out alone, Taylor said, "We've got to get back to the road. My guess is something happened out by the cars." He searched his pockets helplessly for his keys, then realized the pickup was hidden at Shirley Young's. "Rob?" he asked, his voice frightened.

"Yeah. Let's go," Rob said, heading for his own pickup.

"I'll head into the woods and meet you there," Paul Curley offered, hoping that maybe Arnold had fallen on the trail back to the farm and was sitting there waiting for someone to come. By the time the pickup's engine turned over, Paul was already halfway across the blackened field.

On the way out of his driveway, his tires throwing up pebbles and dust, Rob passed David returning in Terry's car. Ethel Card leaned forward in the front seat, waving happily to them as they flew past. "Oh, God," he said, seeing Ethel's joyous face.

They flew down the street to the secret route in and out, then bounced their way over rocks and stumps, short knolls and dips until they reached the secret opening back on to the main road. Rob didn't slow as he plowed through bushes and trees, destroying the ropework they had contrived. Once on the road, the pickup careened through curves and skidded around corners until at last they were heading up the hill to the place Paul Curley had said Bull's men would park. As they came up over the knoll, they spotted the pickups parked along the road, six of them sitting silent in the rosy light of early morning. Rob slowed, coming up cautiously on the last in the line.

"Tires are flat," Taylor said, craning forward.

"Nobody here," Rob said, inching along beside the first two parked vehicles, taking his time to look inside each cab.

"Look up there," Taylor said, pointing to the far end. "Tire marks. Someone peeled out."

"All the others have flat tires," Rob said, drawing his own conclusions.

"One didn't," Taylor replied. "Pull up there."

Rob accelerated slightly, passing the middle pickups without checking their interiors. The pickup engine hummed quietly.

"Shit," Taylor said, opening his door before Rob could even press the brake pedal. "Shit!" he said again, jumping down from the cab.

It took a second for Rob to realize what Taylor had seen. There, just beneath the front bumper of the first pickup, two feet sprawled at odd angles, the toes pointing at each other. Rob rammed the transmission into park, pulled up the brake, and jumped out himself, leaving his door open. Taylor was already kneeling, his hand pressed to Arnold's neck, feeling for a pulse.

"He's alive," he gasped, gently turning Arnold over. "Just barely, but he's alive." Rob saw the panic in Taylor's face as he looked up. "Help me get him into the truck," he demanded, his voice urgent and worried. "Oh, God, Arnold, hold on. We'll get you to a doctor."

They laid Arnold in the bed of the pickup, and Taylor

sat beside him, cradling his upper body. Rob jumped into the cab, making the fastest U-turn he could without throwing Arnold about on the steel floor, then raced as fast as he dared along the same roads over which they had just come. At the hidden cut-off, he had to slow, worrying that too much jouncing could kill Arnold, though in truth, Rob thought he might already be dead. Arnold was pale gray when they found him, barely breathing, unconscious, and cold. No telling how long he'd been lying out there. Rob remembered the shot that had preempted their plan to surround Bull's men. It had surprised them all, for so far everything had gone according to plan. Bull had left some of his men to douse the back end of the field with gas and had headed in closer to the house and barn. They had been surrounded, though they didn't know it, and Rob was just about to tell them to put their hands up. All of sudden, the gun startled everyone, including Bull's boys. Once that shot had resounded, Rob had no idea who shot back, but the result was like a spark in a box of firecrackers. One went off and set the others off as it did. There had been no way to end the confrontation peacefully after that; once everyone started shooting, it was bedlam. Now a dozen men were dead, and Arnold would likely make that thirteen.

When the truck appeared in the driveway, a cloud of dust rising behind it, a crowd gathered near the house waiting for it to reach them. Rob saw Ethel, her face white with fear as she stood next to Laura Block. He pulled up directly in front of them, jumped out, saying "He's in the back!" and hurried to the rear of the pickup with the rest of them. Hands reached out from all directions to lift and carry Arnold's limp body into the house and lay him on the kitchen table, where Doc Lincoln already had her bag opened and ready. Ethel couldn't help but be in the way as she tried to touch him, calling "Arnold, Arnold, darling, Arnold, hold on."

They were ordered out of the kitchen, all except Ethel, who sat beside Arnold, holding his hand, and Carol and Shirley, who, still bloodied from helping deliver Terry's baby were now assisting Doc Lincoln with the other end of life. Both women looked frazzled, yet they remained calm, doing their best to follow Doc's orders.

"He's lost a lot of blood," she said, listening to Arnold's lungs and heart.

"Please, Marianne, please save him," Ethel whispered, her filled with tears. "Please, Marianne." She looked up at Doc Lincoln's face, but saw there only concentration and concern.

"I'll do my best, Ethel," Marianne Lincoln said, "but I'm no surgeon and this is a serious wound."

Outside, the men talked, thinking that Arnold looked too far gone to save. But each of them tried to reassure Taylor and Laura with examples of people they knew or had heard of who had been brought back from the brink. When they ran out of stories, they spoke of Doc Lincoln's fine reputation and Arnold's spunkiness, their voices low and intimate. Finally, someone pointed out that it had to be nearly seven o'clock and he had cows waiting to be milked. Others added to that their own lists of things awaiting them at home and the group began slowly to disperse. Rob climbed back into his pickup; two men jumped in the bed. The truck headed out to the fields to pick up the bodies lying there just as the cool October sun broke golden over the charred fields. Ralph Green climbed on Rob's International and started its engine. He waited for it to warm, quietly gazing at the brightening sun. Then he put the tractor in gear and headed toward the Jamesons' to dig graves. One man jumped up beside him, saying nothing, while others placed Fenn's brother in his truck and, as soon as it arrived, Jake Marks' body in another. Charlie appeared with three shovels and the men began their slow walk to the gravesite. Within a few minutes, the Grant yard had emptied of men and vehicles, and in the distance, only the low moan of the tractor digging graves and the cawing of crows disturbed the calm of the farm.

70

Patterson, October

Depending on the number of storms stirred up in the Caribbean and the fronts blown persistently down from Canada, the foliage in Patterson is beautiful through mid-October. After that, leaves fall like translucent orange and gold teardrops even in the gentlest rain. In no time the ground is a tapestry of hues that rival even the most riotous spring flowers. Sharp and nostalgic is the smell of dried leaves gathering by porch steps, carpeting the lawns and fields, feathering the surfaces of ponds and lakes. Leaves gather along the roadsides, blown there whenever a car passes, while above, the limbs still heavy with bright foliage are like cathedral glass, their branches intricate leading. More leaves drift down to settle among the russet ferns lining vast acres of still young forest floors, forests that only a hundred years ago were open pastureland. The color is spectacular, breathtaking, even awe-inspiring. Around lakes and ponds, often first glazed with frost, deep red maples and birches reflect on the surface like watery conflagrations. Later, only the conifers, the pines, yews, hemlocks and spruces will anchor color to earth.

There is a sadness in such pageantry, rich and lavish as it is, like state funerals, glistening uniforms and sparkling medals, plumes and patent leather boots. The ephemeral beauty of fall is by its very nature a goodbye to the past, a door closing, and a reminder of our own mortality. It is a celebration of and the precursor to long and arduous winters, where death waits with bony fingers beneath frozen lakes and crusted snow, a warning to beware the tenuous time when families are most vulnerable. The alliance farmers have little time to ponder paradox, however, as they prepare to weather the dead time, hoping that they have enough food for themselves and their livestock, hoping they have split enough wood, hoping their water lines won't freeze and their barn roofs won't leak or that they have filled the cracks and mended the slats where the cold might settle in drafty corners and under floorboards already too cold for stocking feet.

What, really, is there to ponder? The worst is over. The crisis has passed. To ride along one of the many country roads leading from Patterson center is to pass farm after farm and home after home gone wild with thorny vines and bittersweet, sour brown hay fields, curling, tenacious weeds wrapping themselves about fence posts and front door steps, as if the earth itself intended to devour the hubris of human order. In their houses the bodies of the dead are now nothing more than gray bones and stained sheets. Houses no longer reek of decay. Even the foul smell has dissipated, dispelled by time and seasons. A few kitchen clocks continue to tick, their batteries flagging. Clothes still hang ready in open closets, shirt arms like proper soldiers in marching formation. Laundry rooms smell faintly of soap. But mice have taken up residence where families once gathered, building nests from gnawed cushion fluff, scurrying about the empty rooms like rebels in the castle. Sometimes floorboards creak, as if ghosts walk about, and when the sun hits the aluminum gutters, their metal expands, clicking like fingernails on the wall. Lives were lost quickly in these houses. The houses will take longer to die. Deep in the forests of Central Massachusetts, crumbling foundations or tumbled chimneys bear witness to the pastoral settlements that were there a hundred years ago. These derelicts will now multiply. The houses aren't needed when the people are gone.

Ethel Card stood in the Grants' upstairs bedroom, considering the spectacle of diminishing color on each successively distant hill, how time and distance dilutes even the brightest oranges, the deepest reds. She had opened the casement window from the top, feeling the crisp air on her face, breathing deeply the freshness of the earth after heavy rains. For two days after the battle, rain had poured down on the house and fields in torrents that at times grew so loud she couldn't sleep. The fields, turned under the day after the fire, lay puddled and soggy, two huge squares stretching from the Grants' yard to the base of the long hill up into the woods. Beneath her window, the driveway was rutted from the comings and goings of cars and tractors. Everywhere else, leaves lay thick and wet, stretched out waiting for the morning sun to dry them.

In the distance, Ethel could hear the faint drone of engines and chainsaws. Today the barricade was to be removed; all the men and children had been summoned to help remove debris and pile firewood so that vehicles could come and go freely. Downstairs, Ethel heard the wee cries of the newborn child and her mother's soft crooning. Terry's muffled voice was gentle and comforting, and if Ethel closed her eyes, she could almost feel her own mother's loving touch and smell the sweet perfume of her talcum. To be young again, Ethel thought. To be just beginning. To start all over. How she wished she had that option.

Behind her Arnold groaned a soft, half-hearted moan that was too weak to be promising. He had been making these sounds for more than a day now. At first, Ethel had been cheered by them. Now, a day later, she feared they indicated deep pain Arnold was unable to express in any other way. She hurried to his bed, as she did each time he made any sound, and took his hand in hers. How many more times could she pray to God for his recovery? Ethel truly believed that God could hear each prayer, even that he might grow annoyed with her whining. Surely he'd be annoyed with her then, for she hadn't stopped begging, pleading, or promising God anything he wanted from her since she'd first learned that Arnold had been shot.

This time, however, something was different. Arnold seemed to be smacking his lips. His chin moved. And beneath his closed lids, Ethel thought she had caught movement, as if Arnold was looking around the inside of his head.

"Arnold?" Ethel said softly. "Arnold, sweetie, are you there?"

Arnold's eye movements increased, though his lids remained closed. His brows flexed, almost imperceptibly, and his tongue peeked momentarily from between his lips.

"Arnold?" Ethel repeated, growing excited. "Arnold, are you there?"

His head jerked to the left and again his tongue touched his lips. "Where else?" he muttered. And then Arnold fell back asleep.

"Arnold!" Ethel urged. "Speak to me, Arnold." Elated, Ethel insisted that Arnold respond. She rubbed his hand; she gently nudged his shoulder.

"Damn fool gut-shot me," Arnold muttered, this time his lids opening just enough to see the tiny slits of his eyes.

"I know, I know," Ethel soothed. "But you're okay. Arnold, you're okay."

Now Arnold's eyes opened wide. He looked about the strange room with wonder. "Where am I?" he asked.

Ethel's smile grew broader. She leaned down to kiss Arnold's cheek, her eyes filling with tears. "Oh, darling, darling, you're going to be okay!"

Arnold ignored Ethel's whimpering, smacking his lips again as if to test whether his mouth worked. "Thirsty," he whispered.

Ethel poured some water from the decanter beside Arnold's bed and raised his head just enough for some liquid to dribble down his chin. "Girlie!" Arnold chided, feeling cranky. Ethel lifted his head some more, this time enough so that Arnold could take a few sips. "That's good," Arnold managed, enjoying the cool, wet feel of water in his mouth. Like a baby bird, he opened wider for more.

"I'll get you some soup," Ethel said, joyous at Arnold's growing return to health. "You stay still, and I'll be back in a few minutes." Ethel bustled from the room, anxious to tell Terry her good news. Arnold listened as she drifted away, falling again into a peaceful slumber that would last several more days.

Arnold slept and woke on nearly the same schedule as the newborn, two hours of sleep punctuated by brief periods of consciousness. Each time he awoke, Ethel was there, waiting for his eyes to open. "Don't you sleep, girlie?" he asked once. "You look frazzled." Always, it was Ethel holding his hand or straightening his sheets, washing his face or smoothing his hair whenever Arnold awoke. By the fourth day, Ethel had grown so exhausted that she fell into a deep sleep while sitting in her chair. Before Arnold opened his eyes, he heard her snoring. He turned his head to see the chair where she always sat and gazed at his wife, all wrinkled and aging, her hair flat and lifeless, her mouth drooping. Arnold thought he could never love anyone more than he did Ethel at this very moment, her devotion to him relentless and unwavering. How could any man be so lucky? He felt his bandage, running his hand across the wrapped gauze on his stomach. He pressed gently the place where he hurt most. He tried turning onto his side and found that he could manage it without undue pain. He felt relief in his back and buttocks, on which he'd now lain for many days. He wiggled his toes and then his feet, feeling for circulation there. He took a deep breath, feeling the skin stretch at his stitches. Downstairs, someone was baking bread. The scent was enticing. He was ravenous for real food, bread and eggs, even some home fries. When Ethel awoke, he'd ask her why she'd been starving him. Arnold smiled, a sense of warmth and well being, like a wave of pleasure, washing over him. Even from his bed he could see the golden tops of trees outside, and before he dozed again, Arnold thought he saw a plane making studied twists and turns in the cloudless blue sky.

71

Patterson, Early October

Arnold sat straight-backed in the wheel chair Taylor had found for him, tucked tightly in a mohair blanket. Though his stitches ached a bit, Arnold managed to tap his toe to the music from Lily Fenn's little group, gathered just across the yard on a jerrybuilt stage. Ethel nodded her head and patted his hand to the beat, herself caught in the happy rhythms of songs she had sung as a child. An October afternoon, Indian summer, and Sunday to boot, Arnold thought.. Could anything be better?

Beside Arnold on the other side, Terry held Little Hope, named after Terry's grandmother. Arnold had told Ethel they ought to leave off the "little," but Ethel had slapped his hand and ordered him to hush. "No sense adding your two cents, Arnold Card. Hope is a fine name," she'd huffed.

"But Little Hope..."

"Shush, Arnold!"

Rob pulled up a folding chair and sat down, patting Terry's knee as he did so. "What's new on the radio," he asked, as he did every time he saw Arnold. "Any news of Bull's son?" After they'd buried the nine dead men, Taylor and Ralph had driven their three prisoners to Worcester, the militia headquarters they'd heard about from Arnold. They'd found there a staff of several enlisted men and the beginnings of a working communication system set up by the state government. They left their prisoners with the militia, for it was the only staffed jail in the region and made their reports and signed their charges against the prisoners. They'd also reported Bull's son among the escaped attackers, leaving a full description just in case.

"Nope. Nothing. My guess is he's long gone," Arnold said. "I just wish I knew who shot me. I'd like to see that fella picked up."

"Can't chase a man without a name or a description," Rob said, shrugging. "Anything else?"

"Reports say the flu has all but disappeared. Swept through and gone," Arnold said. "Washington thinks they've distributed enough vaccine for every survivor. No more worries on that end. Electricity grids might be up and running in a few more weeks. At least some of them."

"That mean we might have lights soon?"

"Yes and no," Arnold said, enjoying his importance. "Well, we'll see, won't we," he added. "At least we all know what to do this time."

Terry, wishing to change the subject, poked Rob. "Look at Charlie," she said, smiling. Charlie had been dancing exclusively with Shirley Young, the two of them sweeping across the yard with every waltz or polka the musicians played. "I knew something was brewing," she pronounced wisely.

Rob noticed for the first time the goofy smile on Charlie's face as he danced by. "Well I'll be darned," he said, surprised.

"I think it's wonderful," Ethel said enthusiastically.

"You think everything's wonderful, girlie," Arnold said, reaching his arm out to hug Ethel's shoulders. "That's why I stick with you."

Ethel pulled up straight, glaring. "Well aren't I lucky," she said.

"Maybe we'll have a marriage soon," Terry mused,

looking specifically now for Laura and Taylor, who lingered together talking with David and Ellen on the far side of the yard. "He's not going back to Wyoming."

"Not without Laura," Ethel said. "They think maybe right after Christmas."

"Look at all these people," Rob said, gratitude welling. "If it hadn't been for them, we wouldn't even have a farm." Rob looked around at the dancers and the people lingering along the sidelines, all of them friends who had been there against Bull and even more who had donated hay and corn to replace his lost feed when the fields burned. The entire town had contributed, arriving with pickups and trailers loaded with donations. If Rob had learned anything at all about life, he thought, it was to value family and friends above all else.

Rob reached down and picked up the puppies jostling about his feet, crooning to the two of them, wrinkled and wiggly, their skin far too big for their puppy bodies. "These guys look just like their daddy," he said, smiling.

"Their daddy came fully trained, though," Terry said with a smile.

Arnold pressed Ethel's hand with his. "Have you ever seen a prettier fall?" he asked, looking west to the rolling hills and valleys, a brief breeze riffling his graying hair. His eyes traced the course of the valley, where grasses and purple loosestrife stretched to the horizon. Beyond the valley, other hills rose and fell in a variety of greens, golds, and reds as far as the eye could see. Above them, the blue sky was cloudless, a beautiful October day. Arnold thought the world a wondrous place, every bit of it alive, each living thing staking out its claim to a piece of time and space. He thought about himself and Ethel, two old people alive here today, and wondered if, in fact, there was a plan to it all, whether God intended that they live while so many billions of others hadn't. And if so, why. What possible purposes could they serve? The two of them had received more than their share of the gift of life. Why had they been given more?

The young girl on the stage stood, adjusting her violin under her chin, then drew her bow across the strings. An elderly woman stood beside her, puckering her lips to prepare them for the flute she held. Just as Lily Fenn's group prepared to play, Hope stirred, waking from the warmth of her mother's arms. Hungry, she wailed for attention and food. The aged woman smiled, bringing the flute to her lips. Her flute, the violin, and Hope's cries became one note. Around them the music caught on the air and danced across the yard and fields. Like a wind sprite, it rolled up and over the treetops, tumbling across the golden expanse of birches and ash, maples and oaks. Diminished by distance, it blended with the rustling leaves still clinging to branches and drifted deep into glistening forest bottoms thick with humus and sweet with decay. In the silences there, perhaps a chipmunk straightened to listen, ears alert, tail erect, assessing the message from Man. Perhaps the notes suggested birds, or the flutter of butterfly wings, or the buzz of bees extracting nectar. Then the breezes rose again in relieved and measured contentment and lifted the sound on heat waves, spinning the notes in lofty cartwheels toward the clouds. The earth sighed as if waking from a long illness.

72

Geneva, Early October

Robert Schultz sat looking out his window at the red sunset. The days were growing shorter; another winter waited in the wings. Schultz was thinking about his old friend Linquist, how only a year ago they would have been watching this together, sharing some brandy and smoking cigars. Only last year he and Linquist had the hubris to be discussing the latest emerging virus and betting on its mortality rate. So much had happened since then. Linquist had flown to Thailand and disappeared. After several initial reports via telephone, he had not been heard from again. Nor had any of his staff. Once rudimentary communications had been re-established, were they alive, someone could have reached Schultz. But no one did. Now, Schultz was certain that Linquist had died with the billions of others who succumbed to the Bangkok flu. He missed his friend and knew the world had lost a brilliant scientist.

But, of course, the world had lost so many people. Too many to count.

"Would you like some tea, Robert?" Edna asked from the doorway.

"No, not now, Edna. Go home. Get some rest."

"Perhaps I will," she said. "Now that it's over, maybe I'll be able to sleep."

Edna turned, and Schultz listened to the familiar rustlings as she gathered up her belongings. "Goodnight," he heard her call softly just before the door to his outer office closed.

Schultz leaned back in his leather chair thinking how simple it all seemed. A virus nearly destroys the world and then, with the discovery of a vaccine, the world is saved. That's what Edna believed, despite how much she had learned as his secretary. That's what the world believed as well. That it was over. That mankind was safe.

Schultz smiled ruefully and nodded his head. Only those familiar with the microscopic world can understand how fragile life is, how easily cells can be attacked and destroyed by marauding armies of bacteria or viruses hell-bent on replicating themselves inside their hosts, and how many forms and strategies those enemies will develop to insure their own survival. Probably at this very moment, Edna was running her hand along the banister leading down to the parking lot, brushing her skin against billions of entities, any one of which could make her seriously ill if she put her hand to her mouth or her fingers to her eyes. Edna was feeling good about life once more. But then, Schultz conceded, feeling relief was better than brooding over the next virus, one they might not be lucky enough to stop at all.

For a time, Schultz guessed, the world would be slightly safer. Schultz knew that the Bangkok flu thrived because it could jump so easily from one host to another and because people lived elbow-to-elbow, unable to distance themselves from the sick. They'd had no way to isolate its first victims and no way to stop its spread once it got going. Now, with the population decimated, perhaps new viruses would not have such fortunate circumstances. For a while, anyway. Until mankind once again began reproducing at rates too great for the earth to accommodate.

Schultz leaned back, closed his eyes and sighed. Outside,

like the dying embers of a fire, the crimson clouds had darkened to purple and blue,. Tomorrow is another day, he thought as he slipped into a deep and peaceful sleep.

VIRUS TERMINOLOGY IN THIS BOOK

Amplification – Multiplication of a virus in a host or population of hosts.

Aspiration – Airborne or in an aerosol

CDC – Communicable Disease Center. Atlanta, Georgia national disease center that conducts research, exploration, identification of international human diseases.

Electron Microscope – A very powerful microscope that uses a beam of electrons to photograph small objects such as a virus.

Extreme Amplification – Multiplication of a virus throughout its host.

Epidemic – Relatively small or contained within a country of a virus or other microorganism outbreak.

Filovirus – Thread like family of viruses such as found in Ebola and Marburg viruses.

HIV – Human immunodeficiency virus connected with AIDS. HHV-6 or Human Herpes Virus reported to be connected with HIV amplification and AIDS.

Host – An organism, cell that serves as a food supply for a parasite or virus.

Pandemic – A multinational or global virus outbreak.

Plague – Outbreak of infections (microorganisms) diseases.

Replication – Duplication or self-copying.

Recombination – Example of two viruses combining to make a new mutant virus. Recombination can help a virus jump hosts.

Viremic – Loaded with viruses.

WHO – World Health Organization

###

UNDERSTANDING VIRUSES

SIZE – 100 million can fit on this period.

A virus is not a cell but needs the cells of animals and plant organisms to grow and multiply.

Viruses are so small they can float and be carried by air

SURVIVAL

-    Some viruses can only survive for seconds outside of the host.

-    Viruses can "go dead", then switch on and multiply if they come in contact with a suitable organism or host.

-    Some viruses can become crystallized and survive for many years.

-    Some viruses prefer dry air, dust and darkness.

-    Some viruses need moisture and can last for hours or days.

-    Ebola virus has survived for five days in distilled water.

TRANSMISSION

-    Viruses can be passed to another host by aspiration.

-    Insects transmit viruses between plants, but also between humans and insects as with mosquitoes.

-    Humans transmit to humans by contact (kissing, handshaking, sexual contact, spitting) and through respiration of contaminated air.

-    Domestic and wild animals and birds have passed viruses to humans – directly or by recombination with a human virus (i.e. mutant change).

VIRAL BAGGAGE

We have lived millions of years with viruses. Many kinds of viruses can be found in or on our body, but healthy immune systems and washing with soap and water keep them in check.

Viruses can remain dormant in the body until triggered by something such as illness, when they begin to multiply and spread to different organs. In other words, a reduction in immunity can reawaken a dormant virus and cause massive multiplication. Fortunately, our immune system is able to handle the vast majority of viruses.